"TACT"

'Do What You Gotta Do, When You Gotta Do It'

Printed in the USA
ISBN 9 78 0 615 29476 6

AUTHOR'S DEDICATION

I was born in Baltimore, Maryland, approximately 6:45am on
a Tuesday morning. Our dysfunctional family moved to
Detroit, Michigan when I was only six years of age. Along with
self-motivation and the need to suppress negative surroundings
I basically concentrated on things I enjoyed.

A special, "Thank you" to the many people I met that inspired
this story. The ones that embraced me and encouraged my will to
survive on the jagged streets of Detroit. Most of all, to the heavenly
angels that were sent to watch over me.

"Hey, life is short and it's up to you to make the best of it."

INTRODUCTION

"We were all so young, so innocent, no clue to the evil that will encourage our need to survive. The childhood promise, the bond that ignites the fire of hell that burns deep in our souls. Revenge was sweet as the blood dried on our hands that night. Some say, 'it was a pact made with the Devil' the night Beauden Hamilson, a member of the Black Connection, Inc., Mafia, was murdered. "Who really killed him? …Well, nobody's talking."

Candice Felioni (Italian-American) the only child of Paul and Audrey Felioni and are extremely protective parents. However, they didn't wean Candice from their bedroom until it was too late. Candice grew up believing sex and love was the same, until…

Elayne Donaldson (Afro-American) comes from a very religious and loving family. She loves singing in her father's church and composing inspirational hymns. She adores the relationship between her parents so much that she prays to The Lord asking that she too would be blessed; but…

Shi Li Kyi (Chinese-American) her father is headstrong and egotistical. His tedious attributes compel his family's destruction; enslaving his wife and child to old customs that Shi Li believes kills her mother. On the day of her funeral Shi Li's little heart began to freeze, becoming darker with each moment - dark as black ice.

D'La Lausen (Afro-American) is one high-spirited little girl and most definitely the neighborhood's bully. Fighting every fight she can find even if she has to start it herself. D'La had her first homosexual experience at the age of fourteen. She would say, "It just don't make sense, why would a woman want a man anyway? Uh, no way. Never…EVEN IN DEATH".

"Yeah we remember, as though it was yesterday."

CHAPTERS

BABES

CHAPTER ONE

"No, I don't want to get up. That darn clock, I wish it would shut up. I don't want to go to a new school. I want to go back to my old one, where all my friends are. Why did we have to move here anyway?"

The dogs barked and the sun shined ever so bright that beautiful morning in Detroit, Michigan, 1962. Even the birds sang a sweeter melody that day.

The alarm rings for nine year old Candice Felioni to get up. Finding it difficult to push back the blanket that covers her, tossing from one side of the bed to the other. Candice knows today is the first day of class at Holtman Elementary School, and still, she refuses to get up. Apparently, today is the day, she is not in the mood of starting over again, even if that means making new friends and meeting her new teacher.

Candice's parents are always trying to move up in the world, 'keeping up with the Jones', in other words, her Uncle Mario and his family.

Paul Felioni, Candice's father, does not want any part of the family business, *'organized'* family business. Paul only want and need for his family is to live a clean life and stay in harmony with his Catholic beliefs. Nevertheless, Paul Felioni struggles to stay afloat. Finding and working many jobs for his most precious gifts, Candice and her mother, Audrey Felioni. He will do anything to protect them, even if that means trading his life for theirs.

At Holtman Elementary, Candice stands silently in the school's office as her mother kisses her cheek. "Now, I want you to be a good girl", she says. Candice's mother pause, but only for a moment, as she tries to catch her breath. She starts again as her words softly flow. Then suddenly, due to nervousness, they gradually become rapid.

"What, I'm trying to say? ...Well, you're always a good girl. Why am I making this so difficult? ...Candice honey, I'll see you after school. I'll be waiting outside right near the front entrance." She pauses a second time. "You know something, baby? I really think you're going to love it here. Everybody seems so nice. Don't you think?"

Candice can only smile, and her reply is very soft. And wanting desperately to believe that those words can possibly be true. "I'll be all right, Mom."

"I know you will, honey. Well, I better get out of here so the nice people can take you to your new class. Remember I'll be waiting outside. Look for me when you get out. Don't' forget, now!"

Candice unhappily watches as her mother walks out of the office. While standing at the entrance, Audrey turn slightly, putting her hand to her mouth and blows her daughter a kiss as the heavy door slowly closes.

Candice doesn't want her mother to see how nervous she really is. So she stands straight and tall like a big girl should, and does exactly what her mother expects her to do, all alone, in a strange new school. She waves her hand and whispers, "I won't forget."

A loud and rough voice echoes over Candice's head, calling her name. She immediately turns and looks up. Candice's mother always told her, 'If you can't say anything good about a person, it's best not to say anything at all.' But what she is thinking at the time, would most definitely put her parents to shame. "Golly, what is that? She looks like the walking dead."

"Candice Felioni, would you come with me, please?"

It is a tall dreary woman, standing at the door wearing a long black dress and orthopedic shoes; she holds one hand out as she signals Candice to follow her. This dreary woman just happens to be the office's attendant.

Candice walks out of the school's office and follows her down the hall, then up one flight of stairs. Trailing closely behind, she can not help listening to the sound of her shoes as they click and knock with every giant step she takes. The woman's tall body keeps motioning Candice through the school's corridor, along with the turning of her head that jerks every so often.

"Follow me. Keep up," she says while peering over her shoulder every few seconds, keeping one eye focus, making sure that Candice is not far behind.

Feeling even more alone, afraid and unaware of what is ahead, Candice's imagination starts to toy with her. It is her way of blocking out the reality of any situation, as she has done so many times before.

"What if...she's taking me to the electric chair? The chair of death...The floor, the windows and the walls all remind me of an old prison movie...Oh boy, this place doesn't look good at all!"

Candice's imagination continues with every second and every step. "This place looks...no, it's spooky."

The attendant's steps quicken as they passed several classrooms along the way. However, Candice can not help noticing how unattractive this woman is.

"I hope my teacher doesn't look as mean and as ugly. Yuck!"

Finally, the office attendant stops, turns the knob, pulls open a door and they hastily walk in. Her rough tone alarms the class.

"Excuse me, Mrs. Neilson. I have a new pupil for you."

Mrs. Neilson looks toward them, "Thank you, Miss Shaw."

The attendant hands Mrs. Neilson the slip, turns, and immediately marches out the door never giving anyone a second glance.

"Umm," thinks Candice, as she observes the woman standing in front of the class, "She looks nice. Nothing like that old dead looking lady who brought me here."

With a warm welcoming smile, Mrs. Neilson takes a looks around the class, as nine years old Elayne Donaldson and her friend Shi Li Kyi, age ten, keeps a close eye on Candice's every movement. Elayne and Shi Li met in their first grade class, while attending Holtman Elementary School and have remained friends ever since.

"Ah...oh," Candice's thoughts are abruptly interrupted by the classroom's instant giggles and whispers.

"Class, class, quiet please?" asks Mrs. Neilson, "As you can see, we have a new student and her name is Candice Felioni...I want everyone to welcome Candice to her new class."

Simultaneously and boisterously the class respond, "HI CANDICE. WELCOME TO YOUR NEW CLASS."

Not knowing what to expect, Candice does wonders about her new classmates. For instance, their thoughts and their expectations of her, because the last thing Candice wants is to make new friends all over again. But the more she wonders the more nervous she becomes.

"Golly, it feels as though they're looking right through my body, watching my heartbeat shake like Jell-O, one beat at a time...Wow, I think...I can hear it and it's...." Candice crosses her hands across her chest, hiding her imaginary heartbeat. "Oh, I think I can feel it shaking too."

Mrs. Neilson picks up the seating chart from her desk. "Now let's see...Where can I seat you!"

While looking around the room, an impulsive shout bursts from the back of the classroom.

"SHE CAN SIT HERE, MRS. NEILSON, NOBODY SITS IN THIS SEAT!"

It is Johnny Burton, the busybody, who always has something to say about something, and the class's bully. It seems as though Johnny has instantly developed an admiration for the new girl. Plus, he is bored with the same girls, everyday the same faces. But Mrs. Neilson is not ignorant to Johnny's behavior and totally ignores his outburst. Johnny repeats himself, this time a little louder, "NOBODY SITS HERE!"

Mrs. Neilson turns and stares at Johnny, placing one hand on her hip. "We know why Johnny Burton. Don't we?"

Suddenly, an explosion of laughter echoes the entire classroom. Embarrassed, Johnny turns away and makes a multitude of ugly faces, and some nasty gestures behind his teacher's back.

It seems that Johnny Burton always has something to do about everything and anything else that has nothing to do with him. Besides, he is always getting into trouble, someway– somehow. He is most definitely true to his name, the troublemaker, and the school's tough guy.

"But...but," repeats Johnny.

Mrs. Neilson quickly replies, "I don't think so, Johnny. Now, would you please be quiet? I don't want to hear or see, and I'm pretty sure your classmates feel the same when it comes to your rude demonstrations; especially, in front of our new student, on how to interrupt my class. Now, sit there and be quite, please?"

Johnny's embarrassment deepens and the only way to retaliate, his moment of revenge, is whispering to himself, "The hell with you, Mrs. Neilson...you heffa."

Mrs. Neilson gazes around the classroom and notices a vacant seat near Elayne Donaldson.

"Elayne, Elayne Donaldson."

Elayne eagerly and proudly answers, "Yes, Mrs. Neilson?"

In a sweet voice, Mrs. Neilson ask, "Would you raise your hand please?"

Elayne raises one arm high, waving it around in the air. Mrs. Neilson identifies Elayne by using her index finger and pointing.

Despite Mrs. Neilson's effort, Candice quickly notices Elayne. She is the girl with the large bangs mashed against her forehead, almost covering her eyes and she has two big white bows that are pinned on two small braids, one on each side of her head.

"Candice take the seat in front of Elayne. Thank you, Elayne." Candice walks modestly to her desk and sits down.

Candice's new classmates constantly stare at her the entire day. And considering the fact, she can't stop thinking about her parents and going home. It seems as if time is moving too slow for whatever reason.

At 11:50 a.m., Mrs. Neilson interrupts and asks the class to put away their assignments and pack up.

"Class...Quiet please! It's lunchtime and as usual we will form one line at the door. Row one, you may line up first. Row two you'll do the same, and we'll continue until all rows are emptied and everybody's in line and ready to walk down to the lunchroom."

Candice can't wait to leave, mumbling, as she slowly eases her bottom out and away from her desk, " Boy, this is going to be a long day, I can feel it."

The class is standing at the door and ready, but standing in line behind Candice is Shi Li and Elayne. They're contemplating, for Candice has a particular air about herself and they really want to introduce themselves. Elayne taps Candice on the shoulder.

"What could she want with me?" Nervously thinking, yet, Candice turns meeting Elayne face to face and looking directly into her eyes.

"Hi Candice, I didn't get a chance to speak to you in class. Mrs. Neilson doesn't like it very much when someone is talking and not listening. My name is Elayne and this is my friend, Shi Li."

"Hi Candice," smiles Shi Li.

Candice speaks ambiguously, "Hi."

Shi Li doesn't hesitate with her questions and gets straight to the point, "What school did you come from?"

Although Candice does answers quickly, "I came from 109 Public School."

"Where is that?" ask Shi Li.

"I know it's not in Detroit," explains Elayne.

Candice justifies her answer, "No, I lived in Pittsburgh before we moved here."

The conversation continues as they follow the class line into the lunchroom.

"Pittsburgh? Ya'll moved all the way to Michigan," Elayne asks.

"Yeah...Me, my mom and my dad."

With so many questions to answer, Candice does understand their reasons, and that Elayne and Shi Li are putting forth an effort to create a new friendship.

With the cutest and sweet smile, Shi Li asks, "Well, we were wondering if you would like to eat lunch with us?"

Candice's mind goes blank for a moment or two, but that really did not stop her mouth from answering for her, "I don't mind. Sure!"

"Great!", replies Elayne.

Several months later, Candice has comfortably adjusted and have become very familiar with her new surroundings and her new friends. That almost everyday before Mrs. Neilson took the class down to the lunchroom, Elayne would sing spiritual hymns in the girl's lavatory while washing her hands. Before you knew it, Shi Li would join in with her Chinese accent, and seconds later Candice would give it a try. Shi Li and Candice would laugh and tease each other on who sounded the worst. Shi Li always argued that she sounds exactly like Diana Ross of the Supremes

Yes, Candice is very pleased with their new blossoming friendship, and as time proceeds, she is also impressed with Holtman Elementary School.

"It's not that bad of a place after all," she thinks.

One Saturday afternoon while sitting on the front steps of Elayne's house, Shi Li ask Elayne about giving Candice a visit, to see if she wants to come out and play for a while. Positively Elayne replies, and suddenly Shi Li adds, "No, lets just walk over there and see if she is at home. If not, we can always go to the playground to see if the new swings are out."

Shi Li and Elayne begin to walk to Candice's house. It only takes a few minutes, for Candice only lives a few blocks away. Once arriving at her house, Shi Li pushes the doorbell and within seconds Candice's mother answers it. "Yes...can I help you, girls?"

In amazement the girls can hardly believe the remarkable resemblance between Candice and her mother.

Elayne ask, "Hi, is Candice home?"

"Yes, she is," says Mrs. Felioni as she looks behind her and calls for her daughter, "Candice...Candice you have company, honey."

Candice runs to the door and she is surprised to see Elayne and Shi Li, though she politely introduces them. "Mom, these are my friends from school. This is Elayne and that's Shi Li."

After the introduction Mrs. Felioni stands at the side of the door listening to the girl's conversation.

Shi Li's asks, "You want to go to the park?"

Elayne adds, "For a little while...have some fun, you know!"

Candice is delighted, "Well, I would have to ask; but I'm sure my mom would say yes."

"Just for a little while," Shi Li reassures.

Candice glances up at her mother and before she can get her question out, Mrs. Felioni gives her permission and Candice kisses her mom on the cheek before leaving.

Elayne and Shi Li admiringly grins at Mrs. Felioni as they leave the house, but before they got completely out of sight, Mrs. Felioni yells out the door, "Candice, don't go too far and be back in one hour... And remember, don't talk to strangers."

"I KNOW MOM! I'm not going to talk to strangers...Which park are we going to?" ask Candice.

"We were thinking about going to the school's playground to swing...I brought my jump rope just in case, maybe we can Double Dutch," replies Elayne as she holds the rope in front of her.

"You know what?" Inquires Shi Li, "I was thinking, summer vacation is only six weeks away. What are you going to do this summer?"

Elayne sucks in a mouth full of air before puffing and blowing it out, "The same thing as every summer," she answers.

"Like what? Are you going on a trip?" Candice ask.

"No, my father says, 'That me and my little sister, Elizabeth, will be attending Bible School again this summer.' He says, 'It just wouldn't look right for the preacher's daughters to run the streets as if their souls were lost in the world."

Elayne was always repeating her father's words. It is as if, she has been brainwashed since birth. Elayne looks down at the ground and continues, "I feel like a prisoner; but, I guess it's okay. He's my father and I'm pretty sure he knows what's best for us. Well, that's what he keeps tell'n Ma mam anyway. Plus, I love my daddy a lot and I don't want to do anything to make him upset...'Cause, he has to keep his mind clear, just in case, The Lord wants to talk to him about somethang with all these sinners running around."

Shi Li's heart hungers for that same kind of attention from her parents, especially from her father. It seems that Elayne's father is always so generous with his affection.

"I don't think my father loves me at all," Shi Li says softly and sadly.

Elayne can not believe her ears as her eyes bucks, almost popping out of her head, her wee voice squealing as she places her tiny hands on her bony hips. "What?"

But Shi Li regretfully continues, "He never looks at me long enough to even notice that I am in the same room. If there is something that needs to be said, he always tells my mother what to say to me. He just stands there and looks at the both of us as if we are strangers. I believe, I have shamed my father's honor."

"Wait a minute?" blurts Candice; she can hardly believe what she is hearing, "That's weird."

"No, not really," Shi Li interrupts,

"Well, it's weird to me," expresses Elayne, throwing her hands high in the air as she shakes her head in disbelief.

After walking several more blocks the girls stop at the corner to wait for the traffic light to turn green, soon crossing, Shi Li compares her native home to her home in America, "That is how it is back home."   "Where is home?" Curiously Candice waits for her friend's answer.

"Far away...China."

Elayne refers to another saying, "My father says, 'That everybody should love one another and have respect. If they did, there would be no wars, no hate, or anything bad in this world. People just need to get along, that all."

Shi Li acknowledges by shaking her head up and down, "That is true."

Candice intervenes, "Well, I know we're not going anywhere this summer. I heard my mom telling my dad that she was thinking about getting a job...and that she's tire of looking at the same old furniture, day in and day out."

Elayne starts to giggle, but Shi Li's mind, her thoughts, drift; she is thinking about another boring summer at home.

"We are not going anywhere, either. I am getting a tutor this summer. In addition, I have to spend more time practicing my karate."

"KARATE," shouts Candice, "You take karate?"

"Yes, my Uncle Chung Kyi, he is my father's brother. He teaches me at his karate school about five times a week. My parents believe, particularly my father, when it comes to disciplining the body and the mind. He says, 'that they both work together, hand in hand, and one can not do without the other."

"Golly," says Candice as she daydreams about taking karate lessons, "Do you like it?"

Shi Li ponders with her answers; "It is not for me to like. It is my father's wish."

Nevertheless, Candice questions keeps coming, "How long have you been taking lessons?"

"Since, I was three years old."

Elayne adds, "Sometimes, when we get together, Shi Li shows me how to do Chinese Splits, she's good."

Candice's anxious to know more as her questions keep coming, "Do you take lessons too, Elayne?"

Sadly saying, "No, my Ma mam doesn't think its lady like. Anyhow, sometimes, in secret, Shi Li will try to teach me when nobody's around. Well...just as long as I don't get caught."

Candice cries out, "GET CAUGHT, why? I think all girls need to know how to defend themselves. Boys act so silly, sometimes."

Elayne adds, motioning with her head, "Yeah, they do, but you know how parents are."

The girls finally reach the playground and run to the swings.

Shi Li yells, "I got the red one because red is my favorite color."

Elayne stops and jokes for a minute, again putting her hands upon her tiny, bony hips. She is her mother's daughter. And this is one of the many things she imitates; "I'll take the blue one. Blue is such a beautiful color. Beautiful like me, if I do say so myself."

With their silly giggles and goofy chuckles, Elayne continues,
"Last summer we went to a Praise Fest. It was in a park under a huge tent and there were so many people a pray'n, and a scream'n, and a shout'n, all day long." Elayne gets off of the swing to

demonstrate, throwing her hands high in the air and shaking them around as she acts out the scene, "Hallelujah! Hallelujah! Praise The Lord, Praise The Lord!"

Elayne is always showing out; yet Candice and Shi Li finds it hard not to laugh at Elayne's silly exhibition. Neither of them has ever been to a Praise Fest or a Baptist Church before.

"That's funny. I've never seen people act like that. Our church, it's so very quiet, nobody says anything," says Candice, "I'm Catholic. All we do is, bow our heads down and make the sign of the cross across our chest." She demonstrates, as she continues to swing. "Last year we went to Italy to visit my Aunt Maria, she's my father's sister. It was so different compared to America."

"One day, I would like to go to Africa," adds Elayne, gazing toward the ball field.

Shi Li smiles, "I would like to go to Africa, too."

"Why Africa?" asks Candice. Candice has always been an inquisitive little girl, and her mother would always say that: 'She was as nosey as a bed bug.'

"That's where most black people come from. My father says, 'That all black people should visit Africa at least once in their lives'. It's our heritage."

"It is also a beautiful country," says Shi Li.

Elayne goes on talking about Africa as if she had actually been there, "Africa's history is very important to our existence here in America and many great men and women have come out of Africa and black people should know the truth about their history, anyway. Not what the white man tell us. So, he too can stand tall in America's society, just like everybody else.' Well, that's what my daddy said."

Yes, Elayne's her father's daughter too, mimicking his personality and quoting his every remark, word for word, as her mind drifts, imagining how it would really be if she lived in Africa.

"Yeah...That sounds great. Maybe one day we should go to Africa."

"We could visit our beautiful native countries together, when we grow up," says Candice grinning.

Elayne nods her head, "That sounds like fun. Yeap, that would be a good idea."

Candice looks out at ball field, "Hey...look, over there."

Looking around to see what she's talking about, Shi Li and Elayne simultaneously answers, "Where?"

Candice stops swinging, "Over there...at that cute boy...on the baseball field."

Shi Li rolls her eyes as she looks at Elayne and before asking, "How can you tell he is cute from here, Candice?"

"Well, he looks cute from here, to me."

"Candice, you are always talking about boys and how cute they look."

"Yeah, every boy looks kind of cute to Candice, says Elayne rolling her eyes upward.

Candice gallantly defends herself, "No, that isn't true...well...okay, and so what? Can I help it if God made so many beautiful things to look at and one of those beautiful things..." Slanting her eyes until they almost look as if they're closed, "...just happens to be stupid boys and smart ones. I believe God gave me eyes, because, he wants me to look at all his beautiful creations, NOW!"

"Sure Candice, whatever you say," Shi Li sneers.

Candice notices that same boy is coming in their direction, she panics, "Oh, here he comes. He's walking this way."

Elayne can't believe Candice's reaction; "He looks all right."

"Yeah, he is not that cute," Shi Li adds, as she continues to insult Candice's taste in boys, "Umm, uh...just all right. I think Candice needs glasses."

Candice eagerly fires back; "Well, at least Johnny Burton doesn't sit in class and stare at me all day long, instead of doing what he's suppose to be doing. He acts like his neck is stuck or broke, or something."

Shi Li confirms, "Yes, Elayne, it is true. He looks at you all the time. He never seems to get any of his work done. Yeah, but I think Candice maybe right about him being stuck...Stuck on stupid."

Elayne reacts to their interrogation. "I don't know why he's looking at me all the time, anyway."

Candice's devilishly smiles at Elayne as she begins to tease her with more insulting remarks, "That boy's in love."

Elayne's lungs tighten, making it impossible to yell, but somehow it finds a way; "IN LOVE...NO WAY... NOT WITH ME... Please set me free, LORD."

"Oh, yes he is," declares Candice, "I heard him talking about you with Tommy Robinson, on Thursday, about how he wish you would be his girl." Candice's quickly begins to sings, irritating Elayne more.

"Elayne's got a boyfriend. Elayne's got a boyfriends...No, Elayne's got a lover."

"Yuck!" shouts Elayne, spiting on the ground.

"The sound of his name makes me sick to the stomach. It feels like, I...I gotta throw up."

"You can say that again," states Shi Li, siding with Elayne.

"I'll never be his girlfriend. He's too stupid. I didn't think anybody could be that dumb."

"What's his problem anyway? Is he retarded?" questions Candice.

Shi Li rest her fist on her chin and answers, "I really do not know what could be wrong with him."

Candice ask, "Is he an orphan? Does he have any family? A father, a mother...and how does she look?"

Elayne replies, "His mother, she looks okay. I've never seen his father."

"I think his parents are divorce," says Shi Li.

"Divorce," Elayne shocking replies.

"I wouldn't know what to do if my parents got divorced," says Candice.

"Me either, if my parents divorce...Please, I don't even want to think about it. It's not the way The Lord planned it to be. People get'n divorced and stuff," says Elayne.

Shi Li continues: "His mother never comes to any of our school programs and I have never seen her at a Parent Teacher Meeting, yet."

"Wait a minute, once, I remember...that day when Johnny got caught smoke'n in the boy's lavatory," says Elayne.

"Oh yeah, that is right, I remember now. She came to the school looking something terrible. It looked as though she was sick or something. She must have had a bad day, that day, because her hair needed combing real bad. She was in desperate need of a beauty parlor; that is for sure," says Shi Li.

Elayne continues, "She was drunk, Shi Li."

"Drunk? ...She drinks?" asks Candice.

"Whisky. Well she smelled like whisky, " replies Elayne, remembering that day very well. Johnny's mother wobbling from one side of the hall to the other, bumping into everything that was in her way and holding on to the walls for support.

"The principal, Mr. Lenowski had to help her to a seat so she wouldn't fall down," Shi Li adds.

"That's terrible," says Candice, who is truly amazed about all the things she is hearing.

Elayne also finds it tasteless, "Let's change the subject, I don't want to talk about her anymore. She's make'n me sick just think'n about her and drink'n whiskey...Yuck!"

"I know what, let's go to the drug store and get some ice cream. I am getting hot sitting in the sun swinging," suggests Shi Li.

As the three girls walk toward the school gate opening, all of a sudden, coming in their direction, the devil himself, Johnny Burton and his little demonic sidekick of a brother, Mark Burton.

Shi Li's first to observe them, "Oh no, look...Do not say one word."

Elayne is quick to respond, "Don't worry, I won't."

Candice has a feeling that there might be some trouble, "Keep walking everybody. Don't even look at them a little bit."

The girls commence to cross the street when Johnny starts to yell, "HEY ELAYNE, ELAYNE, WHERE YA'LL GO'N? ...CAN I GO, TOO? ELAYNE...ELAYNE. DON'T ACT LIKE YOU DON'T SEE ME. HEY...CANDICE...SHI LI...CAN I GO WITH YA'LL? OH, SO, NOW YA'LL GONNA ACT LIKE YA'LL BLIND OR SOMETHANG."

Candice utters, "No, we see you...Go away you demon child."

Mark adds his two cents worth of comments, howling along with his brother, "ELAYNE...JOHNNY'S CRAZY ABOUT YOU, GIRL. WHY DON'T YOU COME OVER HERE AND GIVE HIM A KISS...YOU KNOW YOU WANT TOO, HAA...A...AH."

Johnny and Mark's remarks were loud and shameful; "ELAYNE, ONE DAY, I'M GONNA MAKE YOU MY GIRLFRIEND AND YOU KNOW IT. DON'T YOU? DON'T YOU KNOW IT? YEAH YOU, YOU KNOW IT, I CAN FEEL YOUR HEART BEATING FOR MY LOVE."

Johnny puts his hands over his heart and falls to the ground.

Elayne immediately murmurs, "Oh, no you won't and no you don't, either."

"HELP ELAYNE, HELP ME, CAUSE YOU CAN'T FIGHT MY LOVE. YOU JUST WAIT AND SEE. ONE DAY YOU'RE GONNA BE MY GIRL...THAT'S OKAY, YOU CAN ACT LIKE YOU DON'T SEE ME FALL'N FOR YOU, BUT I KNOW YOU DO." Johnny silly display is so ridiculous, laughing hard, holding his stomach as he gets off the ground and crosses the street.

Candice and Shi Li can not help but to grin at Johnny's demented emotions.

"WHAT, YA'LL SMILING AT? YOU KNOW IT'S TRUE. ONE DAY, ELAYNE, ONE DAY."

Mark's getting bored, "Come on, Johnny. Let's play some ball, the guys are wait'n for us...Come on before they leave."

"Okay. Cool...Yeah, I'm comin, Mark."

As Johnny and Mark go through the school's gate, Johnny turns back and gives one last yell, "ELAYNE...WHEN ARE YOU GONNA INVITE ME TO YOUR HOUSE? I HOPE IT'S SOON...AND MAKE SURE THE OLD PREACHER MAN AIN'T HOME. CAUSE, WE GOT A LOT OF TALK'N TO DO. YOU HEAR ME? DON'T FORGET, CAUSE, I'LL BE WAIT'N."

The girls start to walk faster, trying hard to ignore Johnny's exposition and his sidekick, Mark's remarks.

Meanwhile, further east of Detroit, past the downtown area, across Woodward Avenue, near what was known as Black Bottom. Things weren't so beautiful. Black Bottom, an African-American community, were blacks once owned over 300 businesses in the Detroit area and promising businesses weren't the only things thriving. It also had its share of illegal activities that penetrated through the back doors of the community; one of them was known as the Black Connection, Mafia, and also known as, The Organization, that moved eastward along with the existing community.

Beauden's his name, a member of the Black Connection: profit, pussy and pleasure are his games. On this particular day, he has come to collect on monies owed from a drug addict, by the name of Derrick Morris. Beauden is tiring of Derrick's inability to pay; not only did his drug habit keep him in debt to the organization, but he also had a bad gambling habit, and playing the numbers became a daily activity that really was too expensive for his own good.

Derrick Morris was a nice guy, a family man, everybody thought he would do well in life. He has a wife and one daughter. He married at the age twenty to his high school sweetheart. They were a very happy couple, until things started going bad for the Morris family. Derrick lost his job, due to cutbacks at the auto plant, and with bills coming in faster than he could pay, his wife went out and got a job working at the local five and ten cent store. Due to his layoff, Derrick's pride quickly depleted. He always thought that the man was the head of the household and the breadwinner of the family.

Low self-esteem didn't stop Derrick's search for employment. For months he looked for any kind of work in and around the city and so did many other people in the same predicament. Exhausted, ashamed and broken, Derrick drifted into an unfamiliar lifestyle. First, his casual drinking became an everyday ritual. When he got drunk, he took his frustrations out on his wife by beating her. Second, his thirst for marijuana became so severe that he had to have a J (joint) for breakfast every morning, eventually, lunch and sometimes right after dinner.

Finally, one night after hanging out with his bro's in the hood, he had his first taste of cocaine, then and only then, Derrick found the relief he was searching for. Like they say, "no pain no gain." Derrick was hooked. His habit had taken control of his mind, the difference between right and wrong ran parallel and he cared for nobody, not even himself. His need and his love for cocaine soon became his master, his only reason to live, and the more he used the more he wanted. Sometimes, he would buy on credit and more sooner than later his debt grew larger and his promise to pay faded like the smoke from his joint.

One night, Beauden and a couple of his thugs come to collect monies owed, but Derrick's pockets are empty, not one thin dime can be found in the entire household. Derrick runs frantically through the house checking his wife's belongings. Again, just as before, there's nothing, broke like a three-legged chair. Derrick's wife, Norma, can't keep the little money she makes, working at the five and dime, in the house long enough to do anything. Many times, Derrick would meet his wife on payday and walk with her to the bank, cashing her check then taking what he needed, if not all of it.

There's a knock on the front door. Derrick peers through the peek-hole, but he is too nervous and too scared to answer it. He hesitates on what to do next...should he answer it or pretend he is not home? Two more knocks on the door and this time they are louder, stronger, very aggressive. Shaking like a leaf, Derrick finally opens it, pretending to be cool as if nothing's going on.

"Hey Man, come on in," he says, with a slight grin and acting surprised.

Beauden and his thugs pushes through the door, opening it wider as they walk in, then quietly closing it behind them. Trying his best to keep his cool as the sweat beads on his face. Hopefully, trying to keep everybody around him cool, Derrick sets out on a friendly note.

"Hey, I didn't know you guys were comin all the way over here, today, Man. You could have called or something." Nervously rubbing his head with the most ridiculous smile stretched across his face Derrick starts to joke, "Uh...Ah...ah aha...I'm waiting for my wife to come home, 'cause I ain't got no money right now." He laughs louder, "Ahh aha... aa...She went to get some for me though...But, you fellas got here before she could get back." He laughs again, "He. .e. .e...ah...ta...e...e."

Then Derrick gives a short weak laugh to assure himself that everything's okay, "Ha a ah...I ain't got none either. Ain't that a 'bit..., Man. Ah...a...a...ha"

Beauden and his thugs aren't in the mood for anymore of Derrick's jokes and they did not come to play games; but still, Derrick's frail and bony self continues. "But, but...I'm gonna get your money, Man. Just give me a little mo time, okay? Ha..a..ha...ah okay, Beau, cool?"

Beauden and his thugs stands cold faced and straight.

"Man that's the same sh... you said two days ago," says Beauden.

That's when Derrick realizes he is the only one laughing and he quickly begins to stutter, "Uh...Uh... But...but, but...we're still co...o...o...ol, ain't we-e-e?"

Beauden signals with his two fingers pointing at Derrick, "Break his legs."

The two thugs never said a word as they approach Derrick.

Derrick quickly crawls over the back of the sofa trying to find a safe haven. "Hey Man. Hey Man, no Beauden, Man...I thought we...e...e were co...o...ol," he hollers.

Carefree, Beauden replies, "We are."

Derrick is snatched from behind the sofa, knocked to the floor, socked and kicked as he pleads and yells for his life, "HEY MAN, WAIT...I KNOW...I KNOW...WHAT I CAN DO?" Without a second thought, "How 'bout if I give you Nessa? ...You like Nessa...right? Yeah...Yeah...you remember my baby, my little girl. I know you like her don't you? She's young, sweet, tender and good. You remember Beauden? ...You know, like last time...Cool?"

Derrick frantically hollers for his daughter hoping she will answer him, "VANESSA...HEY...NESSA...GET YOUR BUTT IN HERE GIRL...AND I MEAN RIGHT NOW."

Vanessa never answers her father's call and Derrick doesn't wait for her, either. Without Delay he rushes into her bedroom signaling Beauden and his thugs to follow him.

Derrick aggressively pushes open Vanessa's bedroom door and points at his daughter as she pretends to be asleep. Once more, and like many times before, Derrick offers his twelve year old daughter, Vanessa, as temporary installment, and once more Beauden, a man twenty-four years her senior accepts. Loosening the button on his jacket, Beauden slowly walks into Vanessa's bedroom while his two thugs and Derrick wait patiently outside her door.

Derrick shows no remorse. However, he gives a sigh of relief, smiling, as he closes Vanessa's bedroom door. Once inside her bedroom Beauden licks his lips and whispers to her, "Hey Vanessa...you little sweet thang you."

Vanessa never says a word or look to see who has entered her bedroom. She lays motionless as Beauden removes his jacket and then his pants, making that weird sounding noise he calls a laugh. "Eeee...eee...e...e...u...e."

Within seconds his fat out of shape body covers her. During the intercourse, Vanessa's tears are enormous as they roll onto her pillow. Her bruised and battered mind gradually takes her into a world of her own. A world of darkness, a place where she could always escape, a place where she feels safe and free, a world of sanity as she blocks out the insanity of what is happening.

PEOPLE SAY

CHAPTER 2

After arriving at the drug store, the three friends decide to take counter seats as the waitress approaches.

"Hi, may I take your orders, please?" Her mannerism is very polite and the orders are taken, but that doesn't stop Elayne from thinking back, placing her hands over her face. "Oh boy, I can't believe it. That Johnny Burton has a mental problem and he's teach'n his little brother, Mark, how to be stupid, too."

Shi Li pities the thought that Johnny is not a good role model. However, the hours are quickly passing, Candice realizes that it is getting late and its time for her to go home. After eating and paying for their food, Candice, Elayne and Shi Li begin to walk home, laughing and joking with each other along the way.

"This has really been a wonderful day except for Johnny and Mark," Candice says regretfully.

Elayne agrees, "It sure has."

They decide to walk to Candice's house first, through the side door and then into the kitchen they go. Candice's mother is putting her final touch on the dinner entrees, before she notices the girls standing behind her. She decides to make small talk.

"Did you young ladies have a nice time?"

"Yes Mom, we went to the school ground and swung."

"Good, but don't go anywhere Candice, dinner is almost ready."

Candice replies, "Sure Mom, I won't...But can I have company in my room for a little while?"

"Just for a little while, Candice, " Mrs. Felioni replies.

Shi Li and Elayne follow Candice to her bedroom and while walking through the house, Shi Li and Elayne notice how nice everything looks, and how neat things are placed. All the furniture, even the pictures on the wall was positioned so magnificently.

Astounded by the beautiful displays, Elayne finds it hard not to compliment their home. "You have a pretty house, Candice."

"Thank you, my mom decorates everything while my dad sits back and complains about how she's spending too much money."

Elayne also notices the house is full of plants and statues of people in compromising positions. "When I grow up, I'm going to have a beautiful house just like this."

"My parents have lots of things from China. My grandmother brought them to this country when she moved here. That was before I was born," says Shi Li.

Candice shows Elayne and Shi Li her doll collection and many more toys and games. Another hour has past and Elayne realizes it is time for her leave. "Candice, I have to go now, or I'll get in trouble if I come home late."

"Me too," Shi Li agrees. "My parents will be upset with me if I am not home at a reasonable hour."

"That's okay, parents are like that, all nervous acting and stuff, especially my mom. I'll call you tomorrow." replies Candice.

"Let's walk to school together," Elayne suggests.

"Yeah, we can meet at the bus stop like we always do," says Candice as she walks her friends to the side door.

Mrs. Felioni is taking the dinner plates off the shelf when the girls walk by. "Would you girls like to stay for dinner?"

Even though Shi Li and Elayne would enjoyed having dinner with the Felioni's, they know things are at the beginning stages of their relationship and their parents have not yet met and are strict about eating at strange houses.

"No, thank you. We really have to leave, " answers Shi Li.

"But thanks anyway," Elayne adds.

"Maybe some other time?" asks Mrs. Felioni in a most pleasant manner, still smiling as she reaches for the towel on the table to wipe her hands. "Come back again, you're always welcome...Go straight home and be careful," she adds as she waves.

"Bye Candice, bye Mrs. Felioni," says Shi Li.

Elayne intervenes, speaking a bit louder; "We'll see you tomorrow."

When Elayne arrives home, she walks into the kitchen and sees her mother who's also preparing dinner. Elayne has a three years old sister, Elizabeth, named after her grandmother on her father's side of the family; Elayne was named after her mother's mother. What a coincidence that both grandmothers' names starts with the letter E. Everyone thought it would be a wonderful idea to name their daughters after their mothers.

Mr. and Mrs. Maurice Samuel Donaldson are deep rooted in their religious beliefs. The entire family graciously attends church every Sunday. Mr. Donaldson, Rev. M. S. Donaldson, is the pastor of Mt. Bethel Baptist Church. Elayne and her mother, Gracie loves to sing in the church's choir. Every Tuesday from the day she could remember, when Elayne was just a little tot, and for at least two hours, from 6pm until 8pm, was choir rehearsal.

Missing choir rehearsal or Sunday school, well, that thought never crossed Elayne's mind. Because deeply rooted in her heart, it was equal to sinning against The Lord. Plus, Elayne believes that if you miss any service, especially Sunday service, you would surely burn in Hell. Every Sunday is The Lord's day and it should be given the utmost respect. Beside, Elayne truly loves going to church and writing her own hymns. This was her way of telling The Lord how much she loves and appreciates him for loving and protecting her from Satan and his demonic system of things. Elayne truly hopes and prays, that maybe, one Sunday, she will have the chance to sing one of her songs that she composed to The Lord in her father's church.

Anxious to see what her mother is cooking, Elayne peeks into one of the hot pots on the stove, and not realizing the lid is also hot before dropping it onto the stove-top. The loud noise and Elayne's presence startles her mother that she immediately turns to see what the commotion is about.

"Elayne, get away from that stove before you burn your nose off, girl. The last thing I need is a little brown nose mixed in with those mashed potatoes."

Elayne picks the lid up, this time with a kitchen mitt and places it back on the pot.

"I just wanna see what we're havin for dinner, Ma mam."

"You'll find out soon enough. Now go and wash your hands, dinner will be ready in a few minutes." Gracie fans her hands as if she is shooing a fly. "Go on, now."

"Good, because I'm hungry...I need some food," says Elayne.

Gracie looks inquisitively at her daughter. "Girl, you act like you haven't eaten all day."

Elayne sniffs the fried chicken on the table as she passes.

"Oooo...Ma mam, can I have a chicken leg for dinner? Daddy always eats the legs every time you cook chicken."

"Now Elayne, you know, that's the only part of the chicken your daddy eats."

Elayne pleads with her mother, batting those dark brown baby eyes. "Yeah, I know. I just want to eat a chicken leg once before I die...Or maybe, I can bite a little meat off, just a little piece. And maybe, this'll be the day daddy will be so hungry he won't even notice it. "

Gracie couldn't help laughing at her daughter's silly disposition over a chicken leg. "Girl quit talkin silly like that...Well, you can have it this one time, you hear me, child."

Elayne rushes to her mother, quickly hugging her around waist. Then she closes her eyes as she lays her head against her mother's breast. After their tender moment, Gracie takes a spoon and stirs a little more butter and milk into the pot, for creamier mashed potatoes, the way her husband likes them.

"Elayne we'll just tell your daddy that this chicken was born with one leg", she smiles before asking, "did you wash your hands Missy?"

"Nope, not yet, Ma mam."

"Well, get in there, 'cause, I'm gonna need some help set'n this here table."

Gracie mumbles while taking the mashed potatoes out of the pot with a large spoon and dropping them into a large bowl. "Now lets get this food on the table."

Elayne quickly forgets all about washing her hands, because she enjoys watching her mother maneuvers around the kitchen, she makes everything seem so easy.

Gracie is very familiar and happy with her daughter's behavior: There are no problems in school, people always have good things to say about Elayne; and especially, her beautiful smile that always meant, without a doubt, how much she really cares.

All of a sudden, Elayne is startled by the sound of her mother's voice, it urgently echoes through her head, waking her from her daydream, "Did you wash your hands, Miss Lady?"

She jumps, "No, not yet. Ma mam, I...I was."

"Well, get in there."

"Okay, Ma mam."

Elayne hurries out of the kitchen almost running on the tip of her toes and dashes into the bathroom. She washes her hands vigorously, making sure that there is not even a speck of dirt left under her nails. She dries her hands and then hangs the towel neatly on the towel rack, the same way her mother hangs it, then swiftly rushes back toward the kitchen. Her attention is drawn by the sound of the television in the living room, she looks in and there she sees, Elizabeth watching one of her favorite shows.

"Hi, Baby girl," she says, getting down on her knees and gives her sister a juicy kiss on her forehead. "I love you." Elayne jumps back on her feet and runs into the kitchen, holding her hands out to be inspected. "Ma mam, my hands are clean, look...What do you want me to do first?"

While standing at the sink, rinsing the lettuce, Gracie points at the dish cabinet. "Look up there and get those plates out of the cabinet and set the table...and get some glasses, too."

Eagerly, Elayne dashes to the cabinet. "Yes Ma mam, I will."

Elayne loves helping her mother in the kitchen; she believes the kitchen is where a woman is supposed to be. The reason why: she has never seen her mother do anything else but stay home and take care of her family and the household duties. Contentedly Elayne sets the table, dish after dish and glass after glass, until everything is set neatly into place.

A few minutes later, the front door opens and Elayne glances toward the front room. It is Reverend Donaldson. He has returned after another day of working at the church. People are always coming to him with their problems. His duties include assisting the congregation with prayer, because most of them don't know how to pray, or they are just too afraid to talk to The Lord alone. Mostly, because of their sinful ways, and they really don't think The Lord will listen without the Reverend standing at their sides. Moreover, he loves giving people a helping hand, food and other things they might need. And he even prays for them in silence when he goes to bed at night. When it comes to talking to The Lord, Reverend Donaldson surely knows what to say. Sometimes, he will try to comfort his followers, especially if they believed that they are consumed with too much sin, by reading scriptures from the Bible, trying his best to let them know that 'all are welcome' in the eyes of The Lord. He would always remind them 'All men and women are born in sin.'

Reverend Donaldson walks into the living room where Elizabeth is watching television and picks her up for his daily 'hello' kiss. "Hey, Baby girl. How's my sweet little angel from heaven?" He would repeat those same words to her everyday.

Elizabeth is extremely excited to see her daddy that she screams as loud as she can, almost piercing his ears. "DADDY, DADDY." Elizabeth throws up her arms for a hug. He lifts her from the floor, putting her on his back for a piggyback ride into the kitchen.

The smell of good food cooking when the Reverend comes home always seems to capture his attention and his stomach and he would always tease Gracie by saying: 'That was the main reason he married her, cause she sure knows how to strike a match.' Reverend Donaldson is always joking about why he married Gracie, but Elayne knows that he loves her very much and that is the real reason he married her.

Reverend Donaldson met his wife when they were teenagers singing in the church choir. On that very day, and still today he says, "Something came over me when I first laid eyes on her, she must be the one for me. The one sent down from the heavens above."

Elayne approaches her father as he enters the kitchen doorway, "Hi, Daddy, I love you."
"Hey, my sweet pie, daddy loves you too...Smells like you and your Ma mam are cookin up a storm in this here kitchen." Reverend Donaldson kisses Elayne's cheek before putting Elizabeth in her high chair. Then he makes his way toward his wife, takes her into his arms, holds her tight and plants a huge juicy kiss, one that is full of love, on her lips. And by the way they always looked at each other, Elayne can tell that they are still very much in love. Sometimes, Elayne would over hear her father's confession of his love, as he whispered into Gracie's ears, clutching each other intensely. He'd say, "I love you Gracie, and did I tell you how beautiful you are today?" And Ma mam's reply will always be the same even though she was teasing: "I know...and you better love me, after all this cookin over this hot stove every darn day...Don't let me mention all the clothes I washed and the floors I mopped." Then she would laugh.
"Yes in deedy. I'm surely glad that The Lord has blessed me with a beautiful God fearing family. Praise The Lord. Praise The Lord."
Elayne and Elizabeth take pleasure watching their parents' display of love, affection and true devotion to each other and the entire family.
"Did everythang go well, today?" he ask.
"Everythang went just fine, Samuel," says Ma mam.

That question was asked everyday when Rev. Donaldson came home from work, and you better believe it was expected.

'I guess things wouldn't be the same if daddy didn't ask,' considers Elayne.

Elizabeth looks at the food on the table and points, "Food, food, Ma mam, eat."

Gracie turns and asks, "Why is Baby girl making so much commotion?"

"I think somebody's tryin to tell you somethang," says Rev. Donaldson, as he releases his wife and walks across the kitchen to Elizabeth. "What's the matter with you, now, Li'l Angel? You know your Ma mam is gonna to feed you in just a minute. You can wait another minute, can't you?" Rev. Donaldson rubs the top of Elizabeth's head.

"You better hurry up and bring this girl some food, before she turn this high chair over."

They all laugh at Elizabeth who is sticking her tongue out as far as she can at the fried chicken on the table; unaware of the funny faces she is making.

"Your food is comin right up, Elizie," Gracie says, trying to comfort her.

"Everybody can have a seat now, I think we got everythang, in The Lord's eyes."

"Daddy, can I say grace? I want to thank The Lord for our dinner," Elayne politely pleads as he nods his head.

"Yes, you can. I truly believe The Lord would like that very much."

"May we all bow our heads, please?" ask Gracie.

Elayne closes her eyes, "Dear Lord. We thank you for this food..."

Everyday after dinner Gracie would clear the table as Reverend Donaldson faithfully takes their two daughters into the front room for an hour of Bible readings. Gracie would soon join her family, because she didn't want to miss anything. And after Bible Study there would be a homework review for Elayne, then one hour of television, bath time for the girls, and finally a bedtime prayer with a good night kiss. In addition, every morning at the same time, a little past dawn, Gracie is up cooking breakfast. Reverend Donaldson especially likes grits and eggs, bacon, toast with lots of butter and a large glass of juice. And every morning the Reverend will say, "It ain't nothang like havin a good breakfast before go'n to work, " before sitting down at the table as Gracie places a hearty plate of food in front of him.

Everyday like clockwork, Reverend Donaldson would take a sniff from his plate and continue, "A real breakfast, the kind that sticks to a man's ribs and carries him through the who-o-l-e day, yes Lord, yes Lord."

Sometimes Elayne and Elizabeth would eat their favorite, a bowl of cold cereal. After breakfast, Reverend Donaldson is off to church, or doing some kind to charity work. Elayne is very proud of her family and especially her father's job, working with The Lord and giving his all, trying to save as many souls as he can. During the later hours of the day, Gracie is home teaching Elizabeth her fundamentals, ABC's and counting, while Elayne goes off to school. This daily practice has continued in the Donaldson's household for years.

About five minutes past eight in the morning and Candice's running to the front door. "Mom, I gotta go."

"Candice, don't forget your lunch, honey."

"I got it...Bye Mom; they're waiting for me at the bus stop." Audrey runs behind Candice and kisses her good-by as she rushes out of house. Audrey would always screams to her daughter while standing at the doorway. "CANDICE, BE CAREFUL...AND DON'T TALK TO STRANGERS."

You can say its a mother's instinct, that constant warning that alerts Candice about the dangers of talking to people she doesn't know. But Candice is a loving and trusting person and the warnings doesn't affect her inner spirit one bit.

The memories of how things were played a vital role in Audrey's mind. "This world isn't the way it used to be when I was growing up and the news on the TV don't make me feel any better."

"I WON'T," shouts Candice running faster to meet her friends.

Candice as she stops and grasps for a breath, "HEY ELAYNE," she shouts. Moments later, Shi Li arrives, "Hi everybody...Let's go before we are late for school...Did you do your homework?"

"Yes", says Elayne, "It was easy."

"Me too. It was very easy, but what about the Spelling Bee next week?" ask Shi Li.

Candice contemplates, because she is too intense and apprehensive about the Spelling Bee. Even though, she wants to participate, Candice is lacking self-confident.

"Tryouts are today," Shi Li eagerly says.

"I'm go'n to try out for it, too. I can't wait, responds Elayne.

"I don't know if I will," downheartedly Candice says.

"Why, you do not think you can do it?" curiously Shi Li questions.

"I don't know. I don't want to get up there and look stupid. I know I'll probably mess up on an easy word like KITCHEN or EVALUATE or something like that, I just know it'll be a baby word."

"Let's work together and help each other. Only one can win anyway and it might as well be one of us," assures Elayne.

"Oh, that is a good idea. We can meet after school and practice," Shi Li agrees.

Candice is still uncertain, "If you think it will work."

"It'll work. We'll make it work. We can meet at my house if you want", replies Elayne.

The three girls are very excited with the idea and Candice is thrilled by her friend's offer. "Okay, how about if we meet about four o'clock all this week?"

"Sure, why not? We are friends...and that is what being friends is all about", Shi Li smiles.

"We can do it. We can do anything we want if we work together, right?" asks Elayne. They cheerfully answer, "yes," laughing as they enter the large double doors.

While standing in the school's corridor, in front of their lockers, the three girls notice Johnny Burton talking to Gary Snowden. Gary seems very upset about something. A few seconds later, they see Johnny take Gary's homework out of his notebook. Then he pushes Gary against his locker, reaches into his pocket, takes his money and dares him to tell. Time and time again, almost everyday, this would happen and Gary would never say a word to anyone.

"Did you see that?" questions Shi Li.

"Yeah, that punk Johnny," says Candice.

"Why not fight back or something?" adds Shi Li.

"He's afraid of Johnny and his brother, Mark; that's why." Elayne explains.

Gary embarrassingly looks over at Elayne and her friends, then hangs his head down, hoping to hide his shameful face and the little pride he has left.

"Johnny and Mark follows him home almost every day and beats him up." Elayne continues.

"Well, I am not afraid of Johnny or his brother," declares Shi Li as she makes a tight fist.

"Maybe, one day he'll fight back, " states Elayne reaching into her locker, and all the while, keeping one eye on Johnny.

Johnny senses someone watching him, he looks up and notices Elayne and her friends staring. He releases Gary's shirt collar, "Go." Then takes his hand, kisses it, and blows it to Elayne.

"YUCK, did you see that? I'm gonna be sick...Oh boy, I hope he's not comin over here..." utters Elayne. Before Elayne can finish her sentence Johnny starts walking in her direction. But his devilish intentions are cut short when Mrs. Neilson walks out of the classroom.

"Good morning, girls," she says. They speak simultaneously. "Good morning, Mrs. Neilson." She looks over at Johnny and Gary. "Good morning, boys."

To hide his guilt Johnny promptly speaks. "Good morning Mrs. Neilson, you look very beautiful in that dress."

"Thank you, Johnny Burton."

Still, Gary never says a word, but Mrs. Neilson's no fool about troubled students: she notices a despondent stare on Gary's face. After some of her students have entered the classroom, she confines Gary outside the door, placing one hand on his shoulder and asks, "Gary, is something wrong?"

Too nervous and too scared to speak, Gary shakes his head before answering in a meek voice, then he drops his head, holding it downward, looking at the floor. "No, Mrs. Neilson."

Hoping he would tell what is disturbing him, she decides to ask insignificant questions. Still Gary says nothing as Mrs. Neilson is disrupted by the class' outburst and enters the room.

"Class, class...hurry up and get to your seat before the bell rings. There is Bell Work on the board and I want it completed before 9:20. Do you understand me!"

"Yes Mrs. Neilson."

She walks back into the hallway, with her arms folded at her waist, and stands next to Gary. While observing his behavior, he slowly glances up at Mrs. Neilson and answers. "Nothing wrong."

Moments later, the three friends and Johnny gradually enter the classroom; however, Mrs. Neilson and Gary are still standing outside the door. Mrs. Neilson is determined to unlock Gary's emotional secret.

"Gary, are you sure there's nothing bothering you?"

Again Gary answers, and this time in an even lower voice. "Yes, I'm sure, Mrs. Neilson. Nothing's bothering me."
Mrs. Neilson moves aside as Gary casually enters the classroom. She observes him the entire morning, because Gary's negative mannerism was just to sensitive to ignore. Yet, she doesn't ask him anymore questions, nor does she accept the answers that were given. 'He's lying...I know something's wrong, and after teaching for fifteen years, I can tell when something's wrong with one of my students. If there is a problem, or problems, I will find out.'

Mrs. Neilson enters the classroom, closing the door behind her. And as usual, the students are hardheaded and disorderly, roaming about, throwing paper and shooting spitballs.

"Class, please take your seats. We have work to do and I recommend that you get started this instant." Mrs. Neilson looks around her classroom and again notices Gary becoming more and more hollow. "Class we had homework over the weekend and I would appreciate if you could pass your papers to the front, please."

Shocked by her sudden request, Gary turns and stares at Johnny, thinking, 'Mrs. Neilson asked for our homework. She never asks for homework this early in the morning...We just got here...Oh boy, I was hoping that she would ask for it at the end of the day like she always does. Golly, I haven't had a chance to do it again."

Mrs. Neilson looks directly at Gary. "Gary, would you collect the assignments for me, please?"

Tormented by her request, Gary politely replies as he eases out of his seat. "Yes, Mrs. Neilson."

Gary glances at Johnny as he passes his desk. After collecting all papers and laying them on her desk, he returns to his seat. Johnny pokes Gary in the back with his pencil, he turns, and Johnny gives him a nasty look and his tone of voice is even more threatening. Sending chills through Gary's body, causing him to almost lose control of his bladder, almost wetting his pants.

"If you tell, you know what's gonna happen." Johnny makes a fist and slams it into his other hand.

To comfort himself, Gary closes his eyes, blocking out Johnny's face, because he knows Johnny will do just what he said. Gary is terrified and he doesn't want anymore trouble. Besides, how many more black eyes excuses can he give to his parents? He feels the best thing for him to do is to run as fast as he can, right out of the classroom and never come back. Gary is the class' nerd, has always been and he knows it. Gary doesn't want to hurt anybody or have anybody hurt him. 'Why can't people leave other people alone. Especially me!'

At the end of the day Mrs. Neilson calls to Johnny, asking him to come to the front of the class. "Johnny, I haven't received your homework assignment."

Surprised by her statement, Johnny searches for a good excuse before looking at Gary. "I gave it to Gary when he collected the other assignments, Mrs. Neilson."

Johnny starts to wonder if Gary have said anything to Mrs. Neilson when he went to the front of the class to turn in the assignments, or maybe outside the door this morning. Johnny is nervous as he repeats his statement and hesitates before getting up. "I turned it in with the rest of the assignments, Mrs. Neilson. Yeah, I did. Remember?" He pokes Gary again, this time with his finger and grins. "You remember Gary, I...I...gave it to you, remember?" .

Mrs. Neilson takes the assignments off her desk and runs her fingers through them again. "Well, Johnny I've looked through all the assignments and I don't see yours at all. Why don't you show me?"

Johnny guiltlessly strolls to the front of the classroom, to Mrs. Neilson's desk, as the class anxiously waits for Johnny to dig himself out of this mess. "Here it is, Mrs. Neilson." Johnny stands there, grabbing at the stack of papers, with the most stupid look on his face and hands it to Mrs. Neilson.

"Gary Snowden. Johnny Burton, when did you change your name to Gary Snowden?"

Johnny had forgotten to erase Gary's name off the homework assignment. Startled by the discovery, Johnny didn't know quite how to answer the question. The words from Johnny's mouth jammed his throat, making it almost impossible even for him to speak. He stutters, "I...I...didn't."

"That's what this paper reads, 'Gary Snowden'...And in the other corner it reads 'Johnny Burton' Well Johnny Burton?" Everything becomes exceptionally quiet as Mrs. Neilson takes a long harsh look at Johnny. "Gary Snowden come here, please?" Twisting his pencil between his fingers, Gary slowly paces his way to her desk.

"Gary, is this your paper?" she calmly asked.

Gary says not a word; he is still too frightened to say anything. His toes begin to curl up in his shoes, not even a mutter was heard as the class silently waits. All you can hear are the clock's clicks.

"Johnny can you tell me what's going on here?"

Mrs. Neilson knows exactly what is going on, but she wants to hear their explanation. Johnny boldly interrupts, blurting loudly, with a mouthful of lies. "He must have put his name on my paper when he was looking at it. Yeah, I saw him write something. But I wasn't sure what he was doing. He had to do it, when he collected them, Mrs. Neilson. Yeah, that's what he did. I saw him."

"Gary, is that true?" she ask.

But Gary continues to stand motionless and silent. Finally, Mrs. Neilson is upset with the lies and lays the paper on her desk. "That's it...No other explanation will be necessary. I think you boys better come with me. There is one thing I will not allow and that is cheating...I will not allow any form of cheating in this class, at any time."

Yet, Johnny's mouth constantly continues to fill itself with more lies and they're blurting out even faster. Lies even his classmates are finding it difficult to keep up with. Yet, he tries his best to put the blame some place else. "But Mrs. Neilson, I...I...didn't do any, I..."

Mrs. Neilson isn't in the mood. "I said, explanations will not be necessary! Do you have a hard time understanding English, Johnny?" However, Gary doesn't have a hard time at all understanding Mrs. Neilson.

'Will Not Be Necessary'. Gary knows that Mrs. Neilson only use those words and that tone of voice when she is upset with the class.

"Oh no, am I going to get kicked out of school?" Johnny and his brother, Mark, will surely beat me up, again? ...I hope she doesn't call my parents. I'm going to really get it. I'm a dead kid. Maybe, if I run away everybody would be happy."

Gary constantly thinks the worst thoughts he can. And the fear along with the many questions speeding through his mind, he knows this mean destruction, like a racecar driver crashing into a large brick wall or a crazy person jumping off a bridge. He knows this is the end for him. 'What's gonna happen to me now?'

Nevertheless, Johnny Burton doesn't show any remorse and going to the principal's office is no big deal. He knows his mother isn't going to do anything and this isn't his first time and probably not his last. The class looked on, stoned-still and stagnant as

Johnny and Gary stood there with foolish expressions masking their faces.

Shi Li leans toward Elayne and Candice, whispering, "I knew this was going to happen."

"Why, won't Gary tell the truth?" ask Candice.

Feeling sorry for Gary, Elayne explains, "He's scared."

Shi Li adds, "Scared stupid."

"Class, I want everybody to put their books away and take out your study sheets, I'll be right back. Miss. Edmonds, from next door will be peeking in periodically, so while I'm gone, I want you to study for the Spelling Bee next week. I'm quite sure we'll have a winner from this class."

Mrs. Neilson closes the door and escorts Johnny and Gary to the main office. Meanwhile, reports are filed and parents are called, but Johnny's mother never came to pick him up from school that day, or any other day. Mr. and Mrs. Snowden promptly arrive at the school before the clock strikes three that afternoon. The Snowden's are very upset, after hearing the disappointing news about their son. The threats, stolen lunch money and getting beat up every week, if not every day, by Johnny and Mark Burton. Later, Gary is pleased to learn that his family is moving from the neighborhood and his father is enrolling him in boxing classes.

That evening, Candice regretfully tells her mother everything that happened at school. "Mom, I felt so bad for him. I wanted to tell Mrs. Neilson that Gary was afraid of Johnny and they had been picking on him a lot."

"Why didn't you, Candice?'

"I don't know, I just didn't. I thought..."

"Candice, sometimes, people need a little push, honey, in order for them to see that they may need any kind of help."

"Well, I thought, maybe one day, Gary would just take his fist and sock Johnny in his eye."

Candice is so upset, because, she did nothing to help Gary and promises herself that she will never let that happen to a friend again.

"It's almost bedtime, Candice did you finish your homework?"

"Yes, I did it and I studied for the Spelling Bee we're having next week too.

"Good, you think you're going to win?"

Candice hesitated before answering. "I think I'll do okay. Shi Li and Elayne are helping me study for it."

"That's great," replies Audrey.

"I think it might be a tie between Shi Li and Elayne, they're really smart."

Candice is always elated when she talks about her friends. Audrey gets up from the table and stands behind Candice's chair, brushing her hair away from her face with her hand.

"I think it's time for you to go to bed young lady."

"Can I sleep in your bed tonight, Mom?"

"Candice, you're not a baby anymore."

"I know. I miss sleeping with you and dad. I remember when you used to let me sleep with you all the time."

"That was when you were little, Candice. You're too big to be sleeping with us now, and I'm pretty sure you know that."

"Well, can I sleep with you until dad comes home from work? I miss him. He's always at work when I come home from school."

Audrey always finds it hard to say no to her daughter.

"You can lie in my bed for a little while, but remember, when your father comes home out you go young lady."

Candice explodes with excitement, "Oh, great. I'll be right back Mom." She runs into her bedroom. "I'm going to put on my pajamas."

Candice loves sleeping with her parents, even weaning came late for her, being the only child and all. Candice didn't sleep alone in her own bed until she was at least seven years old and she truly believes that sleeping with her parents means they love her even more. She couldn't understand why her friend's parents didn't allow the same kind of affection. The Donaldson's were always talking about love and how families should stick together, but 'why don't they sleep together, sometimes?'

Another day another dollar, and hours later, Paul Felioni comes home from work and walks into the bedroom.

"Hi, honey." He bends down over the bed, puts his arms around his wife and kisses passionately. "Umm...I see my little star is in our bed, again."

"Yes, she wanted so much to wait up for you. She misses you a lot, you know. Especially, since you've been working these late hours. She hardly sees you anymore, Paul."

"I'll make it up to her this Saturday afternoon, Audrey. There's a ball game at the stadium and my boss gave me three tickets."

"I think she'll like that...Did you eat anything for dinner, Paul?"

"Yeah...I ate at the grill, me and a couple guys stopped after work."

"I think you better take her and put her in bed," says Audrey, pulling back the blankets that covers Candice. Paul picks her up and takes her into her bedroom, tucks her in, and kisses her goodnight. Then he returns to his bedroom and lies down next to his wife.

"You've been on my mind all day, I miss you... Audrey, after all these years you haven't changed one bit. You are a very beautiful woman. Your soft skin and warm body, if only you knew how much I love you...I don't ever want to lose you."

"Oh Paul, I don't want to lose you either... I love you, too."

Moaning starts and more moaning and moaning.

"Ummm...Paul."

Candice is eventually woken by the passionate sounds coming from her parent's bedroom. She lies in her bed reminiscing about the times when she would be in the same room, the same bed, as they made love. Feeling alone and distant Candice finds it hard to go back to sleep. 'I can't sleep. I want to go in there with them...I'm going to go and lie outside their door. I know they're doing it. I don't know why they won't let me in there anymore. I've seen them hundredth of times before, anyway.'

Candice loves hearing the sound of her parents making love and watching them. For years, that was the only way that she could fall asleep. Their body language, rubbing against her, inviting her into their passion, their lovemaking, and their world. Her parents never considered that Candice could be awake. It never crossed their minds that she could be enjoying what she saw and heard.

Although Candice never made a sound, those intimate moments made her feel as if the three of them were making love together, and that made Candice feel exceptional to be present at such a personal time.

Candice gets out of her bed, takes her pillow and blanket, and lies outside of her parent's bedroom door, smiling and listening to the tender screams of her mother. Her mother's moans and groans are considered bedtime lullabies to Candice. She listened that night, until they were finished, before falling asleep at their door. Candice is also a light sleeper, if her parents made any sound she would jump to her feet and dash into her bedroom. If one of her parents did happen to check on her during the night, Candice would pretend to be in a deep sleep.

The next morning, Candice knocks on her parent's bedroom door. But there's no response. She knocks again, putting her ear to the door, but she hears nothing, everything is absolutely silent. Candice opens the bedroom door and peeks in and she sees her parents entangled in each other arms. Locked so tight it looks as though there is only one person lying in bed.

Candice walks into the room, carefully shaking her mother and trying not to wake her father.

"Mom, wake up. I have to get ready for school. Are you going to cook my breakfast? ...Mom!" Candice taps her mother on the shoulder a few more times. "Mom, I'm going to be late for school."

Audrey spontaneously opens her eyes, quickly sitting up. "Oh, Candice. I'm sorry honey...What time is it?"

Candice looks at the clock on the nightstand. "It's almost 7:45."

Audrey forgot to set the clock last night, grabbing the clock off the nightstand and takes a second look.

"Oh, my goodness. I've overslept. You go and get ready for school while I fix something for you to eat. Now hurry, Candice."

"Okay Mom."

Candice runs out of the bedroom and into the bathroom to wash as Audrey snatches her robe off the floor, quickly putting it on, and then dashes into the kitchen to wash her face and hands. Minutes later, Candice comes in and sits down at the table, takes the cereal and pours it into a small bowl that her mother placed on the table. Audrey swings open the refrigerator door, grabbing the milk, and quickly pours it into Candice's bowl.

"I'm sorry, I don't have time to fix you a real breakfast this morning, honey."

"That's, all right, Mom."

"I stayed up late last night watching television with your father."

Candice stares at her mother as she tries to explain why she couldn't get up on time. However, Candice doesn't believe a word she says; Candice knows the truth.

Regardless, Candice isn't paying any attention and her mother, who soon realizes it and changes the subject.

"I've got so many things to do today and I'm already late."

Audrey opens the refrigerator a second time and takes out the juice. Feeling guilty about not getting up on time to fix breakfast, she offers Candice several different foods. "Do you want some orange juice? I got some toast in the toaster. It'll be popping up in a second."

"No thanks Mom, I don't want any toast."

"You don't? I thought you love toast."

"Mom, I do. I just don't want any, but some orange juice sounds good."

"Orange juice it is."

Audrey Felioni sits at the table with Candice, watching her eat her breakfast and rubs Candice's hair away from her face.

"You know I love you very much and I'm so proud of you. You have adjusted so well at your new school. You got new friends and all of you seem to get along so well together."

"Yeah Mom, Elayne and Shi Li are very nice. Whenever I need help with anything, they're always there to help me."

Audrey gently squeezes her daughter's hand. "That's wonderful, baby." Audrey looks at the clock on the stove. "It's time to go."

Candice picks up the bowl, holds it to her mouth and drinks the milk from it. "I'm ready."

"You got your books and everything?"

"Oh, my books." Candice runs to get her books off the chair and then runs for the front door.

"Candice...your lunch." Candice runs into the kitchen to get her lunch off the counter. Then she runs to the front door again where her mother is still waiting.

Audrey reaches for Candice, "Whoa...ops. Where is my hug and my kiss?"

Every morning Candice kisses her mother before leaving for school, whether she is on time or running late. It is a family tradition. Audrey use to do the same when she was a little girl, and she wouldn't have it any other way for Candice.

"I love you, Mom."

Once again Candice starts for school. "Oh. Wait...I have to go and give daddy a kiss before I leave."

After kissing him good-bye then she runs to the front door for the last time. "Okay, I'm ready, this time for sure, Mom."

Audrey takes Candice's sweater out of the closet and hands it to her.

"Shi Li and Elayne should be waiting for me at the corner near the bus stop. We always meet there every morning."

"That's good. I want you girls to be careful, and remember Candice, don't talk to strangers."

Candice is a very foolhardy and loving little girl, which constantly sends chills down Audrey's spine. She knows she will always worry about Candice's trusting heart.

"Mom, I already know not to talk to strangers." Candice steps out, and walks toward the bus stop as Audrey stands in the doorway watching her every step. 'That's my baby. She's so precious. Thank you Mother of God for such a beautiful little girl...If anything ever happen to her, I know I'll die.'

On arrival, Candice sees Shi Li and Elayne waiting near the corner. Shi Li points to Candice. "Here she comes."

With both arms wrapped around her books, Elayne replies. "It's about time, Candice."

"Hi everybody. Sorry I'm late. I hardly got any sleep last night and I almost over slept."

At the end of the school day the girls went straight home. Shi Li walks into the house and she meets her mother in the front hallway.

"Shi Li, my daughter, come? Let me take your sweater."

Shi Li takes off her sweater and gives it to her mother, she ponders, 'My mother never gives me a hug or kiss when I come home from school. My family is very different from most American families. Why is that?'

Mother Kyi hangs Shi Li's sweater in the closet next to the front door as Shi Li takes off her shoes. Walking into the front room, Mother Kyi grins at her daughter.

"How was your day at school, my daughter?"

"It was okay, Mother."

Mother Kyi takes Shi Li's hand and goes into the dinning area. "I have food for you to eat."

"Yes Mother, and I am hungry too."

"Go wash your face and hands my daughter and I will bring your food."

Mother Kyi takes very small steps as she rushes into the kitchen. She brings back a bowl of rice, some pepper chicken, tea and a butter roll. She places the food on the table, then lays the silverware and a napkin at Shi Li's seat. When Shi Li returns, she sits, the aroma from the food penetrates her senses as she sniffs about her plate.

"Mother you are a good cook. The food smells and looks delicious as always."

"My daughter needs her strength. The food will give your body the strength it needs to help it grow." Mother Kyi winks as she tries to crack a joke, but those are the same words, if not the exact words Father Kyi use all the time.

Mother Kyi continues, "...and your brain, too. Ha, ha."

They laugh together, because Shi Li knows this is her mother's way of being humorous, even though, her jokes are stale.

Although laughter in the Kyi's household is not a normal thing, especially, when Father Kyi comes home. The house immediately becomes still, almost lifeless. Father Kyi is a very strict man, and even stricter when it come to education; he believes if you study you will learn. He always says: 'The brain and the body are as one, working harmoniously, but they can easily become your enemy when they are not in tune with each other.'

When Father Kyi arrives home, he walks into the dining area where his wife and daughter sit. He stands there watching them as Shi Li eats, displaying that hardened and selfish attitude. He doesn't say anything to them, never a hello. Then he simply walks to his favorite chair and sits. Whenever he comes home, Mother Kyi would stops whatever she is doing; she always bows her head to him, and speaks softly, calling him 'My husband' because he is the head of the family and should have respect at all times.

Everyday when Father Kyi walks into the house, Mother Kyi would always runs into the bathroom. She would bring back a basin filled with warm water and two clean towels folded evenly over her arm. Then she will bows again before getting down on her knees and delicately cleans his feet, one foot at a time as he reads his newspapers. When finished, she goes and gets his house shoes that she keep near the front door. Everyday his shoes were at the same spot, waiting for him whenever he comes home. She washes his feet very carefully, making sure that they are clean and fresh by putting them to her nose and smelling; she didn't want to make him upset if they weren't clean enough; dishonoring his masculinity.

Father Kyi hates hot, dirty, stinky feet, he thinks it is definitely ridiculous for any man to have nasty feet. Clean feet meant walking a clean life and living a long healthy one as well.

After she would clean Father Kyi's feet, she would hurry, walking as she fast as she can, wearing those restricting clothes, bringing him whatever he wants next. This continued for many years in the Kyi's family while Shi Li endlessly watches her mother chase behind her father everyday, catering to his every desire. Shi Li always wondered if and will her mother ever take time for herself, but she never did.

Shi Li always thought about one thing Candice told them: About her parents having sex during the wee hours of the night. But Shi Li could not relate to something so intimate. She has never heard her parents having sex at night, or anytime of the day, or if they ever did. Plus, she has never seen her father kiss her mother. Personal and private issues are kept among the individual or individuals for which they belonged...and behind closed doors.

This helps Shi Li to realize the difference between Chinese and American families. Shi Li longs for a change, for her family to become more Americanized. Not just to hear the sounds of two people making love, but to see two people enjoy being in love with each other: the caring, the touching, and the telling of how one feels about the one you're supposed to be in love with. Not to be afraid to show love or too selfish to tell someone that you do. Father Kyi refused to show love because love indicated weakness and a man should always be strong and show his family the strength within him. Father Kyi truly believes that a strong demeanor is a survival tactic.

As she dries his feet he asks, "Did you go to the doctor, today?"

Nervously she looks into her husband's cold black eyes. "Yes my husband, I did."

"Did he say what the problem was?"

Mother Kyi holds her head down as she answers him. "He took tests."

Father Kyi's inquisitive nature encourages his questions, forcing her answers. "Are you with child?"

Father Kyi would love to have another child with his wife, especially a son; but Mother Kyi has been having some problems lately.

"No my husband. I am not with child," she speaks softly as her hands begin to shake.

"What did he say?"

Mother Kyi is afraid to tell her husband what the doctor thinks it might be; she hesitates for a moment. "...He said, said...it might be cancer."

Disturbed by what his wife has just told him, Father Kyi practically jumps out of his chair. "CANCER!" He stops himself, immediately taking control of mannerism, again concealing his emotions.

"Yes...Cancer my husband. He will not confirm the results until the tests return."

"When will the tests be completed?"

Due to embarrassment she refuses to look into his face, so she focuses on his shirt collar.

"He said, he would call tomorrow afternoon." Gradually, Mother Kyi finds the courage and takes a quick glance into her husband's face. The disgrace that surrounds her heart shows the humiliation on her face, fearing he will not love her if she has contracted such a deadly disease. In other words, she would be labeled contaminated, because, cancer is not a disease that runs through Father Kyi's family tree.

She looks at him as tears roll down her face; shamefully, she quickly stands and runs into the bedroom, throwing herself onto the bed, smothering her face in a pillow.

Father Kyi gets up from his chair and follows her. He stands in the doorway and listens to his wife cry. He walks proudly and moderately into the room and sits on the bed next to her, refusing to believe, blocking out what she just told him.

Father Kyi knows this disease is not something he has to worry about, because he is a strong man, his wife comes from a good strong lineage and no such thing can happen to his family.

"Maybe, it is not what you think," he says. He put his hand on the back of her head and brushes her hair gently. But Mother Kyi's too perplexed to even look at her husband or endorse his touch, a touch she rarely has a chance to share, or enjoy. She feels deep in heart that she has surely dishonored him.

"Don't worry my wife...I am sure that there is nothing to be concerned about."

Unlike his demeanor, he continues to stroke her hair, and think about what people would say about him, his wife, cancer, and if it is true. "Tomorrow, we will go to the doctor's office and wait for the results."

Mother Kyi continues to cry, and she really doesn't want to go with him anywhere.

"Come now. Go and wash your face. Shi Li must be curious."

She does exactly what she is told; covering her face, her hands, she slowly walks into the bathroom, takes a handful of water and throws it onto her face. Father Kyi follows, and stands outside the bathroom door. Father Kyi hesitates, just standing there staring as she closes the bathroom door. Slightly pressing his ear against the door, listening to his wife as she cries and prays.

'Something is very peculiar, 'thinks Shi Li, inquisitively walking toward her father and eventually gazing up at him. "Father, is there something wrong?"

"Nothing for your little head to worry about."

Shi Li looks at the bathroom door, then at the bedroom door. "If nothing is wrong, why is mother crying?"

He quickly changes the subject. Shi Li's questions are too difficult to answer, even if that means concealing crucial information that may change their family's lifestyle forever. Despite, his voice is stern and strong as usual. "Are you finished with your dinner?"

"Yes, Father I am."

"How was school today?" His bogus smile paste righteously across his face, as he escorts his daughter by the shoulder away from the bathroom door, away from her mother's cries.

"Everything is good at school, Father. Today we practiced for the Spelling Bee."

Shi Li is delighted to have her father finally give some attention to her. 'Conversing with him has never been this easy', she thinks.

"You will have to study everyday for that kind of opportunity; especially, if you're planning to win my daughter."

"I know Father. I study all the time. Sometimes, I study with my friends at school, Elayne and Candice."

His false face hides the truth, pretending to have concern for his daughter's liveliness, though maintaining his opinion, 'that is a woman's job'. He can only ponder regarding the shame his wife will bring to him, his unstained and absolute perfect lineage.

"If you are studying with friends, I think you have made a wise choice of association."

Shi Li can't believe her father is giving her so much attention, and yet she doesn't question it at all. She welcomes his affection with an open heart, tightly caressing his hand and his false emotions. "Thank you Father...I think so too."

Minutes later, Mother Kyi comes out of the bathroom wearing a disgraceful smirk, slightly turning her head, trying to hide her swollen watery eyes.

Shi Li is an only child and her mother would do anything to protect her delicate heart. But Shi Li is nobody's fool; she senses that her father is hiding something. 'What could it be?' She continues to view the emotions between her parents, even though they never spoke a word, though their eyes did reveal some part of the story. Shi Li knows that she will need to pay close attention to her mother. That is, if she really wants to find out what is actually going on in their secretive world, a house of little or unusual love. 'If something happens to my mother, what would become of me?' Shi Li a child who believes her father never loved her because she was born a girl. She acknowledges that deep down in his heart he always wished his first child to be born a boy. Shi Li hopes that maybe one day, he will give her, his daughter, the love she so desperately desire. The same kind of love that he would most generously give if she had been born his son. Yet, deep in her soul and yet unknowingly, Shi Li is most definitely a female version of her father's mode.

The next day, after Shi Li leaves for school, her parents are on their way to the doctor's office, but Shi Li yearn to be near her mother. This situation is a very important to her; but due to family honor, she knows she has to stay in a child's place. If she had not over heard them talking that night, she would have never known that something was seriously wrong. Shi Li remembers what Candice once said, 'If you really want to know, just listen.'

At school Shi Li worries are tremendous, her heart is in deep pain, she constantly thinks about her mother. She closes her eyes for a short moment. 'I will pray for you my mother, and I will keep the prayer locked deep inside my heart along with my love for you.'

The Kyi's arrive at the doctor's office, approaches the receptionist who is sitting at the front desk, and peacefully waits.

She soon acknowledges them standing there, "May, I help you, please?"

With that dominant demeanor Father Kyi takes control of the situation and ask, "We would like to see Doctor Lim, please?"

"Do you have an appointment?" asks the receptionist.

"No", said Father Kyi, "But it is very important that we see him." The receptionist hands them the appointment pad.

"Would you sign your name on the appointment sheet, please? I will inform the doctor that you're here. When you're finished you may have a seat until your name is called."

In a stern voice Father Kyi says, "Thank you, very much."

Mother Kyi signs, then follows her husband to a chair and distressingly sits down beside him. The twenty minutes wait seems longer. Doctor Lim comes out and personally calls Mr. and Mrs. Kyi.

Eagerly Father Kyi answers, "Yes, yes doctor." Father Kyi greets the doctor by shaking his hands.

"Good morning. What can I do for you?"

"We have come to get the results of my wife's tests. You said, you would call her today, but we have decided to come instead."

"No problem, I was going to call Mrs. Kyi this afternoon to come into my office so I could give her the results. Follow me, please."

The Kyi's walks hastily behind Doctor Lim, into his office, and sits in the chairs in front of his desk. Mrs. Kyi looks up at her husband, with the largest swollen red eyes, almost swollen shut. You can hardly see her black pupils. She has been crying all night, thinking and fearing the worst.

Doctor Lim picks up Mrs. Kyi's chart that is lying on his desk. "Okay, let me take a look at this...Umm."

The Kyi's sit nervously, anxiously waiting to hear the prognosis. Father Kyi gives his wife an assuring and sturdy look as if he knows the results will be negative. He knows his wife has been feeling ill, but then again, he refuses to admit even that.

Doctor Lim then looks up at Mrs. Kyi. "I'm sorry...Your tests are positive. You have a severe case of Uterine Cancer. We are going to have to operate as soon as possible."

Mother Kyi immediately looks into her husband's cold dark eyes before abruptly standing, dropping her purse on the floor, and screaming in the most horrible tone that even frightens her husband. "NO o-o-o...NO-o-o-o...IT CAN NOT BE SO...IT IS NOT TRUE. NO o-o-o, I can not have cancer." Mother Kyi's terrifying howl shocks everyone; she brings her hands up, covering her shameful face as she mumbles. "No, no, no..."

Father Kyi's pride is crushed, 'How could I have married a woman with such a physical imperfection? What would people think of me? How could I explain this to my family? It can not be so. Not my wife...CANCER!'

Impulsively Father Kyi grabs his wife, before suddenly pushes her away from him, while suppressing his tears. Mother Kyi is becoming emotionally weak, even standing seems impossible. She soon faints and falls to the floor.

"Oh no. She has fainted," says Father Kyi as he bends down, grabbing hold of her arm while she lies on the floor.

Dr. Lim dashes to the door, pointing. "Follow me to the next room, you can lay her down in there, so I can take another look at her."

Father Kyi hesitates, before lifting his wife off the floor and carrying her into the next room, lying her on the examining table.

"Is she all right?" he asks.

"It looks as though she'll be fine. The shock of the news was too much for her to handle."

"I can not believe it...my wife has Cancer."

The shock instantaneously torments Father Kyi as well, tearing his tiny heart to pieces and at the same time fracturing his manhood and devouring his self-importance.

Dr. Lim cautions Father Kyi of the danger of his wife's condition. "Mr. Kyi, you will have to talk with her very soon. We can't put off the surgery any longer, it's too advanced."

Emotionlessly, he looks at the Dr. Lim, "When she wakes up we will talk. After we talk...we will let you know what we have decided."

Doctor Lim pats Mr. Kyi on his shoulder. "I'm very sorry...I will be in my office if you have any further questions. If you need anything just let the nurse know, she'll be right outside the door." Doctor Lim walks out of the room.

Father Kyi sits next to the examining table, dropping his head into his hands.

Mother Kyi soon regains consciousness, realizing her performance embarrassed her husband so that she apologizes. "I am sorry my husband. My actions were uncontrollable. Forgive, please? "

In a soft voice he says. "It is understandable. I am sorry, too."

Still refusing to believe the news, brainwashing himself, assuring her and gently taking hold of her hands. "Do not worry my wife. I believe everything will be all right after the operation."

He hopes no one will ever find out about the shame his wife has brought to him and to his family.

"I am afraid," she says as her tears begin to fall once more.

"I will be with you every step of the way, my wife."

She is very surprised and confused by her husband words and his sudden change. For many years, ever since the day they met, he has always been self-centered. She was the one who always catered to his every need. This is the first time ever witnessing such a soft caring emotion from him. At that moment, she believes it to be love, never experiencing love from her husband, not knowing how love feels.

The marriage between them was arranged many years before their birth by their parents who had been friends long before they were born. Never experiencing true love, even their sexual relations could be considered forceful by law.

Father Kyi takes his wife into his arms and holds her very close, as his honor eats away his soul, crystallizing his facial expression.

"It is time my wife, we need to talk to the doctor about setting a date for the operation. After we are finished, we will go home and prepare ourselves."

"Yes, my husband, I am ready to go home. Thank you."

On the way home they wonder about that 'what if, when', and how to tell Shi Li about the medical misfortune. She is too young to understand the complete nature of the case, so they decide to wait and pray for the 'right time'.

"We will tell her when all of your impurities are destroyed", declares Father Kyi.

Looking in the kitchen cupboard for cups to make tea, Mother Kyi's heart is rapidly shattering and her thoughts are becoming more and more disturbing everyday as she worries about her young daughter's future. Still the 'what if' bothers her. She wonders, 'what if the operation is not a success?' That question constantly toys with her sanity.

Finally, one day she asks her husband, "How will we tell Shi Li? She needs to know."

Walking to his favorite chair, he drifts into a dimension of self-pity, though her question races through his mind, "We will wait for the outcome of the surgery. She needs not to worry her little

44

head so soon. Besides, it is still too early, anything can happen, things will get better."

Relieved by his remarks, yet hopeful, she agrees, "Yes, you are right. It is too early. Thank you my husband for your concern." She bows her head before lifting a cup of tea to her lips.

Because of Father Kyi's egocentrism, and refusing to believe the seriousness of his wife's condition, the weeks quickly past. And Shi Li is still unaware of her mother's fatal condition, but not her illness. Shi Li runs home from school one day to tell her parents of her success; winning the school's spelling bee, only to find her parents are not at home. When she walks into the house she finds her Aunt Miuki (My-U-Key) standing near the front doorway. Short of breath, but happy to see her aunt waiting, she blurts, "Hi, Aunt Miuki. What are you doing here? Where is mother? ...And is father home?"

Before Aunt Miuki can answer, Shi Li runs excitingly into the kitchen calling their names, "Mother, Mother...Where are you? Father, I have won."

Aunt Miuki scurries behind her, stopping her in the dinning area. "Shi Li...Shi Li, your mother and father have gone to the hospital."

Shi Li wonders and questions, "To the hospital...Why?"

Sadly Aunt Miuki tells, "Your mother has gone in the hospital to have surgery."

Shi Li is very confused by the answer and needs to know more. "Surgery...What surgery!"

"Do not worry...she will be fine, she is a strong woman just like you will be when you grow up. Anyway, your father will call later and tell us how well she is doing."
Distraught by the news, Shi Li goes into her bedroom and sits. She reaches for her parents wedding picture on her dresser, gazing at it, while remembering the good times she and her mother shared. 'Why did she not tell me? How come they never said anything to me? I listened and still I did not know. They think I am a baby...A big baby.'

This whole situation makes her feel even more like an outcast. 'Nobody said a word.' Shi Li begins to cry.

Aunt Miuki sticks close to Shi Li as she trails her into her bedroom and sits on the bed. She gives her comforting hugs, lifting Shi Li's chin and wiping the tears from her eyes. "You are a very special child, Shi Li. You are stronger than what you think you are and you have to be strong for your mother. You have to be patient my child. For your family loves you very much and their only wish is that you are truly happy."

PORK CHOP

CHAPTER 3

D'La Lausen, ten years old, the third born and the only female out of four children. She has three brothers, Michael age 15, Brent age 13, and Anton who is six years old.

D'La enjoys helping her older brother, Michael, rebuild automobiles and fix any broken electrical appliance in the house. Most of all, their relationship is as tight as a large nail being hammered into a small hole; which is unusual for D'La. Everything that Michael does, D'La wants to do or tries to do, In fact, whatever it is, she does it well. You can say D'La is most definitely a tomboy, as well as the neighborhood bully, her prime target 'boys', and their sizes do not matter one bit. D'La believes that the male species are the stupidest and the weakest of the sex and should be kept in their place. Meaning, any place a woman thinks, a man's place should be. Of course, there is one exception to the rule and that is her brother, Michael.

D'La comes home after another day at school, only to find her mother beating up on her father, again. A scene she has seen so many times before.

"You're, home already...I'LL BE DAM...ED," yells Clarise.

D'La listens as her mother speaks harshly and nasty to her father.

Yet Lewis replies are always meek, "Yeah...I wasn't feeling well, so I came home early, baby."

Clarise's voice suddenly changes, getting a little louder and a little nastier with each word.

"LEWIS...What in the HELL do you MEAN? You wasn't FEEL'N well, so you...came...home... EARLY."

Lewis's mild tone continues and still he is calm as the words he speaks; because, after so many years of Clarise's yelling, Lewis has gotten use to it. And most of the time, he tries to ignore her, just like today and many times before, but she is persistent.

"I said, I was sick, Clarise, baby."

Lewis is sitting in the living room on his favorite chair and he never gives his wife a second glance, keeping his eyes focused on the television set. Clarise rushes around and stands in front of the television, yelling. "SICK MY AS...we've got too many BILLS for you to be COMIN HOME SICK or THINK'N 'BOUT COMIN HOME SICK."

Lewis hangs his head low as though he is looking at his shoes.

"You make me SICK. I don't know WHY in the world I MARRIED your AS...in the FIRST PLACE."

Placing her hands on her big wide hips, Clarise' questions keeps on coming. "Did you get your check? ...I SAID, did you GET your check?"

Lewis humbly answers, "Yeah, Honey, I got it."

Clarise gives Lewis another disgusting gapes and waits for only a moment. "Did you cash IT?"

Again, Lewis answers submissively, "Um...uh...yeah, Baby. I cashed it?"

Clarise' patience is growing shorter with every second; she aggressively and angrily steps closer, standing at his side, removing one hand off her hip, and slaps Lewis in the back of his head with an open hand.

"WELL...WHERE IS MY MONEY? I don't know WHAT in the HELL are you wait'n FOR. GIVE ME SOME MONEY NOW? Cause, I gotta go and buy some thangs for THESE HERE KIDS...and ME."

Lewis reaches into his pocket and holds the money up to Clarise and she immediately snatches it.

"I'm go'n to the sto' in a little while...Do you want anythang...or not?

Clarise gives Lewis an unconcerned look, she doesn't care if he wants anything anyway. She places the money in her bra, parading her conceited and snobbish attitude, all the while, holding her head high. "Or, should I SAY...NEED an...y...THANG or NOT."

Beaten down and sad faced, Lewis never says another word. Clarise stops, turns and looks back at him. "What's wrong? You got a PROBLEM? ...If you don't, you sure ACT'N like you GOT A PROBLEM... Uh, all I got to say is...TOO BAD! You should have kept your pants ZIPPED, your funky DRAWLS ON, if you thought that there might be a PROBLEM when it comes to givin ME some MONEY. You know it takes MONEY to keep a GOOD WOMAN

AROUND. Especially if you got all THESE kids run'n around THIS house with this GOOD WOMAN...How else they gonna eat? "

Shaking his head, Lewis continues to look down while answering, "Nah...there ain't no problem, Baby...I'm okay. Everythang is just fine, Darl'n."

Clarise bucks and rolls her eyes as she constantly parades around his chair, badgering Lewis a bit longer. "You betta be fine, OKAY? Before I knock you out of that old raggedly chair, you stinkin as...old man. The next time you decide to get sick, you better call me first, cause, I'll bring you some MEDICINE. Do you here me LEWIS, do you here me talk'n to YOU? Heed these words, before you get SICK again you BETTA THINK ABOUT IT!"

Lewis doesn't respond to Clarise's statements; instead, he just sits there and that bothers her even more.

"I said, do you hear me talk'n to you...MISTER LEWIS LAUSEN?"

Once Clarise gets on a roll there is no stopping her. It is like the devil has taken control of her soul, and she loves every minute. She walks away, still hollering to the top of her lungs and goes toward the kitchen.

"Um...you GOTTA BE CRAZY ...MESS'N with MY MONEY like that...The last thang I NEED is a SICK, BROKE AS... HUSBAND." Clarise lifts her tits, shaking the money into position, inside of her bra. Then she looks back at Lewis, daring him to make a move against her erratic actions. Still Lewis sits quietly, stiff as a stone and docile.

Clarise pushes the door hard, slamming it against the wall as she enters the kitchen, unaware that D'La is standing in the doorway listening to every word. With all the confusion going on, they never noticed her head peeking around the corner.

As her mother approaches, D'La turns and runs out the back door into the yard, throwing her hands over her ears, and sits on the back porch stairs. "Oooo...everyday, the same old thang. Sh.., f..., sh.., dam..., f..., sh... Got dam... it...if this is the way thangs are supposed to be, forget it...I'll never get married. No way...No how...They'll have to kill me first. Kill me dead before I marry any man. Cause, if I do, I just got a feel'n, I'm gonna have to smack him around just like my momma do my daddy."

Looking at the hole in her dress and pushing her finger through it and she goes on. "I can't stand him, so stupid, we can't be related. Huck...He's too dumb and too weak." D'La continues to talk to herself as she sits on the back porch swinging her knees together. "I wonder, are all men stupid...or, is it just my daddy? Well, if my daddy's stupid, I guess he can't be the only one. Yep, before I even notice a man, he gonna have to fall out of a tree right on the top of my head...It just don't make sense, why would a woman want a man anyway?"

D'La picks a stick off of the porch floor and twiddles with it for several minutes, before going to a bottom step to sit. Holding the stick firmly in her hands she begins to punch holes in the dirt. Bored, rigid and nosey, she saunters over to the workbench that belongs to her brother, Brent.

Brent enjoys building things with his hands: for instance, furniture, go-carts, games and toys, just about anything that can be build out of wood and old junk.

Clarise doesn't believe that a man should lie around the house and do nothing. Laziness is a 'No, No' in the Lausen's household and that is the main reason, D'La's two older brothers are very skilled craftsmen. Clarise would always say, 'The Lord don't like laziness...' Then she'll add, 'and I'll beat a dead horse's butt before it happens here in this house.'

While snooping here and there, D'La notices an old knife, she picks it up and wipes it on her dress to clean it. "Ooo...yeah, I always wanted a knife. I'm keep'n it. Yeah, if anybody try to bother me...hell, they won't bother me no more." D'La plays with the knife for a spell, sticking it into the table and pushing it in the dirt and pulling it out, again and again. She even tries throwing it, wondering if she throws it hard enough into the tree would it stay, like the Tarzan movies she seen on television.

D'La plays with the knife and she is becoming attached to it. Every minute she pacifies herself with every excuse she could think of on why she should keep it. "I might have to protect myself one day. You'll never know. Yeah, you'll never know...This world is crazy...And, what if Michael gets into a fight and needs my help...Yep, I'm gonna need protection."

About an hour later, Clarise comes to the back door, calling. "D'LA...D'LA...WHERE ARE YOU, GIRL?"

"HERE I AM...OVER HERE BY THE TREE, MOMMA"

D'La peeks out from behind the tree; she knows if anybody catches her with the knife she will surely be in a world of trouble. And she doesn't like getting her butt woop either, that's bad for her neighborhood tough girl image. D'La quickly put the knife into her pocket.

"D'LA, WHAT ARE YOU DO'N BEHIND THAT TREE, GIRL?"
D'La quickly answer, "NUTH'N."

"You better get your butt in here. It's almost dinnertime, Missy."

"All right, here I come, Momma"

Clarise yells, "I mean NOW... NOT TOMORROW!"

"OK, I'M COMIN, MOMMA."

D'La quickly steps back behind the tree, checking to see if the knife is securely hidden in her pocket.

Clarise yells again, "D'LA...I said NOW, GIRL."

"HERE I COME, MOMMA." D'La runs up the steps, into the house, heading straight for the dinner table to eat. Anton and Lewis have already begun.

Michael and Brent come in a few minutes later talking about the lawn work they did for Mr. Grant. "Momma, Mr. Grant said, 'he'll pay us as soon as he comes back from the store,' says Michael, "Yeah, all he had in his wallet were twenties and fifties."

Shaking his head, Brent agrees with his older brother, as Michael continues, "Yeah, he needed to get some change."

"That's fine. Just make sure he don't try to cheat you this time...like last time," Clarise reminds her sons of a previous incident.

"He won't," says Michael.

Brent adds, "He never tried to cheat us before, Momma. He's just a little slow when it comes to pay'n us, that's all."

"Well, I feel, if you do the job, you suppose to get your money right then and there, not no two or three days later. You hear me?"

"Yeah, Momma we hear you, but Mr. Grant is a little senile that's all...And everybody knows that, he's still cool," says Michael.

"I don't want my boys being cheated by some cool senile old man."

"We know Momma, the last thing Mr. Grant thinks about is not pay'n us," adds Brent.

"I don't know 'bout that man. Ever since his wife died that old fool hasn't been in his right mind." Clarise gives Michael and Brent that demanding glare along with that strong tone. "Now get your plates so you can eat, your pork chops are get'n cold."

Michael and Brent take their plates out of the cabinet, get forks off the sink rack and sits down at the table.

"Ma, Mr. Grant's mouth is always move'n like he's talk'n to somebody," says D'La.

Little Anton gallantly comes to Mr. Grant's defense. "He is dummy. He's talk'n to his wife."

Anton thinks Mr. Grant is the coolest old dude he ever met. Reason: Mr. Grant is always giving him money to buy candy from the corner store.

Michael smiles at his little brother. "And how do you know that, Anton? When she's dead."

"He told me he was, that's how I know, now! We just can't see her. Only Mr. Grant can see her, that's all. Golly, ya'll stupid or somethang?" Anton sticks out his tongue at Michael, and surprisingly, everybody turns and looks at him.

Dumbfounded and stunned by her youngest son's answers, Clarise shouts, "HE TOLD YOU?"

Innocently, Anton answers again, "Ah uh...One day when I was comin from the sto, I sees Mr. Grant on his porch...he was just a talk'n away. So I went up on the porch to see if I could see anybody."

"What!...You did?" ask D'La.

"Yep, umm nope" replies Anton, with the sweetest and most innocent grin.

"Did you say anythang to him?" ask Michael.

"Ummm uh...I said, Mr. Grant, who you talk'n to? I don't see anybody."

"He said, 'Anton...I'm talk'n to my old woman. That wife of mine'. I said, "I thought your wife was dead."

"He said, 'She is, but that don't stop her from drop'n by. I don't know why or what's wrong with her, but she's been comin round a lot lately.' "Yep. He said, 'he thinks it's because, he got him a new lady friend.' He thinks she's jealous, Momma."

Outraged by Anton's performance, mimicking Mr. Grant, Clarise lays down the law once more. "That's it. I don't want you or D'La go'n 'round that crazy old fool anymore."

"But...but, Momma, Mr. Grant, he's my friend and I like him," protested Anton.

Mr. Grant has always treated the Lausen's boys well, especially Anton. On account of, Anton reminded Mr. Grant of his son when he was a little fellow: curious, out spoken and zealous.

"If Anton's his friend, he really got to be lonely," says D'La.

"Lonely...ain't the word. More like LOONY, if you ask me," Clarise shouts.

Brent's love for his little brother was never questioned, even if it came to defending him about something so ridiculous.

"Mom, Mr. Grant's not go'n to hurt anybody."

But Clarise is stern and her mind is made up, repeating herself. "YOU HEARD WHAT I SAID. NOW, eat your food. Cause I don't want to HEAR anythang else 'bout that CRAZY OLD FOOL, or his DEAD wife." Clarise's demand is taken seriously that the dinner table becomes instantly silent.

After all the commotion and rushing his dinner down his throat, Lewis inconspicuously removes himself from the table, walks over to the sink and put his plate into the dishpan. Lewis rarely joins in on dinner table discussions. He turns, looks at his family before leaving the kitchen, then slowly walks back into the living room and sits in his chair. Lewis is a very passive and loving man, and whatever his family wants he would try his best to get it, even if that meant giving Clarise every dime of his money.

As the years past, Clarise has lost interest in her husband, taking his kindness and his love for his family as his weakness; and his heart is slowly but surely beginning to drift.

"D'La, I want you and Anton to get the kitchen together, and this time, when you wash the dishes make sure they're clean."

"Okay, Momma," says D'La giving Anton an accusing gaze.

Clarise leaves the kitchen and D'La points, "Anton, you wash those glasses, first."

Anton hits D'La in her thigh with his fist. "Forget you. You don't tell me what to do. I'll wash what I want to wash, first."

"Boy, I'll break that fist off if you hit me again."

A few days later, Clarise strolls into the front room where Lewis is watching television and sipping on a glass of fruit juice. "Lewis, you need to find another job. The money you bring home ain't enough to support these kids. They're grow'n faster than a beanpole."

Lewis pretends to listen to his wife rambling, but Clarise doesn't think Lewis knows anything about the extra money that she takes from him or what she does with it. Lewis sits there thinking: 'If she quit play'n those street numbers she'd have extra money.'

Lewis has always concealed his true feelings, the pain growing inside heart, hoping that maybe one day his wife will probably change. Change back to the woman she used to be when they first met. A woman's whose love was so strong, that she would do anything to keep him. The same love she once gave him, a love so strong and so tight between them that two semi trucks couldn't pull them apart; and their sex life was indescribable. Who would have thought that things would turn out to be like this?

Lewis married a self-centered, controlling, evil woman, as some would say. It is as if every loving bone in her entire body was crushed or cursed. Yet, Lewis would always ask himself, 'Is she the Devil's daughter or his mother?' It seems that he just couldn't figure that question out.

Days later, on a Saturday morning, Brent has a lot of work to do for one of his neighbors, but he can't find his carving knife he left on the workbench. He hurries through the house yelling and asking everyone. "Has anybody seen my carve'n knife? I left it on the workbench with the rest of my tools, outback, a couple of days ago." D'La listens as Brent runs through the house, raging, and she does recall the day she took it off tool bench. Brent goes to D'La who is mopping the bathroom floor.

"D'La, have you seen my carve'n knife? It was on the tool bench out back."

D'La hesitates before answering, knowing if she confesses to taking the knife she will be in a world of trouble. "No, I haven't seen it. ...Know'n you...you probably lost it."

"No, I didn't lose it. It was on the workbench outside where I always leave it."

Using psychology, D'La tries her brainwashing tactics on Brent. Trying to get him to think he missed placed the knife as she continues to exaggerate her story.

"Maybe, you thought you left it on the workbench outside. People do think crazy thangs like that...You know, totally forgetting just about everythang they might do or touch."

Brent has no doubt, and he is absolutely sure where he left it and nobody can tell him otherwise. "Girl, don't be ridiculous. I ain't stupid."

D'La utters, "That's what you think. All boys are stupid."

Brent notices her silly expression; it is as if she is contradicting him. Brent rolls his eyes and runs downstairs and out the front door calling his little brother, who is playing a couple of doors away. "ANTON, ANTON...COME HERE LITTLE MAN. I WANT TO ASK YOU SOMETHANG."

Meanwhile, D'La runs into her bedroom and takes a pair of pants off of the dresser, checking to see if the knife is still there and it is. "Where can I hide this? I gotta put this knife back on the workbench before somebody finds out that I took it."

Before D'La can put the knife in another hiding place, Michael silently approaches from behind.

"Hey, Li'l Sis, what's up!"

Startled by the sound of his voice, she suddenly spins, holding the knife in front of her and shouts, "MICHAEL!"

Michael can't help but to laugh, as D'La swings, hitting him with her other hand.

"Did I scare you?"

"Michael...Yeah."

He pulls her into his arms for a hug. "I'm sorry Li'l Sis. The last thang I want to do is scare my favorite girl."

D'La suddenly reminds herself that she is holding the knife in her hands as Michael looks down.

"What you got there?"

D'La quickly put the knife behind her back. "Nuth'n...Just, girl stuff."

"Oh girl stuff, okay, I guess, I can live with that. I just want to know if you want to go with me to the auto shop. I got to get some thangs for my engine."

Excitedly D'La replies, "Right now?" Working on her brother's car is better than beating up the boys in the neighborhood and more enjoyable.

"I'll be leave'n in a few minutes."

D'La wastes no time with her reply, "Sure. I want to go. First, I gotta finish clean'n this bathroom floor and my bedroom before momma come in here. Its only gonna take me a few minutes."

Michael walks out of her room, stopping at the top of stairs and hollers, "HURRY UP, YOU ONLY GOT A FEW MINUTES."

D'La yells back, "I KNOW. JUST DON'T LEAVE ME, OKAY? MICHAEL, MICHAEL!"

D'La takes the knife from behind her back and puts it between her mattresses; then she reaches under the bed for her shoes, sliding her feet into them. She runs into the bathroom to pour the bucket of dirty water into the toilet; then she put the mop into the tub to drain. She turns and runs back into her bedroom, throws the blanket over her bed and places her pillows neatly against the headboard, but before leaving, she pats the mattress.

"I'll be right back and don't worry 'bout a thang. Cause nobody's gonna find you under here."

Once reaching the auto store, Michael buys the parts he needs for his old jalopy.

"Li'l Sis, once I get this old car run'n again, I'll take you for a ride."

"Will you teach me to drive, too, Michael?"

"Drive? I never said anythang about teach'n you how to drive."

"Yeah. I know but...I want to learn how to drive. What if you get sick or somethang and you can't drive home. You know you're gonna need somebody."

Michael's delighted with his sister's problem solving and her smooth approach.

"Well, I tell you what. If you help me get it run'n, I'll teach you to drive." Michael always admires his sister's tomboyish attitude and whatever she wants to learn, he is there to teach.

"All right...Yeah, I can hardly wait."

While Michael is paying for his auto parts, D'La walks around the store singing and daydreaming about learning to drive.

Months later, Michael is still working on his car and teaching D'La everything she needs to know about being an auto mechanic. From wheel balancing, putting on shocks and struts, the electrical system and how to rebuild an engine. Finally, it is time to take the car for a test drive. With his head peeking out from under the hood, Michael calls, "D'La, get the key off the seat and start the engine. I want to hear this baby roar."

D'La picks up the key off the seat and anxiously sticks it into the ignition and yells, "Michael, do you want me to start it now?"

"Yeah start it, I want to hear this baby talk to me."

As Michael listens he realizes that the car sounds great, almost as if a new engine was put into his old ride.

"D'La, would you listen to that baby roar? After all this work, this old girl sure sounds good."

With an old rag he wipes the excess oil off of his hands, goes around and gets into the car. "Move over, Li'l Sis."

"Are we go'n for a ride?" anxiously she asks.

"Yeah, as soon as I back this old girl out into the street," he answers. Michael put the car in reverse, out the backyard they go heading for the street.

D'La watch Michael's every maneuver as he drives, hoping she will have a chance soon. She waits; however, driving is so inviting, that she can wait no more. "Can I drive, now?" She impatiently asks as she twiddles with her fingernails, breaking what is left of them off.

"You don't know how to drive yet, Li'l Sis."

"You can teach me. You said you would, one day."

"I'll tell you what. I'll teach you how to drive, but you can't tell, I mean nobody, especially Momma."

D'La is so ecstatic with Michael's reply, for he has always been her knight in shinning armor.

Michael repeats himself, "D'La, I mean, not one soul."

D'La takes her right hand and places it across her chest, covering her heart. "I promise, I won't tell anyone anythang, EVER! ...Even in death."

"Ok...ok, I know a place where we can go. It's quiet and I think nobody will see us."

Michael drives to an old abandon building's parking lot. "All right, its time to learn how to drive...lets see if anybody watching us, first." Michael drives around checking the parking lot.

"I don't see anybody, do you, Michael?"

"No. Everythang looks cool. Com'on De, let's exchange seats."

At ten years old, D'La continues her driving lesson for several weeks, along with practicing how to pitch her knife into the ground, the trees, and in the back of the garage. D'La is exceptionally good, almost perfect.

SWEET 'N TANGY

CHAPTER 4

A year has past, it is now 1963, and it is the last week of school at Holtman Elementary. The girls are preparing for the school's farewell graduating dance and everybody who is passing the sixth grade will be there. Shi Li, Candice and Elayne meet, as usual, at the same corner to walk to school. Once reaching the school's gym the music plays, and their teacher, Mrs. Neilson, one of the dance chaperons, is standing by the record player talking with the principal, Mr. Lenowski.

Elayne and Candice excitedly yell and waves, "Hi, Mrs. Neilson."

Nevertheless, Shi Li's mind is drifting. She worries about her mother constantly. But only for that short moment in time, her thoughts have taking her into a world of her own, as she stares in the opposite direction before noticing her teacher and responding.

As the three girls approach Mrs. Neilson and Mr. Lenowski speaks mildly, "Hello, girls. Are you having a good time?"

"Yes, Mr. Lenowski, Shi Li answers.

"Shi Li won the school's Spelling Bee last year Mr. Lenowski, and Elayne came in second," adds Mrs. Neilson

"Yes, I remember. These girls are, Holtman Elementary, very promising students...Mrs. Neilson, you've done a great job, and I truly believe that a great future awaits these students. Yes, most definitely...keep up the good work girls!"

Mr. Lenowski shakes Mrs. Neilson's hand, but she is hoping, just maybe, he will mention that raise in pay she had been promised.

"Have you girls tasted the punch?" ask Mrs. Neilson.

"No," says Candice looking toward the table.

It is so hot outside, the humidity have left their mouths feeling dry. "We just got here," says Elayne.

"Mrs. Constantine, who works in the cafeteria made it. You should try it. It's delicious!"

"We will, Mrs. Neilson," says Shi Li as the desire to quench her thirst overcomes her.

Mr. Lenowski pats each girl on her shoulder. "Miss Shi Li, Miss Candice and Miss Elayne, congratulation young ladies. I wish you success and a happy future. Keep up the good work. I'll talk to you later Mrs. Neilson."

The three friends spoke simultaneously. "Thank you, Mr. Lenowski." Shi Li, Candice and Elayne suddenly realize things are changing around them and they are growing up.

Tomorrow is Graduation Day and all parents will be there to see their children walk across the stage; all except Shi Li's mother who is too ill to attend. Cancer, have spread through her entire body, her condition is worsening with each passing day. Shi Li's Aunt Miuki has been keeping watch of Shi Li and her family. Aunt Miuki is married to Uncle Chung who is Father Kyi's brother. She has been doing her best to keep Mother Kyi comfortable in her last days. She deeply regrets that Mother Kyi will not be able to attend her only child and loving daughter's graduation, get married or caress any of her offspring's, her own grandchildren.

Yet, Aunt Miuki will have to take her place at the graduation along side of Father Kyi. Aunt Miuki has been a great · help to Shi Li, and she finds it extremely hard to keep the secret, and accept the fact that Shi Li will never see her mother again.

After the graduation the girls agree to go for ice cream at the drug store. On the way to the store they run into Mark Burton who is walking down the street with a pack of cigarettes in his hand.

Holding the pack between his lips, pulling off the paper wrapper with his teeth. "Hey Candice, where ya'll go'n?"

"Why, you want to know?"

"Because, I want to know, NOW!" he says spitefully.

"Well...that's none of your business. Mark, just go somewhere and leave us alone," adds Candice.

"Okay...Okay, girls are dumb, ANYWAY." Mark takes a cigarette from the pack and sticks it in his mouth. Candice turns away from Mark, whispering to Elayne and Shi Li as they continue to walk toward the store. "That boy is as stupid as his big brother, Johnny."

Elayne is feeling regretful. "That's bad to have a stupid big brother. I feel sorry for him."

"I feel sorry for you, Elayne, because his brother still has a serious crush on you, "says Shi Li.

"I know...But he's bad news. He could never be my boyfriend and thinking about it, even today, makes me sick."

Candice continues, "He still has a crush, and he's still in the fifth grade, too."

"That is because he has been living in a boy's home for the last year," says Shi Li.

"A boy's home? ...For what?" asks Candice.

"He robbed a man and tried to steal the man's car."

"How do you know, Shi Li?" ask Elayne.

"I overheard Mr. Lenowski talking on the phone to Johnny's mother a couple of day ago. I could not hear everything, but I did hear that much."

"Yeah, I was wondering what happened to him," Elayne says, putting her hands together and looking up at the sky. "That boy needs The Lord real bad. I'm go'n to have to pray for him, before I go to bed tonight. He's really in need of heavenly help."

Shi Li proceeds, "I saw Tommy yesterday and he said that Johnny got out of the boy's home a couple of days ago."

Once more, Mark yells at the girls, but they're not paying him any attention. He leans against a building, striking a match, as he puffs on a cigarette, watching the girls as if he is a private investigator and waiting diligently to see what direction the three are going.

"Ah uh, I knew it. Wait til I tell Johnny."

Mark wastes no time as he runs home. He dashes up the front stairs of the porch and through the house, hollering. "JOHNNY...JOHNNY. Guess who I saw, today? And only a few minutes ago."

"I don't care who you saw today, Little Bro. I got other thangs on my mind."

Mark replies, "You wanna bet?" Johnny walks out of the closet, over to the bed where Mark is sitting and lay his pants on the chair, then sits on the bed next to him. Nevertheless, Mark persists. "I saw Elayne Donaldson."

Johnny surprised to hear her name, reaching for his socks as he put his foot across his leg. "Elayne Donaldson? That religious bit...."

Mark's smile stretches across his face. "See, I told you. Do you still like her?"

"Nah...She always thought she was too good for this bro." Acknowledging Johnny's true feelings Mark continues talking about Elayne's whereabouts. "They were on their way to the drug store."

"How do you know, that?" Mark immediately stands in front of the mirror, picks up the brush, and brushes his hair with a cocky attitude.

"I kinda stood next to a building and waited, and just as I thought, they were go'n to there favorite place. They go there all the time, Johnny. I seen them."

"Okay...So What?"

"Come on Johnny. Let's go. They're probably still there."

"No. Not right now, Little Bro. I'll deal with those stuck-up bit...s later."

Mark impatiently insists. "But, now is a good time, Johnny."

"That's all right, Mark. Right now, I need to try and find me a ride. I can't lay around here all day do'n nuth'n. I gotta get out and see what's been happen'n. Being lock up, you kinda lose touch of everythang. Plus, I need me some mo-green, some money. You know what I mean?"

"Do you want me to keep an eye on them for you, Johnny?"

"You can if you want too, Bro' Man. But it ain't gonna make no difference right now. I can always see that bit... later."

"Okay, Johnny."

Johnny takes his pants off the chair and put them on. "I gotta lay cool for now. Trouble is not on the menu."

"Yeah, Johnny, I...."

Johnny interrupts Mark. "You hip, man? You down wit it? You cool?"

Mark lays the brush on the dresser and put his hand half way into his pocket. "I'm hip. I'm down. And I'm cool."

"Now, get out of here. I gotta finish get'n dress. I can't be walk'n down the street naked, you know, Little Bro'?"

Mark admires Johnny's cocky and cool attitude. Every word Johnny speaks makes Mark feel as if he is invincible and invincible is exactly his opinion of his brother Johnny.

"Cause if I did, all the babes would be chase'n after me and we don't need the fellas get'n jealous, now do we, Bro'?"

Mark goes to the bedroom entrance, stops and looks back at Johnny, with high regards for his brother Mark shakes his head in favor of his brother's remarks before leaving. "Nah, Johnny."

Meanwhile it is another day and the third day of summer vacation at the Lausen's house. D'La comes home after playing in the neighborhood and after a fight or two, only to hear what she hates most, her mother screaming at her father. This time the argument takes place in the upstairs bedroom.

"LEWIS. LEWIS... YOU DUMB AS...where in the HELL DID I PUT MY WIG?"

"What Clarise?"

Clarise screams, this time in a strong baritone voice. "WHERE ARE YOU?"

"I'm in the bathroom, Honey."

Clarise is in the bedroom throwing clothes and anything else she can grab.

"WHERE IS MY WIG? I know I left it on this here DRESSER next to my LIPSTICK!" As always Clarise calls Lewis whenever she needs something, and again Lewis keeps his composure.

"I don't wear your wig."

"I didn't ASK you if you WORE my wig, LEWIS. Don't be STUPID." Clarise goes to the bathroom door, pushing it open and shouting as Lewis sits on the toilet. "Now get your stinkin old crooked crack up from there and help me find my wig. DAM... Lewis, you gotta stop eaten at THOSE greasy DINERS. Smell like somethang went up inside of you and DIED...HURRY UP NOW, I got somewhere to BE."

Clarise quickly closes the door and continues to yell. The only time when Clarise's tone of voice is low, soft and sweet is when she is talking to herself.

"I can't go anywhere look'n like this. My hair's a mess."

Clarise walks into the bedroom again and looks in the closet. "You crazy old fool. I ain't never seen a man with a brain so screwed up before in my life...or so little. Like bird's brain, ain't worth nuthin."

Lewis slowly mopes out of the bathroom, fastening his pants and goes into his son's room, taking the wig out of Anton's toy box. He smiles, "Anton's afraid of this old nappy, monstrous looking wig. He thinks it'll swallow his mother's head one day. Anton said, 'it's the ugliest thing he's ever seen.' Even more so...it can't hold a curl."

Anton can't figure out why his mother wants to wear something so horrible. Maybe she likes scaring him. So, whenever he gets a chance he will hide it. Lewis has seen Anton with the wig several times before, throwing it around, pretending he is killing it to save his mother's life. Lewis always known that Anton hated that dried up, dusty old thing. And Lewis has a feeling where it might be.

While in bedroom Lewis reaches into one of Anton's toy dump trucks and pulls it out. "Yep, I knew that boy would stick it in here. He always do." Lewis then calls to Clarise. "Here is your wig, right here Baby." Then mumbles, "Umm, I don't blame Anton for try'n to get rid of this old thang. Let me close my eyes for a minute, cause, this here wig can blind somebody if they look at it long enough."

Lewis hands Clarise the wig.

"That boy, if he ain't crazy like his pappy. Just give me the dam... thang, you hold'n it like you're afraid of it or somethang." Unthankful, Clarise snatches the wig and Lewis readily put his head down, looking at his shoes.

Clarise steps in front of the mirror to comb it out. "Wig don't bite; and besides, everybody says it looks good on me."

Lewis turns and goes back into the bathroom to the toilet.

"Love had blinded me when I married your butt. That's the only thang that could have got me to the altar. I had to be blind, that's for dam... sure," says Clarise. Lewis never says another word as he closes the bathroom door, locking it.

All the while, D'La's parents never notice her standing, watching and listening to all that commotion. D'La hurries up the last four stairs and quickly runs into her bedroom, taking out the knife and putting it into her pocket. Then she stomps down the stairs and out of the back door into the backyard behind her favorite tree. She sits there stabbing the ground and grumbling.

"Oooo...they make me so sick. Everyday the same, same, same old thang ... Sh... f... sh... dam..." She keeps repeating these words each time as she stabs the knife into the dirt.

"How come my parents have to act like that? Anybody can see they hate each other. Got dam... it. Please don't even take me there...If this is the way thangs is supposed to be, forget it. Marriage is not for me, EVER! Yep, they'll have to kill me first, for sure."

Later that day Aunt Sharon comes to the back door calling. "D'LA. D'LA...GIRL, WHERE ARE YOU? D'LA...ARE YOU OUT HERE?" D'La pops her head out from behind the tree.
"IS THAT YOU AUNT SHARON? HERE I AM!"

"Yeah, it's me! Com'on in the house for a minute."

D'La runs across the yard, up the steps and straight into Aunt Sharon arms, hugging her so tightly.

"How's my favorite niece?"

D'La can say nothing, her mouth is airtight and all she wants is hold her and never let go.

"Aunt Sharon I'm, fine. When did you get here?"

"Oh, about ten minutes ago. I was sitting in the house talking with your momma."

"Oh," says D'La, dropping her arms from Aunt Sharon's waist, but only for a second before she quickly grabs her again.

"Yeah. We were talking 'bout you comin to stay with me for the summer."

D'La's ecstatic, holding Aunt Sharon even tighter. "Really...can I, can I, please, Sharon?"

"Well, if you want to, you can. Your mother said, it's okay."

D'La claps her hands, jumps up and down, as the back of shoes hits her butt several times. "Oh boy, yes. Yes, I want to go."

"Wait a minute young lady. We got to go in house and arrange everything with your momma, first."

"Okay Sharon, I know. Can we arrange everythang now? Com'on Sharon, let's go and see." D'La takes Aunt Sharon by the hand, pulling her into the house. D'La immediately yells for her mother, "MOMMA...MOMMA"

"Girl, stop all that noise. What's wrong with you holl'n like you CRAZY?"

Nonetheless, D'La is too excited to calm down; her voice is still reasonably high. "Momma, Sharon said, I can spin the summer at her house, if it's okay with you. Can I, uh? Hum, can I?"

Clarise is not happy with D'La's improper and disrespectful behavior.

"Sharon...What did I tell you 'bout...?"

D'La's relationship with her Aunt Sharon is too personal for Clarise, especially when it comes to first names. Sharon or Aunt Sharon, it doesn't matter what D'La calls her. All Sharon wants to be is that special someone in her niece's life.

"I'm sorry, I mean Aunt Sharon."

"That's what you betta mean."

Afraid that her mother might change her mind, D'La wastes no time. "Can I stay the summer at Aunt Sharon's, Momma, PLEASE?"

Clarise hesitates before answering. "Is your chores all done, girl? How 'bout that filthy room of yours...I don't want NO dishes up there under your bed either, Missy. You'd think the roaches are that girl's best friends the way she's always feed'n 'em."

D'La pauses, "Yeah, I can do it real fast. Anyway I'm almost finish, Momma."

"Almost and finished are two different words, D'La. Now hurry up before Sharon changes her mind and leave your butt right here."

That last thing D'La wants to hear. She quickly grabs the garbage from the kitchen canister and throws it into the outside garbage can. Runs back into the house, rushes up the stairs into her bedroom and put her dirty clothes into the hamper. But when she bends over to pick her blanket off the floor her knife falls out of her pocket. She stares at it, pondering on reasons why, before picking it up. "...Yep, I think, I betta take you with me. That way, I can keep practicing. I can't practice if I leave you here...Yep, I go...you go."

D'La then goes to the closet, pulls out her suitcase and packs as many clothes that could possibly fit. She hurries down the stairs, nearly falling and runs into the kitchen, huffing and puffing, where her mother and her aunt are sitting.

"I'm ready, I did all my work and I got my clothes packed. I cleaned my room, I took the garbage out and...I washed the dishes that were under my bed, too. Every last one!"

Clarise cannot help noticing D'La's silly expression as the sweat rolls down her face and neck that she and Sharon, uncontrollably burst into loud laughter.

"Boy, that was fast. The only times I've ever seen her move that fast is when she's go'n some place or she wants somethang. Any other time, I have to knock her on her butt or get my strap to get her to move like that."

Sharon remembers when: "Don't I know...like mother like daughter if you ask me. I remember when Momma used to say the same things about us when we were little. You remember Clarise!"

"Yeah. That's true. We couldn't wait to get the hell out the house, either."

Sharon grins, "Umm...mm, you used to run faster than D'La."

"Sure Sharon, You ain't gonna worry me. Whatever you say, is fine."

Clarise and Sharon cannot stop laughing, reminiscing about the old days, when they were naughty little girls, while D'La hastily heads for the front door carrying her suitcase to put into Sharon's car.

"Bye, bye, Daddy!" D'La waves good-bye as she rushes pass Lewis who is sitting on the front porch. A few minutes later, Clarise and Sharon comes out on the porch. Sharon looks over at Lewis, who is minding his own business; leaning back in his chair with his feet propped up on the porch railing, relaxing and enjoying the day.

"Hey, brother-in-law, you're still sitting out here?"

"Yep. Yep I am."

"This is some beautiful weather. Ain't that right, brother-in-law?"

Lewis eventually looks up at Sharon, replying. "Yep. Sure 'nough beautiful...Yep, real beautiful."

A minute of silence goes by as everyone peacefully looks around the yard enjoying the surroundings.

"Well, Clarise and Lewis I gotta go before I change my mind and spend the day and probably stay the night with ya'll. That'll really make your daughter upset with me. So, I have no other choice but to say, I'll talk to ya'll later...Sis and Brother-in-law. Bye ya'll."

"You take care, you here?" says Lewis.

Impatiently D'La waits in the car, waving her hand, motioning Aunt Sharon to come to the car. "Aunt Sharon, com'on." "Look at her, hollering...ain't she in a rush," Aunt Sharon says with a grin.

"Um uh...that's D'La for ya. Always wanna do thangs when she wanna do 'em. That girl's just a little to bossy for me," says Clarise.

Sharon replies, "She's just like her momma, just like I said earlier. She needs to get out and have some fun sometimes, you know, to hang with the girls instead of hanging around the house all the time. You do remember when you use to hit the streets, hang out all times of the day and night, Clarise?"

"D'La ain't me...She do 'nough hang'n in the neighborhood already. Half the time I can't find her. Anyway, if she ain't fight'n and beat'n up on half the neighborhood, I wouldn't know where to find that girl. I'm tellin you, if it wasn't for those whining kid's parents that keep comin over here talk'n 'bout, D'La did this and

D'La did that. ...Goodness, gracious, Sharon...that's the only way I can find her."

"See, Clarise, you know what I mean. Just like I've been tellin you and Lewis for the longest. D'La needs a little sister."

Clarise throws her hands up. "What...R...R...are you CRAZY? I don't even wanna talk 'bout or think 'bout have'n another baby."

Lewis turns his head and looks in the opposite direction, refusing to listen to Sharon's talk about having more kids.

"You know I'm right. That's why she acts so much like a boy, she ain't got no sister to talk to. You know what I'm talking about. Someone to share her girly secrets with like we used to do, remember Clarise? We used to have so many secrets. I remember when you first met Lewis. How ya'll used to sneak out behind the back of house and do ya'll thang." Sharon demonstrates by twisting her lips as if she is kissing an invisible lover. "And you used to pay me to keep my mouth shut. It started with three cents, then five cents, and a dime and sometimes a whole quarter. Ummm...All that candy, and money to buy candy. Yep, I had a lot of cavities then. Momma and daddy couldn't figure it out, every time I went to the dentist I had so many of them. ...But ya'll secret was safe with me as long as the money kept coming."

"You ought to be ashamed of yourself, Sharon...you're just too crazy for me. No wonder momma and daddy worked long hours, they needed to get away from you."

Sharon stomps her feet and laugh all the while patting Lewis on his back. "I know you remember those days, Mr. Lover Man." Sharon doesn't care one bit. She keeps chattering and teasing, as she laughs herself silly.

Picking at the tiny hairs in his chin, Lewis rolls his eyes as far back into his head after taking a quick glance at Clarise. Anyway, Clarise doesn't want to hear anything about bringing another life into the world, especially if Lewis has anything to do with it.

"I don't care how she acts. She ain't get'n no kind of a sister, big, little, rented or stolen from here...Not out of me."

"Just remember what I said, just in case you guys get sweet on each other one night and change ya'll minds." Sharon takes the first step down from the porch. "You know I'm right. Don't be lookin at me like I'm stupid or something. That's your problem and you know it." Looking back at Lewis, Sharon adds, "Brother-in-law, don't be sitting over there acting like you don't hear me. I see you rolling those big brown eyes back up in your head. D'La wouldn't be acting the way she do, all tomboyish and stuff, if she had a sister in the house. Somebody she can relate too."

Clarise refuses to listen to her sister any longer, "Sharon, get the hell off my porch before I get some rope and tie you to that car of yours. I'm pretty sure, D'La would be glad to drive you the hell away from here if she knew how to drive. You got your nerves comin over here talk'n baby crazy."

"Ha-a-a-ah, okay, okay I'm gone. But remember what I'd said." Sharon takes two more steps down. "I'll call you later in the week, Sis. See ya'll." Sharon goes around to the driver's side of the car, winks at D'La as she gets in. "Are you ready to go?"

"Yeah. I'm ready."

Sharon starts the car and D'La promptly sticks her hand out of the window and waves as they drive off.

"Bye Momma, bye Daddy."

Clarise is the eldest of the two sisters with a ten year difference between them. Growing up with both parents working all the time, they struggled to make ends meet. Clarise was responsible for her little sister's well being, from the time she was born until she was old enough to do for herself and then some. That included cookin the breakfast, dinner, and lunch on every Saturday and sometimes on into the week. Sharon's diapers had to be changed and washed, and Clarise had to clean the entire house too. As well as, school attendance and grades had to be kept up. There was a lot of pressure on Clarise and living in a controlling household she had no choice but to learn how to survive the best way she knew how. Clarise was conditioned at an early age to always be strong, transforming her into the hell-raiser she is today. Everything had to be exactly as she said, 'Put this there', 'get that', 'and', 'I said', 'don't do that'. There were no such remarks as, 'No' and 'I don't want to', 'leave me alone', or 'I'm gonna tell momma on you'. Sharon knew whatever Clarise told her to do, just do it, or get beat. And hesitation wasn't allowed neither, you had to move fast or else.

Deep in her soul, Clarise thought her parent's expectations of her were normal, never questioning anything they said. So the reality to this situation makes Clarise, the Clarise she is today.

D'La wonders, as Aunt Sharon drives closer to her home, if things are still as beautiful as she remembers. It has been about three years since she spent the summer there. Eventually Sharon pulls up in the driveway.

'Finally, I didn't think we were ever go'n to get here,' D'La thinks. D'La gets out of the car heading for the front door. Sharon stands there watching as she runs up on the porch.

"D'La, are you forget'n somethang, Miss Lady?"

Sharon looks at the suitcase.

"What?" D'La asks, observing Aunt Sharon eye motions, as she stares downward.

"Oh, my suitcase." D'La giggles and runs back to the car to gets it.

"I think we'll be needin some clothes, don't you?"

D'La laughs, placing her hand over her mouth. "Yeah, I forgot."

After entering the house D'La drops her suitcase on the living room floor.

"Wait a minute young lady! You need to pick up that bag and take it in the guestroom. You do remember where it is?"

"Yeah...I remember where it is, Aunt Sharon."

"Just lay it on the bed, D'La, we'll unpack later. I want to fix something to eat."

"Okay, Aunt Sharon."

After lying the suitcase on the bed she walks over to the dresser and looks at a photo of her grandparents, Aunt Sharon and her mother when they were children.

"Wow, Momma was so skinny." She time-travels, dreaming of any era before she was born. Soon her thoughts are abruptly interrupted by the sound of her aunt calling.

"D...LA. D'LA...WHAT DO YOU WANT TO EAT?

D'La rushes to the kitchen.

"Ah..." Before she can answer, Sharon adds, "I have hamburgers and fries, fried chicken and rice or we can go out for a Coney dogs."

"Umm...Hamburgers and fries sure sounds good to me...and a root beer?" adds D'La.

"That sound good to me, too. Then, that's what it'll be."

After eating they cleaned the kitchen together Sharon responds, "That's finished!"

While wringing the wet rag D'La asks, "Should I hang the dishrag on the counter?"

"Sure, that would be fine...No wait, hang it on the dish rack it'll dry faster."

D'La folds the rag and lays it very neatly on the dish rack. Sharon's thoughts were rapid, thinking about Clarise who is always complaining about D'La and her disorganized and nasty housekeeping abilities. "We better go and unpack your suitcase before your clothes get too wrinkled, unless you really love ironing, young lady."

"I don't mind ironing, I just hate ironing other people's clothes. Momma always say to me, 'D'La, iron this, or D'La iron that.' Sometimes, I have to iron my daddy's pants before he goes to work. I think momma just quit ironing since I've gotten bigger."

Sharon takes D'La by the chin.

"Let's unpack and when we finish, and if you want too, you can go out to play."

Sharon turns to hang clothes in the closet when D'La asks, "Are there any kids to play with around here, yet? There was hardly any before."

"I'm pretty sure there is, now."

D'La considers Aunt Sharon's every word as she hangs another piece of clothing.

"Don't tell me you're bashful, D'La."

"No, I'm not bashful."

"I didn't think you were."

"I'm just particular," says D'La.

Impulsively, Sharon spins and quickly places her hands on her hips and repeats D'La's words.

"Particular...Uh, aren't we growin up? That sounds like one of those words your momma always use when she's talkin to your daddy."

Modestly, D'La explains, "Some kids act funny to me, that's why I beat them up."

"Maybe you ought to stop beating them up. And maybe, before you know it, you'll find friends with the same interest as yours."

Sharon approaches D'La, placing both hands, one on each side of her face. "Listen Honey, a beautiful girl like you will never have any problem finding friends. You are a very intelligent, spirited and loving person and don't you ever forget that."

D'La grabs Aunt Sharon around her waist, hugging her with all her might.

"Now, get outside and play for a while, it'll be gettin dark soon."

"Okay, I'm gonna sit on the porch."

"That's fine with me."

D'La saunters toward the front door, standing and watching the people as they walk up and down the street. Watching their every move as if she is analyzing them. And wondering if she would find new friends, and will they accept her particular ways. D'La is beginning to have strange feelings and she doesn't understand them, or why.

After standing in the doorway for several minutes, D'La decides to go and sit on the porch. She never says a word to any of the kids as she watch them play. Eventually she gets up and walks off the porch, wandering aimlessly toward the back yard. She looks around to see if anybody is watching her and there is not one person she can see. She eases the knife out of her pocket to practice.

'This knife is really cool, but I'm kinda sorry I had to take it from Brent. When I go home I'm gonna to have to give it back. But, what if he gets mad? Oh...I don't want to think about that right now...When I grow up, I'm gonna buy a bigger one that's for sure. I really do need to practice and practicing is more important then playing with a lot of kids, anyway.'

It's getting dark and Sharon comes to the front door calling. "DE...LA...DE...LA. IT'S TIME TO COME IN. WHERE ARE YOU? D'LA?"

D'La quickly puts the knife into her pocket. "Here I am, Aunt Sharon, I'm in the backyard." She runs along the driveway toward the front of the house.

"D'La it's time to come in and take a bath."

"After I take my bath do I have to go to bed? Can I stay up and watch TV for a little while, Aunt Sharon?"

"That depends on how long you plan to stay in the tub, Miss Lady."

"I'll make it quick. My favorite TV show comes on tonight and I don't want to miss it."

EVEN IN DEATH

CHAPTER 5

The next day after breakfast, D'La goes outside and sits on the porch. There are only a few people on the street, besides its still early morning, about nine o'clock. Everything is quite soundless in the neighborhood, except for a girl who is skating up and down the street. D'La watches for several minutes before actually approaching her. She inspects her carefully, as her steps bring her closer, and before saying a single word. 'She looks like a nice person.' thinks D'La as she toys with the idea of introducing herself. She walks a little closer approaching the curbside.

"Hi," says the girl.

"Hi, my name is D'La. What's yours?"

"I'm Candice. Candice Felioni." Candice also looks curiously at D'La from the top of her head, down to her unlaced high-top gym shoes.

Candice asks, "Do you live around here?"

"No. I'm visiting my Aunt Sharon for the summer."

"Your Aunt Sharon, where does she live?"

"Down the street," says D'La pointing in the direction of her Aunt Sharon's house. "It's right over there." Candice is familiar with the neighborhood, even though her family only lived here a short while.

"Oh...you mean Miss Connell's house."

"Yeah, she's my Aunt Sharon."

"Miss Connell is a nice lady and everybody in the neighborhood likes her...Do you want to skate with me?"

Shockingly surprised, D'La eagerly agrees, "Sure! Why not?"

Candice takes off one of her skates and hands it to D'La. Spending almost half the day together, and ecstatically enjoying each other's company, Candice decides to tell D'La about Elayne and Shi Li.

"I have two best friends and I was wondering if...you want to meet them?"

D'La can't believe how well things are going and her Aunt Sharon was right about just being nice to people.

"We can walk to their houses from here, they don't live that far."

"Okay, but I'll have to let my Aunt Sharon know where I'm goin."

"Me too!" says Candice. "I can't go anywhere without letting my parents know. My mom is always getting upset with me if I leave without telling her where I'm going. Anyway, I'll call to see if they're home before we go. Come on."

Candice and D'La take off the skates at the side door of Candice's house and D'La follows her in.

"Mom...where are you?"

Mrs. Felioni is on her knees cleaning the bathtub. "I'm in the bathroom Candice. Is anything wrong?"

"No, nothing's wrong. I want to know if I can go to Elayne's house?

Mrs. Felioni put the cleaning rag under the sink, hanging it on a pike as the girls enter the bathroom. Mrs. Felioni can't help noticing an unfamiliar face; she has to be someone new in the neighborhood, because Candice is not allowed to leave the block without permission. "Well, who do we have here?" she ask.

"Mom, this is D'La, she's my new friend."

"D'La, how are you?"

"I'm fine, thank you."

"This is my mother, Mrs. Felioni."

Mrs. Felioni admires Candice's cute and very courteous new friend. "You're a pretty one, D'La."

"Thank you, Mamm," smiles D'La.

"She's Miss Connell's niece and she's staying with her for the summer."

"Sharon Connell is your aunt?" ask Mrs. Felioni.

"Yes Mamm."

"She's a very nice lady and the perfect neighbor," adds Mrs. Felioni.

"Thank you," says D'La.

"Mom, I want to know if I can go to Elayne's house, but I want to use the phone first?"

"I suppose so...but be careful and don't talk to any strangers along the way. You hear me, Candice Felioni?"

"Yes, we hear you, Mother!" Once outside Candice replies, "I told you, she's very protective of me. Sometimes, I feel it's a bit too much, but she has to realize that I'm a big girl now...I'm almost twelve years old." Candice looks at D'La as if she is the only person who understands what she is going through.

"Yeah, I know. I guess parents are like that, afraid to let go and stuff. Now, let go to my house and ask if I can go," requests D'La.

"Yeah. I think Miss Connell will say yes," replies Candice.

"I think so too."

They race toward Aunt Sharon's house and D'La sees her aunt washing her car in the driveway. "Aunt Sharon?" calls D'La, running toward her.

"Hi, Miss. Connell." greets Candice.

"Yes D'La?" asks Sharon as she throws the rag into the bucket of sudsy water. "How are you Candice, and how's your mother?"

"She's fine, Miss Connell."

"Okay, I can tell you girls want something. What is it?"

"Aunt Sharon, I want to know if I can go with Candice to her friend's house."

"What friend is this?"

Candice explains, "My friend Elayne from school, she's in my class."

Sharon recalls the conversation she had with D'La about finding new friends, which helps her with her decision.

"Elayne Donaldson, she lives over on Dover Street. It's only a couple of blocks away," Candice says in an assuring manner.

"I know where Dover Street is, Candice."

"Can I go, Aunt Sharon?" D'La asks.

"Yeah, I suppose so...you can go. But, when you see the sun about to go down young lady, you better be back here. I mean long before it gets dark. Don't let me come looking for you, either!"

"We'll be back long before it gets dark...Thanks Aunt Sharon." D'La gives her aunt a hug of gratitude.

"Thanks Miss Connell. I have to be home before dark, too."

Aunt Sharon picks the hose off the ground and squirts water on the car as D'La and Candice walks away. Once reaching Elayne's house, they go up on the porch, and ring the doorbell. Elayne answers.

"Hi, Elayne, can you come out for a while?" Candice ask.

"Hi...Yeah, I can come out." Elayne steps onto the porch looking attentively at the new girl and Candice waste no time introducing her.

"Elayne, this is D'La. D'La, Elayne."

"Hi, D'La, nice to meet you." Elayne is very courteous to the new girl, as they become familiar with one another.

"Hi, nice to meet you, too, Elayne."

"Do you live around here?" Elayne ask out of curiosity.

"No. I live on the eastside of Detroit," D'La answers proudly.

"Oh...the eastside, my grandmother lives on the eastside."

"She do? ...Well, the eastside, it's okay," D'La adds.

Candice interrupts, "She's kin to Miss Connell. You remember her, don't you? She lives down the street from me."

"Yeah, I know Miss. Connell." Both girls realize that D'La must be a very nice person, to be kin to Ms. Connell as Elayne to continue boost: "Miss Connell, is a regular member at my father's church and she's one of the nicest people (The Donaldson's) we know."

Everything is going so well, laughing and playing as the day continue that they decide to introduce D'La to Shi Li. So, Elayne goes into the house and calls Shi Li on the phone, but Shi Li's aunt says that she has gone to the store to buy some things for dinner.

"She must have gone to the one near the school, cause, that's the only store close to her house. Let's go and meet her," says Elayne.

"Yeah, we'll surprise her," adds Candice.

Once at the store, Candice notices Shi Li in one of the aisles. They rushed toward her, and introduced D'La after buying the things needed, teasing each other as they start to walk out of the store. Unfortunately and unexpectedly, colliding with Johnny Burton and his brother Mark at the store entrance, standing face to face.

"Hey, lookey here," says Mark with vengeful intentions and an evil glimpse that slowly covers his face, along with hot thick steam flowing from his eyes. Mark has never forgiven Elayne or her friends for ignoring Johnny's affection, his mating call for companionship. However, the only thing the girls really know about the two boys is wherever they go, trouble follows.

"Excuse us please," states Shi Li.

"You're excused," says Johnny, allowing Shi Li to pass and yet blocking Elayne and the other two girls with his body.

"Excuse me," demands Elayne.

"Elayne, I wanna talk to you for a minute, okay?" Johnny politely asks. Elayne refuse to acknowledge Johnny's request, because bad news is and always will be bad news.

"Excuse me, please." Elayne demands a second time, but still Johnny did not make way.

"Just wait a minute. I just wanna talk to you."

"No, Johnny. I don't want to talk to you. Now, excuse me."

"You heard what she said, move boy," Candice is direct and harsh.

"You shut up. Ain't nobody talk'n to you anyway," aggressively replies Mark.

Shi Li did not say a word. She stands peaceably, listening to Johnny and Mark, while waiting outside the store's entrance. However, her patience is growing shorter and she realizes she can wait no longer. In addition she notices things are not going well that she abruptly interrupts. "Johnny just go away."

Shi Li's statement angers Johnny. "Who ask you anythang, Chink?"

Suddenly, with one hand, Elayne pushes Johnny out of her way and they walk by. In disbelief, Johnny stands there for a moment and only for a moment. Johnny and Mark watch the girls as they leave the store. Spontaneously, the two brothers decide to follow them.

Everybody in the neighborhood knows not to use any kind of force with the Burton Brothers, not for any reason, because nobody has gotten away with it as of yet. Shi Li looks back and sees the two boys coming closer and faster.

"I think we have a problem, trouble is following us."

Looking back over her shoulder, Elayne's nervousness is increasing and it's relatively stressful. "Why don't he just leave me alone? Why don't they just go home or somethang?" she expresses.

D'La is trying hard to be cool but these boys are making it impossible. "Who are those two clowns?"

Candice wastes no time in answering, "Trouble makers, Johnny and Mark Burton. The oldest one, Johnny, is crazy in love with Elayne...or he thinks he is."

Elayne tries to justify the situation. "I've told him almost a thousand times...that I DON'T LIKE HIM."

D'La glances back, "Here they come!"

Hastily the girls cross the street, but Johnny and Mark keep coming, following the girl's every course, walking indeed faster to catch up.

"HEY ELAYNE, WHO DO YOU THINK YOU'RE PUSH'N? NOBODY PUSHES ON ME. NOT EVEN YOU!"

Elayne and her friends continue to ignore Johnny's yells and it seems the faster the girls walk, the faster Johnny and Mark walks, and the boys are getting closer with every second.

"Let's go to my house. We can take the short cut through the alley," nervously states Elayne.

Into the alley they go, and with less than a block away, Johnny takes off running, rapidly sneaking up behind them, throwing his arm round Elayne's neck, pulling her to his body; forcing his unwanted desire and kissing her lips several times.

Mark runs over to Shi Li, grabs her dress and pulls it up. "Let's see...I heard, Chinks don't wear panties."

Embarrassed by Mark's disrespectful and offensive behavior, Shi Li knocks his hand away, he tries again and again and she keeps knocking it away. Eventually, Elayne breaks away from Johnny's clutches, as Candice picks up a big stick and hits him over the head with it.

D'La eyes are focus on the two brothers as she places her hand in her pocket, on the knife. She can't believe her eye. Things like this didn't happen in her neighborhood without someone getting hurt real bad, because where she comes from, nobody in their right mind would ever try something so insane; nobody messes with the Lausen's kids.

Due to the fact, everyone in the neighborhood knew that they would be going home with a bloody nose, crack head or something worse. D'La realizes that this isn't the eastside of Detroit and these people are as strange to her as she is to them. But that is not going to stop her from protecting her new friends and herself.

Shi Li drops her groceries on the ground, makes a fist and socks Mark in his face; then she swiftly lifts one leg and karate kicks him in his stomach. Her kick is so powerful it immediately knocks Mark to the ground, falling on his butt. Amazed that Shi Li could even kick that hard or knew karate, and before D'La can blink, a fight has started. D'La impetuously pulls her knife out of her pocket, releases the safety switch and charges toward Johnny.

D'La comes out of nowhere, slightly presses the knife against Johnny's throat, only pressing it just enough for him to feel the cold blade against his neck. She looks directly into his eyes. D'La is not taking any prisoners; her words are extremely ferocious and her action is even more convincing.

"Hey you dumb ugly punk, back up...before I make you BLEED."

This is Johnny's first time ever being threatened by a knife and a girl, and this is D'La's first time threatening anybody with the knife. Johnny puts his hands up, out, and away from the knife as he wonders, 'Who's this girl? ...Where did she come from?'

He hesitates to make a move, fearing that the strange girl with the crazy face might cut his neck.

She talks in an undertone, almost whispering. "Well, what about it? ...You stupid as... I will cut your throat if you make one wrong move."

Mark fears for Johnny's life. "JOHNNY," he cries.

Johnny is still cool and calm or at least that is what he wants everybody to think especially Mark.

"Stay cool, Bro. Man."

D'La shows no fear, she means every word and somehow Johnny knows this crazy girl will cut him; also, he realizes his life is in serious danger. Shi Li, Candice, and Elayne are in shock, but at the same time, grateful for D'La's quick actions. Relieved by her heroics, they can not believe their eyes, watching fear take possession of Johnny and Mark.

"You and your friend, your brother, or who ever the hell he's to you, betta get the f....' out of here. RIGHT NOW, before you p...ss me off, GOT IT!"

Mark doesn't want any part of this crazy girl; he calls his brother a second time. "JOHNNY."

Johnny slowly steps away from D'La and the knife. "Calm down Mark. Everythang's cool...cool as can be. Com'on Man, forget these nasty tramps."

Keeping his eyes focused on D'La and the knife, Johnny slowly steps away signaling with his eyes and his head for Mark to follow. "I'll deal with your nappy as... head later, bit.... This ain't over."

Mark picks himself up off the ground and runs toward Johnny. Johnny's pride has been cut down and his spirit is scattered right in front of his number one fan, his brother. But somehow he finds a nerve and that one nerve gives him enough courage to yell one final time: "THIS AIN'T OVER...I'LL SEE YOU AGAIN. AND, I MEAN REAL SOON. ...YOU, YOU HEAR ME? IT AIN'T OVER, NOT YET YOU BIT...."

Johnny has lost a fight to a girl and he tries to regain his egotistic reputation by motioning with his fist and his middle finger. Mark has never seen Johnny so furious and embarrassed.

Ultimately, everything seems to have calm down a bit and D'La put the knife back into her pocket while the girls adjust their clothing. Instead of going to Elayne's house they decide to walk Shi Li home.

"Is everybody okay?" Candice asks, before looking at Elayne. Elayne looks grim.

"Elayne!" cries Candice.

"Yeah...I'm all right, Candice," says Elayne.

Candice helps Shi Li and D'La pick up the groceries and before anyone realizes, Elayne starts to pray.

"Thank you Lord for saving our lives...and forgive us of our sin? I mean the knife...Oh yeah, especially...forgive us of that? ...And Lord...please help Johnny and Mark, for they're truly on the road to destruction. Amen!"

D'La hands Shi Li the partially torn bag.

"D'La, thanks for helping us fight those guys," says Shi Li.

"I don't believe it. Boys are the stupidest people on earth...Who are they anyway?" ask D'La.

"The stupidest boys in school, that's who. And the one that was grabbing on Elayne, he was in our class before he got kicked out for fighting and smoking. Everyday he would start a fight with somebody," Candice replies.

The shock from the entire incident weighs heavy on Elayne and her tears begin to fall. Shi Li notices the tension as it slowly consumes her face. "Elayne...Elayne is crying...Do not cry, Elayne." Shi Li dashes to her.

"Do not cry," Shi Li caresses her, holding her with one hand while holding the groceries in the other.

Elayne can not help it. Johnny is really starting to get on her nerves. "Why is he treating me like this? I've never said anythang to him, nor did anythang bad to him. I don't know why The Lord is letting him treat me like this. Somethang got to be wrong with me."

D'La expeditiously responds to Elayne's statement. "It's not The Lord...all boys are jerks, Elayne. That's why they did it...It's in their weak and stupid genes. Even roach spray won't kill 'em. I know, cause, I tried spraying some on a stupid boy in my neighborhood, and all he did was cry."

Candice's heart quickly saddens as she watches her friend's tears fall down her face. "Elayne, Elayne, don't cry, please? Everything is going to be all right," she says.

"Elayne, I am not going to let anything happen to you. Friends through thick and thin, remember! Since first grade!" says Shi Li as she tries to comfort her friend with a smile and a hug.

Candice takes her hands and gently wipes the tears from Elayne's face. "Me neither."

"Don't worry Elayne. If he bothers you again just let me know. I'll kick his butt for you. I can't stand those dumb pitiful creatures anyway. I don't understand why boys have to live on this earth with girls, especially as feeble as they are. They should've all been sent to the moon long ago. WE DON'T NEED 'EM!" aggressively D'La interrupts.

Shi Li and Candice did not understand D'La's statement, and at the time, they did not care, they're too busy concentrating on Elayne.

"We all will," says Shi Li.

"Yeah. That's right, we all will." Candice repeats.

Concern for her friends, D'La adds as she put the knife into her pants pocket. "We better hurry up before we get in trouble."

While walking home, Shi Li starts to wonder about the new girl and ask, "D'La, where did you get the knife?"

Reassuringly D'La replies, "It's my brother's knife...Well it was, anyway!"

Candice also searches for closure as she constantly watches D'La's hand as she holds on to her outer pocket. "Did he give it to you?"

"Nope, he left it on the workbench outside, so...I took it."

Shocked by her answers, Shi Li continues to ask questions. "You stole it?"

"Nope, I took it. A girl needs protection, if you know what I mean. Like today," D'La brags with a cocky attitude.

"Do your brother know that you took it?" Candice is on the right track. Brent did consider D'La as the thief.

"Maybe...I don't know and I don't care. I think he thinks he lost it...Then again, maybe he don't."

"Do you always carry it everywhere you go?" inquires Shi Li.

"Well, sometimes I do...I guess, I like having it around. If I need it, no problem, it's right here!" D'La holds on tight to her pants as she proudly taps the concealed knife. "Right in my pocket."

Candice's mother is always inspecting her whereabouts and her personal belongings that she just has to ask; "Do your mother know that you carry a knife?"

"No way...Are you crazy or somethang! She'll surely woop my butt."

Shi Li interrupts, "Candice, do not ask silly questions."

"If my parents knew that I carried a knife...Ooo...I don't even want to think about it. If Momma don't kill me with it, I know, as sure as I'm standing here, I know she'll make me eat it."

Elayne has finally calmed down a little; yet, her eyes are still teary, and she worries as she takes her dress sleeve to dry them. "If my parents ever find out what happened to me today, they would never let me out of the house again, as long as I live, or until I'm a old lady, twenty or thirty years old, or somethang. I just know it. I wouldn't be able to talk to any of you again."

"Then we will never tell anyone about today, okay? It will be our secret," says Shi Li.

"We will never tell anyone about the knife, either," proposed D'La as she grips her pocket tighter.

With a determined look Candice replies, "Yes, it's our secret...forever."

With a solemn expression masking her face, her eyes focusing into the unknown, D'La adds, "We'll never tell...Even in death."

Without realizing the bond between them, an alliance is born. Embracing one another and promising to always and forever, no matter what, they will never tell.

From the alley and onto the front street they go, Candice notice a car parked at Shi Li's house. "Shi Li look, you have company."

Shi Li identifies the vehicle as they got closer to the driveway. "It is my Uncle's car. My mother and Aunt Miuki never said anything about having company, today."

"Maybe they dropped by, my relatives do that all the time," says D'La.

Shi Li's intense curiosity grows rapidly, and so does her friends, as one step at a time brings them closer to her home, to the front porch.

"Do you want us to wait here until you come back?" ask Candice.

"Yes, wait for me here," answers Shi Li.

Candice contemplates: 'we used to wonder why Shi Li never invited us into her house after school. Lots of time we would wait on the porch until she made sure it's okay to come in. Though, later she did confide in us. Telling us how her mother and her are enslaved by old custom, her father's wish that embarrassed Shi Li so much; yet, still to this day, making sure he wasn't home.'

Shi Li is about to turn the doorknob when someone opens it from the inside. Sadly, standing in the doorway, with watery eyes glaring down at her, Uncle Chung appears.

"Hi, Uncle Chung. I didn't know you were coming back to visit us a second time today, you just left. "

Aunt Miuki quickly comes to the door, taking Shi Li's torn bag. "It is time for you to come in the house. Your friends will have to come and visit another day."

Candice, Elayne and D'La can do nothing but stand and wonder 'what's wrong'. At least Mother Kyi has never sent them home before, well, not so soon, she always invited them in first. Plus she is always pleasant and hospitable as they recall as the door closes in their faces.

Once inside the house Shi Li is even more baffled. "What is wrong? Is something wrong, Aunt Miuki?"

Aunt Miuki takes Shi Li by the hand and sits her down on the couch. "Something has happened."

"What?" asks Shi Li, "What has happen?"

Aunt Miuki looks at her husband before dropping her head; she is finding it hard to express her regrets. She speaks very softly, "Your mother is gone to the hospital. You know she has been very ill."

"What...What do you mean, she is very ill? She was all right when I left for the store. I was not gone that long. What could have happened to her in just a short time?"

"She has been sick for some time now and you know this much. She is very ill. Little One, she wanted to tell you just how much, but she thought the time was never right for you. She wanted your time with her to be happy, so that is why she did not tell, she did not want you to worry."

"I am not a worrier, Aunt Miuki. Uncle Chung she can tell me anything and she knows that. What you are saying can not be so." Shi Li takes her fist and punches the armrest of the chair as her anger increases. "No, that can not be true. She would have told me. I want to see her, now, Aunt Miuki, please?" Please Uncle Chung?

Sadly Aunt Miuki replies, "We will have to wait until your father calls. Then we will know what to do."

A moment of silence overcomes the room prior to Shi Li's next question. "Is my mother going to die?"

Aunt Miuki takes Shi Li into her arms, caressing her as she search for the strength to tell the truth. Yet, Aunt Miuki takes too much time in answering the question. Shi Li breaks away and asks again, "Is my mother dead? Is she? Please tell me!"

Aunt Miuki looks into Shi Li faces, her beautiful black eyes glaring back. "Yes. Your mother has already gone away. She is following the clouds into the sky, behind the sun. Shi Li, it is too late for us to say good-bye."

Shi Li's traumatized by the news of her mother's death, and her horrid screams soon echoes through the house, "NO.... NO... MOTHER...NO."

Finding it hard to believe she gets down on her knees and begs for the truth. "Please do not tell me this, Aunt Miuki. You lie to me, I know you are lying. NO. Oh...o...o...My mother would not leave me like this." Shi Li closes her eyes as immense tear roll onto her cheeks. "Mother please do not leave me. I need you, please." Shi Li runs into her parent's bedroom, throwing her small-framed body onto the bed.

Aunt Miuki immediately runs after her, stopping at the entrance before slowly approaching her. She gently lies next to Shi Li, touching her tenderly, as she pulls her closer, holding firmly as the two mourn together.

The funeral's temple is absolutely beautifully. It is decorated with all kind of flowers, the sweet aroma of jasmine's overwhelming, as Shi Li's mother lies in her ivory casket with roses placed all around her entire body. Shi Li stands completely inert, silent, between her father and Aunt Miuki as thoughts of her mother consumes her. She remembers the good times and the bad times, meaning her father, as she stares at her mother's lifeless body.

'This has got to be a dream. My mother would not leave me this way...she was a good mother. She just would not die and not say good-by, she said...she loves me. No, I can not believe this is happening. I do not want to believe. It is a dream. It has got to be. I want to wake up now...This can not be true...NO.'

Heavy tears pour from her cold black eyes as she grabs hold of her aunt's dress. She looks up at her father, who is standing very erect, that frozen face, that emotionless face, looking as though he is in a hypnotic mindset, the emptiness that Shi Li will never forget and seen so many times before.

She ponders: 'Why is my mother dead and not you? You killed her...Because of you she is dead. You hateful evil man. She died a slave for your love...A love worth nothing.' Her tears were endless, refusing to stop, never the less, Shi Li can not wait to leave, to get away from the man she feels is responsible for killing her mother.

At the Donaldson's home, Elayne's concern about Shi Li, her mother's funeral, is truly troubling her. Also realizing Mrs. Kyi's death will somehow destroy Shi Li's tender loving heart. Elayne knows she has to do something to ease her friend's pain; and she didn't want Shi Li to ever feel that she is alone in this world. What can she possibly do to help her sustain? The Bible teaches us to pray and Elayne knows that prayer is the answer. Moreover, The Lord has always been there when she needed help, so why wouldn't he be there for her friend? She begins to pray, asking to please limit her friend's suffering and heal her broken heart.

"Oh Dear Lord...Please, help my friend Shi Li. Well...her mother is on her way to see you. I know you know that much Lord; but Shi Li is so upset and her heart is broken in half. I just want to do somethang, somethang that will help her feel better. I know she knows I'm here for her always, and that I will be her friend no matter what...But, how can I be there for her now, at this time, Lord? How can I tell her what's in my heart? Dear Lord, please show me? If, there's only one thing I could ask of you, let this be the one prayer that you answer, please Lord...Amen."

Elayne goes to the window and looks up at the sky and within that special moment an inspirational feeling opens Elayne's heart.

"I know what I can do. Thank you Lord. Thank you. For you are truly good."

Elayne goes to her desk and begins writing, erasing, thinking and humming; after gathering her thoughts she starts to write the words to a melody. "Yes Lord we did it. This is the perfect way to tell Shi Li how much I care...Thanks."

The doorbell rings, Candice and D'La have comes to visit and they too are concerned for their friend.

Mrs. Donaldson answers the door. "Hi girls, come on in."

"Hi Mrs. Donaldson. How are you today?"

"Oh, I'm fine. Thank you for askin, Candice."

"Mrs. Donaldson, this is my friend, D'La."

"Hi D'La...D'La, what a pretty name."

"Hello Mrs. Donaldson, and thank you and I'm very pleased to meet you.

"I'm pleased to meet you too, D'La."

"I'll tell Elayne you're here."

"ELAYNE...ELAYNE. You have company, Honey."

"OKAY, HERE I COME MA MAM". Elayne closes her notebook, walks into the living room where Candice and D'La are waiting with her mother.

"Hey, I didn't know ya'll were comin over."

"I know. We thought we would stop by to see what you're doing."

"Follow me, I was just in my room," says Elayne.

The girls follow Elayne as Mrs. Donaldson continues to watch television with Elizabeth.

Once in the bedroom, Candice makes small talk to ease her mind: "I see you've changed your room around."

"Yeah, Ma mam changed it for me; every time she cleans it. It's just her way of checking to see if I left any dishes in here or not."

"Sometimes, my Momma does that to me, she's always checking for dishes, too." says D'La.

Candice sits on the bed while D'La sits at Elayne's desk admiring her nick-knacks.

Although, Candice can wait no longer, "Elayne, have you talked to Shi Li?"

"No, I haven't."

"The funeral should be over by now," replies Candice.

"Yeah, I know. I'm worried about her. She's so upset about her mother's death." Elayne explains.

Candice is starting to worry even more. "I know she is...I hope she's all right."

"Why don't we call her?" ask D'La.

Elayne replies, "No. This isn't a good time and her house is probably full of people."

"That's true. I was just try'n to help. This wait'n is make'n me fidgety," D'La says, picking up a pencil off the desk.

"I know, let's play a game...maybe, that would relax us. How about...Hey, I got it," says Elayne reaching on the top shelf of her closet.

After all, the funeral has come to a close and everyone returns to the Kyi's house. Shi Li is intensely uncomfortable. There are people and more people, her father said their relatives but they're still just people to Shi Li. Plus, everyone is standing around, staring and whispering to one another as Shi Li walks endlessly and soundlessly through the house before going to a window and looking out. It is a cloudy, gray and damp day; it looks as though the rain will never stop. Shi Li tries to watch every raindrop as they fell, and as the memories of her mother flashes nonstop. The laughing and singing together, her gentle touch, and her sweet smile that always met her at the door when she came home from school, most of all, her very best friend.

'I can not remember a single day when I saw my mother upset with me. Of course, there have been times when I have made many mistakes; but mother never got upset with me, she loved me for me.'

Her tears are none stop as her memory replay. 'Now, what will come of me? Who will be there for me? My father does not love me, his heart is cold and dead.'

Shi Li turns and gazes at Aunt Miuki, who is standing behind her husband bowing her head and running behind him, like a shadow, catering to his every need, like her mother used to do.

'She too is a slave to old customs, just like my mother.'

Shi Li's innocent, sensitive heart is growing colder than the north wind, as she try come to terms with her emotions, and realizing that she wants no part of her father. 'My mother's life could have been saved, instead of dying like a slave for a man who values nothing but other people's opinions of his worth.'

Yet Shi Li's thoughts of her mother are not all good; remembering, how her mother ran behind her father day after day, once he entered the house. How she ran into the bathroom to get a basin of warm water and two clean dry towels one for each foot. Approaching him with a bowed head before getting down on her knees to wash his feet as he relaxed in his favorite chair reading his newspaper.

"I can not stand this," whispers Shi Li, " I have to get away from here, away from him."

Without realizing it, Shi Li finds herself running out of the house as fast as she can. Dashing down the steps, running through the rain, confused and seeking the only comfort she knows, screaming her mother's name and begging her to return to life. "Mother, Mother, please come back. I can not go on. I can not live without you, Mother, come back to me, please."

The raindrops increase as they fall upon Shi Li's face as she prays and waits for her mother to answer her call; but there is no answer. Shi Li aimlessly wanders onto the school grounds, sitting in a swing and talking to the sky, trying her best to see beyond the clouds.

"Mother please come back. I miss you so much. PLEASE...E...E...e." Holding her head high to the sky as the raindrops continues to masks her face. "Mother, I have no life without you. What will I do? I love you so, so much."

After wiping her face with her wet hands she looks up again and notices a strange cloud forming, it looks like a lady in the cloud, and she is pointing. Shi Li wipes her eyes again in disbelief, she looks up again, and the cloud lady is still standing in the sky, still pointing.

"Mother?" says Shi Li as she looks in the direction to see where and what. Shi Li replies, "Yes, I will go...and I will never stop loving you. You will always be in my heart, forever."

Shi Li knows she has to go, and she believes her mother has finally answered her prayers.

"Yes, even now you are still with me. Thank you Mother." Shi Li abruptly jumps out of the swing and runs as fast as she can.

Elayne, Candice and D'La are finishing a game when the doorbell rings. Again Mrs. Donaldson answers it. "Shi Li... what...honey, I thought?" She stops herself right at the beginning of her questioning. "I'm sorry about your mother, Shi Li, but if you ever need anythang, I'll be more than happy to be there for you and your family."

Mrs. Donaldson takes Shi Li into her arms, hugging her and squeezing her tightly. It seems as though Mrs. Donaldson can actually feel the pain that Shi Li is carrying in her heart. Shi Li is glad and relieved to hear those words, most importantly, a hug from someone who actually cares for her. Shi Li honestly concludes that she has found a new home.

Mrs. Donaldson has always been a loving person, not only to Shi Li, but to Mother Kyi as well, and that is one thing Shi Li will never forget.

"Thank you, Mrs. Donaldson."

Mrs. Donaldson can't help noticing Shi Li's swollen eyes and wet clothes. She ponders: 'the poor girl looks as though she had been crying for days.' She asks, "Shi Li, do you need me to do anythang for you?"

"No, Mrs. Donaldson...I am all right."

Shi Li impetuously grabs Mrs. Donaldson around her waist again. Mrs. Donaldson squats down, firmly holding Shi Li as if she is her own daughter. Shi Li can feel the love from her by the way she holds her, which brings back one particular memory of her mother and what she once said: 'Shi Li my daughter, you and your friends are all sisters with the same spirits, you will always flow together in harmony.'

"Everythang is gonna be all right, Shi Li. The Lord has his way of do'n thangs and we just have to sit back, wait, and trust in him."

"Thank you Mrs. Donaldson...Mrs. Donaldson, is Elayne home?"

"She sure is. You just go on into her bedroom, and tell Elayne to get you some dry thangs to put on, too. I'll call your father and let him know you're here...And don't worry honey, everythang is gonna be okay."

Mrs. Donaldson points toward Elayne's bedroom. Shi Li hesitates for a moment, that loving hug, lingering, reminding her so much of her mother's hug and her love.

"She's in her bedroom, go on in, honey."

"Thank you Mrs. Donaldson."

Shi Li opens the bedroom door, Candice, Elayne and D'La are delightfully surprised, hurriedly approaching her, but Shi Li voice is meek and sore, "Hi, everybody."

"Shi Li, what are you do'n here? I thought you were at..." express Elayne.

"I could not take it anymore. Every one standing around, staring...I had to leave, so I left. I ran out of the house."

"Won't they miss you?" ask Candice.

"I do not care if they miss me."

Holding back the tears, even around her closest friends is still impossible for Shi Li. Uncontrollably they gush out and she finally breaks down, tumbling face down on the bed. "WHY DID SHE HAVE TO DIE? WHY? ...I do not understand. She was my MOTHER and she was a GOOD PERSON." she looks up at her friends, "Good people should not have to DIE."

Elayne tries to explain, repeating the words she heard frequently during her father's sermons: "Sometimes thangs happen and only The Lord can answer, why."

Shi Li covers her face with her hands trying to conceal her emotions. Then she gradually turns and sits up on the bed. Elayne reaches for her, embracing her. "Shi Li. Shi Li."

Her pain is too strong and Elayne can feel her deepest emotions, she truly understands what she is going through that she starts to cry with her.

Candice and D'La also feel the pain as they wrap their arms around Shi Li and Elayne and within seconds the four are crying together.

"Shi Li you are my friend and I will always be here for you. If you ever need me...no matter what, I'll be there."

Candice wipes the tears from Shi Li's face. "You know we will, Shi Li."

D'La turns her head trying to hide her tears, asking herself: 'How can I be so emotional for someone I hardly know?'

But, D'La did care, a lot and adds, "That's true, always, Shi Li, and forever together."

Holding Shi Li hands, Elayne glances into her eyes. "Shi Li, I have somethang for you. The Lord helped me write this."

Elayne goes to her desk, picks up her notebook, inside is the song she just finished writing. "Shi Li this is for you, always." Elayne starts to sing and her angelic voice captures everyone's heart as the tears continue to fall from their eyes.

> A bond so strong.   It must go on
> A love so real   We needn't feel
> Ever alone under the sky.
> We'll sustain   Beyond the pain
> There lies a peace We're bound to seek
> Ever believing   Under The Sky...

Overwhelmed by the love she is receiving, Shi Li can not help feeling their bond growing, becoming stronger. At the conclusion of the inspirational song the four friends caressed one another and continue to grieve together.

GIRLS DO

CHAPTER 6

　　1967 - Three and a half years later and junior high is coming to an end. D'La has missed several days in the last month, already. The teacher calls her house wondering if D'La is out of school due to illness. D'La is not ill or anything like that, at the moment, she is not interested in going to school. She has other things on her mind: such as smoking cigarettes and gambling with the guys at the pool hall, and most of the time she would beat the pants off of them.

　　Thank goodness Michael took the call that day and he is not surprised that D'La's teacher is calling on her. He knows something is wrong, since D'La has not brought any homework home lately. Momma and daddy are to busy working, paying bills and trying to keep above water, and to busy to keep up with D'La's schoolwork. Michael knows he has to talk with his sister about the call from her teacher because D'La always comes home as usual, about 3:30pm.

　　Again D'La strolls through the door without a care in the world, but this time big brother Michael is waiting. "Hey De. What's up?"

　　Shocked to see him sitting at the kitchen table, she senses an unusual air about him, as if he is mad about something. And D'La has no idea what he could possibly want calling her name like that, so rudely.

　　She answers, "Nuth'n much. "

　　D'La is not in the mood for conversation. Shooting pool for money and hustling is hard work. It takes strict concentration keeping your eyes focus at all times, one eye in the front of your head and the other eye in the back. Never knowing who may want to start a fight and take back their money, especially from a girl who's winning. D'La loves winning and she also loves watching the sorry half-witted faces of the men that loses, a lot more.

　　Nevertheless, from Friday mornings til Friday nights, D'La knows the pool hall will be full of customers who are not perfect shooters. And after watching them drink all day long, D'La knows who are the 'easy pickings' and which ones are not. Some of the players do not know how to play the game or how to hold the stick. Yet, they paraded around the table with their chest all poked out as their big mouths flapped. But that don't stop D'La, the money is still mean green and she wants it all. Still on Thursday nights over half of the auto plant workers get their paychecks and D'La definitely wants to be there. Even if that means, failing her school exam the next day. She knows her teacher will let her make it up. Especially, if her lie is good enough. Plus, after staying out all night she couldn't get up to go, anyway.

Michael doesn't waste anytime with her, but gets straight to the point. His voice is very compelling and spiteful. "De, your teacher called this morning and she wanted to know, 'if you're ill?'"

Again D'La is shocked to hear that tone coming out of her favorite brother's, mouth. That mad face of his could make 'road kill' get up and walk again, but D'La doesn't care.

"And...so what!" Her sassy remark is expected. Putting one hand on her hip she walks toward the kitchen sink to get a drink of water.

"What you been do'n De? ...How come you ain't in school?"

She slams the glass down on the sink, "What you wanna know for, Michael?"

Michael is starting to steam as his face turns a bit sour. D'La is rude yet proud, placing one hand in her pocket. Michael kicks the chair banging it against the table. D'La plays tough, paying no attention to Michael's egoistic exhibition as she takes the glass and drinks.

"Momma and daddy work all day long just to keep a roof over our heads and the last thang they need to hear is that you're skip'n school or fail'n the ninth grade."

"...Okay, okay, I'll tell you...It's no big deal," states D'La.

D'La gently sits the glass down on the sink, walks and stands by the kitchen table looking directly into Michael's face. "I'm not gonna fail, nuth'n...I know what I'm do'n. Got that?"

"Evidently, you don't know somethang. You know how hard it is out here on the streets? If you did, you wouldn't be skip'n school."

"I ain't skip'n school for nuth'n."

"Then what you call it, De?"

"I call it take'n some time out and make'n me some money."

"Money for what? Don't momma and daddy give you money? And if you need money that bad, all you got to do is ask me. Li'l Sis, you're the only sister I got. It would make all of us so happy if you graduated; momma didn't graduate, daddy didn't either, Brent didn't, or me. And Anton got a ways to go before he even get to where are. You gotta graduate. Hey, talk'n about being happy, everybody in this house will jump out of their seats to see you walk across that stage, girl...De, the money I make ain't much, but whatever I have it's yours, girl."

Sympathizing with her brother's feelings D'La sits down at the table. "Michael, the reason that I'm do'n this is so that I can get a little money of my own and momma and daddy don't have to worry 'bout buy'n me thangs I need."

"De, if you need money that bad, like I said, ask me. You know I'm here for you, Li'l Sis. I love you."

"Okay. Okay, goodness...don't get mushy, Michael. I'll go back to school first thang Monday morning."

Michael walks around the table. "Good De, you're do'n right by go'n back to school. I oughta know, okay? Now give your big brother a hug."

D'La holds him firm. "You know Michael, I do want to graduate, but I don't have any nice dresses to walk across no stage in."

Michael's very surprise as he pulls her chin up, looking into her face. "De, I haven't seen you in a dress since you were a baby. This is gonna be some sight, see'n you in a dress, again. When you're ready to go and get that new dress and some new shoes, I'll give you the money."

D'La reaches into her pocket and pulls out three hundred dollars. "I'm ready now, and I already got the money."

Michael's flabbergasted as he takes the money and counts it. "Where you get this money from?"

"The pool hall, I ain't been practicing for nuth'n."

"You won all this?"

D'La demonstrates on the kitchen table, pretending she is holding a pool stick.

"Yep...Them suckers can't play worth nuth'n, I was knock'n those balls in one after another: Pow, Pow, Pow."

"D'La girl, I guess I did teach you well."

"Yep, you did Michael."

Michael's astonished with his sister's determination to survive, yet still he reminds her, "But remember, school comes first."

"I know Michael, and I will finish high school too. You can bet on it."

"My girl...D'La, remember that day when we went to the auto store? The day when we were work'n on my old car, the day Brent's knife came up miss'n." Michael reaches for a bag on the table that he laid there earlier.

D'La is very presumptuous with her answer. "Yeah, I remember. What about it?"

"I know who took it."

D'La takes two steps from the table and leans against the sink. "Yeah! Who?"

"You!

D'La tries to defend herself but Michael isn't buying it.

"Me! Are you crazy Michael? Why would I do somethang like that?"

"Because you're my sister and when you want somethang, you'll take it...True?"

D'La doesn't know what to say; she stands there looking completely bewildered.

"I'm not go'n to tell or anythang like that Li'l Sis." Michael takes the bag off the table and hands it to D'La. "I think it's time for a new one...Happy Birthday!"

D'La opens the bag and pulls out a large hunting knife, a bowie knife. She is ecstatic and relieved that she doesn't have to keep that secret any longer. "Michael...thank you. It's so beautiful and it even got it's own pouch. Dam... look at that sucker shine, Michael."

"Don't let momma know you got this knife."

"Don't worry, I'll keep this a secret even longer than before."

D'La rushes out of the back door to her favorite tree and calls for Michael to follow her. "Michael com'on...see that branch sticking out? ...Watch this?" D'La throws the knife into the tree hitting her target center point. "BULL'S EYE," she yells.

D'La did return to school and hadn't missed a day since her and Michael's talk.

Several months later, one boring Saturday night, D'La is seeking some excitement. She decides to go to the pool hall and once entering, D'La notices that there is a party going on. The party is going strong; there are so many people drinking, dancing and gambling. Even the cheap whores are rolling, making that fast money.

"Yeah, money is up in here tonight," she whispers. D'La walks around checking the place out before deciding to sit at the bar. 'Um...everybody's here tonight and a few new faces, too.'

The bartender approaches her. "Hey D'La, what's up girl? Where's your brother Mike? He said he was coming down here tonight."

"He'll be here later, Zeke."

"You want anything to drink? I got Coke, Seven Up and Squirt."

"Is that all? ...No liquor, Zeke? Not even a drop?" sad faced, asks D'La.

"Hey! Not even a drop for you Miss Minor! I could lose my license serving you, De."

"I won't tell if you don't. You know I'm cool, Zeke."

D'La tries to persuade Zeke, giving him an encouraging sweet girlish smile, but he is not falling for it, that when a stranger in the next seat interrupts: "I'll order. What do you want to drink?"

D'La and Zeke take a curious and long look at the stranger. Her personality seems pleasant, but her clothes are dirty and she is dressed like a man.

'In any case, that's how those factory workers dress.' D'La assures herself.

"All right," smiles D'La. "I'll have a Rum and Coke."

"Bartender, I'll have a Rum and Coke, please." says the woman.

Zeke takes the rum off the back counter, then reaches over head and grabs a glass filling it half way with Coke as he keeps a watchful eye on the stranger and D'La.

"Hi, my name is Kate."

"I'm D'La. Please to meet you, Kate."

"Please to meet you too, D'La."

Zeke sits the drink between D'La and the strange woman.

"Thanks Zeke", says D'La, winking an eye.

"This is my first time here," says Kate looking around the bar.

"Yeah, this is a nice place Zeke got here. Zeke and my brother Michael, went to school together, their best friends."

"Really?" Kate sips her drink while D'La holds her glass all the while twisting the straw between her fingers.

"Aren't you going to drink your drink?" Kate asks.

"Yeah, but I'm a slow drinker," replies D'La as she gets out of her seat to watch the guys at the pool table. "Kate, do you shoot?"

"Yeah I do, but only a little."

"I've been shooting pool for a little while. I would say about...three or four years. I love it."

"Maybe one day you'll take the time to teach me?" suggest Kate.

"Sure. Anytime, but I only teach for a price."

"You're charging me."

"Yeah, but since you got me a drink, I'll tell you what...I'll cut the price in half...this time...but only for today, and only twenty minutes."

D'La's street-smart demeanor, her beautiful smile and sense of humor captivates Kate as D'La leisurely walks in the direction of the pool table with Kate not far behind.

"I'm too young to get a real job, so when I need money...I hustle."

"I like that attitude," says Kate with the most silly smirk that last the entire evening while talking with D'La. In addition, Kate finds it difficult, keeping her focus above D'La's shoulders.

"I don't see too many white people around here. Do you work around here, or do you live in the neighborhood?" D'La small talks while slowly sipping on her straw.

"No. I don't live around here. I do work around here. I work over at the plant on Jefferson."

"I thought so. Once white people move out, they rarely move back into the hood."

Hours later, D'La is teaching Kate how to play and Kate is enjoying being taught by her. During the entire time, Kate eyes are devoted to D'La's seductive body language, her tight jeans and her sculpture posterior.

The Morris Family

Derrick walks swiftly into the house. He slams the front door behind him and yells as if someone is chasing him, "NORMA, NORMA."

His eyes shining like a squeaky clean glass as he passes Vanessa, now fifteen years old, who is sitting at the table reading her homework.

'Oh boy, he's home. Why did he have to come back here? Everything was so peaceful until he walked through the door. Always hollering and yelling at momma and me. Why do she take so much from him? He's not doing anything right. He don't work.

He probably don't know what a job is, it's been so long since he had one. He's just a waste. Momma should just throw him out and get a real man, somebody that can love her and do right by her, by us,' thinks Vanessa.

"Where's your mother?" he impolitely ask.

Vanessa isn't in the mood for any talking, especially to him, so she points toward the hallway, toward the back rooms.

Derrick quickly goes toward the bedroom and looks in; but Norma isn't there. He goes toward the bathroom and pushes the door slightly open, peeking and staring before saying a word. Within those short moments, and this time in a mild voice, he calls her name. She doesn't hear him. The water is running through her hair, over her ears, drowning out the sound of his voice. He continues to watch her for several minutes more. Silently he stands, as she steps out of the shower, wrapping a towel around her head and one around her body. He shouts her name, his behavior is questionable, and his facial expressions appear somewhat crazy. "NORMA!"

He gradually walks toward her, thinking, 'That beautiful body hasn't change one bit.'

She takes the combs off the basin putting it into her hair while standing in front of the mirror.

He asks, "Are you going somewhere?"

"Oh no...When did you get here? I didn't here you come in," she says.

He walks closer closing the door behind him, takes his wife into his arms, first kissing her forehead, then her neck, and finally he removes the towel dropping it to the floor, kissing her breasts.

Norma caresses his head to her chest and wishing he would be this loving all the time. After that short tender moment of affection, Derrick hands Norma the towel off the floor, then ask. "Do you have any money?"

"No, Derrick I gave you all the money I had this afternoon...remember?"

Derrick doesn't want to here any excuses, because the small quantities that once did the job of satisfying his addiction isn't substantial any longer.

"Well, Baby I want you to do me a favor. You know, nothing you ain't done before or use to doing, my love."

Norma is afraid to ask, but she does, "What kind of a favor?"

"I want to take you someplace...And all you got to do is stay in this room and wait for someone to come in. There'll be a bowl under the bed to wash up after you're finished and before the next man comes in."

"Derrick what are you saying?"

"All I'm saying is...that we need some money coming in this house, cause that little bit of money you're bringing home from that job of yours...ain't enough."

"I'm working all the overtime I can, Derrick."

"Yeah, but that ain't getting it, Baby. Remember the day I married you and you vowed...til death to us part. We're still married ain't we? ...And, I would do the same for you if the shoe was on the other foot...you know that."

Norma is shocked and confused as she reminisces about that day, the day of their marriage. Everything was so beautiful, and she remembers how happy they were. She reflects back as Derrick continues to remind her, as he has done so many times before, brainwashing her on the power of their love for each another and their unique bond.

"Well, I...." she says. Norma is terrified but she agrees to another one of his propositions.

Vanessa can't believe that her mother would agree to something so disgusting as she listens to his nauseating request through the bathroom door.

Later that night, while her mother is dressing to go out and do what she feels she has to do. Vanessa says: "Momma don't let daddy do you like this, you're not a whore. Let him find his own way of getting his drugs. Let him go out and get a job if he wants money for that. Momma...No...What, if something happens to you? ...What if you get killed or something? What about me!"

Norma sashays toward Vanessa, smearing red lipstick on her lips.

"Vanessa, you don't understand...that's my man, my husband and I love him. You don't know what it is to have a man in your life, a husband...And if I get killed doing what MY MAN wants me to DO." Pointing her lipstick at her daughter's face. "Then just bury me in RED."

Norma is all dressed up and ready to go, passing Vanessa on her way out the front door where her husband is waiting. He holds out his hand, as if she is a princess and he is Prince Charming, with the broadest grin, escorting her to his old no-gas jalopy. Vanessa is terribly upset. Her mother passing her, and not even giving her second look, as if she doesn't exist. After they drive away, Vanessa goes into her bedroom and begins to pack all her belongings.

Vanessa decides to run away from home. She has no money and she doesn't care, and she never looks back, because she realizes and accepts that she is finally free.

However, within her first year of prostitution, Norma is found dead in an abandon apartment building, throat cut, with red lipstick smear over her face. She is the eighth victim.

The newspaper read: **"SERIAL KILLER STALKS PROSTITUTES" 'Police Baffled.'**

Derrick Morris, a stone junkie, is still running and hiding from the drug dealers, The Black Connection, who he owes money.

The end of summer, 1970 - D'La, Candice, Elayne and Shi Li are having a good day at the fair.

Candice yells, "Hey, look over here, a picture booth. Let's take a picture together."

"Yeah. We don't have any pictures of us together like this," says D'La.

"Yes we do. We have a lot of pictures together," Shi Li insist.

"Shi Li, I mean, with all of us together like this, having fun. Usually, we have our parents escorting us around like little kids. Especially, Elayne's momma and daddy," adds D'La.

Candice positions herself in front of her friends walking backward. "Well, how about it? ...Let's do it."

"Our first time together, on our own, no adults tell'n us what to do," continues D'La.

D'La's right," says Elayne.

D'La starts to laugh at Elayne, hearing those words come out of her mouth is quite a change. D'La actually thinks Elayne enjoys being stuck under her parent's thumb.

"I like the sound of that, Elayne...This is girls day off."

The four enter the small picture booth, laughing, giggling, and hugging one another as they deposit their money and pose for several shots. After taking the pictures they continue to walk through the park acting silly as girls sometimes do.

Shi Li is extremely excited, pointing. "Hey the roller coaster. ...Oh boy...I just love riding fast rides."

Elayne has never cared for all those fast, wild and dangerous rides. "You can have 'em."

"Who wants to get on with me?" asks Shi Li.

D'La slightly glances at Elayne from the corner of her eye, waiting for her next surprising statement. "I will...they don't bother me."

After a long enjoyable day, it is time to go home and Shi Li doesn't want to burn any bridges. "It is getting late. I wonder what time it is."

D'La agrees, "Yeah, Aunt Sharon is suppose to pick us up at eight o'clock and not a minute after."

Looking at her watch, Elayne realizes that Shi Li is correct about burning the bridge. "I think it's about that time, too."

Shi Li insists that they go to the meeting place as soon as possible. Aunt Sharon wants them at the gate at 8pm and no later.

Candice disagrees with the rush back: "We got time, it's only five minutes past."

"Candice, but it's still after 8," Elayne argues as Shi Li takes the defense.

"So come on. Aunt Sharon is a sweet person and the last thing I want to do is to make her upset with us. It was truly nice of her to talk our parents into letting us come here, alone. Candice, you know how they are!"

"Yeah, that's true; and the Reverend, ooh...I don't even want to think about it, Elayne will really get her butt put on punishment if she's late." teases D'La.

"So, if you got a good thing going, do not blow it, Candice," Shi Li explains.

"Yeah...you're right. I'll be glad when I turn eighteen."

Shi Li disagree, "Candice, do not rush life. When you are ready, eighteen will come to you."

LAUSEN'S HOUSE

D'La is in the kitchen leaning against the wall talking on the phone.

"I just wanna know...are you coming tonight?" ask Kate.

D'La hesitates with her answer. "...Yeah, I'll be there."

"What time should I expect you?"

"About seven...Yeah, I should be there no later than seven."

"I'll be waiting D'La." Kate brings the phone closer to her mouth and whispers softly, "I love you."

"What Kate? I didn't hear you?"

Kate immediately changes her statement. "I miss you."

"Kate, I'll talk to you later."

At 7:15pm D'La strolls into 'BUTCHES', a gay establishment and a pool hall. She looks around and she doesn't' see the person she is looking for, but Kate sees her and quietly approaches.

Kate is about three inches taller than D'La, a large muscular frame woman who prefer wearing men clothing - and it is not because of her job, as she would like everyone to think.

"Hey...Who loves you, Brown Sugar?"

D'La turns and embraces Kate. "I was look'n for you. How long have you been here?" ask D'La.

"Not that long, only a few minutes. "Kate puts one arm around D'La's neck, kissing her on the mouth while holding a bottle of beer in her other hand.

"D'La, you want a drink?"

"Yeah...What's that you're drink'n?" Kate gives D'La the bottle and she drinks.

"Do you want one?"

"Yeah...Hell. Why not?" D'La gives the bottle back to Kate and signals for the bartender. "I'll have the same."

"I didn't think you were coming," Kate says as a sigh of relief seizes her face.

Kate is deeply in love with D'La, a love that is becoming more possessive and demanding with each passing hour, and a love so forcible, it is pushing D'La away.

"I told you, I would be here around seven, Kate."

"Yeah, I know Baby...But lately you've been acting kinda funny."

Kate really doesn't' want the conversation to take off on the wrong foot. She knows D'La is spirited, headstrong and the fear of losing her constantly haunts her, especially if she pushes too hard. But this time, Kate can't resist the opportunity; she needs to know what is really going on with their relationship.

"What do you mean, I've been act'n kinda funny, Kate?"

"Like you don't want to be around me anymore, D'La."

"That's not true. And I wish you stop say'n that."

"If that's so, how come when I ask you out, you always gotta think about it? And you've been doing a lot of thinking about it a lot more lately," Kate says as she becomes more agitated.

"Kate, graduation is comin up...Hey, I'm the first of my mother's four kids that's ever finished high school and there are a lot of things I need to do...Remember when we first met? Didn't we go shopping together when I graduated from junior high? And what about all the times after that. WHAT! ...HUM! You can't possibly think, whenever I go shop'n we have to always go together and all the time Kate. You can't possibly believe or think that...DAM...!"

Kate angrily interrupts, slamming the bottle on the counter. "You mean hanging out and shopping with those stuck up hussies you call your friends, don't you?"

"Stop it Kate. I told you many times about how I feel about you, and that you're the only one for me. I love you. Now, stop act'n like a penis head!"

"D'La, when you take time to be with them, you could be spending that time with me. I can help you shop for your dress, shoes, or anything else you want. I love spending my money on you. I love making you happy. But...I...You know, stuff like that makes me jealous, especially when I can't see you when I want to."

"Kate, they're just friends. There's nuth'n sexual go'n on if that's what you're think'n...Now stop it, or I'm leavin."

"If they're such good friends, how come they don't know anything about us?" ask Kate.

"What makes you think they don't?"

"Well, when I'm around they act like they don't like me. Like something's wrong, maybe, I stink or something. Hell, who knows."

D'La lies; "No they don't look at you like that. Stop look'n for trouble Kate. Just drop it! This conversation is make'n me sick."

"Okay I won't say anything else about it, D'La..." Before taking another sip of beer, Kate add, "...for now."

"Good. You're the only one for me...Now drink your beer and shut up," demands D'La.

"I better be," replies Kate as she takes another sip of beer before taking D'La's hand, kissing it. D'La pretends to enjoy Kate's annoying behavior and her public display of affection. Yet before the night is over, D'La goes with Kate to her apartment to share intimate moments.

'RIGHT ON, RIGHT ON'

CHAPTER 7

Mt. Bethel Baptist Church, that same night, Elayne is admiring a newcomer, a young man who is visiting for the first time.

'He's cute, I wonder, what's his name? A religious man no doubt. He's sitting here in church. He can't be all that bad. If he's not a religious man, I don't think he'll be sitting in church this long. He must be some kin to Mrs. Hutchinson. I saw him talking to her earlier. Maybe, after the service she'll introduce us...Oh no, he's looking this way.'

Elayne quickly turns her head and gaze down at her Bible; then she slowly brings it up, covering her face.

Shortly after Reverend Donaldson's sermon, Elayne walks toward the piano, her eyes constantly peering at the cute visitor. The visitor, Raymond Smith, is not ignorant to Elayne's analytical behavior. Besides, he relishes her dark chocolate smooth skin and her beauty.

Raymond has a thing for beautiful women and his good looks make him feel as if can he conquer the world. Yeah, Raymond is a pretty boy. He always wears the latest styles, he has a cool and conservative persona, and he also drives a car that looks almost as good as he does.

"Oh, here he comes." Elayne sits and pretends she is reading her Bible.

"Hi, I don't mean to interrupt, I saw you sitting here and I decided to introduce myself. My name is Raymond, Raymond Smith."

Elayne tries not to be too conspicuous, but it is impossible. She looks away, then back at him, trying her best to act grown up. She really doesn't want to blow this one.

"I'm Elayne Donaldson."

"I know, my aunt introduced me to your father earlier and he told me all about his beautiful daughter..." Elayne looks surprisingly. "...I mean, how you're always helping him with the church and all."

Elayne is very shy when it comes to talking to someone new and someone she may be attracted to.

And Raymond's observation regarding her beauty is embarrassing to her that she feels pressured into changing the conversation.

"Who's your aunt?"

"Mrs. Hutchinson, she's my mother's sister. I'm visiting her this weekend, doing some chores around the house and that's when she invited me to come to church tonight."

"That was very thoughtful of her," says Elayne.

"You can say...she's a very thoughtful lady." With a cool slight grin, Raymond carefully continues to observe Elayne's every move as she looks across the room at Mrs. Hutchinson who is having a lengthy conversation with her mother.

"She's a very devoted member. Never misses a Sunday and she always offering to help people who are less fortunate."

Raymond knows his aunt only do things for a reason and there has to be something in it for her, either now or in the near future.

"Yeah, you can always count on Mrs. Hutchinson."

Elayne wanders toward the piano looking down at the keys.

"You play?" ask Raymond.

"Yes...yes I do."

"Would you play something for me, Elayne?"

Elayne is surprised by his request, she doesn't' have a chance to think of anything or even if she wants to play or not. She is nervous, but her mouth did not waste any time taking control of the situation.

"Well, what do you want to hear?"

"Something special...Hey, I got it, why don't you play your favorite hymn?" ask Raymond with his beautiful smile stretch from one ear to the other.

"Wow, that's going to be tough...I have so many, that..."

Elayne hesitates, her thoughts are many, and within that one moment, Raymond interrupts.

"How about the one you were humming when I passed you in the hallway earlier?"

"You heard me? You were in the hall?"

"Yeah, I did. And I was. You sound so beautiful. Did anybody ever tell you...that you sing just like an angel?"

Elayne blushes while trying to ignore his compliment, "I know which song you're talkin about. I was singin..."

Elayne begins to play and sing and Raymond is mesmerized with Elayne's exquisite voice, her grace, and her loveliness.

The night continues and it is a big evening for Shi Li as she prepares for the annual karate tournament, her third black belt championship fight. Shi Li is in her dressing room conversing with her coach, Uncle Chung.

"You'll be going on in just a few minutes Shi Li. Do you need anything?"

"No. I do not. I am fine, thank you Uncle.

"You look as though you have a lot on your mind."

"I was just thinking."

"Thinking about what my child?"

Shi Li doesn't want her Uncle Chung or anyone to know how much she is missing her mother. Fearing her thoughts can only be unfavorable, especially at this time and still grieving so long after her death. No matter how hard she tries to please her father, she will never be the son he always wanted. His thoughts of her are the same thoughts of her mother, or any woman: weak in heart and fragile like the butterfly in mind.

"Nothing really...just thinking, Uncle Chung."

"Remember Shi Li, watch the eyes. The eyes never lie."

"I will remember Uncle Chung."

There is an abrupt knocking at the door and Uncle Chung answers it. It is the attendant: "Five minutes till show."

"We will be right there," says Uncle Chung.

Shi Li walks to the door as Uncle Chung follows closely.

"Remember my child, relax and concentrate and keep your eyes on your adversary."

Shi Li nods her head before answering. "I will."

As the crowd roars, Shi Li walks into the middle of the rink to meet with the referee and shakes hands with her opponent, then she returns to her corner and waits for the signal. Looking around the place, she sees Candice sitting in the front row. Candice is very excited, giving Shi Li the thumbs up.

Five seconds later the signal is given and the fight begins. With kicks and blows to her face and shoulder, Shi Li defends herself gallantly. She posses the same grace and style of her mother even though her mother never fought in a tournament before. Shi Li's unique, yet, polite characteristics never fails; always remaining the lady that she is, but hidden deep inside, she is a tiger.

Shi Li wins the first competition and now its time to meets her second opponent and the second match begins. She is suddenly distracted.

"Mother!"

Shi Li believes she sees her mother while glancing into the audience. Suddenly, 'WHAM!' a fist hits Shi Li across the face, it was so hard that it turns her entire body around, facing in the opposite direction. Shi Li is kicked in the ribs. She is going down, first dropping to her knees before hitting the floor. The referee stops the fight until she gets back on her feet. Candice is definitely disturbed by the blows to her friend.

"SHI LI...SHI LI...GET UP SHI LI. GET UP," she screams.

But Shi Li's heart and mind is interfering with concentration, she looks at Candice as she slowly gets up on her feet and gives the lady in the audience a second look as well. Candice's screams are getting louder as she moves closer to the ring.

"THAT'S RIGHT. COME ON, YOU CAN DO IT. YOU CAN DO IT SHI LI."

Uncle Chung is stunned. "Why is she putting her guard down? Why? What is wrong? COME ON SHI LI...REMEMBER, CONCENTRATE...AND WATCH THE EYES, THE EYES."

Shi Li realizes that the woman in the audience is not her mother, but only her wishful thinking and before she can blink...WHAM. Shi Li's hit across the face and shoulder and knocked to the floor again. Still looking at the woman and the child that she is carrying reality impels her, strengthening her spirit. Shi Li spontaneously jumps to her feet hitting hard, revenge in every blow of her fist. The excited crowd roars. With backbreaking kicks to her opponent's chest Shi Li's aggression seize control of the ring. Shi Li opponent's knocked unconscious.

The crowd roars for more and Shi Li has won her third karate tournament. Candice jumps up and down, cheering and yelling for her friend's victory.

Overwhelmed, Uncle Chung and Candice run into the ring to congratulate her.

"SHI LI...CONGRATULATIONS...You did a great job my number one student. You were wonderful, but for a moment you had us all scared out of ours minds, and again you came back fighting like the TIGER."

"Shi Li...Shi Li, oh girl, give me a hug. I am so proud of you."

Candice grabs Shi Li as she takes a final look at the woman before she leaves the stadium.

"What's the matter, Shi Li?" ask Candice looking in the same direction that has captivated her friend's attention. "Do you know her from somewhere?"

"No...she reminds me of my mother."

Candice takes a second look at the woman and realizes that she is right.

"She does favor Mother Kyi a lot, Shi Li."

"I know...I just wish she could have been here to see me tonight."

"Maybe she was. I believe your mother is always with you. As long as her love lives inside of your heart she will never go away...Somehow, I believe she's always watching over you...I believe she's watching over you at this very moment."

"Yes, her spirit is always with me...and will be forever."

Shi Li never noticed her father at the tournament, nor did he want her to notice him. Ever since the death of his wife, Father Kyi has found it even more difficult to communicate with his daughter. He fails to realize the pain and the hate that is gradually consuming her heart and the distant that is growing between them.

Later that evening, while Uncle Chung drives Candice and Shi Li home he stops at a red light. Candice notices a somewhat unusual, but not so familiar place. She has heard people talk about these places before, but has never come this close to one until tonight. Candice whispers to Shi Li, tapping on her thigh.

"Shi Li, look at that."

Shi Li looks and sees bright lights and lots of cars in the parking lot. She also notices men, many men, some laughing and some just standing around counting their money before entering the building.

Shi Li also notices a sparkle in Candice's eyes.

"Would you look at that? I want to go and see what goes on inside a place like that. They're having a lot of fun from the looks of things."

Shi Li's eyes nearly fly out of her head listening to Candice rave about visiting that kind of establishment.

"You got to be kidding, Candice."

"Don't you want to see what it's all about, Shi Li?"

"No I do not. Ladies do not go to places like that."

"There's nothing wrong with looking is it, Shi Li?"

"The question is: Who is looking at you? ...Candice, do not even put it in your crazy head about going into a place like that. Do you understand? You can not be that moronic."

"Shi Li, I was just thinking, that's all."

"Well quit thinking. Your thinking is worrying me."

The traffic light turns green, Uncle Chung attempts to listen to the girl's whispers.

"Is something wrong with my driving?" he asks.

Immediately the girls stop talking.

"No Uncle."

"Your Aunt Miuki says, my driving is terrible...ha ha. And I thought you girls were agreeing with her."

"No Uncle Chung, we were talking about something else."

"You're a good driver Mr. Chung. Better than a lot of people I know."

"Yes Uncle Chung...a whole lot better."

Uncle Chung glances at the girls through his rear view mirror.

"Ha-ha...Okay girls, you don't have to rub it in. I get the picture." Soon Uncle Chung stops in front of driveway of Candice's house.

"Thank you Uncle Chung for bringing me home. And thanks for inviting me to the tournament Shi Li."

"You are quite welcome, Candice."

"Bye Shi Li, I'll talk to you tomorrow?"

"Sure and do not forget to call me in the morning Candice?"

"I will."

Candice opens the car door, gets out and runs to the top step of the porch, waving before she goes in.

Two months has already past and Elayne has been spending a lot of time with Raymond, especially at her father's church. He seems to be the perfect gentleman and Elayne has falling head over heels in love with him. Nevertheless, Raymond is persistent, making sure that he keeps Elayne's heart on his pedestal, something he's never done before with any of his girls.

The Donaldson's have invited Raymond to their house for Sunday dinner. During dinner Raymond and Elayne are trying to figure out a way to ask her father about going with Raymond on a date: Elayne's first date. Raymond can not help questioning himself, whether the Reverend and Mrs. Donaldson can see through his suave demeanor, them being spiritual people and all. He is really curious about how close are they to The Lord, and has The Lord given them a sign about not trusting him due to his reputation?

Raymond continues to toy with his thoughts, and he feels this is the right time to compliments Mrs. Donaldson's cooking; maybe that will help take his mind off of The Lord and The Lord connection with the Donaldson's. He knows most women love when someone talks about their cooking and how good the food is, whether you like it or not.

"That was a delicious dinner, Mrs. Donaldson," he says, wiping his mouth gently with his napkin.

"Why, thank you Raymond, you're welcome to come for dinner any time."

Another seal of satisfaction as Mrs. Donaldson grins at her husband.

"No...I thank you Reverend and Mrs. Donaldson for inviting me, and don't be surprised if I take you up on your invitation real soon."

Mrs. Donaldson begins to clears the table. Elayne tags along side of her father and Raymond as they walk into the den. Standing very close to him, she nudges Raymond in his ribs, they have secretly been discussing their plans for the rest of evening as well as how and what to say to her parents.

"You ought to taste Mrs. Donaldson's fried chicken. Umm...The Lord has truly blessed this woman with a fry'n pan; especially, when it comes to fry'n some chicken."

Rev. Donaldson speaks extremely boisterous and haughty about his wife's cooking, she hears him while walking into the den.

"Don't pay my husband no mind. He's a country boy and everybody knows that country boys love 'em some chicken. Whether it's fried, boil, steam or raw, I know the Reverend will eat it."

Everybody laugh and the tension in the room is low, in addition, everybody seems relax. Raymond believes this is the perfect time to ask.

"Rev. Donaldson, I was wondering, if I could take your precious daughter to an early movie this evening? I know it's Sunday and I promise to bring her home as soon as it's over."

Raymond has a sweet way of putting words together when he wants something.

"Please Daddy, can I go? ...Please say yes?" Batting her sweet brown eyes, Elayne makes an emotional appeal.

"Well, I guess it'll be fine. But she got to be home early, young man. She's got school tomorrow...Can you believe in the next few weeks, Elayne will be graduate'n high school? Yeah, we are surely proud of her."

"I'll be home early Daddy, I promise."

Elayne waste no time in changing the subject before her father has a chance to change his mind. Elayne quickly kiss her father's cheek, then she and her mother goes to the closet to get her something to throw over her just in case the whether gets a little chilly. You can never really count on Michigan's weather, it's always changing, some days it can be hot and later that same evening, it's cold. Mrs. Donaldson then reaches into her pocket.

"Here's some money."

Elayne takes the money and counts it. "Ma mam..."

"Just in case the car breaks down, Elayne."

"Ma mam...thanks...But I don't think Raymond's car is going to break down, he has a nice car."

Mrs. Donaldson takes out two dimes more.

"Here's twenty cents for the phone. A young lady should always carry extra change for the phone, especially, when she's out on a date."

"Ma mam, Raymond will take good care of me. He's not going to let anybody bother us."

Elayne stares at Raymond from a short distance and he is still talking and joking with her father.

"Don't you think he's nice, Ma mam."

"Yes, I do. I believe he will take care of you and bring you home safe...but take it anyway child." Mrs. Donaldson pushes the money into Elayne's hand.

"Sure Ma mam, I love you and thanks."

The Donaldson's seem pleased with Raymond's personality as they escort them to the door, Reverend whispers to his wife:

"Gracie, he's such a perfect gentleman...praise The Lord."

She agrees, "Yes...praise The Lord."

Elayne waves as Raymond opens the car door, as a gentleman should. The Donaldson's watch their daughter as they drive off.

Elayne turns on the radio. "What movie are we going to see?" she ask.

With that innocent, boyish, charming smile, Raymond answers, "Any movie you want to see."

"I got an idea...let's go downtown, they have lots of nice theaters we can pick from."

"That sounds good to me. Tonight is your night and what ever you want, it's yours Elayne."

Elayne is exceedingly pleased with Raymond's mannerism.

"I don't know what it is, but downtown lights are so beautiful," she says as she lays her head on the headrest.

Elayne adores her relationship between her parents so much that she prays one day she would have the same blessing in marriage as well.

'Raymond's so perfect, just like daddy....'

But before Elayne can finish her thought Raymond makes a suggestion. "Instead of going downtown right away, I want to stop by a friend of mine's house first...If that's all right with you, Elayne?"

"Oh...I don't mind...Sure."

"It'll only be a minute," says Raymond.

Shortly after arriving at his friend's house, Raymond parks and gets out. Elayne opens the door to follow him but he quickly stops her.

"Wait here Elayne, and keep looking beautiful for me. I'll only be a hot second...cool baby?"

"Oh, don't take too long Raymond, I don't want to miss the beginning of the movie," says Elayne as she closes the car door.

"I won't...And if the movie starts before we get there, I'll make them start it over."

Raymond blows her a kiss, then runs up on the porch and as he knocks on the door a voice shouts from within: "WHO IS IT?"

"It's me Man, it's Ray."

A tall, skinny man comes to the door, only opening it halfway as he peers out. "Hey Man, come on in. I ain't seen your as... in a good while, then all of a sudden, 'BOOM' here you come bangin on the door like you some dam... poe poe." He giggles. "Nah, I don't think the police will knock that dame crazy. Hey Man, what the f.... been happen'n?"

"Ain't sh... go'n on...I come to get a small bag, Percy."

Percy looks out of the door at Raymond's car.

"Who's the Brown Sugar?" he asks as he holds and squeezes his crotch.

"That's my baby. She's sweet, ain't she?" Raymond replies.

"She sure looks sweet from here and that's on the real side...Where you guys go'n?"

"Thinking about go'n downtown to a movie," says Raymond, walking into the living room.

"To a movie, Man. I thought you might be do'n your usual thang."

Percy squeezes his crotch again while making circling motions with his body then adds. "The nasty."

"Nah Man, this little honey, she's special."

"Ray, Man, don't give me that sh..., please. I ain't never seen you with a special, not unless it was a buy-one-get-one-free...and that's a dam... six pack special. And we know that ain't hap'n no time soon, not the way this economy is all f... up."

"Man, I'm tell'n you. It ain't like that. I really like her. She ain't like the others, she's good people."

Raymond sits on the couch, leans back and crosses his legs.

"Meaning you done had some and the smell of it got your nose blown wide open, right? ...Bull...Don't tell me, nigga.

"Man get the stuff." Raymond tries to change the subject but Percy won't let up.

"How long you been see'n this special girl?"

Again Raymond tries to direct Percy's attention away from Elayne.

"Man, quit be'n nosey. You gonna sell me some weed or not?"

"Dam... Don't get sen...si...tive, Brother Man. We've been know'n each other too long for you to be get'n all mushy over some coochie. Please nigga, don't even play that sh... with me."

Percy puts his hand under the couch and pulls out a shoebox full of marijuana.

"Come on Man, before she starts get'n suspicious and sh...," urges Raymond.

"I'm get'n it, just hold up...don't be comin over here ramp'n and ravin and actin crazy Man...show'n out and sh... Cause you gonna see some movie with your new special honey."

Percy continues to aggravate Raymond. "You can't fool me, I know what you really want nigga. You want some of that chocolate stuff. Weed might calm your nerves, but it won't cure your urge."

Raymond reaches into his pocket and hands Percy some money.

"Man, these bags are get'n smaller and smaller every time I come over here. What's the problem? Don't tell me inflation is f... with the weed neither?"

"Inflation is everywhere. I'm tellin you, and I can hardly believe it myself. But this sh... right here, is good, inflation or no inflation."

Percy leans back on the couch folding one legs over the other, then grabs a pillow to relax his head.

"You're still crazy. I think you better stop smokin and just focus on sell'n the stuff," Raymond explains.

Percy picks up a pack of cigarette papers off the table, pulls out two sheets, licks one of them, puts them together to roll a joint.

"Man, I want you to taste this sh... and then tell me it ain't worth your tight as... dollar. Just hold up and sit tight for a minute."

Percy lights up, hits it and passes it to Raymond, who puffs it. Percy starts to smile, "Now, what you gotta say 'bout that sh...?"

"It's cool." Raymond hits the joint a few more times.

"Yeah, it's cool, you got it, Man. You got it."

"Right on, Brother Man. Right on." Percy inhales and squeezes his nose, holding his breath as he tries to stop the smoke from escaping; leaning back to enjoy the aroma and the taste.

Percy and Raymond are good friends; they met at a party that Percy had given several years earlier. Percy was supplying, dealing drugs, mostly marijuana and a little cocaine that night when they were introduced. Raymond had an instant joy for that kind of a high. Yet, he wasn't a heavy smoker and he would only purchase marijuana on special occasions. He didn't want anything in his system that was too addicting. Moreover, he didn't want anything effecting his precious sex drive.

Raymond nicknamed himself 'Sweet Daddy Ray' because he knows exactly how to get any girl he wants. He said, 'They were easy prey, and he really did not have to try to win their hearts. They were drawn to him as if he was The Sweet Mack Daddy of Love.'

Raymond loved playing the mind games, especially, with the girls that thought they were hard to get. He and his friend, Percy, would joke on who had the most girls chasing them.

Percy has never married, but lived with his old lady, Yvonne, until she walked out a few weeks ago. Plus, Percy never had a nine-to-five job. Working for the white man was too confining. He believes selling drugs was much easier and faster money. Percy's main product is marijuana and sometimes, if demands are high enough, he would sale hash, some girl/cocaine or some boy/heroin to his favorite customers.

Percy and his old lady have one set of seventeen months old twin daughters. Yvonne always argued about his occupational habits with him nearly everyday. She insists that Percy is not being a good role model.

"My kids ain't growing up in no drug house. Strange people coming and going all day long. Percy, this kind of lifestyle isn't right for the kids."

However, Percy's main focus is on the money. He believes he is doing the right thing for his family and Yvonne should be more understanding.

Percy would say, "Baby, this money could open doors, we can buy all the thangs we need. Anyway, I can't see myself or my woman struggl'n like we used to do...NO MO! Those days are over!"

The fast money also encourages Percy's unfaithfulness, having affairs with other women, which he blames on Yvonne's nagging.

Raymond and Percy continue puffing on the joint when Percy decides to shares the latest information about Yvonne.

"You know man, my old lady done moved out and took the kids. She says, 'I was a f...up role model, a dead-beat daddy.' ...Can you believe that sh...? Well, all I got to say is, 'let by-gones, be by-gones'. You know how that is?"

"Nah Man, I don't know about nuth'n like that. Ain't, no woman ever walked out on Sweet Daddy Ray. Percy I don't know what it is, but those women out there, they love me, Man."

Raymond replies arrogantly, rubbing his hair back from his face as he passes the joint back to Percy.

"I gotta go before my sweet stuff starts wondering what in the hell I'm do'n in here...and thanks for the sample Man."

Percy takes a couple more puffs as the smoke penetrates his system.

"No problem Man...Yeah I got you, that's the last thang you need is a woman who wonders. Cause if they start wonder'n too long, ain't no woman go'n to put up with your sorry as...no way no how."

Raymond stands and adjusts his pants, "I'll talk to you later man with your crazy butt...Peace Brother."

While shaking hands at the front door, Percy gazes at Elayne once more.

"Umm...mm...Man..an...n...dam... That's some deep dark brown sugar there. You sure you don't need no help with that? Orgies or sharing ain't my thang, but it can be...Yeah, I think I better take some of that chocolate stuff off your hands. She's too sweet for you alone nigga. Ain't nuth'n like dark chocolate that sticks to your teeth, and melts in your mouth, no-way on earth you won't get a mouth full of cavities when it comes to licking on a woman like that. I'm tell'n you Brother, you better make you a dentist appointment, now...Dam.., black is beautiful."

"Man. I'm gonna tell you one more time, quit smoke'n that sh... Hey, I'm start'n to wonder 'bout you Bro anyway," says Raymond.

With a slight high, Raymond strolls off the porch and to the car. Elayne is not familiar with the smell of marijuana, even though Raymond carries its scent and she never asks any questions about the strange odor.

Feeling relaxed and satisfied from his high, Raymond has a sudden change in plans.

"Elayne, I want to take you some place special."

"Some place special?"

"Yeah Baby. Somewhere we can be alone. So, I can spend some private time with you. You know...I've been see'n you for almost two months and we have never taken time for ourselves, yet. It's always me, you and your momma and your daddy."

Elayne's curiously ask, "But...I..."

"Don't get me wrong, mom and popsy are cool peeps and all, but how are we go'n to get to know each other if everybody's always hang'n around? ...Now you tell me, how?"

"Well...I," inquisitively states Elayne.

"Baby, if you really want to go to a movie tonight, we'll go."

Seductively, Raymond reaches over the armrest for Elayne's hand, bringing it to his mouth, kissing and embracing it gently, as he toys with her emotions with his gentle touch, his charismatic smile that lures her innocence.

"Or tonight can be our first night together...alone. You're my woman now, and Baby your wish is my command."

"Where will we go? Are we go'n back to your friend's house?"

"No. I know a place and I know you'll like it too. It's real co-o-ol."

Raymond squeezes Elayne's hand once more; she is bewitched by his appeal, which instantly captivates her even more. Unknowingly drifting into the hands of a certified Casanova.

114

"Baby, why don't you move a little closer to me? You don't have to sit that close to the door. Your man's over here."

Elayne likes what she hears and slides closer, laying her head on his shoulder.

After securing the motel room, Raymond comes back to the car as Elayne nervously looks around. All motels are foreign to her and she is not stupid to what goes on inside. She constantly looks about to see if anybody notices her as she slowly saunters up the stairs to the room. With each step she takes she feels uneasy, somewhat weird, because everything is absolutely new, absolutely unfamiliar.

Raymond verifies the number on each one as he passes several doors.

"Now let's see."

Raymond looks at the number on his key, using his jazzy dialect, which belies the perfect gentleman Elayne has been witnessing for some time, and yet his charisma becomes even more potent.

"Room 124...Yea...aa....aah. This is it, Babe!"

Raymond assures her as he put the key into the lock and opens the door, then quickly taking Elayne by the hand.

"See...what did I tell you?"

Elayne steps into the room looking around.

"Well, how do you like it? I told you it was co-o-o-ol.

Raymond slowly closes the door.

"I've never been to a place like this before."

Raymond approaches and seductively whispers into her ear.

"I know, that's why I want your first time to be spec...i....al and with me, your man."

Raymond moves closer, looking into her eyes, kissing her about the face.

"Because you're a special lady, umm...my special lady."

His passion is too irresistible and his soft touch is so imperative.

"Let me show you around the place, Babe."

Raymond gently takes Elayne's arm and pulls her around the room presenting all the latest luxuries the motel has to offer.

"Look here, Babe. We got television and a rad-i-o. Maybe later we might wanna watch a little TV, or listen to some music."

Raymond turns them both on and starts to dance.

"And they work, too."

Naturally, Elayne focuses on the bed behind her and Raymond notices that Elayne's uneasy about the room; she is getting cold feet, so he pulls her toward to bathroom.

"Look in here, Babe, even the bathroom's clean. Just look at that toilet, all wrapped up with san..i...tized pay...per. We even got our own little soap...These are called...personnel com...mo...di...ties."

Using reverse psychology, Raymond gently pulls Elayne by her hand, this time taking her toward the bed and alluring her.

"Babe, if you don't like it we can leave."

Elayne is afraid to say no. Raymond is her first real boy friend and she doesn't want to disappoint him. She knows if she does, she will certainly lose him.

"No...it's fine. It's just...that everything's..."

Not knowing what to say next Elayne simply shrugs her shoulders.

Raymond slowly moves a bit closer, a bit more, and bit more.

"Don't worry, I'm not go'n to let anythang happen to you...my lady. That's for real."

Raymond hot breath flows over her ears, her face, then onto her neck. His passionate kisses cover her lips as he pushes his tongue into her mouth. Then laying her gently down on the bed he rolls on top of her, consuming her body with his, as one hand strokes her breast and his other hand slowly guides its way under her dress. Surprised, as well as, excessively apprehensive by his behavior she jumps up, murmuring.

"Wait."

Raymond whispers in a sensual soft voice as his warm breath and hot body comes closer.

"I'm not go'n to hurt you, Baby...No way, no how. I love you Elayne....And that love is locked deep DOWN in my soul."

Before Elayne can say anything else, Raymond puts his lips over hers and swiftly slips his tongue deeper into her mouth, her throat.

AT THE TIME

CHAPTER 8

The chase is on and the police are hot on his trail. Speeding cars force their way onto the small residential streets in Detroit. Mark has stolen a car and the smell of burned rubber from the tires has over power the scent from the garbage the trash collector didn't pick up again this week. Mark Burton is losing control of his vehicle as he turns the wrong way on a one way street, hitting a utility pole.

Disoriented and confused as the blood gushes out of his head. He gets out of the car with a gun in his hand. The siren still screaming as Officer Peck and his partner, Officer Mulligan, the first cops on the scene. With their guns pulled Officer Peck yell. "DROP THE GUN, BOY...DROP IT."

Suffering from a slight concussion, Mark is unresponsive to the officer's request and doesn't realize that the gun is still in his hand. Holding it loosely, Mark aims at the ground. Officer Mulligan then yells louder, but Mark doesn't seem to understand what he's saying, he looks around, he is shaking and spinning, walking in circles.

"DROP YOUR GUN, BOY."

Mark slowly turns toward the officers, raising his hands up with the gun barrel slowly pointing toward the sky. It looks as though he is going to shoot, but he is not. The warm blood is blinding as it streams down his face. Mark tries to toss the gun to the ground, but the police are not sure what Mark's intentions are, nor do they care. As far as they are concerned, he is just another stupid black troublemaker. Without hesitation the two officers anxiously press their triggers and Mark is shot not once, not twice, but less than ten times.

"That boy should have dropped his gun like I told him," responds Officer Peck. Officer Mulligan agrees as he returns his gun to his holster. "Ain't no nigger, like a dead nigger, if you ask me. Just one less worry for the city's taxpayers."

After the shooting, Johnny is notified by a neighborhood friend, Gilbert, who has witnessed the entire incident.

Gilbert and Johnny met before Johnny was released from the boy's juvenile detention center. Gilbert's nickname, "Gil-man," but everybody calls him "Fish-head" because he resembles a fish. He has large balloon lips and ears that protrude at least an inch and a half from his face.

Gil-man knows exactly where to find Johnny and he immediately dashes down the street and through the allies, never stopping, not even to catch his breath. He dashes up the front steps of a house, knocking on the door as hard as he can, yelling from the top of his lungs with sweat pouring down his face, completely masking and blinding him. "HEY JOHNNY... JOHNNY."

Beauden opens the door slowly, with a crazy look on his face; he wonders what could possibly be wrong. He has never seen Gil-man so emotional. "Is Johnny here? I need to speak to Johnny, Man."

"Yeah Man, he's here. What's wrong with you?" Beauden ask as Johnny comes to the door. "What's up, Fish-head?"

"It's your brother, Man. He's been shot, I think he's dead, Johnny. The police shot Mark," hyperventilating as he wipes the sweat from his forehead and eyes with his hands.

"What...What in the HELL are you talk'n 'bout?"

Johnny pushes his way pass Beauden and grabs Fish-head by his shirt. Shaking and trembling, he franticly describes the horrible scene.

"Yeah, the police shot him down like a mad dog. He wasn't trying to shoot the gun and everybody knows that. It looked like Mark was dazed or something. Like he didn't understand English, Man. He had so much blood running down his face, all in his eyes. Johnny, blood was all over him, it was everywhere...Then they just shot him down. They just kept shoot'n and shoot'n, Man."

Johnny pulls Fish-head closer. "WHERE?"

"Right down the street, about three blocks..."

Johnny runs out of the house with Gil-man's close behind pointing the way. After reaching the scene of the crime, Johnny runs over to his brother, uncontrollably falling to his knees. Shocked as he looks at his little brother's bloody body lying lifeless on the dirty cold street in the city. Johnny quickly goes into a hysterical surge, spontaneously grabbing his brother, vigorously shaking him and shouting his name. "MARK, HAA...MARK, MARK...GET UP, MAN. COM'ON GET UP, LI'L BRO."

Pulling his brother by the arm, wishing, hoping and praying that Mark's only kidding around, playing dead, like they use to do when they were kids, but still, Mark doesn't respond to his brother's voice. Emotions run high, blinded by his tears doesn't stop Johnny from seeing the two officers and he begins to yell: "YOU DIRTY PIGS. YOU KILLED MY BROTHER...YOU MURDERING SONS-OF-B...s."

Fearing for his friend's life, Gilbert grabs Johnny. "Johnny. Johnny, cool it. Stay cool man, I know it's hard, but don't be cussing at the police."

Mark's dead body lies on the ground for at least thirty to forty minutes before the ambulance arrives. Johnny finds it hard to swallow that Mark is lying on the ground so long without any attempt to save him, no emergency medical attention, nothing at all. It seems as though, if Mark had a chance to live the police just blew it. Johnny can't help shaking like a leaf as the paramedic's place his brother's body into a body bag.

Johnny's eyes are frozen on the police as they put Mark's gun into a plastic bag. Every second that Johnny's heart beats the thought of revenge grows stronger, eating away his soul, as he falls to his knees again, watching Mark's blood drying on the street next to him. Gil-man bends down next to Johnny patting him on his back, but Johnny refuse to move from the spot where Mark died. With a strange look about him, a look that is very familiar to Gil-man, and the people in the neighborhood who witness the shootout, he knows exactly what Johnny's thinking and what has to be done as he whispers into Johnny's ear. "Johnny, Man...don't try anythang stupid. They just killed your brother, don't give them a reason to kill you too. We just go'n to walk a little closer, real cool like, get their names and numbers off their badges and we'll deal with these punk mother-f.... police later, cool? ...Just lay low for a second; you know how we do this sh... You know what I'm say'n is real, Man."

Johnny turns to Gil-man, crying. "Mark...Mark. Fish...they killed my baby brother. They killed him...Mark."

As the angered words mumbles out of Johnny's mouth, Gil-man takes Johnny by his arm. "I know Man, com'on. I know."

Wobbly legs make it difficult to stand up. Gilbert tries to console Johnny holding him close by the arm as Johnny stares into Gilbert's face. Yet Johnny continues to tremble. "We'll deal with these white peckas, later. Now, keep do'n like you do'n. Just be cool, Johnny."

"Pay-back is a mother-f...., Fish. You dig where I'm comin from, Man. Later, with this sh... Pay-back will be a mother f...this time for real."

Johnny finally stands on his own and walks over to the ambulance, looking at his brother one last time. He pulls the zipper back slowly, opening the bag, leaning over Mark's body, as his tears fall from his eyes onto his brother's body shirt.

He reaches for his hand, squeezing it, as he whispers into his dead brother's ear. "I promise you...Mark. I promise you, Man. ...Yeah, somebody's go'n to get f... up. You'll see...Mark. I promise you, Little Bro. The war is on in this mother f...n city."

"Johnny, what 'bout your momma?" asks Gil-man.

Johnny keeps staring at Mark's bloody face, slowly zipping the bag, closing it, before answering. Gilbert understands Johnny's hesitation and waits patiently. Without changing a single facial expression Johnny looks at Gilbert. "Momma can't take this, Man. I don't know how in the hell I'm gonna tell her somethang like this. Mark was her baby, Man."

"Johnny, we'll think of somethang on the way back. Com'on let's go before someone else tell her."

"Yeah, I gotta tell Momma. I gotta be the one to tell her...This sh... is all f... up. I know this is gonna kill her, Fish."

Gilbert accompanies Johnny home. Once arriving at his house, Johnny stops for a second looks around, then gradually takes one step at a time. With one hand on the doorknob, he pauses, without making a sound, standing there holding it and shaking.

"Do you want me to go in with you, Johnny?"

"Nah, Fish...I gotta do this myself."

"You sure?"

"Yeah...go on home, Fish...I'll talk to you later, Man."

"I'm sorry this had to happen Johnny, Mark was a cool little brother."

"Yeah, I know Fish. He was."

Gil-man runs off the porch and down the street and with every second that past he looks back at his friend, still standing there holding the doorknob. Gil-man turns around, walking backward, looking at Johnny and yells:

"DAMU DARAKA...DAMU DARAKA," squeezes his fist tight, raising his arm high and giving a soulful gesture.

"Thanks Man...Damu Daraka," says Johnny.

He walks slowly into the house closing the door behind him.

Lucille Burton was in the 11th grade when she got pregnant with her first child, Johnny. And when she told Johnny's father about his arrival in seven months, he disappeared. So one day she decided to go to his house to see what exactly was going on and why. When she arrived, his parents were very hospitable; they invited her into their home and offered her a drink of water. Even though they seemed like nice people, Lucille noticed that they kept their distant. Never telling her where her baby's father was, if he was out of town or not. When was the last time they had seen him, or what time he would be coming home that day, or if he was. Nor did they give Lucille any information about their son's whereabouts during her entire pregnancy. They didn't even want to acknowledge their grandchild.

A single mother, no job, no money and no father for her unborn child. Ashamed and disgraced, Lucille eventually went south, living with an aunt and gives birth to her first child. A year after Johnny was born she meets another young man who falls in love with her and Johnny. They relocate back to Detroit, living as a family and Lucille gives birth to a second son, Mark. They never married, even though they talked about it many times. When Mark turned four, and Johnny six years old, almost seven, he moves out, leaving Lucille to raise their two sons alone.

Years later, things got extremely hard for Lucille, her finances quickly depleted, changing her and her children's lifestyle tremendously. Lucille tried to hold on to what she had, but couldn't. Even though her sons loved her very much they were becoming difficult to handle, ultimately, Johnny is taken away and put into a boy's home. After Johnny gets out of the boy's home, Lucille moves further east, selling almost, if not all, of her personal belongings and furniture to make ends meet; but that money only lasted so long. At that point, Lucille registered for government assistant, and moved into something more affordable, government housing, and a.k.a. The Projects, low income, housing, apartments.

Upon entering the house, Johnny sees his mother, Lucille, in the living room dancing in front of the stereo with an 8-track tape playing. The volume hit high levels as she holds tight to a half-filled glass in one hand, while a bottle of gin and juice sits half-full on the cocktail table.

She is singing and prancing around as if she is the opening act in Broadway show; she always wanted to be a star, a dancer. Ms. Burton is so drunk that she doesn't notice Johnny standing less than four feet in front of her. Her eyes are half shut as Johnny walks closer. His eyes are swollen from crying and tears are still rolling down his cheeks. Johnny hesitates, while searching his heart for the right words to tell his mother that her youngest son is dead.

Another black mother's son shot down by the white police: The Big Four, Nazi in disguise. A very familiar scene of blood and death that haunts black families that live in predominant poor black neighborhoods, The Ghetto.

Struggling to speak, even a tiny whisper he finds extremely difficult. "Ma...Ma."

Lucille ignores Johnny, spinning and kicking her legs high as she dances.

"Ma," he says, and still she ignores him. He grabs her, immobilizing her. "Ma."

"What. Sh... What you grab'n me like that for, boy?"

Johnny closes his eyes for a second, exhaling before telling her the news. "...Mark's been shot."

"What...What you talk'n 'bout, Johnny?"

This time he looks into her face, repeating the most difficult words he has ever had to say to his mother. "Mark...he...he's...been shot." With tearful eyes, uncontrollably he blurts out, "Mark's dead Momma."

"What the hell are you talk'n 'bout...dam..."
Lucille stumbles as she pushes Johnny with one hand.
"Boy...don't be play'n no dam.. games. Now...what in the hell are you talk'n 'bout? You come in here talk'n stupid and sh...and holl'n."

"Momma please." he begs her.

Lucille stops and looks in Johnny's face. He repeats, "Mark is dead. The police killed Mark...They shot him."

Lucille stares into Johnny's face. She notices the tears in his eyes revealing the pain within. "Mark...Mark is what?"

Johnny hesitates before repeating those horrible words again. Struggling with his emotions, trying to stay calm, but it's impossible, he screams horridly, "HE'S DEAD, MA...HE'S DEAD...MARK IS DEAD."

Lucille aggressively snatches Johnny by his collar, pulling him toward her, and smacking him several times across the face.

"Don't be talk'n no crazy sh... You hear me, Johnny? I don't want to hear no sh... about Mark being dead. Cause he ain't DEAD. You got THAT?" Lucille still refuses to believe Johnny's bad and unwanted news. "Nah...Johnny, my baby ain't dead. Who told you some sh... like that anyway? Mark's dead."

"Ma...I know. Ma, it's true...I saw him. He didn't move or nuth'n. I tried to wake him...but...but." Johnny breaks down, howling even louder than before and that's when Lucille realizes that Johnny is telling the truth. The news hits her even harder, and without warning Lucille starts to scream losing all bodily control, dropping her glass on the floor, her tears gushing as the saliva spatters from her mouth. "NO...OOO...OO...NAH...HE CAN'T BE. NOT...MY BABY. MARK...MARK. WHERE IS MARK? I GOTTA GO AND GET MY BABY...WE GOTTA BRING HIM HOME, JOHNNY...HE CAN'T BE DEAD. HE'S JUST A BABY, HE'S ONLY SIXTEEN."

Johnny grabs holds his mother, wrapping both arms around her as they mourn Mark's death.

Lucille whispers, "Johnny, go get Mark, bring him home, please...e...e...e. Please Johnny, I want Mark to come home, now. He's still a baby."

"I know Momma. I know." Johnny continues to clutch his mother, wishing he could squeeze the pain out of her frail alcoholic body and bring Mark home again, alive. "Don't worry Ma, Ma...don't worry one dam.. bit. Those two officers will pay for Mark's death...I promise you."

The next day the newspaper read: "**POLICE CRACK DOWN ON CITY STREETS**" - *Car Jacker Killed In Chase.*
And in the sports section: "**GARY SNOWDEN WINS MIDDLE WEIGHT CHAMPIONSHIP FIGHT.**"

Graduation day and Elayne is standing at her seat in the school's auditorium, waiting impatiently for the ceremony to come to a close. She isn't feeling very well, her head is spinning and her stomach is upset. She stands quietly in her cap and gown, trying hard to keep her sickness a secret. Finally, the ceremony ends and Elayne speeds through the crowd and into the restroom.

"Oh thank you, Lord. I don't think I could've stood there any longer."

Like a thief in the night, slipping out of the auditorium, before anybody notices her. But someone did see her, D'La, who wonders about Elayne's peculiar look, she immediately follows her into the restroom.

From a distance, Shi Li and Candice are watching Elayne and D'La, and they too have concerns, so they hurry out of the auditorium, following D'La.

"What could be wrong with them?" asks Candice.

"I do not know," replies Shi Li.

Elayne pushes through the stall door. With her legs wobbling and her head spinning faster with each breath, she practically faints as she falls to her knees. Bending over the toilet, vomiting. The loud sounds echoes through the restroom as D'La walks in; she is shocked by Elayne's illness. D'La leans against the sink, listening to the sounds from Elayne when Shi Li and Candice enters, but before they can ask any questions, D'La quickly puts one finger to her lips, silencing them, and whispers, "Shhh!"

Shi Li whispers, "What is...?"

Before she can complete her question she hears the weird sounds coming out of the stalls.

"Who's that?" ask Candice.

"It's Elayne, she's throwing up, "explains D'La

"Throwing up. No...She can not be," says Shi Li.

Candice asks, "Be what?"

D'La whispers to Candice, "I think Elayne's pregnant."

Shi Li covers her face, "Oh no."

Candice sympathetically whispers the shameful secret she promises not to tell. "She said, 'she only did it that one time."

In dismay, D'La shakes her head, "Candice, it only takes one time."

Elayne finally comes out of the stall, mouth twisted, wiping it with a piece of toilet tissue as a small piece sticks to her bottom lip. Looking as if she just ate some old sour meat, dumfounded, embarrassed and speechless.

Shi Li says, "Do not tell me you are pregnant."

Candice takes a paper towel from the canister, wets it and wipes Elayne's hot moist face, then she asks, "Tell me. Are you? ...I wanna know."

"Candice I told you we only did it that one time."

D'La finds it hard to believe that anyone can think something so ridiculous, throwing her hands up, and with that tough sassy look as she strolls toward the stall door, approaching Elayne.

"Well, did you get your period?"

Elayne doesn't know how to respond. First, she stands there, with a blank expression, looking around at her friends. "No. ...I'm ten days late."

Shi Li is unhappy, but she inquisitively asks, "Have you ever been late before?"

"No...never! I've never been late before in my life."

"She's pregnant," blurts D'La.

Shi Li continues to question Elayne. "Well if you are, please tell me it is not Raymond's."

Elayne's intense, nervous, her body stiffens. "It's Raymond's".

"OH DAM..." shouts D'La.

"I can't tell my parents. I'm afraid of what they might do. I'm pretty sure daddy's go'n to kill me. I just know he will."

D'La abruptly replies, pointing at Elayne's stomach, "You won't be able to keep that a secret. You'll be sticking out in about three months."

Shi Li wraps one arm around Elayne's shoulder, comforting her. Do not worry, we will think of something...Does Raymond know?"

"No, just us. I'm afraid to tell anybody else. I'm hoping my period will come."

Candice continues to wipe Elayne's face as Shi Li figures out a plan.

"First, let's go back to the auditorium before our parents get suspicious, and try to look as though nothing is wrong. Elayne, do you think you can do that?"

"Yeah, I feel a little better now since everything came out."

Shi Li continues, "Later I want all of us to meet at my house, say about six. "

Elayne expresses a sigh of relief, due to the fact that, Shi Li has always been a person that can handle pressure.

Shi Li continues to map out the plan and everybody agrees. "From there, we will call Raymond and invite him over. Right now, I want everybody to stay calm and cool."

"I'm always cool and calm," says Candice as she throws the paper towel in the trashcan.

"Yeah. No matter what, just be cool," replies D'La putting her hands into her jacket pocket.

"Elayne, if you start to feel ill again, just let us know," says Shi Li.

"I will."

The four girls return to the auditorium reuniting with their parents, teachers and friends.

But that evening at Shi Li's house the tension is high, Raymond arrives in his Cadillac, a slick cream shark-skin suit, shiny cream alligator shoes, with a camel silk hanky in his top pocket and two pinky rings, one on each hand. As usual, he is smooth as smooth can be, dressed to kill, from his head to his toe.

D'La, Shi Li and Candice waste no time informing Raymond that he is going to be a daddy. Overwhelmed by the news, Raymond sits quiet for two to three minutes, thinking. He has never been a daddy before, but he has come close many times. Out of all the many girls, he have knocked up, he always made a way for them to be taken care of. Yet this time is different; he knows Elayne wouldn't think of doing something so horrible, being a child of 'The Lord' praising him with her every breath. An abortion is out of the question.

"Dam...dam...dam. I got to get the hell out of this here. ...Well, I guess Elayne is an okay girl and all, but a baby, and me...a daddy... Dam... this is some tight sh...."

As the four friends focus on Raymond, waiting for his response, D'La's patience is growing short, abruptly and in a harsh tone. "WELL, what you gonna do, DADDY?"

As D'La continues, Elayne's self-esteem shrinks, fearing Raymond will walk out of her life and the baby. She takes under consideration, that maybe, she is just another piece of booty, a notch on his belt: "Raymond the Conqueror." She holds her head down low, her eyes almost closed, thinking and finally understanding what her mother told her so many times before. "All a man wants from a young innocent girl is to be her first, in other words, her virginity."

Her mother's statement echoes more times than she can count in that one moment in time. "Remember honey, a man ain't gonna buy the cow when he can get the milk free."

Without any facial expression, Raymond stands, constantly cracking his knuckles. "Well ladies, you want to know what I'm gonna do about this situation? Well you see, it's like this."

Elayne is afraid to listen, blocking out his voice, refusing to hear what Raymond might say. She always thought her first time would be on her wedding night. At least that is the way she planned it would be.

"Raymond, you have to do what's right. Elayne's a good girl," demands Candice.

"He knows that Candice, "says D'La." That's if he knows what the right thang is. Hell, that's why he took her virginity anyway, cause he would be her first. Any and every man dreams is 'bust'n a virgin'."

"Shi Li agrees, "Yes Raymond, it would be very honorable if you would take Elayne for your wife. Your son will not have to be born a bastard. Do not leave her in disgrace, because if you do, it would surely come back to haunt you later in life."

"You reap what you sow," says D'La.

"Hold up, hold up, what makes you think, and how do you know this baby's mine?"

D'La aggressively answers, "AIN"T this some SH... HOLD UP, HOLD UP, one DAM... minute Mr. Raymond Smith. Are you try'n to say, what I think you're try'n to SAY? I know you ain't go'n there."

"Well, a man has to be sure now-a-days. Women are always try'n to capture us, men. Look at me. I'm pretty sure you can see my dilemma with women and them always chase'n after me. They say, Raymond this and Raymond that. You dig where I'm comin from!"

"Do you believe Elayne wants to capture you?" Shi Li asks.

Raymond takes his combs out of his pocket and starts to comb his hair. "Well, yeah, like I said, ...I've been through this here before. You know how it is."

"No. No we don't know how it is. Why don't you tell us so we'll know?" declares Candice.

D'La sees right through Raymond's 'game plan' and her composure is wearing even thinner. "Stop right there...I don't want to know how it is and I don't have the patient or the time to listen to this AS...talk that bull-sh... neither. All he's try'n to do is play with our heads and I don't appreciate it one f...n BIT. Now, do you understand where we girls are comin from, RAY?"

"D'La calm down and let the man talk." Shi Li interrupts and Raymond sarcastically agrees. "Yeah D'La, calm down girl."

Raymond opens his jacket putting his comb back into his pocket. "I know ya'll are tight and everything, but this is between me and your girl, Elayne."

Elayne suddenly looks up, too nervous to say anything. Shi Li walks toward Elayne. "Elayne, tell Raymond what you think he should do, or what you want him to do." Shi Li caresses Elayne's hand.

"What ya'll need to do is leave us alone so we can talk this out...just me and her, together. We don't need ya'll influencing her, she's a big girl," Raymond charmingly says, with that same cool daddy smile stretched across his face.

"Is that okay with you Elayne?" asks Shi Li.

"Yeah, it's okay with her," Raymond replies.

"Didn't nobody ask you," says D'La as she moves slowly toward Raymond, that when Candice quickly grabs her by the arm.

"Yeah, ya'll get her out of here so me and my girl can talk privately about this sit...u...ation."

Smiling from ear to ear, Raymond continues to control Elayne by answering for her, even though, she wants her friends to stay with her every step of the way. Reason: because she is still afraid. She understands deep down inside this is something she has to do without her friends, and with Raymond.

"It will be fine. The Lord is watching over 'me and the baby'. I know he is."

"If the Lord was watch'n over you, you wouldn't gotten knocked up by that dam... fool...He musta had his eyes closed that day when you were do'n it with him," declares D'La.

"D'La be nice. How could you say something like that?" asks Candice.

"Well, he had to have been do'n somethang else. Look at who's the father."

"D'La...Let's give them time to discuss this matter," says Shi Li as she pulls D'La and Candice by their arms escorting them into the kitchen.

Raymond couldn't help noticing Elayne's delicate demeanor glaring from her sad eyes. Judging from his previously sexual experiences, Raymond knows he's Elayne's first. Standing with her arms to her side, his eyes probe her body, her stomach, pondering: "How would it be, to be a father?" Still Raymond toys with the question: "Is he the baby's daddy?" It seems that question must have run through his mind a thousand times as it constantly lingers from the shock of the entire situation.

"What in the hell am I go'n to do about it?" he thinks as he signals Elayne with his head to come to him. She hesitates, but she reconsiders his every gesture as she gradually walks in his direction.

"What do you want to do Raymond?" she asks in a meek voice.

"Well, let me see," says Raymond still smiling from ear to ear. "First I want you, us, to sit down so we can talk."

Elayne turns looking at the couch before sitting next to Raymond. Meanwhile, standing at the kitchen entrance, Candice peeks around the corner every so often at Elayne, ducking her head out and in.

"Do you see anythang? What are they do'n in there? It sure is quiet," says D'La.

"Shh..." whispers Candice. "She's sitting next to him but she's not saying anything."

"She's probably pray'n," says D'La, rolling her eyes around.

"Candice, D'La, give them a few minutes, just be patient. I am pretty sure Elayne will tell us what he said when they have finished."

D'La goes to the kitchen table takes a chair turns it around throwing her leg over it to sit. "Yeah, you're right Shi Li, there ain't nuth'n we can do anyway but wait and see. I still can't figure out what she saw in him in the first place."

Candice also sits at the table. "I think he's cute, if you ask me."

Simultaneously: Shi Li and D'La utters, "Candice, you think everybody's cute."

"Here we go again," says D'La.

"So, I don't care what you two think about him, he seems to be a nice person. He came over here, didn't he?"

Taking Elayne by her hands, Raymond decides to accept his responsibility. Nevertheless, he considers, the majority of his friends are fathers. Standing there squeezing her hand, glaring into each other's eyes, the same way they did before making love that night.

"Girl, you don't have to worry about a thang. I'm with you all the way." Raymond then takes Elayne into his arms and kisses her. Then he gets down on one knee and proposes marriage.

Elayne accepts. "If I knew the reason for my visit, I would have stopped at the jeweler's and got a ring."

Astounded, Elayne runs into the kitchen to tell her friends the good news. Everything seems to be going perfectly, but there's one critical question remaining: How are they going to tell Elayne's parents?

Reverend Donaldson always believed Elayne would set a good example for her little sister Elizabeth; getting married before getting pregnant or going to college.

Coming home pregnant is an epidemic in black communities. Fatherless children are everywhere and he didn't want his daughters to fall victim to a trend that society has welcomed with open arms.

At the right time and with Raymond by her side, Elayne tells her parents about the new addition into the family. They are not happy with the news, but ultimately, Raymond does marry Elayne in her father's church and everything seems to be going well for the newlyweds...well, Elayne thinks so.

But as for Raymond, he is not happy with his decision or position as a husband and an expectant father. All his friends can't believe as they continue to tease 'The Sweet Daddy', Raymond Smith, who they thought would never marry.

He is the lover of many women, and many women still follow him around like lost dogs in heat. There were many times when Raymond would loan one or two of his girl out to his bro's, especially, if the brothers were looking for a little companionship for the evening. The women didn't mind sharing at all, whatever Ray say do - they do. They even supported him, giving him money, paying his rent, buying him anything he might need or want. Just as long as 'Sweet Daddy Ray' is happy, they're happy.

Four months have past in the so-called happy home. One morning after having sex with his wife Raymond lies across the bed watching Elayne and thinking as she put on her clothes, piece by piece, examining her every move, and he doesn't care for the view. No, not one bit. He is disgusted, and her pregnancy is very unappealing. 'I can't take this. This family stuff ain't for me. Look at her, looking like a fat cow. Swollen feet and a fat swollen face to match.'

Elayne starts to rub her stomach, the baby's moving. "It kicked. Raymond I felt the baby move. Touch right here, you can feel the baby's little feet. Owoo...That was a big kick that time, Ooo...Raymond put your hand right here, honey."

Elayne hurries to Raymond, sits on the bed beside him, takes his hand and lays it on her stomach. The baby kicks again.

Raymond doesn't want to share the happy moment; he impetuously pulls his hand away. "Dam... that feels like some kind of space creature trying to break out."

However, every day Elayne becomes more excited about the life that is growing inside of her. She sings spiritual hymns and thanks The Lord for blessing her with such a happy family and a good husband. She expects to spend every new and exciting moment with her husband until 'death do them part'. Yet, every day Raymond is becoming more disgusted, her out of shape body, and those ugly old fashion clothes that her mother has given her. It is getting to the point that every time he looks at her he becomes more discussed with his life, particularly his hasty decision.

Raymond ignores her enthusiasm and throws the blanket off of him. "I gotta get up and get ready for work...I don't wanna be late."

"Ahh...It's still early. Do you have to leave so soon, honey?"

"Baby, if I stay in bed any longer..." Raymond puts his arms around Elayne, kissing her, pretending all is well, "Ummm...I'm gonna have to lay you down and start where I left off."

Elayne giggles and kisses him once more. "I love you, Mr. Raymond Smith."

He is faking, and every word that comes out of his mouth chokes him.

"I love you, Mrs. Raymond Smith."

LOST WITHIN

CHAPTER 9

Candice's dream has finally come true: Candice has been secretly dancing at the Wild Cat, A-Go-Go Nightclub, for a couple of weeks, now.

Her schedule only allows her to dance part-time, three nights a week and it is not that far, only about twenty miles from her dormitory at the university. She loves the attention she is receiving from the men and especially from her boss, Sam.

Sam is very fond of Candice, he treats her as if she is his own daughter, and she turns out to be one of his best dancers. Yet Candice is afraid to tell her friends the truth knowing how they feel about something so immoral. Of course, she lies to everyone, including her parents; they actually think she is studying with a tutor, trying desperately to keep up her grade point average. Candice doesn't need the money; her parents are paying for everything. In other words, curiosity has killed the cat. Although, she should be ashamed of herself, but she is not. Candice really wants to do something on her own without everybody having 'a say' about whatever she does in her life, for once.

"What the heck. People enjoy watching me when I'm up on stage and I enjoy them enjoying me."

Candice, the topless dancer; she loves the men, the music, and especially the money they throw at her feet or slip into her G-string. It is her night off and Candice is a bit restless, she tries studying, but that's not working. Plus, studying all day is somewhat boring, so she closes her books laying them on the night table next to her bed. Then she lies down again, trying to relax but it is impossible. So she gets up. "I think I'll go and see what's going on at the club."

After arriving at The Wild Cat Club, she observes Sam talking to some customers.

"Hey Sam, what's going on?"

"Candice, nothing much, you got it kid...It's just the same old same old...What you doing here, ain't tonight your night off?"

Candice replies, "I know Sam, I got bored, thought I'd come and see what's going on in here tonight."

"Candice, I dig it, baby...Come on over here, I want you to meet some people."

After spending several hours talking with old and new friends, Candice realizes it is getting late. Naïve to her surroundings Candice is being watched by three non-suspicious looking characters and before she leaves, she saunters around saying her good-byes. Enticed by her beauty, one of the men signals the others. "Look, I think she's about to leave."

The second man agrees, "She's coming, lets wait for her in the car."

The three men quietly get up from the table and walk out, with their engine running they sit and wait.

Candice doesn't notice anything unusual as she goes to her car, as she done so many times before, alone and without any problems. Nor has she seen or heard about anybody having any trouble at the club. Once reaching the dorm's parking lot, she gets out of her car, and suddenly a car pulls up next to her.

"HEY BABY. HEY...DO YOU WANT A RIDE?"

Candice ignores the question, locks her car door and begins to walk toward the dorm's entrance. The men drive along side of her as she starts to walk faster. "Hey...All I'm trying to do is be nice."

Candice shakes her head as to say no. One of the voices speaks very nice at first, "I just thought I'd ask."

Candice then turns and answers hasty, hoping they would drive off, "No thank you."

Another voice makes a remark, "A pretty girl like you could get hurt out here walking all by her lonesome. What's you name, baby?"

"Maybe she don't want to ride with you, Josh," says the third voice coming from the backseat of the car.

"Yeah, maybe she don't like your car...or maybe it's your face Josh," says the third voice again as he starts to laugh. The more he laughs the more Josh gets upset with his friends and with Candice's refusal.

"Stop the car," Josh yells, but the car doesn't stop fast enough. He yells a little louder. "AYE ...I'M TALKING TO YOU...Cal, pull over and let me out. I said, pull over!"

"What are you going to do?" asks Cal, the second voice.

"I'm going to get out of the car for a minute. I wanna talk to the beautiful lady."

The car stops. Josh gets out and quickly adjusts his pace with Candice as she walks faster toward the dorm's walkway. And soon enough they are walking side by side. Cal continues to follow them, driving as slow as he can. Unaware of the potential danger, Candice does not run. Her destination is not far and nothing could possibly happen to her this close to the front entrance, especially with dorm security standing there.

"I don't need an escort," says Candice.

"I didn't ask you what you need, Bit... I know what you need with your stuck up as..."

Josh's harsh remarks send chills through Candice. He grabs her, signaling Cal to bring the car closer. Candice starts to scream but Josh quickly covers her mouth with his hand, threatening her, then pushes her into the back seat of the car and they speeds off.

They waste no time when it comes to having their pleasures satisfied, driving through back allies and parking in a closed city park. Candice is raped and beaten by all three men numerous times. One after another as the hours past, her virginity stolen and her self-respect degraded two weeks after her eighteenth birthday. After gratifying themselves, they drive into an alley to rid themselves of their victim. They lift Candice's weak, bruised and battered body out of the car, throwing it on the ground. Candice begin to scream again. Josh hits Candice across her face to stop her. "I said shut-up bit..." His fist just keeps coming, hitting her on one side then the other.

The sounds of Candice's screams alert a hooker on the stroll. She sees a girl being beaten and thrown out of a car, a scene that she has seen many times before in the area. Feeling sorry, afraid and understanding for the strange girl, she begins to scream.

Josh and his nervous friends, Ed and Cal are shocked by the sound of another voice. They panic and quickly gets back into the car, hit the accelerator, the wheels spin and rubber burns. Within a few seconds they were gone.

Her voice is extremely loud as she hurries toward Candice. She looks unconscious, and the hooker is not strong enough to carry her; she is only five feet and four inches tall, about 105 pounds. Consequently, all she can do is yell. "HELP...SOMEBODY HELP. PLEASE, HELP US...POLICE...POLICE. She bends over to check Candice's pulse while talking to herself, "In this neighbor at night, that's last thing you'll find is help."

She realizes that nobody is responding to her cries; she rubs Candice's face, "Poor girl...It's got so a girl can't make a decent dollar these days without some punk john getting all rough and sh..."

Sympathetically, she calls to Candice; "Hey...Can you hear me? Are you all right?"

Candice open her eyes, screaming very boisterously, "NO. NO. THEY RAPED ME...ME"

Almond Joy tries to calm Candice, "I believe you honey. Sh... like that always happen to girls who work the street around here! Those animals have no respect for the working woman. I don't know what kind of mother could've raised a man to do something so terrible."

Nonetheless, Candice keeps repeating herself, placing her hands between her legs, touching her torn jeans, that covers her vagina area, "They raped me. No-o-oh."

It seems that is all Candice can say.

"Girl, you...you gonna have to get up out of this alley, just in case they come back. Com'on now! ...Do you want me to call the police, or your family, anybody, somebody? Just get out of this alley."

Candice goes deeper into an emotional frenzy and it seems as though her words are coming out of her mouth before Almond Joy even notice her lips are moving.

"NO..." Candice yells.

Almond Joy reaches out, gently touching Candice, "Com'on now, please? All I want to do is help you."

Candice's mind is shattered as she wonders who the strange woman is with the white eye shadow and the deep burgundy red lipstick. Still not realizing that Almond Joy is there to help, Candice snatches her arm away, and again she repeats: "NO...don't, don't touch me. NO. NO!"

Almond Joy knows she has to be persistent because the young girl is not thinking straight, "Com'on...you can't stay here.

I'll take you back to my place. You'll be safe there, I promise. I don't stay too far. I live just down the street."

Extremely distorted, frightened, and confused Candice agrees to go with her.

Almond Joy reaches out again, helping Candice to her feet and they slowly walk about two blocks before reaching Almond Joy's apartment.

At the apartment she opens the door and helps Candice to the couch. Candice is bleeding from her head to her toes. Psychologically her condition is quite obvious, like an egg's shell, very fragile; she could crack at any time.

"Is there anything I can do for you? Can I get you anything?" asks Almond Joy.

Candice mumbles, "I just want to sit here for a minute, okay?"

"Sure, that'll be fine. You can sit there as long as you want."

Candice looks up at Almond Joy and starts to cry again as she describes what happened, "Those nasty punks, they kidnap me...They raped me...They stole my virginity."

Surprised by Candice's statements, Almond Joy grabs the phone, "I think we better call the police."

With swollen twisted and out of shaped lips, cuts around her eyes and on her face, Candice refuses, "No...I can't."

"Why? It's probably best to go on to the hospital so they can run tests and to check to see if you're all right. You know, make sure you're not torn or damaged, and to check to see that you don't have VD or something. Listen, I don't want to get into your business or anything, but you really should make a police report while everything's still fresh in your head."

Candice ignores Almond Joy as the incident keeps repeating itself in her mind. It seems as though she can not stand the touch of her own skin. Suddenly she jumps up off the couch, raises her hands up away from herself and begins to scream frantically.

"NO...NO...I NEED BLEACH. I WANT TO STERILIZE MYSELF. JUST SIT IN SOME BLEACH AND WASH THEIR FILTHY GERMS..." This time she screams louder, and in a deeper tone, "...OFF OF ME! If bleach don't kill their germs, VD or whatever, I'LL JUST GIVE IT BACK!"

Almond Joy realizes that Candice is not thinking at all, so she backs off only for a minute, giving her a chance to compose herself.

"Okay...if you don't want me to call the police, how about seeing a doctor?"

Candice turns away from Almond Joy, ignoring her and her questions. Almond Joy realizes that talking to Candice is not getting very far, so she stops trying; because Candice is not in her right mind to be persuaded. Almond Joy gradually moves away once more.

"Okay, it's your life." Almond Joy then goes into the bathroom and fills the tub with warm water as Candice requested, but when she returns she notices Candice staring at the wall, staring at the wall as if she is hypnotized.

Almond Joy kneels in front of her, hoping to break the horrible spell, trying her best to get Candice's attention somehow. Yet, the brutal images that replay in her mind are overpowering, but that did not stop Almond Joy from trying. "Hey..." Almond Joy gently taps Candice on her shoulder, "Ah...your bath's ready."

The language that comes out of Almond Joy mouth is somehow strange to Candice, because she is only a hair away from drifting into a world of darkness; a world of insanity.

"Uh...uh..." is all she can say.

Almond Joy pleasantly repeats herself, "You can go and take your bath now."

Candice's zombie-like body stands slowly as if someone is calling her from beyond. She walks even slower, taking small steps into the bathroom. Almond Joy refuses to give up on the stranger. For some reason or reasons something is guiding her inner spirit to stick with Candice, not to fail her at her time of need, "Girl you're really messed up. Don't go and crack up on me now. Just hang in there, you can do it. You're a woman and we women are much stronger than we think. We're not gonna let any man take or control our destiny. We're in charge...You hear me? Our destiny is ours...Hey, everything is gonna be fine."

Almond Joy takes Candice by the arm and escorts her into the bathroom. "Take your time, now. Okay?" Almond Joy continues to speak to Candice as she closes the bathroom door, "I'll make something to relax your nerves."

After the door closes, Almond Joy knocks before she walks away, "Hey...do you want something to eat, or...just something to drink, or would you like both?" Almond Joy waits for an answer, yet Candice says nothing; she waits a few seconds more, just in case, before walking away, but still she says nothing.

Almond Joy returns about five minutes later and knocks on the door again; nevertheless, there is no response. Almond Joy places her ear to the door listening for a sound, but there is none.

Gradually she opens the door and peeks in only to finds Candice standing in front of the mirror, fully dressed, staring at her swollen disfigured bruised face and at her bruised body. In addition, Candice does not recognize herself, the strange girl in the mirror, or the stranger within, "Who is she? I don't know her. I'm not sure. No! That girl, her face, her hair, she's ugly. I don't know her. The poor thing, I feel so sorry. "

Yes, the girl in mirror isn't Candice at all. Because Candice is beautiful, her hair is always in place, she is very neat in appearance, and she has a very attractive nature.

"Who is this person who's looking at me?" Staring as hard as she could, Candice can't identify the person in the mirror and don't want to.

Almond Joy cautiously walks into the bathroom and takes a deep breath before saying anything, "Ooo...okay girl friend...I see I'm going to have to do this for you." Almond Joy patiently assists Candice in taking off her torn dirty clothes and getting into the tub.

Almond Joy gently washes Candice's face, and keeps talking to her hoping to keep her from falling deeper into a trance, "You know...after all that commotion I don't even know your name."

Still there is no sound from Candice, not even a murmur.

"What's you name?" Almond Joy asks. It's been a while since Almond Joy asked her last question. Then minutes later she hears something, but she is not sure, she lays the wash rag on the side of the tub to be certain. Candice whispers something again and Almond Joy is not sure what she just said this time either. Without warning, Candice speaks again, "Uh..."

"It's about time, that's one word that's finally comes out and I understand," Almond Joy says in a low tone.

Almond Joy starts to converse even more, "That's a start. Let's try to keep it going. My name is Joy..." she tries to add a bit of humor, "...Almond Joy. That's what the people in the neighborhood call me...What's yours?"

To her amazement Candice speaks five more words, "Ah... my...name...is...Candice." Her speaking is extremely low and her words are so far apart and mumbled that Almond Joy does not understand what Candice is trying to say. She mistakenly calls her by another name, "Candy. That's cute...Hey, Almond Joy and Candy."

Almond Joy fakes her laugh as she tries to take Candice's mind off of her situation; off her attackers, "Is that Candy with a C or a K?"

Again her words are docile, "It's...Candice with a...C."

"Oh, I thought you said, Candy. I'm sorry Candice. I didn't mean to get your name all screwed up and stuff...That sure would have been something though, Candy and Almond Joy."

Remarkably, Candice is starting to slowly regain some normalcy. She is getting stronger as she willingly buries the evil deep within her soul, concealing her true thoughts.

"Candice, those bastards who attacked you tonight, did you know them?"

"No! I've never seen them before." Shamefully, Candice begin to cry.

"Hey, you just go ahead and let it out. Nobody's gonna to bother you here. HELL NAH! Not while I'm here."

Candice promptly stares into Almond Joy's face, feeling relieved and thanking her with every glance.

"Come on, it's time to get out of this tub," says Almond Joy.

"I have some sandwiches on the table too. Would you like some coffee or tea with them? Umm...Hey, I got it. I got some gin in the cabinet. I was saving it, hoping one night me and my old man might wanna have some fun. That night never came. Uh... my man...that fool, he left one day...about seven months ago. He said, 'he'd be right back.' Sh...The next thing I knew he had moved in with my sister.

My sister had the nerve to call me and tell me not to wait for my man cause he ain't coming home, he already was home. That bit... she was always going after everything I had, even when we were little kids. As if she was too dumb to go out and find her own man, her own anything. Huh...every time I think of her, I could just kick her as... and his as... Then the next day Mr. Greenboro, the landlord, with his old dusty ugly looking as..., come knocking at my door asking for some rent money. I said, what rent money? He said 'the rent I owe for living in this beautiful apartment.' In that case the mice, and those hideous cockroaches, should be paying rent for this old piece of sh... too. So I went to the kitchen cabinet to get the money, and all I saw was nothing, the rent jar was empty. That two-bit sucker stole the money, all of it! Every dam... dime! I could have knocked my old man's head off his neck if he had been standing next to me. You know what Candice? The rent hadn't been paid for over two months, almost three, and I needed to do something fast. I needed some money. Everybody I asked said, 'they ain't got none.' So, I decided to turn a trick, then another one and another one...And here I am...still hook'n. If you ask me, men ain't sh... Well, forget all that, how about that gin?

After telling you my sorry as... story, I think I need one right about now myself."

"Gin is good, answers Candice while shaking her head.

"Then gin it is. Dry off and I'll go and get it. There is a robe on the back of the door. You can put it on if you like...it's clean. It was my old man's. After all the bull he gave me, that's the only thing he left." Almond Joy goes toward the bathroom door, pointing to the robe that is hanging on the back of it.

"Well, if you need anything else, I'll be in the kitchen."

Almond Joy leaves and few minutes later Candice walks out of the bathroom and into the kitchen. She sits, with her eyes fixed on the glasses sitting on the table. She asks, "Is this mine?"

"Yeah", says Almond Joy. "Did I pour too much?"

"No," replies Candice. "No...this is fine." Candice picks up the glass and sips.

"Sometimes I forget that everybody don't drink like a fish," says Almond Joy with a delightful smile.

Candice put the glass to her mouth again sipping slowly.

"If you need anything just ask, or if you change your mind and would like to make a call...the phone is on the wall over there." Almond Joy points to the wall behind her.

"I'll call in a few minutes...My friends will come and pick me up." Candice instantly starts to stare again, gazing at a roach that crawls into a crack in the wall. Almond Joy immediately interrupts her as she takes a can of bug killer off the sink and sprays the crack.

"Candice," she calls. "Candice," she calls her name again, "If you'll like to spend the night, you're welcome. My couch is a sofa bed. I'd pull it out for you if you're not ready to leave."

Candice looks at Almond Joy. With a silly smirk Almond Joy adds, "Don't worry about the roaches, they won't bother you. ...Everything's clean. I just washed."

"Yeah...I think, I 'd like that...I'm not ready to see anyone right now."

Almond Joy hesitates for a moment, "If you don't mind me asking, were those guys johns? How do you know them?"

"No. I'm not a hooker. I was visiting some friends at a club...The next thing I knew they were calling me...I go to school."

Even though Candice's answers are jumbled and not fully true Almond Joy persist. "School, that's great. What school?"

"I go to the university..."

Almond Joy asks, "Did you meet them at the university or at the club?"

Candice answers, "I think they were at the club, I really don't know. That's...well...I was at the university, in the parking lot, they started following me with their car...I was on my way to my dorm."

Almond Joy's questions continue, "Were they watching you while you were in the club or did you notice them there at all?"

Candice takes her hand to her face, touching it, "I don't know, maybe, I don't know...remember them. I think I remember. I'm not sure."

"Candice, what about your family...I'm pretty sure they're worried about you by now, especially being out here this time of night and alone. Somebody's gotta be worried out of their head."

Candice swallows the last drop of gin from her glass, "That's why I can never tell anyone about tonight. My parents would go crazy if they knew about this. And my father would probably kill somebody and wind up in jail or something and that would break my mother's heart. I couldn't let that happen to them, they tried so hard...not for something I caused."

Almond Joy pours more liquor into Candice's glass, "Candice, you'll never have to worry about me telling anything to anybody. A girl in my position, a prostitute, at least you got people, family that care. My momma, uh, she don't give a dam... 'bout nobody but her own dam... selfish butt. With her evil as... I don't even want to think about her either." Candice gives a snicker as she watches Almond Joy silly facial gestures.

"Almond Joy thank you... Thank you for everything."

Almond Joy places one hand on Candice's wrist, and without warning, Candice's voice gets heavy, demonic like tone, and her eyes close slightly as she begin to squeeze her fist tighter and tighter, "I promise myself tonight and all other nights to come. Before I lay down with any man ever, HE WILL PAY!"

A sinister grimace possesses Candice's face, gritting her teeth with each and every word that comes out of her mouth, "From now on every man that wants me, whether he wants to TOUCH IT, SMELL IT, or F... IT, he will PAY BIG TIME! TONIGHT was my ONLY and LAST free night!"

Almond Joy lifts her glass, toasting to Candice's proclamation, "You won't get an argument out of me on that one that's for dam... sure. You wanna lay, you gotta pay...You can go home to you wife or girlfriend if you want free pus... Special pus... like ours, that wild street pus... its gonna cost ya."

"If anybody ever touch me again like that..." Candice's eyes expand wider, her voice deepening even more. "I'LL KILL 'EM."

The next day Almond Joy gives Candice money to take a cab back to her dorm. Feeling guilty, dirty and excessively ashamed, she calls Shi Li, "Shi Li, I need to talk to you."

"Candice, is that you?"

"Shi Li, I need to talk to you, now. It's important. Please hurry!"

"Candice, are you in any trouble?"

"No, I'm not in any trouble."

"Your voice...have you been crying?"

"No, I'm not feeling very well. I need to talk to somebody, please come."

"I am on my way. I will be there soon."

The phone rings less than a second after hanging up and it is D'La. "Hey girl, What's go'n on? I called you all night last night. I was go'n to come over, but nobody answered the phone. What's up, uh?"

Candice speaks very soft. "Nothing."

D'La notices an eerie tone in Candice's voice. "Candice, are you all right? You don't sound right."

Candice can not pretend, holding back her feelings is extremely impossible and she starts to cry, "I... I..."

"Candice, Candice what's wrong? I'm on my way over there. You hear me? I'm on my way. I'm hang'n up the phone, Candice. Bye. I'm hang'n up the phone. Bye."

D'La hangs up and immediately calls Shi Li.

"Hello, Shi Li."

"D'La, I was about to call you."

"Shi Li, I just spoke to Candice and she don't sound right, somethang's wrong."

"I know D'La, I called Elayne and I am on my way to pick her up and from there we are going to Candice's."

"Ok cool, I'm leave'n now. I'll meet you there."

D'La arrives first, coincidentally, while she is pushing the elevator's button Shi Li and Elayne walks into the lobby. After the ride up to her floor, Shi Li knocks one time on the door. Candice moderately opens the door, slightly turning, hiding her disfigured face; she hangs it downward, before turning away from the door as her friends enter. Elayne easily paces toward Candice, gently lifting her face, alarmed by her appearance. "Oh...my Lord."

Shi Li and D'La make their comment simultaneously, rushing to Candice and inspecting her face, arms and legs. D'La is so angry that she wastes no time hollering and her question is right to the point. "WHAT IN THE HELL HAPPEN TO YOU?"

Candice goes to the bed and sits down. Shi Li follows her and stops D'La from saying another word; she can see that Candice is hiding something, "D'La please."

D'La throws her hands up and hurries to the other side of the room, hitting the wall with her fist. Shi Li calmly sits next to Candice questioning her. "Candice, what happened to you?"

The room becomes instantaneously quiet; everyone is motionless, waiting for an answer. Instead Candice begins to cry, but that does not stop the outpouring of her words, "I...I..." Shamefully looking into her friends faces her words burst outward. "I GOT RAPED LAST NIGHT!"

Immediately, Shi Li grabs hold of Candice and refuses to let go.

"Oh, my Lord." cries Elayne as she starts to pray.

All that emotional outpour is fine and dandy, but not good enough for D'La as she grabs a chair turns it around backward and sits, searching for more information, "All I want to know is who in the f... is he? ...Did you know him? ...How did you meet him and where? Most of all, where did it happen? ...THAT NASTY PUNK-F...." D'La stomps her foot. "DAM..."

"I don't know...I never seen them before. They were in the dorm parking lot when I was parking my car last night. They wanted to talk to me, but I refused them. Then one of them got out to the car and grabs me, pushing me into their car. They drove me around for a long time and then they took me to a place, I think it was a park or alley or something. It was dark. All I know is that there were lots of trees and bushes everywhere."

"THEY? There was more than ONE?" shouts D'La.

Candice doesn't say anything, motioning her head, agreeing. Elayne's dishearten, as tears fill her eyes, listening to Candice as she talks about that night, "Ohoo...Candice, I'm so sorry."

"Elayne don't you go get'n all up set. You're gonna make that baby up set. The last thang we need right now is for that baby to be popping out...No way, I ain't ready for that," says D'La.

"How many were there?" Shi Li asks. Candice hesitates before answering, "...Three...it was three of them and I heard two of their names."

"YOU DID?" yells D'La.

"What were the names, Candice?" Shi Li's questions were soft spoken as she continues.

"One was Josh and the other was Cal. I believe Cal was the driver."

"Did you call the police?" Shi Li asks.

"No. I didn't." With Candice every word D'La is becoming more upset, especially, the way Candice is handling this situation and again she shouts, "WHY IN THE HELL, NOT, CANDICE?"

Candice starts to shake because the pressure of telling is too overwhelming. She screams extremely loud, jumping up off the bed, looking at D'La, Shi Li and Elayne.

"I WAS SCARED...I DON'T WANT ANYBODY TO KNOW...I DON'T WANT MY PARENTS TO FIND OUT WHAT I'VE BEEN DOING. DAM... YOU, D'LA."

D'La aggressively comes back, demanding more information, "WHAT...FIND OUT WHAT? CANDICE THERE'S SOMETHANG GO'N DOWN AND YOU BET-TA TELL US, NOW!"

Still hanging on to her emotions, Shi Li speaks even more softly than before, trying to calm everyone in the room by agreeing with Candice, "All right, Candice we will not tell anyone. We will do it your way."

D'La gets up and kicks the chair across the room as Shi Li continues, "Remember always and forever no matter what."

"Somethang ain't right. I can just feel it," says D'La irascibly.

Elayne closes her eyes as she prepares to pray once more. "Oh Lord, please...please help us."

Yet, D'La interrogation becomes more demanding, "Just tell me what kind of car it was and when did you first notice they were follow'n you? ...What were you do'n for them to follow you anyway? Where were you comin from, and who were you with Candice?"

Intensely nervous, Candice knows the truth has to come out. She knows D'La will not stop until her curiosity is satisfied. That means, every question has to be answered. Nothing gets past D'La, a self-educated, street-smart individual. When it comes to surviving, D'La know just about every game being played on the streets.

So Candice tells, thinking back, as her mind gazes into her own mysterious world, revealing the secret fantasy to her friends, the lie she has been living, "It all started when I was working The Wild Cat Club as a dancer. I..."

The three friends are astonished as they listen to Candice's revelation. Deep within their hearts they know Candice is right, she cannot tell her parent about anything so discussing. This would definitely break their hearts, as well as, discovering their little girl's innocence has been stolen in such a horrible manner. Even with her friend's love and support Candice still refuses to see a doctor.

They spent the entire day and night talking about old times, when they were little girls and how they met. However, their relationship has taken another step closer and the bond has become even stronger.

After many hours of studying at the library, Shi Li arrives home only to finds her father in her bedroom, shuffling through her personal belongings.

She quietly watches him as he thoroughly examines everything he touches; searching through her jewelry container, her make-up kit and even her drawers, looking through every pair of knotted socks, her panties, bras, anything and everything he could find.

"Is there something wrong, Father?"

He is startled by the sound her voice and quickly closes the drawer, "I was just looking," he says with the most ridiculous grimace that accented his stupid reaction. If looks could kill, Father Kyi was late for his own funeral.

"Looking for what?" she suspiciously ask.

"What can I say to my daughter?" he says to himself, but all he can think to do is to lie and Shi Li is no fool, she has seen this man's game many times and knows exactly how he plays them. Yet, still he proceeds with his lies: "Pictures of your mother. I can't believe how much you are starting to look like her. She was very beautiful like you, Shi Li."

Aggressively she answers as she slowly walks toward him. "Father, all pictures of my mother are on TOP of my dresser, not in my drawers! I know you know that much."

Father Kyi looks at the pictures on top of the dresser as he begin to leave her bedroom; but Shi Li is not in the mood for any more of his lies or even trying to reason with him any longer. "WAIT!" she says in a stern voice, "Father, this is not the first time I caught you inspecting my things. Now tell me, what are you searching for?"

She steps closer to him and looks directly into his eyes, challenging his authority. He moves away from her and tries to leave the room once again. Shi Li moves along with him, her look is stern, a side of her Father Kyi has never seen in his daughter's face before. He pauses: It is a standstill between the two, facing her eye to eye as he answers the questions.

"You are right my daughter. I do not look for pictures of your mother. I look for evidence."

"Evidence of what?" ask Shi Li.

"Of your purity," he proudly says.

Shi Li is outraged with his reasons, his voice so rude, cold, evil, but that does not scare Shi Li. Not one bit. Patiently she listens, waiting until he is finished.

"I don't want my daughter to be like those, you call...friends."

"My friends? What are you talking about?" she asks.

Father Kyi's eyes grew larger as the ice within him grew colder, "The friend that sleeps with man and make baby too soon in life. THE NASTY WOMAN."

Shi Li is not surprise to hear her father's answer, yet, she knew this day would come, the day she fights for her independence and her mother's.

"HOW DARE YOU QUESTION MY JUDGEMENT! Father, I will not give you pleasure when it comes to defending my friends. I will not attempt to satisfy that selfish thinking of yours for one moment."

"Shi Li, you are speaking to your father."

Shi Li voice becomes more stern disrespecting him for the first time in her life.

"Instead of worrying about me and my nasty so called friend or friends, you should have been taking better care of my MOTHER!"

Father Kyi is appalled by his daughter's disrespectful attitude, but the longer Shi Li speaks, the more she thinks about her mother's death. Shi Li takes another step closer. Almost nose to nose, as she aggressively continues to stare into his eyes. The hate that has been growing inside her iced heart finally encourages her to continue, "Because of you she died so young. Running around, catering to your every wish, your every need and all you did was treat her as if she was your slave, a dummy who could not even think for herself. My MOTHER, who waited on you hand and foot, every day of her life, not thinking of herself or her needs. Because, all she wanted was to make your every wish come true. All she wanted was for you to love us, as you loved yourself. My MOTHER died making your life happy and you thanked her by killing her. She was the only parent that loved me, the daughter you never wanted. The daughter you wished was a son every day of my life; so you could stand proud among the family and those so-called friends of yours and now you spy on me? ...You want to

146

know about my purity, to see if I am having SEX? Now you wonder if your daughter is a NASTY WOMAN!"

Father Kyi is aggravated by his daughter's behavior; he interrupts, yelling at her, "SHI LI, YOU ARE SPEAKING TO YOUR FATHER...HOW DARE YOU!"

Immediately she turns the table, "MY FATHER! ...What is this, FATHER'S DAY? HOW DARE you pretend to be a concerned FATHER after so many years after you KILLED MY MOTHER AND TREATED ME AS NOTHING, as though I was INVISIBLE! You have never been a father to me...NEVER...Oh yes, about my sex life, my purity FATHER ...that is NONE OF YOUR BUISNESS!"

Father Kyi can not say one word as his daughter speaks the truth. He stand emotionless, as he watches tears fall from her eyes. Still refusing to show his love for her, he proudly turns, holding his head high and walks out of her bedroom. Shi Li soundlessly closes her door behind him. Father Kyi never realizes the pain he has caused his family until now; and still he does nothing.

RA`H SILK

CHAPTER 10

Early spring of 1971, Beauden is making his usually rounds collecting monies owed to the organization. He stops at one of the number houses in the area run by the Black Connection. He knocks on the door of Edna Simmins, an older woman about sixty-five years of age, she is the neighborhood street number lady, a bookie, and has been for many years. Edna has had a crush on Beauden for a least twenty years and at one time they were serious about each other. That is until, Beauden decided to take on a few young girls to work the streets, eventually turning it into one of the largest stables on the eastside.

She peers through the peek hole of the door. Beauden senses her presence, "Hey it's me...open the door."
Without hesitation she opens it.

"Hey Beauden...what's go'n on, baby? I didn't expect to see you til at least after ten tonight...you know, same as usual," she says while grinning and batting those eyes of hers. Beauden is accompanied by two of his thugs who follow closely behind.

"Edna baby, you know I can't stay away from you too long...Eee..e.e.e...Cause you got somethang I want, somethang I need and you got somethang I like," says Beauden with a grin of greed that sparkles even in his eye.

Edna walks toward a desk near the kitchen doorway, "Yeah Beau, it's all here. You can count it if you want too."

She hands him a brown paper bag filled with money. Beauden intentionally spills the money on the desk then points his finger at his two thugs, Maddog and Griz. They sit down at the desk counting it and comparing their records with hers.

"It's all there...you know I ain't gonna try and cheat you...I ain't gonna do no sh... like that, Beau."

Beauden's grin gradually turns into a laugh, "Edna, I know you ain't, but business is business...Eee.e..e..e. Edna Baby, I don't want nuth'n happ'n to you if it's a little short. You know what I mean?" He takes a sniff and smells soul food cooking. With his cool 'Cat-Daddy' stride he strolls into the kitchen, "Cause, can't nobody make hot buttered cornbread, cooked ham hocks and collard greens with 'fat-back' the way you do woman."

"Sh... Beauden, that's all you think 'bout is some dam... food every time you come over here." She fans her hand at him as he goes over to the stove and glances into the pot.

"Edna, I wouldn't say that. This man got a-lot other thangs on his mind too...You got that baby?"

Edna is hungry for some love and affection; it's been a while since her last intercourse with Beauden. Seductively she walks toward him and opens her robe, pulling up her nightgown revealing her nude body, "Thangs like what? ...You mean thangs like this?"

"Oooo Baby...Edna, you make it hard for a man to choose. Dam... woman what you do that for? I ain't got that much time, but a quickie ain't never failed me yet. Sh... Edna, it's either your ham hocks, or these here ham hocks in this here pot. E..e..e.e.e, Edna baby, but a man gotta do what a man gotta do...Why don't you fix me a plate to go?"

Edna is a little agitated with Beauden's refusal that she quickly drops her nightgown and closes her robe, but it is not the first time he has turned away her sexual advances.

"The hell with you Beau...You know you want this sh... here. In my day, not too many men could turn this here thang down. And not too many men is turn'n it down now, except for your old crazy as..., for your info."

The two thugs give thumbs up to Beauden.

"Edna baby, it's all there and I gotta make a move. I'll catch up with you later, just keep look'n good for me and stay sweet." He kisses her cheek then pats her butt.

Beauden and his thugs leave the house and drives to another business location, a whorehouse. They get out of the car, Beauden runs up the stairs into an apartment while Maddog and Griz wait outside. Pinky is Beauden's main lady whore, as well as his recruiter for young girls into his stable.

"Hey Baby...I've been waiting for ya," she says.

"You got me some money?" he asks as he places his hand around her throat.

"Yeah, I got you some money baby...and I got you something else, too." Pinky goes into the dining room where a young girl is nervously sitting. Pinky whispers into Beauden's ear.

"She's a runaway and she needs a place to stay. So I told her she might could stay here, but it's really up to my old man."

The young girl stares at the plate of food Beauden is holding in his hand. All the while, he is checking her over from head to toe and he like what he sees.

"Did she eat anythang?" he asks Pinky.

"No...from the look of things she ain't ate nuth'n in a while."

Beauden put his plate of food on the table as the young girl watches its every move.

"Aye, how you do'n?' he asks.

"Fine," her answer is so low, a meek and sweet voice, almost whispering.

"What's your name?"

"Tiffany."

"You live round here, Tiffany?"

"No, I'm from Ohio."

"How you get here...in Detroit?"

"I ran away from home and I hitch-hiked all the way here.

"Why you come here?"

"I don't know, I just did."

She looks at the plate of food again, Beauden leans toward Pinky and whispers, "Take her out and get her somethang to eat, and make sure you bring her back to me."

"Okay Beau, sho'nuff. I'll take her to the twenty-four hour Coney down the street. "

They walk out of the door, all the while Beauden's mind is going a thousand miles a minute on how much money Tiffany can bring in. Licking his lips as he sits back and relaxes in a chair, kicking his legs up on a footstool, and planning Tiffany's future while making that disgusting sound he considers a laugh that echoes through the room, "Ee.e.e..eu....e."

Beauden, true enough loves all women but he has a strong fetish for young girls between the ages of eleven and twenty years. Their soft, smooth, tender and firm body makes his blood boil every time he penetrates them, especially if they're virgins. Beauden doesn't fear any retaliation from the legal system or anybody else, due to the fact that some police officers, a few judges, and a handful of city officials have dealing with the organization. Numerous molestation cases, murders, drug related cases are either thrown out for lack of evidence, lost, or charges were dropped due to coercion from prosecutors that are on their payroll, the disappearance of witnesses, the death of the victim and, or their family members.

Johnny and Gilbert walks into Dexx's Place, a pool hall, one of many fronts for the organization's daily business activities: drug dealing, weapons dealing, street-numbers running, prostitution and murder, just to name a few.

Gilbert searches the room, walking and looking around until he sees Beauden standing at the bar conversing with a small group of people.

"Johnny, there he go...over there."

Gilbert nods his head, pointing in Beauden's direction. "Com'on, Fish."

Gilbert heedlessly follows Johnny to the bar, "Hey man, what's up?"

"Johnny...Johnny and old Fish-head," says Beauden putting out his hand, "My Man. What's been happen'n with you?"

Johnny and Gilbert give Beauden a soulful handshake.

"Nuth'n much. Just chill'n," says Johnny.

Gilbert adds, "You got it, Beau Man."

Johnny gazes at the people standing around and he is somewhat uncomfortable, "Man, I gotta to talk to you...alone", he says pushing his way through the people and leaning toward Beauden.

"Ah, Johnny Man, everythang's cool. Just hold up...I want you to meet somebody."

Beauden with his slick stride steps over to Dexx Barone, one of the people standing around the bar with him. Johnny and Gilbert's anticipation grows, watching Beauden shifts from one side to the other, as he speak confidentially, whispering into Dexx's ear, "Dexx, Man, I want you to meet somebody." Dexx takes one step away from the bar.

"Dexx, Man...I want to meet Johnny...and this is his sidekick, Gilbert. They're cool peeps."

Johnny and Gilbert give a soulful gesture, the brotherhood salute.

"Hey Man, please to meet you," Johnny says.

Dexx replies, "Likewise I'm sure."

"Dexx, these are the fellows I was tell'n you 'bout."

Dexx casually nods his head, "Um...okay."

Out of nowhere, Beauden takes another looks at Gilbert and starts to laugh uncontrollably. "Ha...aha, Eeee.e.e.e, Man, every time I see your as... I think of fish. Dexx, look at him, look at him Man. Now...don't his as... look like a fish? E.e.e.a ah...look at those lips! Dam... he even got fish lips."

151

Simultaneously, everyone takes a quick look at Gilbert.

"I ain't try'n to be funny man, but what in the hell was your momma think'n when she was f...'n your daddy?"

Gilbert puts several fingers to his lips, stroking them, reassuring himself. "Man, all the women love these lips. I don't know what in the hell you're talk'n 'bout."

"Fish, you got those pus... sucking lips," Beauden adds.

"Man gone, ain't a dam... thing wrong with my lips."

Beauden slaps Gilbert across his back, laughing, almost knocking him off his feet as he grabs hold of the bar's railing for support. "Hey, you know...ha ah e.e.e...how I know? Cause I got 'em too, eee..e..e..ah."

"Man, leave the man alone," says Dexx.

"Eeeeuu..e...eu ah...okay...okay. Ah...ah. I'm just tease'n with you. We still cool Man, ain't we? Fish, there's one thang I do like and that is some good pus... There ain't nuth'n like a good piece of as..., hot and juicy, lay'n up and wait'n for me."

Dexx interrupts, "Beauden...one day, pus... is gonna get your horny as... killed."

Beauden continues to laugh, gazing around the pool hall. Ultimately, he sees a big-busted, big booty woman standing by a juke box, wearing a mini so short you can almost see her panties when she leans, dropping her quarters into the coin slot of the juke box. "Look-a-here...Look-a-here...Do you see what I see?"

Beauden sticks out his tongue, licks his lips and points with it, wiggling it up, down and around. "Look at that piece of as... over there. Whoa...Come and get me, baby...Umm..um..um. Daddy's waitin over here. If I ever get stuck up in that, I would have no choice but to believe, I've died and gone to heaven...Umm Um, " continues Beauden.

"Man, I didn't come all the way over here to hear all this BS. I got business to take care of," declares Johnny.

Beauden agrees, "You right Man...No problem. That's cool. Business is business and business always comes first, right before pus..."

Dexx stands up. "Let's go into my office, we can talk there." The three men follow him into a back room office.

"Come on in and have a seat."

They all sit together, encircling Dexx's desk. "What can I do for you fellas?" ask Dexx.

"Dexx, these are the guys I was tell'n you 'bout. They need a Roscoe," answers Beauden.

"So, you guys need a piece. Am I right?" ask Dexx.

Johnny quickly answers, "Yeah. What you got?"

"Hold up, nigga...First things first. How much are you talking? Then you'll know what I got."

"I got two bills," replies Johnny pulling his money out of his pocket and laying it on the desk. Dexx takes out a small suitcase; he opens it, holds up a gun for Johnny to view.

Johnny gets up and goes to examine the piece. "Let me see!"

Dexx hands Johnny the gun and he aims, looking into the picture mirror on the wall, at his reflection. He smiles, "Yeah...This is cool. Real sweet."

"Johnny, you can blow a mother-f... head off with that baby," responds Gilbert.

"Two mother-f...," says Johnny as he continues to point the gun at his reflection. "I'll take it. Yeah, this baby is gonna do all right." Johnny pushes the money closer to Dexx.

"You guys need some shells with that?" ask Dexx.

"Hey. You can't shoot no gun without bullets," laughs Johnny.

"That's true Johnny, Ha aha," says Gilbert, also Johnny's yes man.

Dexx reaches into his suitcase and hands Johnny a box of bullets. Johnny admirer his new found status, feeling like a big man. "Hey, baby...you and me are gonna be all right." He squeezes it tight.

Gilbert gets out of his chair and walks toward Johnny with a ridiculous smirk, "Hey...Dexx, you got another one like that?"

"Aye, you guys ain't plan'n on knock'n over no gas station? Ee.e.e," Beauden ask, relaxing back in his chair, swinging one leg across the other.

"Nah Man, that's kid stuff, we're in the big league now," Johnny replies with a cocky attitude.

Without thinking, Gilbert blurts, "We gonna kill..."

Dexx abruptly interrupts him, "Fish, I don't need to know your business, all right. You want a Roscoe. I sold you a Roscoe and that's all I need to know."

Johnny and Gilbert reply, "That's cool Man...No problem. Yeah, no problem at all. Our business is our business."

Dexx defines the gun's short history, "Don't get stopped by the police, these guns are cheap for a reason." Dexx takes another gun out of his case. "Now this bit... here, she's still hot. A mother-f...er got his head blown off last month and they're still wondering how she come up missing from the police station; this baby here, she's been missing for two weeks now."

"Yeah, all that was left was his neck. His own mother couldn't identify his as... E....e.e..e," laughs Beauden.

Dexx hands the gun to Gilbert and he is extremely impressed, "Would you look at that, Johnny? She's sweet, a pretty thang, and smooth as silk... Yeah. Ra`h Silk."

"How much?" inquires Johnny.

"I'll tell you what...give me another bill and we'll call it even." Gilbert instantly reaches into his pocket for the money.

"Hey...that's straight. I got that, thanks Man. Dexx you're real cool peeples."

Johnny and Gilbert's dream is about to come true, they have been watching the donut shop for weeks. But this particular morning Gilbert is standing on the corner adjacent from the donut shop, scouting out the place, waiting patiently. This is the same donut shop where Officer Peck and Officer Mulligan stop almost every morning around 3am for a snack.

At 3:05am, Gilbert notices a police car driving into the parking lot and stopping at the front entrance, he looks callously at the officers. Gilbert walks back to their car parked across the street where Johnny is asleep in the back seat. Gilbert softly knocks on the windshield with his knuckles.

"Johnny...Johnny wake up." Gil-man keeps his cool and his eyes focus on the officer's every move. "They're here."

Johnny quickly sits up, hitting himself in the head with his own gun and glances across the street at the police car. Officer Peck gets out of the car and goes inside the donut shop.

Gilbert assures Johnny, "The one who shot Mark first is still in the car."

"Then, that's the one I want first. I've been a wait'n for that punk as... pig. Uh...wait'n too long."

Slowly Johnny gets out of the car and they hurry across the street to the police vehicle.

Gilbert takes his stand at the side of the shop's entrance waiting for Officer Peck to come out. Johnny bends slightly, holding the gun behind his hip, approaching the vehicle's front passenger window and looks in. He eases his gun hand up, pointing the gun at Officer Mulligan who's writing on his report pad. Suddenly he turns looking into Johnny's face. But before Officer Mulligan realizes anything is wrong, Johnny says, "Hey mother f... this is for my brother, Mark."

Johnny hurriedly pulls the trigger twice. Officer Mulligan is shot dead with two bullets to the head.

Johnny's taste for revenge is finally satisfied, as he watches the blood pour from the officer's head just like it poured from his brother, Mark. "That's for my Momma too. That's right, you punk cop you'll never kill another brother again...nobody's brother."

Officer Peck runs out of the shop with his gun drawn and notices Gilbert standing at the side of the building entrance aiming a gun at him. Gilbert hesitates with his shot, he is having second thoughts, and Officer Peck shoots Gilbert in the chest. Johnny quickly looks up at Gilbert and notices him falling to the ground.

Officer Peck turns toward Johnny and starts shooting. Johnny quickly squats behind the police vehicle and returns the shots, shooting Officer Peck in his leg and then in the chest.

Officer Peck is also killed. Johnny rushes to Gilbert, trying to lift him up off the ground, but he is too heavy to carry.

Johnny drags him across the street to the car as his blood trails. "Fish...you okay? Fish, com'on Man. I got you. I got you, buddy. You gonna be all right. Everythang is gonna be all right, just stay cool, Man. You'll see, just wait, everythang's gonna be cool Fish." Johnny opens the door, immediately pushing Gilbert into the car, runs around to the other side and gets in, pushing his pedal to the floor and expeditiously drives away.

"Johnny take me home! Nobody's there."

Johnny parks the car in the alley behind Gilbert's house, pulls him out of the car, one leg drags as he carries him through the backdoor.

"Johnny, take me down in the basement...downstairs there's a couch."

"No problem, Fish. I got you," Johnny lays him on the couch and franticly looks around for a rag.

"I gotta find somethang, anythang to stop the bleed'n, Fish."

"I ain't gonna make it, Johnny Man."

"You'll make it, Fish."

"No, I know I ain't...I can feel it, Johnny."

"Stop talk'n like that Fish."

"Johnny...I'm gonna die."

"Fish, shut-up, you're make'n me nervous...you ain't go'n nowhere, you hear me, we're partners, remember? Don't nobody bother us no mo."

Johnny dashes to the sink and takes an old rag that is hanging, he runs cold water over it, then twists it just a bit. He hurries across the basement floor as the water steadily drips, pressing it against Gilbert's wound and sorrowfully looking at his friend and trying his best to help him.

"Man I can't stop the bleeding. Gilbert I gotta...let me get somebody, we gotta get this bullet out of you, that's the only way the bleed'n will stop. I gotta call Beau." Johnny stands, he is about to go for the phone, but before he could take one step Gilbert grabs hold of Johnny's arm.

"No, Johnny, don't leave me...please. I...I...don't leave yet."

"Fish, I gotta do somethang."

"They're gonna come look'n for ya, Man," says Gilbert.

"I know that Fish...Let's not talk about that right now."

"Give me your gun, Johnny?" ask Gilbert.

Johnny surprised and frightened, "What...my gun? What you gonna do?" Johnny hesitates before realizing what Fish is trying to do and he refuses.

"No, I can't do that, Fish."

"Johnny, I'm already dead. Now give me the gun. This way the police will never know...who killed who."

"Fish...Man, I can't. You're like my brother, Man. I can't let you go down like that."

"Dam... Johnny it's the only way...Now give me the gun."

Gilbert is right, he was dying and they both know it.

"Man, go home," says Gilbert, coughing up blood that is starting to settle in his throat. "Hey, take care of your momma, you're all she's got left."

He coughs again as the blood spatters, quickly he covers his mouth with his hand, "Now give me the gun."

Johnny wipes the gun down, clearing it of his fingerprints with the rag and hands it to Gilbert. Gilbert takes the gun, gripping it as tight as he can with both hands.

"Thanks Man, I'll never forget this," says Johnny.

Taking a short breath, Gilbert coughs one last time as the gun falls from his hand. Johnny sadly drops his head into his hands, his tears spontaneously fills his eyes as he says, "Damu Daraka. Damu Daraka, Fish, my brother."

Raymond seems to be moving up in the world and fast; he has a new job in the accounting office and all his co-workers thinks he is a pretty nice guy too.

Ms. Connie Landull is Raymond's boss and she is very pleased with his performance, especially, his overtime performance, on and off the job. Raymond has been secretly having an affair with his boss for several months.

Ms. Connie Landull has been divorced for approximately two years due to her extra marital activities. She finds it very difficult, especially when it comes to keeping her hands off the new male employees. Connie will always tease her friends by saying: "It's only the good-looking ones I can't resist." Connie is a sex addict and she has continuously found reasons for Raymond to work late at least two or three nights a week. She wants him and there is nothing stopping her from getting him. She is the boss.

Landull Construction is a family-owned business started by her grandfather some years ago. And after her father's death, being the only child, she inherited everything. Connie's mother didn't want anything to do with the business because it reminded her of Connie's father and the memories they shared, building the business up to what it is today, those memories were just too impossible to bear.

Raymond gathers the finished production performance sheets from his desk and heads for Ms. Landull's office. Discreetly, he knocks on her door before entering, even though all his co-workers already know what's going on. Raymond and Connie's behavior has never been the regular employer-employee relationship.

"Here's the report you asked for, Ms. Landull and everything looks great."

"Come in Mr. Smith, and close the door behind you, please?"

"Sure...Ms. Landull." Raymond does exactly what he is told. She takes the sheets from Raymond never giving them a glance.

"That's true. Mr. Smith, everything looks great." Connie's directly focuses on the crotch of Raymond's pants. So she gets out of her chair, seductively approaching him, getting as close as she can, gently and sensually pushing her thigh between his legs, pressing her mouth against his.

"What time do you want me to come by tonight?" Raymond asks.

"The same time as usually...bed time. If not sooner."

They kiss and converse for several minutes. "I'll be there with wine and roses."

"I know you will...but what about your little, wifey-poo? Won't she miss you again tonight?"

"Let me worry about her."

The phone rings, but his alluring embrace is too irresistible to let go. Raymond's heart and mind is all tied up in knots about Connie.

"You better get back to work, before..."

"Umm...I know...I know. It's so hard to leave someone so beautiful," he says. They kiss several more times before Raymond leaves her office.

Raymond never calls Elayne to tell her when or if he is going to be late, nor does he inform her on those certain nights, that he is not coming home. The one morning after waking up in Connie's bed, Raymond slowly rolls onto his side passionately placing his lips on Connie's breast, kissing each nipple one after another, as he lies there fantasizing and enjoying her every touch. Raymond is truly living the life, every man's dream - one woman at home and another woman in his arms whenever he wants.

At least that what he thinks, until Connie makes an unexpected request, "I can't stand it when you leave me like this, Raymond. It never fails, whenever you stay the night you always rush out of my bed and back to hers. Raymond, I feel nasty and cheap. Don't you love me? You can't make love to me like that and say you don't love me, and yet love her too. Anyway she only gets the little bits that I leave between us...seconds."

Raymond is stunned by Connie's accusation and statements, lying there as if he is frozen to the bed, all the while staring up at the ceiling.

"What Connie? What are you talking about?"

"I want you to move in with me," she says.

"What? Move in. But I'm married."

"You said you love me...I don't want to share your love with any other woman, nobody at all. I want you all to myself, Raymond, every first, second, and third of you. "

Raymond quickly sits up, ceaselessly rubbing his head. 'This wasn't in the cards,' he thinks. He ponders, trying to figure this whole thing out. 'What in the hell am I gonna do or say now?'

Connie eases behind him, kissing his naked back, setting her sexual trap as she convinces him to leave his pregnant wife. Raymond pulls her around in front of him laying her across his lap.

"Connie. I..." Before Raymond can say another word he is bewitched by her kiss, her touch and her perfectly beautiful contour body pressing against his. She holds him, teasing him with erotic foreplay, touching him in his most sensitive area before placing it into her mouth. Then she slowly moves on top of him, sexually propositioning herself, devouring him as she takes total control of his senses.

It is late morning, almost noon when Raymond returns home. Elayne and her three friends are out shopping for baby necessities. Elayne's due date is approaching fast, only five and half weeks to go before their new baby arrives.

Elayne gets out of the car waving good-bye to her three friends. "Bye ya'll."

"Oh, wait Elayne, let me feel it one more time? Is the baby still kicking?" ask Candice, impatiently getting out of the car with her.

"Candice, by the time the baby's born it won't have a hard time recognize'n you at all. That baby will know Candice," says D'La.

"Yes, Elayne you better watch out, I think Candice thinks she is having this baby for you," laughs Shi Li.

"Candice don't pay them any attention. You can touch my stomach anytime."

"Elayne you do not look very good, you are starting to look weary," says Shi Li.

D'La adds, "That's because she's hardhead. She knows pregnant women need sleep. Lots of sleep...So get your butt in the house and lay down before that baby come out look'n tire and goofy...The last thang we need is for that baby to come out look'n like Raymond."

"Elayne, D'La is right. You do not have very long to go. You will need all the rest you can get," says Shi Li.

"You all sound like a bunch of mother hens. I'll talk to ya'll later," replies Elayne.

Candice gets back into the car as the three yell their good-byes.

"Call us if you need anythang and get some rest," says D'La, waving and yelling as they drive off.

Elayne rushes into the house, dropping her bags on the floor, heading for the bathroom. Once in the bathroom she hears a noise, someone is in the house. After adjusting her clothing she peeks into the bedroom. She is startled by Raymond presence because he is supposed to be at work, she rushes toward him, "Hi,

Honey, did you miss me? Happily she hurries into the front room, picks up her bags and rushes back into the bedroom to show him.

"I was out shopping. Shi Li and Candice picked out some beautiful baby things. Look!"

As she lays the baby clothes on the bed, she realizes Raymond is not paying any attention and she also notices the suitcase on the bed.

"Raymond, are we going somewhere?'

He answers irascibly. His tone is heavy and rude, "NO! I'm going somewhere."

Disturbed by his answer Elayne instantly drops the baby outfits. Raymond's heart has turned cold and she didn't understand his reason, yet he continues to pack and ignore her.

Elayne fearfully realizes that she is being abandoned, but she has to ask to be sure. Maybe she is wrong about what is happening; maybe she is imagining the entire situation. "You're leavin me?"

He says nothing. He didn't even look up.

"Raymond, are you leavin me, why? ...Why Raymond? ...What did I do? Tell me! What did I do to you? ...What about the baby?"

Raymond goes into the closet, removing any and all clothing hanging there. "This kind of a life ain't for me. I should have never married you in the first place. I only married you cause I was trying to be nice...Trying to do the right thang."

Raymond's answers are becoming even ruder by the minute and his behavior was worse than his words. Shocked, distressed and confused, Elayne vigorously throws herself in front of him, clutching tightly, kissing him and whispering into his ear.

"I thought you loved me. You said you would always love me...Remember on our wedding day, you vowed, you promised. Don't leave please Raymond! Don't go...I need you, our baby needs you.

He shakes his head and still he ignores her as she continues to plead.

"WHY RAYMOND...WHY...WHAT DID I DO WRONG?"

Raymond snatches his head away; rejecting her, refusing to hear another word, then abruptly pushes Elayne onto the bed.

"STOP! DON'T PUT YOUR HANDS ON ME!"

Elayne quickly jumps to her feet, tossing her pregnant body at him again, "RAYMOND...NO...DON'T DO THIS! I love you so much. PLEASE...give me one more chance? I can be a good wife...Please Raymond, okay? ...My whole world evolves around you and our baby. Don't walk out on our family...All I need is just one more chance! I'll make it up to you honey, baby. You just wait and see. Please Raymond PLEASE?"

Raymond grabs the baby clothes off the bed. "You see this? Look around you. This house, that baby, all this...this ain't me. I'm not the husband type...And I'm dam... sure not the father type. It's not in my blood, Elayne."

Raymond throws the baby clothes across the room to the floor. "IT'S NOT IN ME, WOMAN...You should know that."

Elayne reaches for her husband, still Raymond's heart is cold as he yells louder at her, "NOW, GET OFF ME AND DON'T TOUCH ME AGAIN."

Elayne can't believe his iced demeanor as he pushes her, this time to the floor. Elayne screams his name again, "AHHA...ahaa, RAYMOND, RAYMOND...WHY...WHY? Tell me what did I do wrong? Baby I love you, please NO, NO...Just tell me."

Raymond squats down in front of her, taking her by the arm, then by the wrist, he squeezes it as tight as he can before twisting it.

"Why...you wanna know WHY? ...Because I DON'T LOVE YOU, that's WHY. All those nights when I didn't come home, did you actually think I was working LATE?"

"I thought you were workin late so we could have extra money for the baby," cries Elayne as she struggles to free herself.

"How foolish can you be?"

The look of insanity overwhelms his face and his eyes expand, rolling around in his head. Elayne has never seen Raymond act so crazy.

"Every night of the week, Elayne, you can't be that stupid. WAKE UP, ELAYNE...There's another woman and she makes me feel like the man you can't. Now, since you can't see what's going on for yourself, maybe you better go and ask The Lord...YEAH...he'll answer you...pray Elayne, cause I'm gone...SEE YA."

Raymond walks out of the bedroom carrying his suitcases, heading for the front door. Feeling degraded and with that deep pain inside that hurt so bad, Elayne leaps off the floor holding her arm, hollering as she runs after him. Raymond continues to ignore her pleas as he opens the front door. Elayne throws her body in front of the door.

"Raymond...Raymond, wait...Please, Raymond." She screams as loud as she can, "NO...DON'T GO...WE CAN TALK IT OVER, WE CAN WORK THANGS OUT, CAN'T WE? ...I LOVE YOU.

No, please. You're making a big MISTAKE, I CAN FEEL IT...NO...o...oh... oh"

Raymond grabs Elayne by her blouse, pulling her toward him, then pushing her against the door slamming it close. Then he grabs her around the neck and squeezes it, choking her. She can't breath. Elayne gasps for air as Raymond whispers in a mild and scary voice, "You love me. You love me. One time with you and you're PREGNANT. How in the HELL do I know that's my baby? As far as I know, that could be ANYBODY'S baby. You and your friends, you're all a bunch of HO...S."

Raymond releases Elayne as she slaps him across the face. "THAT'S NOT TRUE AND YOU KNOW IT."

For that one minute 'only' everything's silent as Raymond's blood begins to boil. Outraged that Elayne would even think about laying a hand on him, his gorgeous face.

"BIT... ARE YOU CRAZY?" Raymond grabs Elayne around the neck with one hand and beats her with the other, hitting her as hard as he can, knocking her over the telephone table. Then he snatches her by the blouse collar and drags her into the living room where the beating continues.

When he finishes, he goes into the bathroom to check his appearance, "Nope not a scratch." He continues to admire himself as he washes his hands, his face, before neatly combing his hair back into place.

"Yeah, everythang's still cool, you handsome dude...you."

In less than five minutes, Raymond returns to the front room, peeks at Elayne who is semi-conscious and laying on the floor in a fetal position. With no remorse, his head high and his chest out, he takes his suitcases and walks out the door.

Confused and broken-hearted Elayne made not a sound as the sharp pains traveled through her bleeding body. Silently praying and asking, "Lord, tell me, what in the world could I have possibly done to deserve such treatment from a man who promised to love and cherish me forever? ...He's my husband, Lord. Please tell me?

Then she adds, "And why Lord did YOU turn your back to me when I needed YOU so desperately? Lord it seems...No matter how hard I try to do right, I'm always wrong." Elayne instantaneously blacks out.

Hours later, Elayne is waken by sharp piercing pains charging through her body, practically immobilizing her every move. She fears for the baby, but still she crawls toward the phone that has been knocked to the floor during the fight. There is no dial tone; it's dead. She presses the receiver several times, then finally, dialing.

She moans, "Oh...ooa. Hello, Shi Li. Yaaha..ow...ooo," she moans again.

"Elayne is that you?" Shi Li asks.

"Shi Li help me. It's the baby, hurry; Oaaooa."

"I am on my way," says Shi Li hanging up the phone. She runs out of her dorm room and gets into her car. Shi Li is terrified because all she can think about is what could have happened, when and how, she knows it is too early for the baby to be born. Something has to be wrong.

When Shi Li arrives, she finds the front door slightly open. So she walks in and sees Elayne lying on the floor curled in a knot, her knees and arms circled around her stomach. Her clothes are bloody and torn, her face swollen, there are bruises everywhere, and small cuts on her neck, arms and legs.

"Elayne...Elayne...I am here. Just lay still. I am going to call an ambulance."

Not only does Shi Li call the ambulance but she also calls D'La and Candice. The ambulance stops in front of Elayne's house, the nosey neighbors watching and pointing fingers talking about all the screaming they heard as the paramedics carries Elayne out rushing her to the hospital. Within thirty minutes Elayne gives birth to a tiny beautiful five pound one ounce baby girl; and she looks just like her father.

Things are finally peaceful as the three friends encircle Elayne's hospital bed and longing for answers.

Shi Li is the first to ask, "Elayne, what happened at the house?" But Elayne ignores the question and says nothing.

"That dam... Raymond did this to you, didn't he?" demands D'La, staring at Elayne as she rolls her eyes at Shi Li. "Shi Li, that's what happened, it was that dam... Raymond. I can just feel it. Elayne is hiding somethang...That no good nigga."

Still Elayne keeps silent, protecting him. She acts as if nothing happened. She is traumatized. And still, Elayne refuses to give any details to the circumstances surrounding her ordeal. She only stares at the wall every time Raymond's name is mentioned, as if she could see right through it and he is on the other side.

Candice walks into the room, approaching Elayne's bed. "I called Raymond's job but he didn't come to work today. And I even called the house, but he's not there either. I tried everyone I could think of. "

D'La isn't letting up. She is determined to get answers, "I wanna know where in the hell is that f...? That's all I want know? Gotta wife laid up in a hospital, who just gave birth to his baby and he's nowhere to be found. This is some f... up sh..., if you ask me."

Without batting an eye D'La gazes at Elayne. "Elayne, you betta stop protecting that as... and put that mother behind bars where he belong. Anytime a man do some sh... like this, he don't love you. A man always acts an as... when he's got another woman, especially if he's gonna beat you like this. And a lot of times, men do stupid sh... cause they know a woman ain't gonna do anythang about it, anyway."

Despite D'La's words, Elayne ignores her. "I wanna see my baby. Ask the nurse if she can bring her to me?"

Candice goes to the nurse's station and the baby is brought to her mother. The girls intimately gather around Elayne's bed admiring the sweet bundle of joy.

"She is so beautiful...Elayne", says Shi Li.

"And so tiny too," says D'La.

"Ooo, she looks just like a baby doll I had when I was a little girl," admires Candice.

Brokenheartedly Elayne interrupts; she stares at the baby, while kissing her tiny fingers, as her heart continues to tear apart as the pain consumes her. "Raymond's gone now...and if anything happen to me, I want all of you to take care of her," says Elayne as she continues to play with the baby's fingers. Yet, her thought, her inner emotions carry her deeper within, wondering: 'Why, did The Lord turn his back to me? And how could a man beat a woman so badly? He said he loved me.'

"Ah, Elayne, ain't nuth'n gonna happen to you, girl. Don't be talk'n like that," assures D'La.

"I know, but just in case...cause her daddy don't care nuth'n about her. I want my baby to know that we love her. I don't ever want her to feel alone or lost in this cruel world...Just as all of you have been there for me, I want you to be there for her. No matter what!"

Shi Li gently touches the baby's hands, "Don't worry Elayne, we will be there for her always...What are you going to name her?"

"Well, I'm think'n about naming her Janal Chimaia Smith."

"Dam... how in the hell do you spell that?" ask D'La.

Elayne finds it hard not to smile because it never fails; D'La and Candice are always asking ridiculous questions.

"D'La, don't worry, I'll write it down for you later."

"Funny...real funny, Elayne," replies D'La.

"I think that's beautiful. Different, but beautiful." agrees Candice.

"I want something different. I think it's time for a change."

"I think it fits her well. A unique and beautiful name for a unique and beautiful young lady she will grow up to be," expresses Shi Li.

Elayne continues, "I know...That's why I'm asking all of you to be her guardian mothers."

Everyone smiles, shaking their heads, in absolute agreement, all except D'La who is seriously contemplating before shouting, "GUARDIAN MOTHER...You lost me on that one. I don't know how to be a mother, burp a baby, or change diapers. What if I stick her with a pin or somethang? No, I can't be a MOTHER...All I know is how to wire cars, and build thangs. Can I be the guardian father?"

The room is filled with silent as everyone quickly stares at D'La; then suddenly they all burst into laughter.

"Yeah, it's funny. Okay, okay. Yeah, ya'll just keep laughin'", says D'La before smirking.

Within the first year of Janal's birth Elayne starts to drink. The memories of her marriage to Raymond keep taunting her, reminiscing on how things were and could have been and what cause it to fail. Many days and nights went by, and yet she wonders why Raymond has not called to inquirer about his daughter. Elayne finds it hard to believe even to this day. 'Did he really mean the things he said? The sound of his voice so angry so full of hate. Where did it all come from and why? Everything went sour in such a short period.' Nevertheless, her heart has started to rot, still believing that The Lord has turned his back to her. Elayne finds the reality of the situation hard to deal with. With each day of Raymond's absence soon turns into weeks and then months her drinking becomes heavier. Feeling sorry for herself, her religious beliefs shortly becomes her enemy and she inevitably abandons her father's church, and barters with the Devil.

ONLY DEAD MEN CRY

CHAPTER 11

The year is steadily passing and everything seems perfect for the two lovebirds; Raymond's just rolling over from a good night sleep and an incredible night of lovemaking. Yet another day, another dollar to be made as he toys with the idea of getting up and going to work. Connie is already preparing for her day, after taking her shower she comes out of the bathroom and goes to Raymond who is pushing back the blankets as he rolls over on his side. Her towel drops while bending over him as her breasts gently strokes him across the face.

"Good morning, sleepy head."

Raymond reaches for her, taking her into his arms and pulling her down on top of him, "Ummm...Hey Baby, good morning to you."

"You better get up before you're late for work."

"How can I be late when I'm sleeping with the boss?" Raymond smiles, "But true enough, I must admit, it's about that time for me to be getting my butt on outta here."

He kisses and licks Connie's breast a few more times before letting go.

"Yes it is. Now, hurry up, Ray."

Connie sits next to him. "Oh...I got some errands to do this morning, so I won't be in the office until noon."

"What kind of errands?" with a mesmerizing smile he asks.

"Just some errands. If I tell you everything I wouldn't have any secrets my love."

Connie is a captivating and sexy woman, her beautiful creamy white skin, her sensual touch, and the lovemaking is always hot and steamy.

Raymond takes Connie by the hand and sucks one of her fingers at a time before placing his hand between her legs. "Umm...Baby you are so delicious. I hate getting up when you're tasting so good."

Connie kisses Raymond forehead then goes to the closet to get her clothes. After getting dress, she slowly turns and blows him a kiss from her hand. "I love you, Ray."

"I love you, Baby."

Raymond's exceptionally happy with his relationship with Connie. He smiles as he returns a kiss from his hand. Yeah Raymond's the man, he has a beautiful, wealthy, intelligent woman all rolled into one 'hell of a package'. Most of all, Connie is very generous, giving Raymond everything a man could ever want.

That afternoon Connie didn't get to work till one o'clock and Raymond is worried out of head. He has been watching the clock, counting every minute until she arrived. He follows her into her office as she walks through the door, "What took you so long? I was starting to go crazy."

Raymond is relieved to know she is all right and he can hardly wait to put his arms around her. "What am I going to do with you? Ummm...Baby...I miss you."

"I had to get some things changed."

"Yeah...some things? Like what kind of things?" he asks.

Connie's stride is delightfully sensual, smooth like at a cat, and very pleasing to any man's eyes as she slowly eases away from Raymond. She reaches into her blouse pocket and hands him a note. He reads it. Within that one short breath, her warm and beautiful personality instantly changes right in front of Raymond's eyes. Connie becomes cold and lifeless as her facial expression quickly freezes.

Raymond is outraged, "WHAT...A PINK SLIP? Connie, you gotta be kidding me, Baby."

"No...you're fired! You'll find all your belongings packed and waiting to be picked up outside the house, at the garage door."

Raymond laughs, he is in disbelief, "You can't be serious, ha..a..a. No woman has ever turned down Sweet Daddy Ray".

"Oh, but I am, Mr. Raymond Smith."

"Are you cracking up or something, woman? I'm the man. Every woman wants me. Look at me. Connie, you're been smoking too much weed, now you can't be serious!"

Connie immediately responds, "I'm bored with you and that little fellow you call KING. He's just not living up to his royal duties and I can't fake it anymore. I'm bored with it and you...and I don't want to waste anymore time pretending. Ray Baby, as one lover to another, I'm pretty sure you understand how I feel, don't you, Sweetie! So take your things out of your desk and get out."

Raymond temper immediately explodes. "You...YOU...BIT...!"

But Connie's disposition is laid back, very cool, and that outrages Raymond more. He becomes hysterical, and with a tight fist he rushes toward her. But Connie's no fool, she knew Raymond would act ridiculously violent and she was prepared. Security is readily stationed outside of her office door once Raymond entered.

In a mild tone she says, "At...At...At...SECURITY!"

Quickly three security guards enter the office.

"I gave up my wife, my family for your as... I don't believe this sh... Connie this has got to be some joke, right!"

Connie continues to be as cold as ice. "Believe it, if you don't, you soon will...Security, show Mr. Smith the way out please."

Infuriated, humiliated, his ego cut down like tall grass, with one hand Raymond pushes everything off of Connie's desk knocking it to the floor. Security grabs Raymond. He tries to break free as the hit one in his mouth. Almost dragging Raymond, they escort him out of the building, practically throwing him on the trunk of his car. Raymond leaps at one of the guards, punching him in the stomach. Security gladly retaliates. Raymond is knocked to the ground, kicked and dragged to the driver's side of his car. Holding his chest, he gets up on his feet, opens the door and yells, " F... YOU CONNIE...F... ALL OF YOU. I DIDN'T LIKE WORKING HERE ANYWAY." He cusses all the way to Connie's house.

After picking up his belongings outside of the garage, Raymond realizes that the player has been played. Feeling like a fool, he finds himself thinking about his wife and the baby he has never seen.

"I'm going home."

When he arrives at the house he parks across the street, approximately three doors down, just in case Elayne is sitting or standing on the porch. He does not want her to see him, not yet anyway. Remembering the circumstances of how he left, how he beat his wife so severely, Raymond is afraid and too nervous to get out of the car. So he sits, thinking for over two hours, what can he possibly say and possibly do after all he had done?

"I don't even know what to say to her or how to say it. Dam... I don't even know if the baby is a boy or a girl." He hits the dash-broad and says, "Hell, she probably hates me by now, anyway."

So Raymond sit, thinking and watching the house where he once lived, as all kinds of thoughts run through his head. "F..., this sh... is all f... up. How could I be so stupid? Hell nah, I ain't going in there. She probably got another man in her life by now. And my baby probably thinks that man is its daddy. She probably found somebody who is treating her right...Plus, after all the sh... I did to her, I know she don't want to see me." Raymond starts his engine and drives away.

Candice is becoming very emotional, unstable after her rape. Flashes of that horrible night torments her with each passing day and she is finding it almost impossible to sleep. It feels as though something is eating away at her soul, something evil, and her self-esteem is breaking down fast. Everything she once thought was so beautiful, all of a sudden, was not. And all she wants and needs, is a change of scenery, and she knows that leaving the city is the best thing to do, a least for a while, so she decide to move to Paris, France to continues her education.

August 1971, Metro airport: Shi Li, Elayne and D'La are saying good-bye to Candice near the terminal.

"I'm going to miss you so much. But, it's only for a short visit and I'll be home from school during my fall and summer breaks," cries Candice.

"It's not gonna be the same without you," cries Elayne, holding Candice tightly.

"Remember, Candice, if you ever need anything, do not hesitate to call. We will be there faster then you can say...well anything, just call us if you need us," declares Shi Li.

"I know you will, but I won't need anything. My heart is always with you. All of you," replies Candice with eyes full of tears.

"Yeah, and ours will be with you!" D'La smirks as she tries to camouflage her tears by poking her finger in her eyes.

Candice bends down and picks up Janal, now six months old, out of her stroller. "Now, this little princess here, I will certainly miss. Janal, I love you with all my heart. I'll sell my soul for you." Candice kisses Janal several times before putting her back into the stroller.

"Yep, that's a true statement Candice, we all will," agrees D'La.

"Look how she's lookin at you Candice, I believe Janal understands what you said," with joyful tears, expresses Elayne.

"Of course, she understands, she is apart of us all, and the spirit of the dragon will protect her too," explains Shi Li.

"Well, I think I'm gonna need some of that dragon stuff in my life, Shi Li," grins D'La, "Can you sprinkle a little bit of that dragon stuff my way when we get home?"

The four friends embrace one another, saying their good-byes, as Candice attempts to board the plane.

"I love you. I love you all. And take care of each other," waves Candice as she gradually enters the terminal. "I'll call you when I get there. Take care...Bye. I'll be back soon."

It's been six months since Candice's arrival and enrolling in one of Paris' finest universities. It looks as though Candice is finally letting go and trying to move on with her life. The change of scenery seems to have worked wonders.

One day while studying in the university's library, two young ladies have come to introduce themselves; Candice has seen them around the courtyard many times before.

"Hi, we don't mean to be rude or anything, but we've been admiring how beautiful you are and you seem to be a nice person, so we thought that we'd come over and introduce ourselves. You know, say hello!"

Candice's quick to set things straight, "Sorry, but I'm not gay!"

"No. No. We are not gay! Don't get me wrong, there's nothing wrong with gay people if that's your preference, but we're not, truly. You're in my calculus class and I thought we'd say hello. My name is Monique and this is Sheri. We noticed that you are new around here, so we thought that you might need to know someone. You know, maybe we can be friends or something. I remember my first day here at the university and how hard it was for me to meet nice people.

"Then she met me," says Sheri, interrupting.

"That's very polite of you to think of me, but..." Candice shows no interest in their conversation and before Candice can finish her sentence, Sheri intervenes by sticking out her hand.

"Here's our number, just call if you ever want to party."

Candice takes the piece of paper and puts it into her purse, "Well, thanks," smiles Candice.

A month later, while Candice is walking through the university's corridors, "Candice, Candice," calls Monique.

Candice stops and waits as Monique and Sheri hurries to her, "How did you do on your exam?"

"I think I passed," replies Candice.

"Great, let's celebrate. There's a party at a friend's house on Friday night and we want to invite you. It'll be a blast...Say you'll come, please say you'll come," expresses Sheri.

"Well, I don't know...I'll think about it," replies Candice.

"Just in case you decide to come, here's the address," says Monique while writing the address on a sheet of paper in her notepad, then quickly tears it out and hands it to Candice.

"It's really not that far from the university. I would say, it's about, fifteen to twenty minute cab...just on the other side of town," adds Monique.

"The place will be loaded with lots of wealthy gents, great food, and a live band...And as beautiful as you are, Candice, I know you'll love it, " says Sheri as she gives devilish wink that accents her sinful smile.

"Well, as I said before, I'll have to think about it Monique and Sheri, but thanks. "

It is Friday night and it seems that everyone in the dorm has plans; bored and lonely, Candice decides to go to the party. Once there, Candice catches sight of Monique and Sheri, and soon the three are truly having a good time; the best time since Candice left the states. And now, their next task is getting beyond the dorm mom, due to the fact, that they are five hours past their curfew, and foolishly drunk. Despite the task, sneaking back into the dorms was as much fun as the party.

While sitting in dining hall, one afternoon, Monique and Sheri decide to tell Candice about their extra curriculum. It has been their secret for a least three years and Candice would be the perfect candidate to join their private society; besides, they truly enjoy Candice's companionship. Moreover the questions remain, 'How would they go about it? What would they say to convince her to join? Mostly, can they trust Candice with their secret if she refuses?' Again, if anyone ever found out they would automatically be expelled from school. Yes, many questions roved their heads before presenting them to Candice.

It's been seven months since they met Candice and they have finally made up their minds that tonight would be the perfect night. Absolutely, because finals are over and everybody can, at last, relax.

About ten o'clock that evening, Monique and Sheri goes to Candice's dorm room and knock. Once opening the door Candice is surprised, yet happy to see them.

"Hi, Candice, were you asleep?" asks Monique.

"No, I was just reading."

"Good! Can we come in for a moment? We won't take long," assures Sheri.

"Sure, come in."

They confide in Candice, telling her all she needs to know, making her promise never to tell anyone about what she heard as they try to convince her to join them.

First, Candice is shocked to hear all about their secret fantasies and she most definitely refuses. Though after thinking about it for several weeks, Candice eventually accompanies Monique and Sheri during one of their ventures. Candice convinces herself into believing that this will also be the perfect opportunity to relieve her parents of their financial burden of paying the high cost of her tuition. Candice toys with any and every excuse she can think of, finding ways to clear her mind of what she is about to do. Moreover, what is truly bothering Candice, is that shameful night. The night that still haunts her to this day, the day of her attack, the day she vowed that every man would pay for that one night. The night her virginity was stolen. Now she realizes this is the perfect opportunity for 'pay back'.

It is not a house like Monique described, but an exquisite mansion. The servants are exceptionally polite, dressed accordingly, wearing black bow ties and black pants with stiff white shirts. There are lot of men and young beautiful women everywhere as she wanders.

"Oh Candice, I'm glad you made it. I was hoping you'd change your mind and come tonight," says Monique.

"Follow me Candice, I want to show you around," says Sheri. Candice, Monique/now Sylvia and Sheri/now Fawn walk out to the patio, as Monique promptly introduces Candice as Carmen to the lady of the house.

"Madam, this is Carmen."

"Carmen, what a pleasure to me you. I have heard so much about you. I'm Madam Brigitte...I see, Sylvia /Monique and Fawn /Sheri weren't lying, you are a very beautiful girl, Carmen."

"Thank you," says Candice.

"You'll do very well here."

Candice begins to looks around, she is nervous and apprehensive, having had any sexual contact since that horrible night and she is having second thoughts.

"Thank you," says Candice.

"Make yourself at home Carmen and if you need anything, don't hesitate to ask, the servants will be pleased to assist you," says Madam Brigitte.

"Thank you," repeats Candice.

"Sorry for introducing you as Carmen, but everyone here is someone their not, if you know what I mean", says Monique, "even us and we're regulars."

"Yes, even if you see them on the streets, you act as if you do not see them and never have", adds Sheri, "So enjoy, we'll talk to you later."

As Monique and Sheri disappear in the crowd, Candice begins to stroll around the grounds watching everybody and everything. People are talking and laughing as though they are all having a good time, while some of them make their way upstairs into private rooms.

Candice doesn't say a word to anyone at first; that is, until a sophisticated well-dressed man approaches her.

"Bonjour mademoiselle, my name is Monsieur Fatz," he says.

Looking at him you can tell why his name is Fatz. He is about 300 pounds or more, however every strand of his hair is perfectly placed, and he is perfectly dressed as well.

"Bonjour monsieur, my name is Carmen", says Candice, 'It seems as if everyone is somewhat familiar yet unfamiliar with each other just as Monique and Sheri said.' thinks Candice.

"I've never seen you here before."

"Non, I've never been here before," states Candice.

They talked for a while before he propositions her, first offering her five hundred dollars for one hour. Even though that is a lot of money and the going rate, Candice refuses. She wants more, double than what her friends are being paid.

"Excused me, Monsieur Fatz, but that would only pay for thirty minutes. However, one thousand dollars will get you the entire hour."

Candice constantly reminds herself of that night as she waits for his answer, her heart is beating fast and turning colder with every second as she remembers what Almond Joy once told her: 'If you wanna lay, you gotta pay. If you want free pus..., you can go home to your wife or your girlfriend. Special pus..., wild street pus... is gonna cost.'

He smiles, "Carmen you must be the special one, Oui?"

Candice smiles back, her facial expression frozen, "Oui, very special."

He agrees as he follows her, making their way upstairs. His eyes constantly focus on Candice's seductive, elegant stroll and the swaying of her hips.

October 1973, Janal is twenty months old, with a liquor bottle in one hand, and a spoon in the another, Elayne is having a hard time feeding her daughter her dinner. Additionally, Elayne is too drunk to hold the spoon steady and the food is all over Janal's face and clothes. Every time she drops the spoon, or misses putting it in Janal's mouth, Elayne finds a reason to take another gulp from the liquor bottle.

"Oops, Janal, what kind of a baby are you? Girl you gotta help mommy. You can't keep movin your head like that."

Elayne belches and tries again and this time the spoon hits Janal in the side of the head.

"Janal, do you want to eat this nasty stuff or not? Now keep your head still. All that movin around is makin mommy dizzy."

The doorbell rings and Elayne is too drunk to get up to open the door, instead she gives a loud drunken holler.

"WHO IS IT?"

She doesn't hear anyone so she hollers again.

"I SAID, WHO IS IT? Janal, I think we have invisible people at the door...Maybe it's ghost...What do you think?"

The bell rings again, this time Elayne gets up, bumping into the walls several times while walking to the door. She opens it slightly and peeks out. Disgusted but not shocked with Elayne's appearance, Shi Li invites herself into the house.

"I said who is it! How come you didn't say anythang?"

"You're drunk...I thought I would come over and see how you are doing."

"Well as you can see, we're do'n just find, if you ask me. How you been do'n, Shi Li?"

Shi Li shakes her head with shame, "Where is Janal?"

"She's in the kitchen eat'n her food, at least try'n too. Seems we can't get that nasty food to go in her mouth, it keeps fall'n off the spoon. Oh boy, maybe 'cause...it's a day old...No, I'm kid'n you. Haaa...how can those companies make somethang so nasty and call it baby food? Alley dogs don't want to eat this stuff." Elayne laughs, "Really Shi Li, you wanna know what go'n on, we don't know...we don't know nuth'n right now." Elayne belches and it is loud and it smells, "It just keep fall'n and fall'n, hah-ha." Elayne gives a loud drunken laugh before closing the door."

Shi Li goes into the kitchen and finds Janal sitting in her highchair with food covering her from head to toe.

"Come here little princess."

She takes Janal out of the highchair and into the bathroom, "Auntie Shi Li is going to get you all cleaned up. Would you like to put on some clean clothes, Janal?"

Elayne follows, stumbling with every step, using the walls to support her drunken condition.

Bath time is over and Shi Li sings a Chinese lullaby that her mother use to sing to her when she was a small child as she rocks Janal to sleep. She lays her into the crib then goes to talk to Elayne about her drunken condition. Shi Li can not help but to feel sorry for her friend, seeing her like that, destroying her life so disgracefully.

"Elayne we have to talk about your drinking, it is a terrible problem. Janal is too young..."

Instead of having that heart to heart talk, Elayne has past out on the couch and Shi Li is worried out of mind about her friend and her goddaughter's safety. Shi Li realizes that Elayne's heart has been severely crushed and the pain has blinded her judgement. In addition, she refuses to seek counseling. Sharing in her friend's pain Shi Li takes the blanket off the back of the couch covering her and wondering what can she possibly do in a situation like this.

For approximately one hour, Shi Li sits on the floor next to the couch, wondering, watching and stroking Elayne's head as she sleeps.

'What is happening? Please Elayne, pray to your Lord before it is too late. Between your god and my god one of them should answer us, because I do not know what else to do. What do you need me to do? Please, just tell me, please? And I will.'

In addition, Elayne's sexual appetite is growing out of control. She has had many on and off relationships, inviting promiscuous behavior into her life, too many to count; it seems as though there is nothing her friends can do. Elayne is self-destructing.

Miserable and depressed, her drinking has turned out to be a daily ritual and Elayne's self-esteem is at its lowest as her sexual appetite peaks. The bad thing about it, Elayne is having sex with just about every man she meets. At her place of work there is a sign on the wall in the men's restroom that reads: 'BLACK AND FRISKY.' That is a nicknamed given to her by her male co-worker and at times they will draw straws to see who is going to ask her out next; gratifying themselves, taking turns with her. And it is not just her co-workers it is any man she meets, anywhere.

Elayne is not hard to look at, but like the old saying goes, 'The Blacker The Berry, The Sweeter The Juice.' Elayne could have settled down and had any man she wanted, but Elayne is afraid to love again. Fearing she might be kicked around like 'day old trash', the same way she was when her husband, Raymond beat her and walked out.

She never stops wondering, 'why?' That question still nibbles at her soul, devouring it a little at a time as the years go by. 'Why did The Lord turn his back to me? And why he never turned around to look at me again? What did I do to deserved such treatment from my husband?'

She questions herself many days and many nights; nevertheless, that never stop her from taking off her panties and giving her body to men she hardly knew. Relations with these strange men somehow boost Elayne's ego and in return made her feel beautiful, loved, and all in all, in control.

The year is 1975, Janal is now five years old, too young to understand what her mother is doing behind closed door, but she is not stupid. She knows that the men her mother brings home have no resemblance to her. However that does not stop Janal from questioning her mother about them or about the father she longs for.

Many times she would say, 'Mommy when is my daddy coming home? ...All the other kids at school have a daddy!'

In any event, Elayne is too ashamed to answer Janal's questions truthfully.

Regardless of her daughter's feelings, Elayne keeps bringing new faces home. On many occasions, Janal would run to the mirror to compare her facial features with the strange men sitting on the couch in the living room, drinking with her mother.

While looking in the mirror one day, Janal begins to talk to herself, "Umm...nope, he don't look like me...He can't be my daddy, either. He's too, too, ugly...yuck. When will my momma let my daddy come home? She always brings everybody else home but not my daddy...how come? I don't think my daddy wants to come home. I don't think he loves me, that's why he don't want to come back." Janal starts to cry.

Now seven-year-old Janal is assisting Shi Li with dinner at her apartment. Again Shi Li baby-sits; this is the fourth night this week as the two prepare one of Janal's favorite food: Shrimp fried rice, egg rolls, and green tea to rinse it down.

Janal goes to the kitchen drawer and takes out the silverware, she gets a couple of napkins from the holder and places them neatly on the table.

"Too bad momma had to work late again, because I know she would love to eat this food."

"Yes, I am sure she would."

"Auntie Shi Li, can we save her some?"

"Yes, Janal, we can."

"Momma gonna be surprise when she finds out that I helped cook...I just wish she didn't have to work so long, so much, Auntie Shi Li."

Elayne is not working long hours. She is on another date with another man she hardly knows at some hotel she frequently visits. And she has been drinking heavily, and there is a possibility, when morning comes she won't remember him neither.

A mother's love for her daughter, Mother Kyi's memories were passed on through her teachings, their spiritual belief, and the herbs that heal the body and cleanse the soul. These memories and remedies Shi Li holds very close to her heart as she generously teach Janal.

Raymond Smith the man who once had everything now has nothing, finally finds himself searching for a way to make ends meet by going to as many businesses he can find and looking for work. For some reason, Raymond's luck has run out. It is as if something is holding him back. Something is causing all kinds of trouble for him and he can not figure it out. He believes he is cursed.

Then one day, after finding work at a fast food hamburger restaurant he is convinced that things are about to turn around. Raymond's duties are: cleaning the restrooms, mopping floors at least three times a day and after the restaurant closes, restocking the shelves, and any other work that has to be done.

However, Raymond's position is soon terminated, over and again, this time because of his tardiness and absentees. He has been late twenty-three days in one month, due to his lack of transportation. Raymond had to sell his lovely convertible a while back, because he needed money to pay for necessities. In addition, to catching the bus around town, he often stole food from his job, then sell it to the residents at the shelter where he lives.

Trying hard to make ends meet, when he had a job, Raymond did not make a lot of money cleaning bathroom and mopping floors. Still holding on, refusing to let go, dreaming of the times when he had so much, the times when he lived the so-called 'good life'. Nevertheless, he still wonders about the wife he once had and a child he has never seen.

Surviving the streets and trying to stay above water is difficult when you have nothing or nobody to turn too. At one time, Raymond believe he could counts on his old buddies he use to hang with, his friends at the shelter, and the friends he thought that would be there when he needed them most. Yet, it turns out they really wasn't his friends at all. Whenever Raymond confided in them, they would back-stab him every time, whispering behind his back, laughing and making jokes about him, and stealing the little belongings he still own. After the jokes and teasing, Raymond is pushed around, kicked and beaten down during his stay at the shelter.

Whenever Raymond comes across anything of value, the residents would straight-out take it and dare him to do, or say anything about it. Raymond was not a total jerk he did try to defend himself. Despite it all, Raymond has been seriously hurt from fighting during his stay at the shelter, some he won, and yet, many of them he lost.

Eventually, between the rumors and lies, he is kicked out of the shelter for his violent behavior. With no where to go, Raymond finds himself living in a large cardboard box in a park not far from the river. Although his convictions never abandoned him, the memories of the good life he once lived, a family, and most of all, a warm home all taunt him.

Nasty, dirty, in ragged clothes, who would have ever thought that cool, smooth, the ladies' man: Sweet Daddy himself, Raymond Smith, would be holding a sign in the middle of rush hours traffic that reads: "HUNGRY, I'LL WORK FOR FOOD." Raymond has hit rock bottom.

On a Saturday afternoon, nine years old Janal runs into the house after playing with friends.

"Mom...Momma, I'm home."

Janal closes the front door and goes into the living room and finds her mother asleep on the couch. She shakes her, but there is no response. And judging from the position of her body, one leg draped over the edge pointing to an empty liquor bottle lying on the floor next to her, it is truly obvious, she is drunk again.

Janal picks up the liquor bottle and puts it to her nose. Feeling lonely, ashamed and neglected, Janal ask herself as she has so many times before 'Why do she drink so much? Is she drinking because of me? I don't think she loves me. Maybe that's why my daddy left, because he didn't love me either and my mother is getting sick of looking at me everyday. Anyway...daddy never calls to see how I'm doing. That's got to be the only reason, it's the only reason I can think of. I don't even know how he looks. Yeah, I think my parents aren't together because of me. Why was I born? Why didn't they just give me away? Then my momma wouldn't have to drink herself drunk.'

Sad and confused, Janal slowly walk to her bedroom, closing the door quietly as she blocks out the thoughts of her parent's disapproval of her existence.

Two days later, Janal is outside in the backyard sitting on the back porch playing with her dolls when D'La pulls up in the driveway. She runs to the car, shouting, "Hi Aunt D'La."

"Hey Janal, what's up?"

"Nothing," she says leaning against the car door, "Momma's in the house."

"Do you wanna go with me to get somethang to eat?"

"Sure! My place or your, Auntie D'La, " she joking says.

"Umm...Yours of course. Let me check with your momma and see what's go'n down."

Janal waits on the porch as D'La enters the house, calling to Elayne who is throwing clothes into the washing machine.

"I'm down here...in the basement."

D'La runs down the stairs: "Hey girl, what's up with you?"

"Nothin. Tryin to get Janal clothes clean. Seems like all of her new things look so old. Sometimes, I can't tell what's new and what's not," Elayne holds up a pair of jeans, "Look at these pants." Tossing them to D'La.

"I think these are the ones I bought last week, but I can't tell it. That girl, she ain't nothin but a little tomboy."

"And what's wrong with that?"

Elayne answers with a roll of the eyes and a shake of the head.

"Look at me Elayne, I was a tomboy and I turned out just fine."

"Yeah D'La, okay...sure. What ever you say. D'La, the only time my baby gets this dirty is when she's with you."

"Hey, what can I say! Can I help it if we have big fun when we're together."

"Havin fun and comin home this dirty and nasty, smell'n like a lost puppy is not the same."

"Elayne let Janal have some fun. If clean clothes is the problem here, hell, I'll buy you some more wash'n powda."

"D'La please."

"Okay, Elayne, I'll tell you what...I'll wash Janal thangs next week, deal!"

"D'La you said that last week, and the week before that, and before that."

"Yep, that's true Elayne, and that's cause next week never comes...it's always this week, " giggles D'La.

"Funny, funny! One day I'm gonna tie you and Janal to this wash'n machine, so I can take a break." Elayne tosses more clothes into the machine as she continues to complain, "Shoot, this girl got too many clothes."

"Elayne relax. Take a break. Me and Janal is gonna get some hamburgers, then we're go'n to the park, cool?"

"Yeah, yeah, yeah...but make sure she's clean when you bring her home, D'La, " Elayne stares into D'La's face, "I mean it!"

"She'll be clean, don't worry," hollers D'La as she runs up the steps and out the back door to the porch, "Okay, everything is cool with your momma, let's go."

Janal runs around and opens the car door. D'La gently closes it and secures the lock before she gets behind the wheel. Janal observes closely as she takes her knife out of its pouch that's fastened to the back of her hip. Without a blink, Janal continues to watch D'La as she pushes it between the seats.

"Aunt D'La, how come...I mean, why do you always carry that big knife? Did somebody make you mad? Are you gonna cut somebody?"

"No Janal, nobody didn't make me mad...and I'm not plan'n on cut'n anybody."

"When I grow up, would you buy me a knife like that, Aunt D'La?"

"Sure thang, but only when you grow up. Got it!"

"Got it! Aunt D'La, can you show me how to throw it like you do? You know, just in case some stupid creature tries something with me. Okay? We girls have to be safe."

D'La is surprised and impressed with Janal's survival instinct. "Sure Janal...You know, you're gonna be all right. After we eat I'll take you to the park and we'll practice behind the trees; but, we can't tell your momma or anyone about this."

"I cross my heart...I'll never tell momma. I'll never tell anybody."

"And Janal, we'll practice on our tumbling and rolling to the ground some more too. Cool!"

"Cool Auntie D'La!"

Kate's accusations have finally destroyed the relationship between her and D'La. One hot summer night while lying in bed, Kate makes sexual advances toward D'La by gently places one hand on her breast. D'La pretends to be asleep, and rolls over on her stomach to end the proposal. Kate removes her hand and lies on her back and looks at the ceiling. Minutes later, D'La gets up, puts on her clothes and starts to walk out of the bedroom; but before she can leave Kate quickly sits up.

"I thought you were asleep. Where are you going? "

"No, I'm not asleep or in the mood, Kate."

Aggressively Kate adds, "What! ...You haven't been in the mood a lot lately."

Courageously and straight face, D'La answers, "Yeah, I would say you're right."

Immediately, Kate crawls across the bed. "Is something wrong, D'La?"

Trying hard not to argue with Kate, D'La tries to evade her questions, but she knows Kate will not let up if she didn't answer.

"I don't know."

"What do you mean, you don't know? You ought to know if something's wrong or not, D'La."

"Kate, I'm not in the mood for this sh... tonight, okay! I'm go'n out."

"What do you mean you're going out? Out where?"

"Kate back off...I need some air."

"Hey, I need some air too. Do you want me to go with you?"

"No Kate, I don't want you to go with me. I'm go'n by myself. I need some space, too.

"D'La, you act like you got a secret lover or something...do you?"

"No! Dam... it Kate, I'm not see'n somebody else."

"Yeah, right...You expect me to believe that, when you act like you are. I see how men look at you when we're out together. And the way you look back at them. WHY IS THAT D'LA? My dic... isn't real enough for you anymore? All of a sudden, you don't like the way it makes you feel, how it use to get your body all hot and juicy...WHAT, you want a real one, NOW!"

"YOUR JEALOUSY IS DRIVIN ME CRAZY, KATE. I JUST CAN'T TAKE IT ANYMORE. I have never been with anybody. I gave MY VIRGINITY TO YOU. YOU'RE THE ONLY ONE I EVER BEEN WITH...AND YOU KNOW IT. So DON'T go there, with THAT BULLSH..."

"Maybe, if we made love more often, I wouldn't think the things I do."

D'La takes her jacket off the chair, her knife off the dresser and slides it into her low cut boot.

"You see...this is what in the hell I'm talk'n about, your accusations all the time. Day in and day out, I can't take it anymore, Kate. I'm leave'n you."

Kate quickly loses her temper and starts yelling, "I KNOW THERE'S SOMEBODY ELSE, BIT... YOU JUST REMEMBER THIS, WHOEVER HE IS, HE CAN NEVER LOVE YOU THE WAY I LOVE YOU. NO MAN CAN LOVE A WOMAN THE WAY A WOMAN NEEDS TO BE LOVED, D'LA, AND YOU KNOW IT!"

D'La tosses her hand upward, shakes her head and that is when Kate realizes that she is losing the argument. She tries to calm herself down as she gets off the bed and goes to the bedroom doorway, blocking it.

In a sweet, soft and low voice Kate expresses, "D'La I love you. I love you a lot and it scares me to think that somebody else might take you away from me. And when I think like that, I just starts shaking all over."

"Kate, I know you love me...I know you do. But that somebody is you who's chase'n me away. Don't you see that?"

Kate pleads, "I'm sorry. Forgive me? I know I've asked this question many times, but I have to ask again. D'La, can you forgive me? All I need is one more chance...Okay?"

"No...because there will always be a one more chance, and another and another. Kate there has been too many 'one more chances'. I gotta go. I'll be back tomorrow to pack my thangs."

Kate's heart aches as she silently begs from within, trying to control her emotions.

"You're leaving me for good this time?"

"Yeah, I think it's better if we call it quits for good this time."

Kate spontaneously takes D'La's hand and pulls her closer, wrapping her arms around her, squeezing her tight, kissing her lips, but D'La does not respond.

"You'll be back. You always come back to me."

"Not this time, Kate."

Feeling confident that D'La will return, Kate still conceals her emotions, smiling as D'La walks by, she stands in the doorway holding on to the knob, twisting it.

"Bye Kate."

Kate hastily follows D'La to the front door. She is so close that all you can see is one shadow on the wall. Brokenhearted, Kate watch as D'La leaves the house. Kate hurriedly walks onto the front porch, standing there, watching D'La walk away.

In a soft whisper Kate states, "She loves me. I know she do. So I'll wait for her...Yeah, she'll be back."

With all the emotional turmoil surrounding Shi Li's life, she never lost focus of her dream. Her determination and long hours of obsessive studying for her medical exams every night for over six years. Trying hard to make her dreams a reality, by never dating, or associating with anybody other than her three friends and her god-daughter. Neglecting her happiness, that is, to be loved by a man.

It is Shi Li's first few weeks on the job in the hospital's emergency room. She is daydreaming as she saunters through the corridor, accidentally bumping into Dr. Chou Tsetung, Head of the Emergency.

"OH! I am sorry."

She immediately gazes into his face and then at his nametag pinned to his jacket, "Oh. Oh...Dr. Tsetung, I am very sorry. Forgive me please. I was not paying attention to where I was walking."

Dr. Tsetung is startled by Shi Li's interruption and very pleased with their encounter. However, Shi Li feels very foolish.

"How could I be so clumsy?"

"It's, okay. It was my fault. I was not looking where I was going either. I too, I'm sorry."

Shi Li glances into his face but all she can see is his smile, yet she still insist.

"No, it was all mine Dr. Tsetung."

"Well, lets say we're both at fault. Anyway, there was no damage done...Do you work in this department?"

Surprised by his question and his wanting to have a conversation with her, Shi Li drops her medical pad on the floor. Impetuously, she bends down to pick it up and answers him, "Yes, Dr. Tsetung, this is my first day."

He stoops down, "Your, first day. Welcome aboard." Dr. Tsetung extends his hand to greet Shi Li. "Your name is?"

"My name is, Shi Li Kyi, Doctor Tsetung."

"Shi Li Kyi, that's a lovely name."

Shi Li quickly stands and so does Dr. Tsetung. Shi Li is a very beautiful woman and Dr. Tsetung likes what he sees.

"Thank you, Dr. Tsetung."

"I would like to show my humble apology by buying lunch. Shi Li would you like to have lunch with me this afternoon?"

Shi Li becomes even more nervous. Her fear of relationships, even dating, makes her extremely uncomfortable as constant memories of her mother's life and death replay themselves. Still taking control, and denying her every chance at any relationship.

"I appreciate your asking, Dr. Tsetung, but I am going to have to decline."

"May I ask, why? ...Oh, I'm sorry, I did not think to ask...Are you married?"

"No, I am not married, but studying takes much time and then there are tests, too...many, many tests."

Dr. Tsetung interrupts her, "Okay, later, after studying, after tests, we will have lunch, agreed?"

"I will think about lunch," says Shi.

Her shy demeanor is extremely breathtaking and attractive to Dr. Tsetung.

"And, I will wait patiently while you think, Shi Li Kyi."

Shi Li remains nervous as she mediates on how to get out of this situation, 'Maybe, I should run fast down the hallway.'

But before Shi Li can say anything else, Dr. Tsetung quickly adds before he delightfully walks away, "I will be patient, and it is a pleasure meeting you, Shi Li."

Shi Li is mesmerized, 'Dr. Tsetung wants to take me out for lunch? I can not believe it! Every nurse, every candy striper, every female that works in this hospital wants to go out with him, even the married ones...and he ask me. Oh boy!'

DAMU DARAKA
' BLOOD OBLIGATION '

CHAPTER 12

Several years have gone by and the year is 1982. It is the 'same ole same ole', nothing has changed that much, except for D'La who has been working long hours at the U.S. Postal Service. It is very exhausting and time consuming, overpowering her personal life, but the money is good. She works ten to twelve hours a day, sometimes two and three weeks at a time before she gets one day off. She barely has enough time to spend with her family and friends, or even to sit back and relax.

One night while driving home from work, D'La sees a sign, she has seen this sign many times before, but never took any interest. The sign reads "DEXX'S PLACE," so tonight she decides to park her car and go in. She wants something else to do, instead of her usual ritual, that is going straight home every night when she gets off work.

"Dexx's Place", a pool hall, and not the best place in town to drop in for a visit; it is also a cover for The Black Connection's illegal activities. A place many people avoid, but it is something different, 'a change is a change', and D'La is not afraid to go anywhere in the hood, alone. Besides, "Dexx's Place" reminds her of the kind of places her brother, Michael, use to sneak her into when she was a little girl. In addition to, this is the perfect place where she can get away from her problems, for instance Kate, whose persistence is becoming increasingly annoying.

D'La walks over to the bar, orders a beer as she probe her surroundings. She notices the place is packed with people drinking and dancing. Even the drunks are trying to convince the prostitutes to bring their prices back down to two dollars, because five dollars is too much money for a quick piece. The pool tables are occupied as the balls speeded across the dirty green fabric and into the tattered pockets. D'La can not help noticing a loud mouth man standing by of the pool tables yelling. He is constantly sticking his tongue out, endlessly licking and wrapping it around his mouth, all the while, stroking a whore's butt. It seems as though, he is searching for money that she denies having.

'Don't tell me that nasty old thang is her pimp,' thinks D'La.

He pushes the whore up against the wall, quickly snatches at her mini dress, pulling it up to her waist as he put his hand into her bikini panties.

'Dummy, you never hide money in your bras or panties, that's the first place a pimp's gonna look. And when did whores start wear'n panties anyway! Umm...she gotta be new to the business,' thinks D'La as she continues to observe her surroundings.

D'La feels a little remorse for the young whore as her pimp takes the money out of her panties, then smacks her across the face several times.

'It doesn't look like much, only a couple of dollars she's try'n to keep', perceives D'La.

"What I tell you 'bout hold'n out."

He is loud and crude, yet he demands answers. The young whore does not make a sound at first, nor does she shed a tear. She only looks at him for a moment of two before she starts to beg.

"Beauden, I'm sorry baby, I just needed to keep a couple of dollars. I was hungry, that's all."

His eyes enlarge as he grabs her arm, vigorously snatching her, pulling her toward him.

"When you bring your daily quota to me, then you'll eat; just like all the other ho...s! Do I make myself clear?"

His mouth is vulgar as he twists the girl's arm behind her back and forcefully escorts her to the door, pushing her outside into the street. The entire incident is so disgusting that D'La turns her head and looks in another direction.

'I can't take look'n at this stupid nut', thinks D'La.

But as she puts the bottle of beer to her lips she notices a high-yellow woman watching her. She is not as young as the other girls are. She has to be at least in her late twenties. Surprising the woman winks at D'La. Then the woman gets up from her chair and saunters toward her.

"Hello, hello, my name is Pinky."

"What's go'n on Pinky?" replies D'La as if she really care.

"Oh, nuth'n much," she says as gradually admires D'La's frame.

"Well, what can I do for you Pinky?"

A moment of silence overcomes Pinky; cautiously waiting before making what she considers complimentary remark, "My man would sure love you if I brought you home. Um, uh...he'll take real good care of you."

D'La is cool. She listens while observing Pinky's attire. She is wearing a cheap vinyl leopard jacket, a brown crooked-hemmed mini skirt that is as short as her faded blue blouse, black fish net stocking, you can see where she stitched several ragged holes with green and gray thread. She is wearing shabby hi-heeled shoes and a heel plate missing off one of her shoes, and her wig is old as antique furniture, dingy, dried up, and nappy. Looks as though her pimp shops for her clothes at the Salvation Army on 'give-away-day.' Her make-up is caked on her face; two shades lighter than her complexion, maybe she is trying to pass for white. And she has the nerves to wear light blue eye shadow traced with white hi-lighter and bright red lipstick paste on and over her lip-line. After critiquing Pinky, D'La realizes that she is one of the poorest looking whores she has ever seen.

Abruptly D'La declares, "How in the hell is he gonna take real good care of me, when he can't take care of you? No offense Pinky, but no man owns this pus... And ain't no man put'n a price on this pus... or tell'n me what, when, where, or how to use it!"

Pinky did not say another word, you can tell she is upset as she hurries back to her table, sits down, and swiftly crosses one leg over the other.

D'La continues to watch the guys shoot pool before deciding that she wants to play. So she goes over and lay her quarter on the side of the pool table. She waits patiently for about thirty minutes. The winner always plays the next player. Trey is one of the players and he loses, and the winner happens to be that big mouth pimp, Beauden.

Trey watches Beauden as he picks up the money off the table.

"It might not look like it, but pool's a crafty game, a man's games; and you young brothers betta listen to an old pro. You gotta have some insight, know'n your longitude and your latitude when it comes to hold'n your stick. You gotta hold it like you're about to make love, just like you do with a woman. Not too tight and not too loose...but just right," says Beauden talking his jive talk.

The waitress walks up to Trey, a.k.a., "Ty Baby," with a tray of drinks and looks directly into his face and winks, "Here your drink, Ty Baby."

He nods his head to the waitress as she hands him a napkin with her phone number written on it.

"Thanks," he says as he tosses a big tip onto her tray.

Trey is one of Dexx's connections to the Italian Mafia; he is also a good friend, always honest, proving himself worthy in many of Dexx's misfortunes. He is a gentleman, and the rumor is, Trey is an extraordinary lover. And once the word got out about his enormous blessing, many of the whores wanted to give him some for free. Simply to experience, just how big it really is.

The rumors about the Caucasian men sexual inability does not apply to Trey not one bit, but then again, he is Italian.

"Beauden Man, I got to give it to you. You're good with that stick...You say hold it like a woman, right. Yeah, I'll remember that next time. Thanks Beau," replies Trey as he pats Beauden on his back and heads for the waitress.

Beauden yells, "ALL RIGHT, WHOSE NEXT? Bring your ugly as... on over to the TABLE, so I can WOOP it and take ALL your money too, SH...! Oooo wee..e...e...I'm hot tonight."

Beauden giggles as he continues to talk his jive and walk with a stride, nonetheless, his big mouth doesn't scare D'La.

"E...eee ah...eeee. Com'on who's next? I ain't GOT all day. I gotta a HOT beauty wait'n on me tonight. She says to me, 'Beauden daddy, you sure got some good lovin.' So, I gotta GO, so I can get it and so I can give it...E...eee....ah...ee."

D'La steps over to the table with her stick in her hand and Beauden is overwhelmed on how gorgeous she is.

"Baby, are you sure you wanna play? Cause I don't want you messin up those pretty wavy afro-curls, cry'n and scream'n, cause you lost all your money to me," he says while walking around the table.

Yet D'La is cool, "You wanna play, let's play."

Beauden pushes most of the balls across the table.

"Here they come...Ooo...you don't know how much I wish those were my balls comin your way, Li'l Darlin." Beauden grabs his crotch of his pant, showing out in front of his friends; then he rolls the rest as D'La racks them.

Beauden tries to sweet talk her, "Li'l Darlin, I'm not in the habit of take'n any woman's money. I usually give women money so they can buy themselves pretty thangs...Eee...so they can look pretty for me when I come to visit. You know what I mean?"

D'La ignores his proposal, looking across the table straight into Beauden face.

"Play!"

Beauden bends down with his stick in hand, positioning himself for the shot.

"I guess there is a first time for everythang...E.e.e.e."

The game begins and fifteen minutes have past and Beauden is losing. D'La never says a word during the entire game. She is always cool and very laid back. Beauden does not appreciate her calm demeanor one bit. It bothers him a lot that he talks the entire time. Calling her bluff with every shot. Finally he makes her an offer, by doubling his money on the table. There is only one ball left and that is the black ball and he knows D'La will miss the shot. Still he keeps his fingers crossed. He does not want to lose to a woman, especially to a woman in front of his friends and his whores.

"Call your pocket, Li'l Darlin."

D'La calls, "Black ball in the right corner."

Everybody and everything becomes solemnly soundless. D'La positions her body and then her stick. She maneuvers her posture a bit more, eyeing the ball, the pocket, and the tip of her stick. Surprisingly to everyone, she hits, slamming the ball across the table and knocking it into her desired pocket. She wins. Beauden is not happy at all about this. But as soon as D'La goes around the table to picks up the money, she reaches out. Without warning, Beauden grabs D'La's hand, giving her an evil grimace.

"What do you think you're do'n?"

As usual D'La's cool, she stares into his face, positioning her body for the kill as she slowly reaches behind her back for her knife that is attached to the waist of her pants, under her jacket.

"What do it look like I'm do'n. Now, take that ashy hand off me!"

An unexpected, yet a strong and demanding voice urgently echoes from the crowd, "HEY, MAN, that ain't NO WAY TO ACT. The lady won fair and square...NOW CUT THE SH...!"

Beauden immediately releases D'La's hand as the strong voice continues, "We're all here tonight to have a good time, even if that means, you lost."

Beauden retreats, smiling and grinning, showing all of his front teeth, at the man with the strong demanding voice, "Ah...Man. I wasn't gonna do anythang to her."

"I know you weren't...but the lady don't know that."

Beauden nods his head, then takes his stick, practically throwing it on the table. Immediate he yells at the bar tender for another drink as D'La collects the money off the table.

"Thanks," says D'La to the stranger.

The man with the deep powerful voice is tall, dark and handsome, a perfect specimen of a black man, and every woman's dream.

"I hope he didn't scare you."

"No, he didn't scare me," D'La is very unconcern with Beauden, his attitude and anyone else who has a problem with her winning.

"Is this your first time here?" the stranger ask.

D'La answers discourteously, "Maybe...Maybe not. Who's asking?"

All Dexx can do is grin, he knows right away that this one is a real fighter, nothing like the women who visit his place regularly. The ones that constantly throws themselves at him and who will do anything and everything for him.

"Oh, excuse me. I don't mean to be rude. My name is Dexx Barone. I'm the owner of this establishment.

"Please to meet you, Dexx Barone. Ahh...its get'n late, I gotta go, says D'La.

But as she turn to walk away Dexx quickly ask, "Umm...what's your name."

D'La pauses, looks back, before answering, "D'La...D'La Lausen and I'll talk to you later."

Dexx gradually sits on the edge of the pool table, "Is that a promise?"

Sweet and innocently D'La smiles, "Yeah...Maybe."

Dexx Barone is 6'4" tall, handsome, with the most gorgeous smile you have ever seen. His complexion is as black as sweet black liquorice, a strong masculine physique and he is extremely sexy. The kind of man you would see on the covers of a fashion magazine.

Most of the women that visit his establishment are visiting for one reason, and that is for his personal attention. Sometimes, hoping to spark up a conversation with him, all the while, keeping their fingers crossed that he would find them attractive enough to spend some time with. Plus, the women always went crazy whenever Dexx wore those tight fitted sleeveless shirts that revealed every muscle in his chest and arms. And when it comes to sex, his stamina is no problem. Women were standing in line just to be the next one in his bed. Yes, the women are crazy about Dexx Barone, his power, and his money.

Dexx's father was married to another woman and already had a family of his own. When Dexx was a little boy, him and his mother never knew when his father would come for a visit, or bring money to help support them. There were many days and nights that Dexx watched his mother sit by the phone waiting for him to call. Sometime the phone would ring only once before she grabbed it. Due to her anxiousness, the phone never had a chance to ring a second time. But as the years past, the phone calls started to lessen, and eventually they stopped, and that when Dexx's mother started to cry herself to sleep almost every night. On one cold windy night she finally 'come to term' that she and her son had been abandoned.

Dexx lived part of his young life growing up on the streets of Chicago. Dexx was about nine years old when his father stopped coming around, and Dexx too cried himself to sleep as he longed for his attention, a father-son relationship and his love. Ultimately, Dexx started misbehaving in school and was kicked out several times.

By the time Dexx was eleven years old his mother moved them to Detroit, Michigan. With her constant persuasion and talks about being somebody in life, Dexx graduated high school and found a job making minimum wage, but not enough to give his mother the kind of life he thought she deserved. Dexx was developing into a strong, healthy, and smart young man and he learned fast how to survive on the streets.

As a boy and to earn money fast, Dexx starting running errands for the pimps and prostitutes. Soon he got involved in illegal activities: collecting money for the neighborhood's number man, then a short time later he started selling drugs.

As the years continued, Dexx inevitably became a member of the Black Connection Inc., a black organized crime family, that mostly consisted of the brothers on the streets, and he later gained status as 'The Boss'.

Six weeks later D'La returns to Dexx's Place and she is just finishing her first beer.

"Would you like another drink?" ask the bartender.

"Yeah, thanks," says D'La.

Another twenty minutes goes by and D'La's surroundings are becoming tiresome that she decides to leave. Before she could swallow her last drop of beer, Dexx humbly walks up behind her, tapping her on the shoulder. His deep strong sexy voice surprises her, she swings around on the bar stole.

"Look what the wind blew in. I didn't expect to see you around here any time soon."

"Surprise," says D'La.

"Yeah, I think I like this surprise...a lot. And if you don't mind, may I ask, what brings you back?" Standing and grinning, Dexx is very delighted to see her.

"I just got off work and this place is on my way home, so I stopped."

"You're welcome to stop by anytime you get off work and more," says Dexx.

"Is that a personal invitation?"

Dexx was about to answer when one of his members approaches.

"Hey Boss"

"Ty, what's up?"

Dexx leans forward, seriously listening to Ty's discreet whispers. Then Ty promptly walks away.

"D'La, I got to go and take care of some things, but I'll be back as soon as I can. That is, if you don't mind waiting."

"I guess a few more minute won't hurt," says D'La.

Dexx signals the bartender, "Skippy, get Miss Lausen another drink on me and take good care of her."

"Yeah Boss, no problem."

"D'La, I'll be right back, don't go away."

"Would you like another beer, Ms. Lausen?"

D'La pays no attention to the bartender. She is watching Dexx and Ty enter another room on the other side of the bar as they slowly closes the door behind them.

Inside Dexx's office all hell is about to break loose. Skunk, one of Dexx's long time friends, now a member of the connection has been skimming money out of his collection owed to the organization. Every other week, for the last six weeks, he has only turns in half of what he collected. Dexx is not in the mood for any more excuses.

"Skunk, Man what in the hell's going on? This sh... you doing ain't roll'n this time. You're coming up short, now, all the time Man."

"Ah...Ah...Dexx, I was gonna pay you back. All I need is some time to get on my feet, " says Skunk as he starts to sweats. Soon he is shivering so severely that it looks as though his chair is shaking.

"Yeah Skunk, just some time to get on your feet. But what I'm I suppose to do until then? You gotta remember...business is business and you've been mess'n up with your end of the business for some time. Hey, I can't let things like this just keep happening, Man...you understand. And you had enough time to get it together, Skunk."

Dexx points to Ty Baby and Beauden and three other thugs, Bubba, Maddog, and Griz who are standing behind and alongside of Skunk's chair.

Ty Baby taps Skunk on his shoulder to escorts him through the backdoor, but Skunk quickly pleads for his life.

"Dexx, please Man, I won't do anythang like this again, I promise you, Man. I just needed to get on my feet, that's all...I'm sorry Man, I'm sorry. Hey, Dexx Man, wait...wait, memba the time, Man, memba, when we did a raid on those white folks when they where short-changin the worker at that truck company. They were try'n to hold a brother down, under cut'n, steal'n our money. Memba, how we got those suckers run'n back to the suburbs after they repaid all that money?"

Skunk jumps up out of his chair with his fist raised high over his head, shouting, "DAMU DARAKE...DAMU DARAKE...Yeah, those were the days. Memba Dexx, me and you, we were like real brothers and thangs were real cool than, memba, memba? Dexx Man for old times, Man, don't do this, please?"

"Sorry Skunk, a man's gotta do what a man's gotta do."

Prior to Skunk getting caught, it was reported by members of the organization that he was seen around town in a new flashy car, designer suits, and throwing the organization's money on fast women and dope. After fifteen years as a member of the Black Connection, Skunk has become a victim of his environment and could no longer be trusted.

"Get him outta here...and take him out the back door," orders Dexx.

The four thugs, all except Ty, escorts Skunk out the backdoor, into the alley, putting him in the back seat of a car. From that day onward Skunk is never seen again. However, the rumors around town say that Skunk's mixed in with the hamburger possibly at your local supermarket.

Shortly afterward, Dexx returns to D'La and she asks, "What was that all about?"

"I see you're the curious type," states Dexx.

"What's wrong with the curious type?"

Dexx's finds D'La courageously amazing, she doesn't seem to be afraid him, and to ask such personal questions.

"Nothing, except curiosity killed the cat...,"he adds before quickly changes the conversation "...Would you like another drink?"

"No. It's get'n late. I think I betta be go'n on home."

"Can I walk you to your car?"

"No, that won't be necessary. I'll talk to you later, Dexx."

"This time I'm gonna hold you to that...And don't wait another six weeks, your beauty makes this place look good."

D'La gets out of her seat, "It won't. I'll see you soon."

D'La walks out and into the parking lot. Dexx is impressed and finds D'La hard to resist. An intelligent, brave, beautiful black woman, all rolled into one that he follows her out into the parking lot anyway.

"HEY...let me be a gentleman and walk you to the car. That's if you really don't mind. I hope you really don't mind."

"Maybe I do, maybe I don't," says D'La in a sassy tone.

"Wait just a minute Ms. D'La Lausen...what's up with this, maybe?"

D'La faces Dexx, "Ain't nuth'n up...but what's up with you Dexx Barone? Do always follow beautiful women that make your place look good into dark parking lots?"

"Dig this, I just want to get to know you, that's all."

"Umm uh, that's all!"

"Yeah! Is that okay with you?"

D'La gives a goofy expression before answering, "Maybe!"

Dexx starts to laugh. His loud outburst is so comical that he falls on hood of D'La's car. D'La soon joins him, laughing and giggling at this grown man's silly exhibition.

"I wish you could have seen your face. Aaah ah...you look so funny. I haven't seen anybody look that stupid, aha ah, not in a long time." D'La's impenetrable laughter impels Dexx.

"Wait just a minute!"

Despite his sudden egotistical response, D'La could hardly stand straight for laughing so hard.

The relationship is starting to build between them, bringing their friendship to another level. Still Dexx has many disturbing questions and he really needs and wants them answered. However he hesitates before asking. "Are you married?"

"No," she grins.

He hesitates again, but there is still one more question that eating at him.

"Is there a special someone in your life? Someone that you might have a interest, or seeing at this time?"

"This time, Ummm...." D'La hesitates before answering, toying with his emotions, "Well...let me think...ummm...Is there somebody ...I'm interested in or seeing at this time. Golly, that's a tough one to answer. Why are you ask'n such difficult questions, Mr. Barone?"

Glancing at him from the corner of her eyes, enjoying his anticipation, watching him as her questions takes him by surprise. Scrutinizing him before answering. "Umm...No! There's not one person I can think of at the moment, Mr. Barone."

Impulsively he blurts out, "GOOD!"

Dexx doesn't want to frighten D'La by acting too anxious so he quickly controls his emotions. And a man of his status, that wouldn't look good if somebody were watching him act so out of character.

"What's so good about it? Are you on the hunt for lonely women?"

"No. No, that's not what's up, not at all. You seem to be a nice person and nice people are very rare these days," defensively speaks Dexx.

"Is that so," replies D'La.

"Yeah, except for that laugh," Dexx makes screeching sounds with his mouth, mimicking D'La's laughter.

"Okay, okay you wanna go there...?" says D'La.

He interrupts, "...No, I don't want go there...It's just that...forget it. Do you live around here?"

"Wait a minute, question after question, who are you Dexx Barone, and what makes you think I'll answer every question you ask?"

Placing her hands on her hips D'La steps closer, facing him, head to shoulder and that is only because he is much taller.

She is aggressive and straightforward with her words and Dexx is enjoying every bit of her. Even more, delightfully grinning at the fiery and spirited woman standing in front of him, facing him head on.

"I'll tell you what, any night you want to come back and visit my place, you're welcome. We can sit down and talk properly and after we get to know one another we can have a night on the town, dinner, dancing, and..."

Before he finishes D'La asks, "AND WHAT?"

Dexx smiles at her goofy behavior.

"D'La would you let me finish, woman...as I was saying...and a bottle of Dom Perignon, you name it."

D'La is embarrassed but cool, "I'll keep that in mind, Mr. Barone, if I come back to your place." She reaches for her car door.

"Let me do that."

Dexx is very polite. Again he is the perfect gentleman, just as his mother raised him to be. He opens the car door for her. D'La gets in and starts the engine while Dexx hangs on to the open door.

"Drive carefully."

He closes it tightly and pushing down her lock.

"I will."

Once reaching the end of the parking lot she put one hand out the window and waves.

Candice made many trips to Detroit, mainly because, she miss her friends, and especially her goddaughter, Janal.

One day while shopping at one of the most exquisite suburban boutiques, Candice takes a cute two piece outfit off the rack.

"Janal look! Oui, Oui, I believe this is the one. Oui!"

Candice holds the outfit in front of Janal as she glares into the mirror.

"Well Janal, what do you think?

"Aunt Candice, it's so beautiful."

"A beautiful outfit for a beautiful girl, Oui."

Janal's ecstatic. She rubs her hands against the fabric, then takes hold of the price tag and reads it.

"Aunt Candice...it cost a lot of money."

"I do not care about the cost. Whatever you want, I'll buy. You're my only little girl, and I will spoil you whenever you want me too."

Janal looks over at the make-up counter and ask, "Can you buy me some lipstick like yours?"

An innocent face and a girlish smile, Janal waits for Candice to answer.

"I'll tell you what, since you're almost eleven, I'll buy you some chap-stick for now. And when you get a little older, say maybe sixteen, then I'll buy you lipstick. I'll buy every shade to match every outfit, Oui!"

"Oui...Aunt Candice, I love you."

Candice bends over and kisses Janal on the top of her head.

"Janal, I want you to remember...D'La, Shi Li, and your mom, we will always love you. And we will always be there for you. Oui."

Janal giggles with joy. "Oui Auntie Candice."

SPICES OF LOVE

CHAPTER 13

The year is 1982 and Janal's standing at the kitchen table watching her mother put the final touches on her birthday cake, she is twelve years old today.

"This cake is going to be so good, I can tell by the icing, Momma."

"Yes it is honey. And that's because the icing can tell it's your birthday and it knows you're just as sweet."

"Momma, is Aunt D'La and Aunt Shi Li still coming to my party?"

"Um uh, they wouldn't miss your birthday for the world. You know that, Janal."

"I wish Aunt Candice was here. I miss her a lot. Is she ever going to come back home and live, Momma?"

"Well, she might, one day. Maybe she'll surprise us both and come home unannounced and this time, stay for good. Your Aunt Candice is always full of surprises."

"Today is a good day for a surprise," says Janal as she licks the icing of the spatula.

Elayne calmly picks up a glass off the table and eagerly puts it to her mouth; hoping Janal believes it to be a glass of water. But Janal is not ignorant. She is aware of most of her mother's deceitful tactics when it comes to booze. She knows it can only be liquor, and her reason, because water is one of her mother's rarities. Still this is very disappointing for Janal as she snatches at the glass, gently removing it out of her mother's hand. Impetuously she takes a tiny sniff.

"Momma, you promised you wouldn't drink any liquor today."

Janal is right, Elayne did promise not to take a drink on her day. No matter how much she wants to, Elayne can not fight the overpowering force. The thirst for liquor controls all moral senses as it and speeds through brain and her veins. Humiliation covers her face; sorrow pierces her heart as she shamefully gazes into her daughter's eyes. Nevertheless Elayne quickly searches her soul for another excuse.

"It's only a little bit...little bits don't count...do they baby?"

Janal is lost for words. Silence overwhelms the kitchen. Respectfully, Janal stares into her mother's face, before looking at the half-full glass of liquor in her hand; sadly she places it on the table.

"Okay...I won't drink anymore. I promise...Today is your day just as we planned."

Elayne takes the glass, walks over to the sink, emptying the entire content. Quickly turning on the facet, rinsing the lustful aroma that somehow lingers within the drain.

"Now, see. It's gone," Elayne says with an insincere smile.

Janal's relieved, believing her mother will respect her and cherish her special day.

But as soon as Elayne turns off the facet the phone rings. Janal runs into the living room to answer it, "Hello."

"Bonjour, Janal...Happy birthday."

Janal exceptionally excited, screaming and hollering to the top of her lungs as she jumps up and down.

"AUNTIE CANDICE...MOM, ITS AUNTIE CANDICE."

Janal has so much to say to Candice and Elayne knows she will be on the phone for a while. Elayne truly think this is the perfect opportunity for her sneak another drink. So she goes to one of her secret places, the bottom kitchen cubboard, hidden inside a large pot is a fifth of liquor. She eases it out and opens it, drinking straight from the bottle, all the while, listening to Janal's converse with Candice.

"Did you get my surprise, Janal?"

"Oui. Merci, merci, Aunt Candice."

"How is school?"

"Well it's okay, I think."

"Oh, you think?"

"Yeah," Janal says grinning from ear to ear.

Do you have a boyfriend, yet?"

Embarrassed by her question Janal voice squeaks before she giggling, "No Aunt Candice, boys act too silly."

"You'll change your mind soon enough, Janal."

"How's your la mere? (*mother*)"

"Oh, she's all right, she's in the kitchen finishing my birthday cake."

"Let me speak with her for a moment."

Janal yells for her mother but Elayne does not respond right away. Janal wonders what could be taking her so long to come to the phone. She lays the phone on the couch and peeks into the kitchen. Even though her posture is blocking the view of what she is actually doing, Elayne's unaware of her daughter's tactfulness. She quietly put the top on the bottle, closing it, and sneaks it back into its hiding place.

Elayne's instinctive nature impels her. Suddenly glancing behind her, she yells, "I'm comin," as she eases the cubboard door shut.

Janal isn't sure what to think; watching Elayne easily places something under the sink behind the tall pots. Janal wonders if it is her birthday present. Even though, she does not want to spoil her mother's surprise, she quickly turns away before her mother realizes she is watching her every move.

"I'm comin," Elayne holler once more.

Janal dash back to the phone, "She's coming Aunt Candice. I love you."

Janal hands Elayne the phone, "Hello...Okay, okay...Bonjour Candice...Yeah, everythang's go'n well. Janal is so happy and thanks for sendin her that beautiful gift."

Unexpectedly and disrespectfully Elayne belches as she continues to talk. The liquor is starting to take effect.

"Auu...You know she misses you very mu...us...ch."

"Elayne, you're not drinking on Janal's birthday, are you?" asks Candice.

The liquor seizes her every word, her every thought. Elayne tries to conceal it but Candice is no fool.

"No...ooo...No way, not today. My little girl and I are go'n to have a swell birthday. Some of her friends are comin over. Shi Li and D'La are comin, too."

"Elayne, don't spoil it for Janal. This is her special day."

"Oh, no. Everythang is going swell." Elayne place her hand over her mouth covering up the sound of another belch. "Of course, Janal's very excited."

As Elayne talks, Janal curiously goes into the kitchen to see what her mother is hiding. Carefully the doubled cubboard doors opens, one at a time. Slowly she pulls so the door does not squeak.

"I bet she's hiding my birthday present under here, yep, I bet she is."

Janal looks behind a large pot and finds a half-filled bottle of liquor, Gin. Janal's devastated. "How could she do this!"

"Candice, I love you, too. Bye."

Janal pays strict attention, listening to her mother as the conversation ends. Swiftly closing the doors, she quickly sits at the kitchen table as her mother enters.

Elayne's smile is senseless as it is phony, pretending everything is well, "That Candice, she'll talk your head off if you let her...I'm tell'n you; that girl...Baby, what time is it?"

Overwhelms with disgrace Janal closes her eyes. Though difficult she tries to hide her tears from her mother before glancing at the clock on the stove.

"Boy, it's get'n late, " Elayne unexpectedly belches again, "We better hurry up. Do we have everythang? ...Oh! I know Janal".

Brokenheartedly, Janal gets up from the table. "I'll be back."

Stunned by her action, Elayne ask, "Is something wrong, baby? Janal, honey!"

Janal completely ignores her mother and her questions, taking small and moderate steps, almost dragging her feet as she walks out of the kitchen into her bedroom, closing the door.

The Paris Hilton, a cab stops at the hotel entrance. Gorgeous long legs extend from the opened door with the most expensive silk stocking hugging firmly. Her hair is blond with a short sassy cut and curls that only the best salons can accomplish, and she is dressed in the most exquisite designer apparel.

Enhancement is not a fair assumption, but things have definitely progress for Candice Felioni as she pays the cab driver. She strolls into the lobby passing the front desk, then into the elevator. Pushes the button and patiently waits for the elevator to stop. Candice soon gets out on her desired floor. Her sensual, uninterrupted rhythm of her hips has developed greatly over the years, turning any man's head that catches sight of her.

She knocks on the door twice before realizing it is already open and walks in.

Inside the room is one of her client who is lying nude on top of the silk quilted bedspread. In view, there is fifteen hundred dollars on the night table next to the lamp. Candice takes the money; counts every dollar before placing it neatly into her handbag. Silent is the room. Only speaking the words necessary, Candice approaches the bed, the client, and begins to take off her clothes very sensually.

His thirst for her is overpowering as he moistens his lips with the spit from his tongue. His burning desire is unquestionable as he gently places his hand over his most precious jewel. Though patient, he diligently watches each second advance on the clock that sits on the desk against the wall. Waiting for Candice's young, tempting and ravishing body to fulfill his sexual craving. Hushed as he watches every piece of her clothing slowly sheer off, as she neatly places them on a velvet davenport. Anticipation defeats him. He swings his body toward hers and immediately puts his head between her thighs. Inflamed with fervor he provocatively kisses each leg one at a time. Her sweet and seductive scent captivates his mind as he maneuvers his kisses toward her vagina. She reaches behind her back to unfasten her bra, then tosses it on the dresser. Loosening herself from his firm hold she slowly gets into bed, promptly straddling him. He places his hand on her proportioned breasts, lifts his head and gently kisses them before placing one in his mouth.

Only one hour of foreplay and sex, his dream is her command. Candice then gets out of the bed and dresses herself very exotically, but in some strange way, with a sense of innocence. With the taste of her body still fresh in his mouth and in his mind, he continues observe her every move. In the midst of absolute delight he ponders on the last hour, like many hours before as Candice completes her dressing.

"Can I see you again? ...Soon!"

With her cold brown seductive eyes, Candice stares at him before answering, "Oui, but remember Monsieur, advanced appointments require a 'no refund' deposit."

The client reaches for the chair that is next to the bed and grabs his pants, pulls out his wallet and takes out a hundred dollars bill then hands it to Candice. Unsatisfied with the hundred dollars, Candice delicately removes his wallet from his hands and takes an additional two hundred dollars out. He is pleased with his deposit; besides, money is no object, all of Candice's clients have money to burn.

"I'll be back next month...same time Oui," says the client.

"Oui," repeats Candice as she completes her dressing, fastening the last button on her expensive silk suit.

Serenely, observing Candice as she picks up her designer handbag and leaves, confidently closing the door behind her.

Jacques Crozier was born in Paris, France, with a silver spoon in his mouth and the only child born to Armand and

Dominique Crozier. He is an elderly gent, about fifty, a multi-millionaire with a compassionate heart.

The family's business is importing and exporting many products internationally. A single man. He has never married. His colleges consider him handsome even, and he is absolutely a ladies man. Many women of all ages from all over the world, some beautiful, some not, have tried to seduce him. Many have scheme numerous plots, but none were successful. They tried every trick in the book that they could think of to get Jacques' hand in marriage, yet they failed.

Although a bachelor, Jacques never forgot what his father once told him when he was a young man: 'As long as the milk's free, why buy the cow?' Jacques never thinks about marriage and sowing his wild oat seems to fit his lifestyle excellently. Plus, he never liked answering to anyone about his whereabouts. Jacques Crozier is a very intelligent, soft spoken, and you may say a 'perfect gentleman'. Jacques has no preference when it comes to dating, single, married, young and older women they all have a unique beauty. And of course, he knows exactly how to treat the gently flower and how they wish to be treated. He gives the world to every woman he dates or at least they thinks so; by showering them with diamonds and furs, shopping sprees, vacations around the world and other luxuries. That is because Jacques believes all women should be spoiled and he prefers to spoil them all the time, then some of the time. He acknowledges: 'If the men in these women's lives are not able to take care to them, Jacques is always willing to do it for them.' In any event, Jacques has enough time and money to do whatever he wants.

At a young age, Mr. Jacques Cozier has convinced himself that he was born to wear Casanova's shoes.

One morning while sitting at an outdoor café, starting on his second cup of coffee, Candice Felioni walks in.

Jacques is intrigued with her beauty, her grace and her elegant taste in clothes as she passes by. One by one and step by step, with each moment Jacques becomes extremely fascinated. He has met many women over the years, but he is confident he has never lay eyes on anyone so exquisite and lovely as Candice. He concludes that he has to find a way to make his acquaintances without seeming improper.

Contemplating on ways, Jacques can't resist the view. His anxiety increases because she is very inviting. Although Candice is not a stranger to admiration, her sensual perception alerts her as she casually looks over her menu observing the inquisitive stranger who is of course, examining her long crossed legs.

Jacques realizes that the lady he is looking at is looking back at him. He smiles, then he gets out of his chair and make his way toward her to apologize for his impoliteness; also realizing this is the perfect opportunity to make his acquaintance.

'An introduction is essential. And there is no better time than now,' he wonders. Jacques soon walks over to Candice's table.

"Bonjour, mademoiselle."

"Bonjour, monsieur," replies Candice.

"I want to apologize for staring so. It's not every day that I see someone as lovely as yourself."

"Merci, monsieur," smiles Candice.

"Non, merci. With your permission, I would like to introduce myself."

"Oui."

"I am Jacques Crozier and you are?"

"My name is Candice Felioni."

"It is such a pleasure to meet you Miss, or should I correct myself and say, Mrs. Felioni?"

"No, it's Miss."

"Miss Felioni, may I join you for a cup of coffee?"

"Oui! You may, Mr. Crozier."

The introduction and the conversation went beautifully. Candice sense that Jacques may be a well-mannered gentleman, someone she has not come across for some time now, and especially in her profession. Although Candice has made up her mind that relationships are not the best thing for her, and it has been many years since Candice even considered the thought.

After her kidnapping and raped, she vowed she would never give herself to any man - for free. Candice has kept that promise ever since. It would take a hell-of-man, a very understanding man to accepts and understand her reasons why she do the things she do.

Months have past and Candice and Jacques have been spending a lot of time together. Candice's uniqueness has finally captured Jacques' heart. But Candice's ice cold heart has only melted a wee bit for the man who has been so kind and generous. Accompanied by her hidden obligations she ponders over the relationship as each day goes by.

'What's to come of this situation?' Candice is apprehensive to tell Jacques about her lifestyle. She continues to suppress the dark secret deep in her mind and her cold heart where it has always been; where it has always felt safe.

A night on the town, a champagne dinner and the theater, Candice's natural feelings: the need for love and the want to be loved are developing overwhelmingly. Though gradual, even her emotional restraint is weakening. Candice is becoming fond of the strange man who has been so good to her. Moreover, he never asked anything of her, and she is very happy with the ways things are going. She never thought anything - like this - could be so wonderful, or a man could be so caring. Their unusual relationship is unquestionably perfect for a girl who has quite a few differences, that is, until she runs into one her clients as she is coming out of the ladies restroom. This encounter makes her extremely uncomfortable. Within that one breath, he greets her and asks for an appointment.

"Carmen...How are you?"

"Bonjour," nervously Candice replies.

"It's been quite a while since I've seen you. Is everything still the same?"

"Somewhat, the same...Oui!"

"Good. You don't know how much I've missed you. Can I see you soon?"

Candice speaks before realizing she has said anything. "Oh, of...of course...you know the number."

"Oui. I do know," smiles the client before rushing away.

Deep within, the fear and uncertainty about her future with Jacques somehow plays important role in her decision. She knows Jacques will eventually find out what kind of a woman has seized his heart sooner or later, and once he does he will throw her back to the streets like the trash she is.

Lying in bed that night, Candice can feel her nerves twisting and tightening through her entire body. She knows it is time to reveal her secret, that deep dark secret that she has suppressed for so long.

Slightly tapping Jacques several times on his shoulder Candice sadly states, "I have something to tell you."

She hesitates, as her throat muscles seems to tighten around her vocal cords which block the flow of air and her words. It is as if she has instantly become mute.

Jacques sits up, bracing a pillow behind his back wondering what could it be, 'Is Candice finally going to end their relationship?'

"Please, whatever you do I want you to understand...I thought about this day many times...I just didn't have the nerve to tell you...before. Now the time has come," says Candice.

Jacques can feel Candice's sadness as he watches each and every neurotic gesture.

"Candice, you're shaking! You know what, if this is bothering you so, I don't care to know...Candice darling, nothing can turn my heart away from you. So whatever it is..."

Candice immediately covers his mouth with her fingers, "Jacques please, listen!" Holding her head downward, immediately closing her eye before looking him in the face.

"Did you ever wonder about what I did before we met? The kind of person I was or the kind of work I did...where I've come from?" She slowly removes her fingers from his soft lips.

"I don't care about that...everything about the past is irrelevant. All I know is that we are here and the time is now...and most of all, I love you. That's all I need to know," Jacques states. He quickly takes her hands, kissing her palms many times.

"Jacques, you're making this very difficult for me."

"Sometimes, love is difficult my dear Candice."

"It's extremely difficult for me at this very moment."

"Then we'll wait...And I'll hold you in my arms until you are relaxed. And later if you wish, I'll make love to you all night and when the sun rises in the morning you can tell me while the birds are singing your name."

"No! Jacques...I want to tell you tonight. Then you can hold me, make love to me tonight if you still want too."

"D'accord, if you insist on telling me tonight, tell me, Candice!"

Candice continues to twiddles with her fingernails, "Well...I don't know where to start."

"My darling, start where your heart tells you to start."

Candice takes a deep breath, than she pauses..."I'm a professional...a professional. Looking into Jacques eyes she declares, "I'm a prostitute, call girl."

Jacques isn't surprised by what Candice has just told him, because he had a private investigator look into her background the first week they met. He knows everything he needs to know about Candice and her secret life style.

"Are you one now?" solemnly he ask.

"Sometimes...I think I am. I was in the business for so long. Sometimes...I wonder about myself."

"Do I make you feel like you're doing your business when we're together?"

"At first, I tried to think of you as a business arrangement. Then it was easy. Now...suddenly, things started to change. Things became very difficult for me. Something had changed inside me, inside my heart. Now my heart belongs to you...But tonight, tonight at the theater, I stumbled into a former client of mine and he asked me for an appointment..." Tears begin to fill her eyes and fall to her cheeks, "...and I agreed."

Jacques' composure is questionable as the conversation proceeds.

"Why, did you agree, Candice?"

Candice can no longer look into Jacques' face. She is extremely embarrassed and ashamed to say anymore as this kind-hearted man sits in front of her for fear of breaking his heart.

"I don't know why. It's like my mind agreed, but my heart did not."

"Here and now, I have a question for you, Candice!"

Instead of hearing him out, Candice turns and gets out of the bed, doubting, fearing that Jacques may say nothing good to her.

"Candice, where are you going?"

Jacques grabs hold of Candice's nightgown.

"I'm going to get my clothes," she utters before glancing into his face, his eyes.

"WHAT! ...WHY?"

"I...I thought that...that might be your next statement or question. I'm afraid to hear any other words," Candice sadly states.

Jacques pulls Candice into his arms.

"Do you think that those things you tell me, I don't already know."

Candice's astonished, severely shocked as her eyes overflow with even more tears.

"Candice, I already know about your past; from the day you were born and where, your childhood, your three special friends and your beautiful goddaughter, everything I need to know about you, I know. I love you Candice, not what happen to you or the things you've done because of it...We all make crazy decision and take crazy chances in life. And yet we must move forward...But when it comes to you Candice, my love is only for you," he sincerely says, giving her heartening smile.

Candice faces him and instantly seizes the moment; throwing her arms around his neck, pushing him down on the bed as his head falls between the pillows. Gazing deep into his warm eyes and with a sigh of relief she graciously pronounces, "Jacques, everything is out. It's finally over...Finis. Finis!"

Jacques continues to shower Candice with everything a woman could ask for and all she could ever want. He surprises her by moving her out of her old apartment and into a beautiful villa. Candice honestly has stolen Jacques' heart. Incredibly she has fallen deeply in love with him as well. Candice never thought a man could be so magnificent. A kind of love she never thought possible. Now she realizes that Jacques is most definitely one of a kind. And he is truly a dream come true.

Dexx and D'La have become such good friends. Dexx has promised to help D'La paint a couple of rooms at her place. Dexx is knocking on the door of D'La's apartment. She peeks through the peek-hole before opening it.

"It's about time...I thought you got lost or somethang."

"No, I wanted to make sure that I had everything that was on your list."

"Oh yeah!"

"Yeah. I didn't want you to get p...ss off or anything...I know from experience...never make a black woman mad. I'm telling you. She will..."

"Ha...a..a," D'La laughs at Dexx's ridiculous explanation. "Sure Dexx, that sounds like a black man's issue to me."

D'La takes one of the paint cans and a bag from Dexx as he carries them into her apartment.

"Just put them over here for right now, Dexx."

They put the cans of paint and bag next to the wall.

"I was fix'n me some lunch, peanut butter and jelly. Do you want a sandwich?"

"Peanut butter and jelly...you know, I haven't had a peanut butter and jelly sandwich in a long time, since I was a little guy."

Dexx follows D'La into the kitchen and sits down at the table, she reaches for the bread, the knife, the peanut butter and jelly. She sticks the knife into the jar and pulls out a huge batch of peanut butter.

"Yeah...umm, don't make it too thick, D'La."

"I know how to make a peanut butter and jelly sandwich..."

"...Ah, I know, but that's too much."

"Dexx...now, quit act'n like a baby."

Teasingly, D'La slaps another huge amount of peanut butter on the bread.

"D'La...if it's too thick it'll make me throw up," Dexx replies.

However, D'La finds Dexx's defensive display hilarious that she begins to laugh.

"Throw up...throw up...Ha...ah. I don't believe you, Dexx Barone. Mister Big and Strong Dexx Barone!"

"I'm serious, D'La. I'll throw up...really."

D'La takes more peanut butter out of the jar and slaps that on the bread.

"This, I gotta see," she says as she continues to laugh.

"D'LA, NO! You crazy girl. What's wrong with you? I told you..."

Dexx spontaneously grabs her by the wrist trying to prevent her from putting more peanut butter on a slice of bread.

D'La can not believe what is actually happening. Everything is so hilarious and her laughter is so severe that she falls from her chair to the floor all the while holding the knife with the peanut buttered stuck on it.

"Ha...a...a...I don't believe it...you. Ha...ah...you gonna throw...up...He...eh. Dam... you are so goofy...ha..aha."

Dexx is so embarrassed that he impulsively tosses his body on top of hers.

"What's so funny? Uh uh."

Dexx takes the peanut buttered knife from D'La, wipes his finger across it.

"Let's see how you like having a mouth full of peanut butter stuck in your throat."

Dexx smears it all over D'La's mouth as she continues laughing. D'La starts to make seductive sounds while motioning her body very suggestively as she licks the peanut butter off his finger, a little bit at a time. "Mm...umm...Ooo this is good...umm so delicious...Dexx, this is real good. Yeah, real good baby. Feed me. Feed me baby."

Unaware of their compromising position Dexx begin to squeeze D'La. Suddenly he realizes that something more is happening between them and it is hard to resist her. Abruptly he stops, quickly releasing her, looking into D'La's face as she continues to tease him and moan.

"Umm Dexx baby, feed me. Don't stop...umm."

Dexx glares into D'La's face, her seductive facial expression makes him want her more as her moaning continues for a few more moments. All at once the playing stops, they're motionless, and everything is quiet. Even the humming from the noisy refrigerator seems soundless. They stare into each other faces, then into each other eyes.

Finding one another's touch very stimulating, they continue to stare before Dexx jumps to his feet, leaving D'La lying on the floor. Quickly finding his way back to his chairs, pretending nothing's happening and all is well. D'La silently admits that something more has just occurred and she too slide into her chair. Trying their best to ignore the situation by looking at the furnishings around them, then eventually at each other.

"D'La just put a little bit of peanut butter on my bread...okay?"

"Sure. No problem...Just a little...I know."

D'La lays the knife on the table and hands Dexx the sandwich on a paper towel then goes to the refrigerator.

"How 'bout somethang to drink? I got some milk to go with that sandwich, if you want some. You know...so it won't get stuck."

"That'll be great, milk and peanut butter has always worked perfect for me, thanks."

Again, resisting her is tremendously difficult and the same thoughts are D'La. They're trying their best to ignore the passionate hunger that is developing between them. Inconspicuously, they begin to eat their sandwiches, as well as, finding it impossible to keep their minds off of the sexual desire growing within.

Dexx wipes his mouth with his napkin, "I think we better get started painting before it gets too late. Cause, I'm going to have to leave soon...I got a lot of things I need to do," states Dexx in low but pleasing resonance.

"Yeah...you're right. We better get started," repeats D'La.

Dexx stands up at the table and D'La finds the view, Dexx's physique, even harder to resist. Starting with his face her thoughts of him begin to imagine every aspect of his body.

Dexx also gazes at D'La as she lifts herself from her chair, standing only an arm length away. D'La's eventually gazes at Dexx's chest. Soon her eyes travel to his waist, then his pelvis area. She stares for several moments, roaming that one particular area before looking upward again; at his chest, his face, and lastly his eyes.

The passion burns as Dexx indiscreetly pushes the chair into the table. He takes D'La into his arms and gently lies her on the floor. Kissing her numerously about the face and lips before snatching at her blouse, struggling and savagely pulling it upward, practically tearing off at each others clothing. Ultimately, their passion sculptures their bodies; from the kitchen floor to the living room, from the living room to hallway, hours later and with few breaks in between the lovemaking finally reaches the bedroom. With her arms tightly bound around his neck, D'La moans and calls his name.

"Dexx...Dexx...I...umm...yeah."

Their passion is intense. Dexx can't resist her love, deeper and deeper, fashioning her around him, holding her and squeezing her in his arms as their minds journey into a world of their own; inevitably becoming one. "Aaah...D'La."

Shi Li has just arrived at work and she is about to punch the time clock when Doctor Tsetung approaches.

"Dr. Kyi, how are you today?"

"I am fine, Doctor Tsetung, thank you for asking."

"I want to let you know that you are doing a great job here at the hospital."

"Thank you Doctor," Shi Li speaks very shyly, still refusing to acknowledge the doctor's interest and still afraid to set free her feminine emotions.

"I have to get to work Doctor Tsetung. Thank you again."

"You're very welcome Dr. Kyi."

Shi Li rushes away, down the corridor of the hospital, never looking back.

MY ONLY   MY LAST

CHAPTER 14

Saturday afternoon and Elayne is about to drop Janal and her friend, Nicole, off at the movies. Nicole is Janal's friend from school; she is a very level headed, intelligent, and pleasant individual.

Elayne always drop the girls off at the movies every Saturday, providing that all Janal's homework is done and her chores are finished. The girls are sitting in the car with the door slightly open.

"I want you to call me when the movie's over and wait for me right here, at the front door...And don't be out here talkin to strangers, Janal," demands Elayne.

"Momma, we know!" says Janal in a slightly rude tone."

"I know you know. That's why I'm tellin you so won't forget that you know. And call me before the last movie ends. Do you understand me young lady?"

"Okay, Momma."

"I mean it, Janal, before the movie ends."

"We will Mrs. Smith, don't worry," says Nicole in a modest tone.

"Here's fifty cents. Twenty-five cents to call me when it's time to pick you up and twenty-five cents more, just in case you loose the first twenty-five cents," says Elayne.

Janal puts the money into her pocket. Then both the girls get out of the car and walk to the window booth to pay for their tickets. Elayne always drives away once the girls enter the theater.

"Let's get something to eat before we look for seats, Janal."

"Yeah, because I don't want to get up in the middle of the movie neither."

At the counter the girls look to see what to buy.

"May, I help you?"

"Yes, I'll have a box of candy," pointing to her favorite kind, a small popcorn and medium soda, please," says Janal.

"What would you like?" asks the clerk.

"I'll have a hot dog, a small bag of popcorn and a medium soft drink too...and a box of Chocolate Bars, please," says Nicole.

Nicole always had a hearty appetite, that is one of the main reasons that she is a little chubby.

After paying the clerk, Janal puts all her money into a different pocket, picks up the food, then the two walks into the dark auditorium.

"I think, this is going to be a good movie," says Janal.

"I can't wait until it starts," ecstatically replies Nicole.

"Me either!"

"Janal, let's get close to the screen. I just love to watch scary movies up close, don't' you?"

Janal and Nicole sit four rows back from the front row of the theater's screen, placing their drinks into the arm holder of the seats and wait attentively for the movie to start. Hours later, as the last movie is coming to its end, Janal makes a comment about calling her mother.

"Wait until the movie's over Janal, then we'll go and make the call together."

"Okay, 'cause I really don't want to miss the end anyway. That's always the best part," declares Janal.

After the movie the girls go to the lobby to make their telephone call, only to find Janal's money is not in her pocket.

"Oh my lord...my money is gone. I lost my money!"

"Are you sure?" Nicole curiously asks.

"Yeah, I must have put it in the wrong pocket. This pocket has a hole in it. Nicole, do you have any money?"

"I think...yeah! I got some," Nicole reaches into her pocket and all she can pull out is nine cents. "Ahh...shoot, I knew I shouldn't have bought that last box of candy during intermission. I'm seriously going on a diet, for sure...What are we going to do now, Janal?"

"I'm going back there to see if I can find my money. Maybe it fell under my seat. I gotta go back to see if it's still there."

"We better hurry before somebody finds it first, Janal."

"Come on Nicole. Everything will be okay. We'll find it."

The two girls rush back to their seats, franticly looking around the floor, behind the seats, kicking over trash left by other movie-goers and wondering where could it have fallen; but there was no money to be found.

"Oh no, Momma's going to kill me. Especially if she finds out I lost all my money, even the emergency money."

"Your momma gonna kill you, my momma is gonna kill me too, we'll both be two dead girls. I wish I could just throw that last box of candy up and get my money back, " apprehensively speaks Nicole.

With their sad faces and their mouths nearly dragging the floor, Janal and Nicole goes to the lobby again.

"I got an idea. Wait here," says Janal.

"What are you going to do?" Nicole's inquisitive nature alerts her, because Janal is always thinking up something.

"I'm going to ask somebody for twenty-five cents so I can call home."

"Janal, are you crazy or something, a stranger!"

"Which would you rather do? Ask a stranger for twenty-five little cents and not tell anybody, don't get in trouble. Or get in trouble, because we lost our money? ...And what if our parents tell us we can never go anywhere else alone, again, uh...Did you think about that Nicole?"

"Okay Janal, you're right...I really don't want to get into any trouble. I know how my father would react. He'll probably make me sit on the porch for the rest of the summer like he did last year."

"Yeah, and you know how stupid you looked last year sitting up there, Nicole?"

Janal looks around and she sees a well-dressed man standing alone in the middle of the lobby. He seems like a nice person and it look as though he is waiting for somebody.

"Wait here Nicole."

Janal walks toward him.

"Janal, Janal..." Nicole blurts in whispering tone. Suddenly she has a quick change of mind and calls for her friend to come back, but Janal is too far to hear her.

"Excuse me, sir," Janal politely says.

Composed, the man turns toward Janal.

"What's up, Li'l Momma."

"I was wondering if I could borrow twenty-five cents please?"

Janal hesitates momentarily before continuing, "...I lost my money and I need to make a call. I was wondering if you..."

He interrupts before she could finish, "Ain't no thang, Li'l Darlin. Sure you can borrow twenty-five cents. Matter of fact, you can keep it."

She was right, the stranger is a nice person, believes Janal, as he reaches into his pocket and takes out a quarter and gives it to her. Although, before she could walk away he stops her. He reaches into his pocket and takes out a pen and pad.

"Just a minute, Li'l Darlin...umm, take my number, you know, just in case you ever need anythang else. My friends call me Beauden, but you can call me Poppa Beau."

Janal looks up at him, takes the phone number and walks toward to Nicole.

"See, we're not going to get into any trouble after all, Nicole."

Nicole looks at the man who has just given Janal the money and asks, "What else did he say to you? What did he write on that piece of paper?"

With a sassy attitude Janal says, "His name is Poppa Beau and he gave me his phone number."

Janal's action and her irresponsible attitude seriously disturb Nicole.

"His phone number! ...Why? You're not going to call him, that Poppa Beau, are you?"

Calmly, Janal answers, "No, don't be crazy Nicole."

"Good, cause Poppa Beau, he's old enough to be your great grandfather."

Beauden keeps a steady eye on Janal, 'a fine and tender roni like that needs somebody to take good care of her...umm,' as she puts the money into the phone slot. Soon Beauden is approached by his date for the evening; she is a big-busted woman with a large butt.

"Hey baby that didn't take long," she says she approaches him.

Staring at Janal he replies, "Nah, everythang is everythang." Beauden gives Janal one last glance before leaving the theater.

It is past closing time at Dexx's Place, about 3:10 am: Dexx and D'La are inside his office closing down things for the night. D'La has been doing Dexx favors, by helping him calculate the weekly sale receipts and several small office jobs. Unexpectedly, the door buzzer rings. Dexx throws his pencil down on the desk.

"Who in the hell could that be?"

D'La looks at Dexx as the door buzzer rings one more time. He is not expecting anybody. Dexx takes his gun out of the office desk and tucks it into the waist of his pants, behind his back. Then he goes to the door, looks through the peek hole, he recognizes the person at the door, so he opens it.

"Hey, Man, what you doing out here this time of night?"

"Dexx my man, I need some money. I thought that..."

"Johnny, I told you not to come around here anymore; you're too hot. I don't need the man sticking his nosey butts up in my business cause of you. You trying to get me locked up. This is some bull...?"

Even though some city officials are on the payroll didn't mean all of them were.

"Nah, Dexx Man, I ain't try'n to do anythang like that...dam... I gotta get some money from somewhere, somehow. All I need is a little cash so I can get the f... out-a-here. Anywhere just as long as it's away from Detroit. Dexx, my man, you dig where I'm comin from, don't you?"

Dexx pulls fifty dollars out of his pocket.

"Johnny I'm telling you...this is the last time, man."

"Dexx, is that all you got?" asks Johnny.

Dexx couldn't help noticing Johnny's clothes, how nasty and dirty with many soiled spots all over them.

"Johnny Man, you're going to have to find you another hustle. What in the hell have you been doing all this time, anyway? You look terrible and you stink."

"Things ain't been so great. Every time I turn around, BAMM, sh... hap'ns. Ever since I smoked those two pigs for kill'n by little brother, Mark, all kind of thangs just keep on comin my way. So Dexx I figured, I'll get some money and get the heck out of the city for a while. You know...til thangs calm down a bit. Cause man, every time I look up, I see the Big Four, Little Four, all kind of nigga killers...I think they even got little killer midget police out look'n for my butt. Everywhere I go those mothers pop up. I ain't got no kind of peace. You know how they always try'n to lock a brother up. A black man ain't got a chance round here anymore."

"Johnny you out shooting up every dam... thing you see nigga. Acting like you some wacko, lunatic or something, you just gone crazy, man!"

"Dexx you know how that sh... jumped off. I wasn't try'n to do nuth'n that time. But that punk can't be talk'n 'bout me to my face and keep walk'n too," cocky Johnny replies, nervously shaking as he adjust his dirty clothes.

"That's why you gotta keep your narrow as... from around here. I can't be getting mixes up and going to jail for no dumb sh...."

Dexx goes around to the other side of the counter to the cash register to get Johnny a few more dollars. Dexx opens the drawer to the cash register as Johnny takes a quick glimpse into it and he sees enough money to take him far away from Detroit, real fast.

Little balls of sweat begin to bead on Johnny's face as he watches Dexx take out the money. Nervously and swiftly Johnny pulls a gun out of his jacket.

"Man, I'm sorry, but I gotta do this."

"WHAT THE F...! You crazy bastard...Put that dam... gun down!" calmly but angrily Dexx responds.

The longer Johnny points the gun at Dexx the more nervous he gets as the beads of sweat quickly turns into balls that dripped from his face.

"I can't...Now, ain't nobody gonna get hurt, okay Dexx? Just take all of the money out of the register and give it to me. All I want to do is get the f... up out of here, man...Now...do what I tell you."

The sweat rolls faster, covering Johnny's face completely, as he watches Dexx take all the money out of the register.

"Okay, Johnny Man, you know you're screwing up, don't you? Just quit sh... while you can. You come here asking for help and his is the bull sh... I get in return."

"And...uh...I want the money in the safe too, Dexx. Now, go get it, " demands Johnny.

"You're really going too far with this bull sh... Johnny."

Johnny is getting agitated and his voice level starts to deepen. Dexx turns around slow and easy, then heads for his office.

"Dexx, DON'T F... WITH ME...NOW, hurry up and get the money out the safe."

D'La hears the outburst and she rush to the office's entrance to see what the commotion is about. She is shocked to find a man with a gun, and he is aiming it at Dexx, also they're coming in her direction. She looks around the office for a place to hide, but there is nowhere to go. She hurries behind the office's desk and lays silently on the floor, waiting patiently, her heart beats uncontrollably as she fears for Dexx's life.

"Okay, man just hold up. I'll get you what you want. Just quit waving that dam... gun."

Dexx knows he has no choice but to do what Johnny wants, he turns his back, all the way around, facing the opposite direction and that is when his gun is exposed.

Be that as it may, Johnny notices the gun in Dexx's pants and jerks it out. "You won't be need'n this Mr. Bigman. I'm the head nigga in charge now. Ha, uh, ah."

Johnny laughs as he seizes control of Dexx and the situation. D'La observes their shoes from the floor as they enter the office doorway; Dexx's feet are walking toward the wall safe, he opens it.

"Okay Man! Take the money and get the f... out," says Dexx.

Johnny looks around the office, his attitude flare a bit high, and a bit cockier; being in charge makes him feel good again as he boasts, giggling, waving the gun in Dexx's face.

"Nah, it ain't go'n down like that brother man. You take the money out of the safe and put it in that bag, right there."

D'La peeks out and the gunman looks familiar, but she can not remember exactly from where. Dexx takes the bag off the desk, putting all the money into it, emptying the safe entirely, including books with important names and addresses. Once the bag is full, he hands it to Johnny, as the reality of the circumstances hits him, Dexx seriously worries about D'La's safety.

"Okay, Johnny you got the money, now leave."

Johnny continues to sweat, "Sorry Man, but I can't do that, either...leave you stand'n. My momma didn't raise no fool, not when it comes to Johnny Burton anyway; not here. Cause, as soon as my black as... walk out of that door about fifty dudes will be on me like there's no tomorrow."

"So what, you going to do...shoot me, Johnny?"

"Now, you know how that bull goes...You know exactly how this sh... works, Dexx."

D'La listens as the conversation heats up and she does not like what she is hearing. She fears for Dexx's life. She knows that somehow she has to do something and something fast. So she eases her bowie knife out of her low cut boots, peeks out from her hiding place and slowly stands up. She signals Dexx by nodding her head. She takes the tip of the blade and quickly throws it precisely into the center of Johnny's back.

He's traumatized as the throbbing pain captures his attention. He turns slightly to see what, who threw the knife, looking around all the while trying to keep an eye on Dexx. But it is too painful and impossible. His focus is lost, and without warning Dexx grabs Johnny's gun hand. Knocking over furniture while aggressively struggling Johnny to the floor. Without hesitation, there is a fight for life, the gun goes off and within that one precious moment, everything is still.

D'La wonders: 'Whose been shot?' It is the longest second of her life as Dexx eventually stands up over Johnny's body. And at that moment, D'La is gratified, surprised and relieved as she rushes toward him, throwing her arms around his neck.

"Are you all right?" she asks while kissing him numerous times.

"Yeah, I'm cool, De."

"That crazy nigga...What are we gonna do with his body", she asks.

"Ah...Get me a plastic tarp off the kitchen shelf. I gotta wrap this sh... up fast, throw him the f... out of here before he bleeds all over the dam... place."

D'La approaches Johnny, looking downward as he lies on the floor.

"Is he dead, Dexx?"

"If he ain't, he will be."

She pulls her knife out of his back and wipes the blood off, cleaning it with Johnny's shirt, he moans. She abruptly looks over at Dexx.

"He's still alive!"

Dexx is highly surprised with D'La's demeanor, cool and courageous, that this woman could be so much like him, as if she is his own shadow, standing a hundred percent behind him. Yet, thinking only of her and what she witnesses tonight really bothers him. In reality, he never wanted her involved in any of his illegal activities. This is one relationship he wanted to keep clean and clear from corruption.

"D'La baby, go get the plastic tarp off the kitchen shelf, NOW!
I'll call a couple of the boys to come and get rid of this crazy nigga."

"But Dexx?"

"D'LA," he shouts.

D'La runs into the kitchen and while looking on the shelf for the plastic tarp, all of a sudden, there is a shot and then another one. She yells, "DEXX." She runs back into the office and sees Dexx sitting in a chair in front of the desk; his shirt is covered with blood.

D'La looks down at Johnny who is lying on his side and pointing a gun at her. She hesitates, standing motionless, without making a sound, or even batting an eye; unexpectedly, Johnny Burton collapses.

D'La is not taking anymore chances as she pulls the knife out of her boot one last time. Expeditiously dropping down on one knee, she stabs Johnny in his chest abundantly, screaming hysterically, "DIE YOU NASTY MOTHER F...er DIE...DAM... YOU, DAM... YOU...CRAZY NIGGA."

When finished and knowing for sure that Johnny is dead this time, she crawls to Dexx, sobbing, her tears streaming down her face and screaming his name: "DEXX, DEXX, are you all right."

He says nothing.

"Please don't die...DEXX...DEXX...DON'T DIE. I love you...Please, Dexx. LIVE FOR ME."

Dexx's semi-conscious and does not fully comprehend what D'La is saying as he opens his eyes and sees her tears falling.

"D'La...Baby."

D'La then smiles, she is relieved that Dexx seems all right. "Dexx, Dexx I gotta get you outta here."

She tries lifting him but before she can do anything Dexx collapses.

"DEXX...DEXX." Tapping his face she continues to call his name. Frantically she grabs the phone off the desk pulling it to her and dials for the operator. After placing the call Dexx regains consciousness.

"I'm sorry baby...I had to call the ambulance," hysterically she cries, "I have to do somethang. Dexx, I don't want you to die."

"You called the ambulance? You gotta get out of here. I don't want you to get caught up with this sh... Go D'La please? Get the hell out of here, NOW!"

"Shh...Don't talk. You're gonna be all right. The ambulance is on its way, Dexx? Please e...e, baby just relax. I'm not gonna leave you like this...I'm with you all the way, one hundred percent, whether you like it or not...no matter what. You hear me!"

Her tears cover her face, blinding her as she runs to the bar and grabs a towel and ice. Applying a cold compact and pressure to his chest trying to stop the bleeding, trying to stop Dexx from dying. She tries comforting him by wiping the moisture from his face, but before she knows it...within that one second, Dexx Barone dies.

D'La's dumfounded; wild with anger as the pain stabs her heart. She screams and yells his name, shaking him vigorously, trying to wake him from death, to bring him back to her, "Dexx...Dexx...DEXX... DEXX...NO...O...Ooo...YAA AH...NO.O.o.o."

D'La falls to her knees, pushing her body between his legs and kissing his bloody hands as she prays for a miracle, while promising to make changes in her life, but Dexx does not make a move or a sound. Twenty minutes pasts, D'La still sits on the floor, with her head lying on his thigh, with one arm wrapped around his legs and the other hand squeezing his hand tightly. She talks to him and kisses his hands constantly, one bloody hand after the other.

Finally, she hears the sirens and the ambulance is not far away. She gets up, but instead of leaving as he warned, she bends over him and continually kisses his lips. The sirens are getting louder, realizing she has to leave soon she walks toward the door, but she finds it impossible. She can not leave him like this. She looks back, turns around and dashes back to him, again falling to her knees, pushing herself between his legs, kissing him, crying, squeezing him and calling his name, "DEXX ...DEXX."
The longer she lingers the more difficult it becomes, leaving him dead in a chair and knowing she has no choice. Still, her tears continue to flow as she tries to leave, kissing his lips again and again. Finally forcing herself, she creeps to the door. But as soon as she reached the entrance she stops, she turns, realizing that a future together - is no more, and blows him one last good-bye kiss before saying, "Dexx...You're my first and my last. I'll always love you," she whispers, "Even in death," before walking away forever.

The day is just gorgeous, the birds are singing, the sun is brightly shining with only a few clouds in the sky and everybody and anybody has come. The procession is huge; approximately fourteen or fifteen stretched black limousines all distinctively polished as the sun's radiance reflects every object they pass.

D'La continues to weeps uncontrollably as the driver opens the limousine door. She slowly walks toward his grave, covering her face with wet tissue she holds tight in her hands, squeezing and twisting it. Though her small hesitates steps bring her closer she refuses to acknowledge his death, by refusing to get closer to his casket.

Yet, Janal's heart is filled with deep sorrow, watching her aunt's emotions as she cries so severely for a man she had only a short time to love. No one ever thought D'La could love any man, then Dexx Barone walks into her life. She was so excited and at times so gentle-hearted. Although, she tried to hide her true feelings behind that sassy and tough girl image, we knew.

However, crying is something Janal has never seen D'La do before as she too slowly walks closer to his grave. D'La stares at his casket, his gravesite, she is almost lifeless, she recalls their good times, their intimate moments, his tender touch as well as his loving heart.

She gently wipes the tears from her face, but that doesn't stop them from falling from her eyes, the more she wipes the more they fall. Janal releases her mother's hand and gradually approaches D'La. Immediately throwing her arms around her, holding her tightly, trying her best to comfort Aunt D'La as she too begin to cry.

From a distant, Shi Li, Candice, and Elayne notice an older woman wearing a long black dress. She has a black lace hankie that she holds close to her face that she uses to wipe away her tears. And she has a lovely black hat with a large black veil that drapes onto her shoulders, covering her entire face. For some reason, she slowly eases her way toward D'La. Even though this woman has never met her before, D'La's dramatic and emotional outcry identifies her, capturing the woman in black attentions.

'This has got to be the young lady my son told me so much about. Her honey brown complexion, small frame, she's a little taller than what he described, and the way she wears her hair, a curly Afro. ...Yes, this has to be her...the one, Dexx loves so much.'

The woman keeps a watchful eye on D'La as she gets closer.

'Yes, he said he wants me to keep in touch with her if anything ever happens.'

The woman continues to recall the conversation that she had with her only child, Dexx Barone.

"Excuse me...I'm Ms. Barone, Dexx's mother. Are you D'La?"

Sorrowfully she gazes up, " Yes, yes, I am."

She reaches for D'La's hand, though her touch is gentle she takes a firm hold.

"I just want to thank you for caring enough to come," she says as she places a small piece of paper into D'La's hand.

"Here's my number. If you ever want to talk or need any thing, please, call me please!"

"Thank you very much, Ms. Barone, and you have my utmost and deepest sympathy."

"And you mines, D'La."

D'La gives Dexx's mother a sincere hug before she walks away.

Despite death, his love whispers from the grave. Whispers that entangled with the breeze that folds the leaves on the trees around its branches. Whispers that bend with the grass and the flowers that grow near by. Whispering the words only the soft wind can hear.

The whisper say: "D'La, I'll always love you."

CHAPTER 15

Candice stays a couple of weeks longer in Detroit after Dexx's death, she wants to offer any help she can to D'La who has emotionally and physically falling apart. D'La is so distraught that she doesn't return to work for almost a month. Yet, her three friends and her goddaughter are always by her side, consoling her every step of the way and caressing her every emotion.

Eighteen days after Dexx's funeral D'La becomes very ill. She believes it is because she has not been taking care of her physical needs: she has lost her appetite and she can't sleep at night.

Ultimately, she starts to feel a little better, but not totally. Early one morning, with some convincing from her friends she decides to go to the doctor for a check-up. After her examination and the return of her test results, the doctor calls D'La into his office. This was one of the most appalling days of her life.

"Congratulation, Miss. Lausen, you're going to have a baby."

D'La is shocked and frightened by the news, "WHAT...are you sure? That can't be true. I don't know if...I can't have a baby...I don't know...What am I go'n to do with a baby? ...No way!"

"Just relax Miss Lausen, new mothers always get excited or scared by the news at first."

"No, you don't understand...I can't be. I can't have a baby."

"Now calm down, Miss Lausen, everything is going to be just fine."

The doctor tries every way possible to reassures her, but D'La is so uncomfortable with the news of having a baby that she quickly springs up out of her chair.

"I gotta go...I'll call you...Uh...Just send me the bill!"

Confused, D'La dashes out of the doctor's office and into her car and drives around for hours thinking and crying about Dexx and his baby that is growing inside of her.

Afraid of the future, afraid of what her life is becoming, she never thought about having a child. She actually thought bringing a child into this crazy world is insane. Nor did she ever dream it would happen to her.

D'La is drained at this point and decides to go home and take a bath. Several hours after her bath, while relaxing on the couch D'La begin to cry more. Hopelessly thinking and occasionally pacing nonstop about her apartment, walking from room to room she is drawn to the closet. She opens the door and notices one of Dexx's shirts hanging on a hook. D'La takes the shirt off and stares at it as she remembers the beautiful times they spent together. She squeezes the shirt in her hands. Then she puts it against her face, lays across the bed, holding it to her breast.

Even though its Dexx's baby, D'La is still confused about the entire situation and she is considering giving the baby up for adoption. She thinks, 'Maybe someone could be a betta mother than me. Perhaps someone could raise Dexx's baby to be somebody, far better than what I have to offer. And what do I have to offer...what do I got? ...Nuth'n, nuth'n at all'.

She truly believes that she is worthless. Especially after everything that has happen, not acting soon enough to save Dexx's life that night. And at this very moment she asks herself: 'how would he feel about me being the baby's mother? Am I woman enough to raise his child? No, no way...I'm not woman enough."

Her thoughts are quickly interrupted when the phone starts ringing. She picks it up. She hesitates before saying anything.

"Hello...D'La, are you there? Hello."

"...Hello, Shi Li." D'La voice is extremely meek.

"D'La, I called to see if you are all right...Are you? And do you need me to do anything for you? Did you eat anything today?"

D'La's words were slow to answer. She has been crying nonstop for the last three hours.

"Did you go to the doctor?" asks Shi Li.

"Yeah, I went," mumbles D'La.

"What did the doctor say?"

"Dam... Shi Li, he said I'm pregnant."

Shi Li's overwhelmed with the news. "WHAT? ...You are pregnant? I knew it. How did that happen? ...Well I know how it happened. I mean, I thought you were not going to have any children and that you were so against bringing a child into this crazy world. Did you not use protection?"

D'La becomes deeply stressed as Shi Li questions and comments continue.

"I don't want any kids. I'm butch...a dyke, and bit... like me don't get pregnant, Shi Li."

"D'La, you are not making any sense. Remember, you are still a woman."

"A woman that likes pus... You know...other women. Dexx is dead, the only man I ever been with...And, now I'm pregnant. How can I go on with my life if I'm knocked up? I can't get a woman if my big stomach's stickin out over everythang. And besides, how would Dexx feel about this? Can you tell me that, Shi Li, can you?"

"D'La...D'La...This is wonderful news and there is a good reason for this, I am pretty sure."

"What in the f... kind of a good reason could a big stomach pregnant dyke be? What kind of a reason is that? I would sure like to..." D'La shouts, "KNOW!"

"D'La, calm down, you are just upset right now, just relax, please. I spoke to Candice yesterday, even though she just left, she said she will catch the first flight from France tomorrow evening, and then we can all sit down and find a solution to this situation; the four of us, together."

"I already know what to do with this situation."

Shi Li is disturbed by D'La's attitude and it is sending chills down her spine.

"Do not do anything stupid, D'La. Just go to bed and we will talk tomorrow, okay?"

The doorbell rings.

"Hold up, somebody's at my door."

Shi Li listens to the background noises as D'La answers it.

"Who is it?"

"It's me, Elayne, open the door, girl."

D'La pushes the buzzer, before returning to the phone.

"It's Elayne. Shi Li, I'll talk to you later."

"D'La, remember, we love you and we will always be here for you. And D'La, stay calm please, everything will be fine. Bye."

"D'La hangs up, opens the door as Elayne saunters in with a paper bag in her hand.

"Hey girl, I thought you be need'n somethang right about now, so I brought you somethang right about now."

"Brought me somethang, like what Elayne?" Elayne chuckles as she holds up the brown bag, "Somethang to relax your nerves. It really works and I ought to know...it relaxes me all the time and every time, without a doubt. When I get upset, I go in the kitchen, get a glass and pour me a little bit. Sometimes, I just drink right out of the bottle. ...You know, sometimes it seems to taste betta when I drink it straight like that. Then I'll sit back, relax for a few minutes...TA-TA, I'm feel'n fine honey-child, just fine. It's like magic. Nerves relaxed, yep...everythang's relaxed."

D'La swing close the apartment door, slamming it shut.

"Elayne...you're drunk."

"Nope...not yet, but I'm work'n on it...ha ha ah..."

"Elayne, you should be try'n to get off of that stuff."

"Yeah, yeah, yeah...I know, I know, I know...Ma mam, the Reverend, and everybody else keeps say'n that...they even got my little sister, Elizie, talk'n I should come back to church. And all I got to say is, ya'll probably are right? But I ain't, I need this magic medicine in a bottle. Once you get use to it, it has great incentives. Hey, I know what I'm do'n. I don't need no babysitter. "

Elayne belches, then drags her feet into the kitchen and takes a glass out of the cupboard.

"I'm not in the mood for drink'n anyway, Elayne," says D'La.

Elayne jokingly ask, "How come? I didn't spit in it or anythang." Elayne looks through the bottle, "And nuth'n fell out of my nose when I was drink'n out of it either." Holding the bottle to her face she gazes at its content, "I don't see anythang. Anyway...if so...it still looks good," she sips from the bottle, " and it still taste good too...And it can make you and me feel good, together. Come on D'La take a little sip."

"I'm pregnant," D'La grumbles.

Elayne quickly sits on the living room couch next to D'La.

"Now run that by me again. You're WHO?

"Pregnant! And I don't know what I want to do. I'm confused."

"YOU'RE WHO...PREGNANT!" Elayne giggles. "...Girl, go for yourself...I knew that fine deep dark chocolate delicious looking black man would get next to your butt. He was one good-looking brother if you ask me...Umm uh...Now that's a piece of as... a girl would fight for."

Elayne is so excited that she puts the glass on the cocktail table.

"D'La, I'm so happy for you. The Lord has blessed you and it's about time, if I do say so myself. And you know what, I don't care what you say. There's a woman in that body behind all that butch and she's just beg'n to come out...How long have I been know'n you...uh? Just about all my life and I knew it would happen one day. I knew it would take a hell-of-man, a strong man to bring her out. You know what? ...I'm glad 'cause this is what you need. That's for Dam... sure!"

D'La is baffled as she toys with her emotions, "I'm not keep'n it...I'm givin the baby up for adoption."

"WHAT'S THE MATTER WITH YOU GIRL, ARE YOU OUT OF YOUR MIND OR SOMETHANG! That baby would have NEVER found its way up in your BUTT if it wasn't meant to be. D'La don't be talk'n crazy like that."

"Elayne, I feel if Dexx knew that I was carry'n his baby before he died, he would have told me to get rid of it. Go see a doctor, D'La, cause my baby's momma will be all woman. Not a half-n-half, a man in a woman's body; a wanna-man."

"D'La, no he wouldn't have and you're make'n excuses. He fell in love with the first time he laid eyes on you, ever since he met your silly butt that man has be hog-wild over you. And he would've been so happy that you're that baby's momma compared to those wanna-be heffas that was run'n behind the man every minute of the day, try'n to do anythang and everythang to get in his bed. I believe, if Dexx was alive today he would marry you in a heartbeat just to give that baby his last name." Elayne takes another sip of liquor and belches twice.

"I don't know, Elayne, everythang was great between us, but I can't help wonder'n."

"Well stop wonder'n before you get sick or somethang. I didn't come all the way over here to see you throw up and talk all stupid and stuff. Umm, talk'n crazy like that will make any woman sick. Heck, all this talk of relationships done spoiled my appetite...done killed that sweet booze taste I like in my mouth too. Darn, all this talk, it really don't taste that same right now, pew! " Elayne belches a short one, then a long one. "...D'La you know what, after listen'n to you talk about being pregnant, I ain't upset no more. My blues done gone away...I feel kinda special."

Elayne puts the top on the liquor bottle, "D'La, I remember when I was pregnant with Janal, I was so happy."

"I was too. I was so happy it was you and not me."

D'La and Elayne start to laugh as they reminisce all night long about the good old days.

Approximately eight and a half months later, D'La gives birth to a son and he has a lot of his father's features.

Candice, Shi Li and Elayne have come to visit D'La at the hospital and she is still an emotional wreck. Due to the fact that, her pregnancy was a difficult one. She suffered with one or the other constantly: dizziness, fainting and vomiting at least two or three times a day. Her delivery was even worse. It seems as though her pregnancy has been cursed and the doctors thought that they would have to delivery by cesarean section. Thank goodness and just in the nick-of-time, D'La's baby decides he was ready to come into the world and when he felt like it, and all by himself. He has the same temperament, just like his mother.

Later that day the nurse brings D'La her son, he is all wrapped in a soft blue blanket and a cute tiny blue knit cap.

"Miss Lausen, I have your baby boy and he wants to see his mother, besides he's ready for his dinner."

The nurse gives D'La the baby as Shi Li, Candice and Elayne is overcome with enchantment.

"He's so beautiful, D'La...Look at those little hands," says Candice.

Knowing exactly how D'La feels, Elayne just has to ask anyway, "Are you plan'n on breast feed'n him?"

Shi Li and Candice couldn't hold back their giggles. D'La looks at Elayne as if she is losing her mind.

"No, Elayne, no!"

Yet, Elayne continues, "Ahh...isn't it amazing, that when you see a baby this small it kinda make you want to have one of your own. Don't it ya'll."

No, it don't Elayne," responds D'La.

"Of course, not you D'La, you just had one, " smiles Candice.

"D'La, have you decided on a name?" asks Shi Li.

D'La hesitates, "...No."

"Why not? Don't you think you betta name the little fella before you take him home?" replies Elayne.

D'La hesitates again before answering, "...I'm not take'n him home with me. I just want to look at him one time before...I make my decision."

Out of curiously Candice ask, "What decision? What are you going to do with him, D'La?"

"I'm put'n him up for adoption so he can have a real mother."

Candice is extremely surprise that D'La can give away her own child, a sweet innocent baby and after holding him so close that she expresses her dearest feelings, "You can't!"

Shi Li agrees, "D'La, you cannot do that. He is a part of you...your own flesh and blood, Dexx's son."

D'La is outraged that Shi Li would try to explain who the baby's father is.

"I know WHOSE SON he is, Shi Li."

"Yes, he's Dexx's son, D'La. And you talk about how much you loved Dexx. If you did love him so much you would never let that child out of your sight," argues Candice.

"I'm not ready to be a mother," D'La starts to cry, her feelings pour as her fear reveal themselves, "I don't know how."

"I didn't know how either and sometimes I think, like today, I don't think I got it right yet," agrees Elayne.

"It takes time, sometimes a mother never learn, and that is when her instinct kicks in to teach her. D'La, all that is required of you and for that beautiful little person is, that you give it your all," explains Shi Li.

"Well my instinct tells me that I'm not ready," replies D'La.

"D'La, if you give that sweet little boy away you will be sorry for the rest of your life. If you want to know, how I know, just say, I have known you long enough to know. Now, he is here and you act like you do not care about his life and refusing to face those true feelings inside of your heart," says Shi Li, "Now, deal with the facts!"

D'La screams and cries as she clenches the baby's blanket, "I care...I care, but I don't know what to do. DEXX IS DEAD. Yes, I loved him, but I'm not ready to be a mother. I'M AFRAID!"

"You're still grieving for Dexx and this is a very emotional time D'La, " says Candice as she spontaneously embraces D'La.

"We love you D'La as always, we're always by your side, " Elayne says.

Candice adds, "So don't worry, we're here to help. Just take some time to think about this, please, for Little Dexx."

Elayne agrees, "Yeah, for Li'l Dexx...and you can always count on us through thick and thin, remember!"

Shi Li replies, "Always."

"You know, thank you, thank all of you...and it's true. You have always been there for me. We have always been there for each other...You know what? ...I think I like that name...Li'l Dexx and I will give it some thought," D'La tenderly replies.

Eight weeks later, D'La walks up on the porch of her brother's house, rings the doorbell and waits patiently as the door quickly swings opens.

"Hey De. What's up girl! Come on in."

"Hi Michael."

D'La sits on the couch and lays Li'l Dexx next to her as Michael gently removes the blanket from his face.

"Is this the little rascal...Let me see him?"

"This is him," says D'La.

"De girl, he looks just like his old man. Look at him. Look at that nose. That ain't your nose on his face and that nose sure don't run in our family."

D'La grins as Michael admirer the baby's features.

"Wait a minute, come and give Big Bro a hug girl, and quit act'n like a stranger."

As Michael caresses D'La, Tina and Pamela, Michael's two young daughters come running from the kitchen heading straight for D'La.

"Aunt D'La," shouts Pamela as her sister Tina mimics her every word, "Aunt D'La."

"Hey...my two best girls, come on over here and give me a big hug."

D'La holds out her arms as the girls run to her, they're squeezing her as D'La showers them with lots of hugs and kisses. Pamela is first to glance at the baby. "He is so little."

Tina replies, " ...and he's pretty, too."

Pamela's inquisitive as she looks up at her father, "Boy's aren't pretty, they're handsome right daddy!" she says.

"He's pretty to me," replies Tina, sticking out her tongue before continuing, "Can we keep him Daddy, forever and ever?"

"No, I don't think so, Puddin."

Tina continues, "Ah aha...Daddy, but he's so little. He needs me to take care of him."

Tina glances at D'La and ask, "Aunt D'La, can we have him? I love him and I want him to live with us forever, all right?"

Big sisters Pamela intervenes, always a miss know-it-all.

"Tina don't be stupid, he's only going to live with us for a little while, until Aunt D'La feels better. Ain't that right, Daddy? Tina, don't know nothing!"

Michael readily interrupts, "Hey...did you two finish your breakfast?"

Guilt instantly covers Tina and Pamela's faces. Holding one arm straight out, Michael points to the kitchen, "Get in that kitchen and eat your food. Go on...get!"

Tina and Pamela run into the kitchen, as D'La sadly glances up at her brother Michael and her eyes are swollen and red.

"They're grow'n up fast."

"Yep, too fast if you ask me, "Michael replies."

"Michael, I want to thank you for take'n Lil' Dexx for me. I'm all dazed out or somethang. I'm terribly confused. I feel like I'm crack'n up. Right now, I need time to think. Some space, before I really go crazy."

"Sis, do what you got to do. He'll be fine here. I'll take extra good care of him. I'll treat him as if he's my own son. You know that."

D'La's begins to cry. "I know you will. You have a good heart Michael and that's one of the reasons I love you so much."

"De, as you can see, boys are scarce around here. I'm gonna need somebody to watch my back from all these females. I just hope Tina doesn't try to kidnap the little fella."

Michael jokes somehow compels D'La to smile, she immediately stands up and put her arms around Michael's necks.

"Thank you...Thank you for be'n there, again."

"What are big brothers for if they can't be there when their little sister needs 'em, uh um?"

D'La takes her purse off the couch.

"Well, I better get go'n before you get all mushy on me. I can only smile so long...ha ha," says D'La trying to laugh.

"And Sis, don't worry about a thang. Sophie can't wait to have a little man in the house. She'll be so happy to see Lil' Dexx. She always wanted a boy, now she got one...At least for a little while anyway."

"Where's Sophie?"

"She had to go to her parent's house and do some errands for them. Yeah, that arthritis has her father feelin real bad and her mother don't want to leave him alone in the house."

D'La slowly walks to the front door.

"Kiss the girls for me and tell Sophie thanks, and I'll call her later, " says D'La as she gives Michael another great hug.

"I will...And De, take care."

D'La gets into her car, waving good-bye as Michael stands on the porch watching. He shouts, "See you later, Sis...And don't worry, everythang is gonna be just fine."

THE DEVIL'S HAGGLE

CHAPTER 16

It is Thursday night, about 9 o'clock, Janal, now twelve and a half, is in the hallway on the telephone whispering as her mother sleeps on the couch. Janal has been secretly spending time with Beauden ever since she met him at the theater.

Today has been an extremely long day, tax season, and Elayne has been working overtime at the office for the last two weeks; it has really taken a toll on her. After dinner, around 7:30, Elayne has fallen asleep on the couch in front the television as it plays.

"Poppa Beau, I called to thank you for buying me such a beautiful dress...No! My mother doesn't know who bought it. She hasn't even seen it...Well, I was thinking about coming over there tonight...Nah, I won't get into any trouble...I...on the bus...Oh, yeah...she asleep on the couch...She won't even know I'm gone...okay...Bye."

At 9:05, Janal hangs up the phone, peeks at her mother to confirm that she is still asleep, and she is.

"Good...I'll leave out the side door, that way she won't hear me."

At 9:12, Janal quickly and quietly dashes out of the house, heading for the bus stop and gets on. About 10:30 Janal arrives at her destination, she knocks on the front door.

A stern and ragged voice yells from within in.

"WHO IS IT?"

Leroy drags himself to the door with his cards in hand.

"It's Janal. Is Poppa Beau home?"

He opens slowly. "Hold up hold up." Leroy calls Beauden to the door, "Hey, Beauden...Man, it's for you."

"Who is it, Leroy?"

Beauden leans back in his chair just enough to peek toward the front door where Janal is standing.

"It's me Poppa Beau, Janal!" she blurt outs, looking pass Leroy.

"Oh, let her in, Man. She's cool."

"Sure thang, Beau," smiles Leroy with a devilish grin.

Janal walks into the house, sees two men sitting at the table with Beauden playing cards, gambling and drinking whiskey. She is so young, so innocent and confident as she joyfully walks toward him. Believing he is such a good person, her new friend, a father figure she can look up to, something she never had yet longs for.

"Hi Poppa Beau. See! I told you I was coming. You didn't believe me, did you?"

Beauden smile gradually stretches across his fat face, "Everybody, I want you to meet Janal. Janal these are some card play'n fellas of mine. You already met Leroy, he opened the door for ya."

"Hi everybody. I'm very pleased to meet you." Gazing around the room she continues, "You have a nice house Poppa Beau," Janal says as she moves closer, standing next to Beauden's chair, swinging and slapping her hands together.

"Thank you Miss Janal. Hey, if you want to watch TV you can, you know just till I finish my game. You just go right ahead. Me casa is your casa."

Janal charmingly walks into the den and sits on the sofa. Yet naïve, she waits ever so patient for Beauden's game to end.

Time is quickly passing and Janal is getting sleepy, furthermore, Beauden's game is finally coming to an end. Two of the men are leaving out the door, but Leroy's concentration is strictly on Janal. He can not seem to keep his eyes or his nasty thoughts, off of her either.

"Hey Man, what are you plan'n on do'n with Brown Sugar over there?"

Simultaneously, they both turn and look at Janal who is peacefully watching television.

"Beau, is she a hooker or what? Are you plan'n on break'n her in."

Both men are intoxicated but they're coherent enough to understand their situation, although, Beauden does not like Leroy's questions concerning Janal.

"Why Leroy?"

"I want to know what she'll charge for a little piece. Dam... if she don't look good...and dam... tasty too," Leroy replies as he scratches his head with two fingers.

At 11:47, Beauden and Leroy continue their conversation about Janal as they clean the table. Beauden with his chest all stuck out jive talks and boast about his manhood and urging Leroy to confess that he is still a ladies man.

In a low voice Beauden proclaims, "That's my pretty piece of booty. She brought that all the way over here for me...The Black Stallion, nigga...and I don't rememba say'n anythang 'bout you get'n some of anythang, Le."

Leroy is frustrated and disappointed, because there have been times when the both of them would share a woman or a girl, especially if they were breaking her into the business.

"Man, I thought we were cool."

"Man dam... we're cool, but not that dam... cool. Not tonight anyway...I ain't got to share every piece...do I? ...Eee.e.e.e," disputes Beauden.

"What if I ask her, would you mind then, Beau?"

"Just as long as I'm first...I don't care what ya'll do later."

After Beauden and Leroy takes the last batch of dirty glasses to the sink, Beauden comes back into the room trying to impress
Janal, walking his cool daddy stride, abruptly stumbling over the floor rug. He tries to play it off, as though it is part of his natural stride before approaching Janal. Leroy is not far behind, he too, pretends to be cool, and half-wittedly bumps into Beauden.

Janal, smiling, thought they were just being silly, staring at the two pushing at each other.

Immediately she says, "Poppa Beau, I got to go home before my momma finds out that I left the house...anyway it's getting late. Can you drive me home, please?"

She looks so sweet sitting there in front of the television, holding her hands, playing with her fingers.

"Sure, I'll take you home in a minute, as soon as I show my man Leroy to the door."

Leroy leans and whispers, "Man, I thought we were go'n to get it on, like last time when we broke in that little filly from Texas. You rememba! Umm...that was one of the sweetest and longest ride; yeah, that night was a good night."

Beauden is a sly fox; despondently he looks at his friend then says, "I'll talk to you later, my man."

Irritated with Beauden's decision, Leroy stomps out the door.

It is Beauden's first time ever being alone with Janal and he has no intentions on sharing her with Leroy or anybody else. Beauden locks the front door after Leroy leaves then returns to the den where Janal is still sitting. That frozen smile pasted on his face, every second his tongue encircles his big lips as the saliva moistens his shabby mustache. Walking with a lean, with one leg dragging behind, he strides closer.

"Eee...e.e.e...I know you didn't come all the way over here Brown Sugar, just so I can drive you all the way back, so soon. Now did you?"

Unaware of Beauden's intentions, Janal smiles and agrees with his every word. Also, she is very pleased that he is showering her with so much attention and has given her so many beautiful gifts.

Softly she speaks, "Well okay...I can stay a little longer but not too long Poppa Beau. I have to go to school in the morning," then giggles.

"Don't you worry my little tender roni. What I'm about to teach you, you can't learn in no school, tomorrow or any other day."

Janal doesn't understand Beauden remarks, or why he is suddenly talking in riddles. Unexpectedly, he grabs her by her legs and drags her to the floor.

"Poppa Beau stop! What are you...?

Quickly tearing off her pants and soon her panties. Janal is horrified. "BEAU, STOP!"

She screams and screams, but nobody hears as he throws his overweight body on top of her. "YOU'RE HURTING ME...STOP"

Janal first scream ends a few minutes after midnight to be exact, just as Elayne's motherly instinct wakes her.

To suppress the sound of her screams Beauden takes his hand and places it over her mouth. Janal struggles, but she is no match for him. She is repeatedly raped in every way imaginable and beaten severely.

At home, Elayne frantically runs into Janal's bedroom, turning on the light, but there is no Janal.

Elayne is horrified as she runs through the entire house calling her daughter's name.

"JANAL. JANAL...JANAL where are you baby?"

But still no Janal. Elayne panics, she goes to the phone and calls Shi Li and D'La to see if Janal is with one of them. But still no Janal. No one has seen her, or talked to her. Elayne is getting even more worried and scared out of her mind. She goes to the police station, but the police refuses to file a missing person report unless the person has been missing for at least twenty-four hours. They say, 'teenagers are always running away for a day or so, and they didn't see any real concern'. Nonetheless, they did take a brief report of her disappearance.

Early that morning, approximately 3:30, Beauden's sexual gratification is fulfilled. He wraps Janal's helpless body in a blanket and carries her out the back door, putting her limp body into the trunk of his car. Discreetly he gets in and drives to a secluded field and quickly tosses Janal to the ground. Beaten, bloody with a couple of teeth knocked out, Janal frantically cries as she pleas for her life.

"Please...please Mr. Beauden, don't hurt me anymore. Take me home please? ...I won't tell anybody about tonight or anything. Okay, I promise!"

Beauden's heart is hard, iced cold and true to his notorious nature.

"Take you home. Ain't that some sh...! I'm look'n at jail time, if I take you home Brown Sugar...Eee...e...Take you home. Dam...!"

Nevertheless, Janal continues to plead, but Beauden is not taking any chances on letting Janal testify against him. So he snatches the blanket off of her naked body, takes out his gun, step three steps back and aims.

"Brown Sugar, I hate to do this, umm...you're such a good piece. Though I hate to waste all that cash you could bring daddy...Dam... this thang is all mess up...The money, money, money you could bring home. Whoa! ...But, what it is, is what it is. I gotta do what I gotta do. Cause, I ain't go'n down for no bull sh... like this. I got too much to lose, and I gotta consider my reputation, Li' Darlin. I hope you understand, you win some - you lose some."

Janal's pleadings are becoming meek but she begs once last time. One last time before Beauden pulls the trigger.

"Please...no, no, don't...MOMMA," she screams.

Janal is shot twice. The bullets speed through her body. One in her lower stomach, the other one travels through her chest, slightly misses her heart. Janal lays quiet; the pain is traumatic and she is too impaired to move even a finger. Though she remembers what her Aunt D'La once told her, 'Always be cool, and, or play dead.' So she pretends to be dead. Beauden quickly gets into his car and drives away, laughing as if nothing happened.

The moon is fading behind the clouds as the sun starts to shines its way through. All night long, worried out of her head, Elayne sits on the floor by the phone. Everything is so confusing as she wonders: 'Why, oh why?' Still waiting for her daughter to come home, to call.

That same morning about 7:45 a young boy on his way to school crosses a vacant field, he sees something lumpy lying on the ground. He can't quite figure out what it is, so he goes closer to get a better look at it. He is horrified. He sees a naked girl and she looks as though she is dead. He hurriedly runs home to tell his family. The police and ambulance arrives on the scene, Janal is barely alive.

The hospital's emergency room, a voice carries over the intercom. "Dr. Kyi, you're wanted in emergency. Dr. Kyi you're wanted in emergency."

Shi Li hurries to the emergency room unaware that her patient is her goddaughter, Janal Smith, who is clinging to life. Shi Li is terrified. Shi Li Kyi tries everything possibly to save her, almost losing her twice. But, Shi Li refuses to let her go, trying everything possible to save her. After hours and hours of surgery, though emotional Shi Li finds the strength to assist some of the top-notch doctors on call. Time is everything, and with time things are starting to look a bit favorable for Janal. But Shi Li has no choice but to wait. She wants to be positive. She has to be sure. She refuses to leave Janal even for one second. Sadly waiting, trying her best to stay strong; not just for herself, but for Janal and her three dearest friends. Janal is eventually places into intensive care, on the critical list as Shi Li diligently concentrate on her vitals.

No matter how hard she tries, Shi Li could not hold back her tears any longer. Pouring like rain, her tears evidently makes it almost impossible for her to see as she makes her way to the telephone.

On the first ring Elayne grabs the phone, hoping it is her daughter who is on the other end.

"JANAL...JANAL, IS THAT YOU BABY? ARE YOU ALL RIGHT? ...JANAL!"

Although the pain in her heart is too strong, Shi Li mumbles in a sad and crackling voice, "No...it is Shi Li."

"Shi Li...you found Janal. Have you heard from her? Is she with you?"

"Elayne...you got to come to the hospital...Janal is here."

"Janal there! ...WHY? Did she...is she okay? Shi Li is Janal okay?"

"I...It is hard to say right now. Elayne, you got to get here fast."

Elayne is even more horrified from the shock of the news and the sound of Shi Li's voice.

"OH MY LORD...MY BABY. I'M ON MY WAY. All right, I'm comin. I'm comin...I'm on my way, Shi Li. ...No Lord, please...NOT MY BABY, NOT MY BA...A...BY! ...Shi Li."

Elayne quickly hangs up the phone, grabs her car keys and rushes out the door, speeding ever so dangerously.

Meanwhile, Shi Li is sad and very emotional as makes another call. "D'La, Janal is in critical condition. She has been shot, raped and beaten. I do not know if she is going to make it through the night."

"WHAT, WHO, JANAL! ...I'm outta here, in a minute, Shi Li." D'La quickly runs out of her apartment heading for the hospital. Then Shi Li makes another call, this time to Paris, France. The phone rings many times before Candice answers. Because, Candice is getting out of the shower, wrapping a towel around her dripping hair. Brokenheartedly, Candice listens to the news about Janal. She is shocked, she screams in terror, "NON, NON, OUI, OUI. I'm on my way!" Candice hangs up the phone immediately runs to the closet, quickly grabbing any clothes and her luggage.

Detroit, Elayne frantically arrives at the hospital first and rushes into Janal's room, practically fainting when she sees her only child who is being assisted by a breathing machine, clinging to life. Elayne uncontrollably burst into tears. Shi Li quickly takes hold of her as D'La enters, and she is in total dismays.

Distraught by the sight of her goddaughter, "I don't believe this sh... A bastard that would do somethang like this has to be insane!" D'La becomes iced cold and within that very moment evil seduces her soul.

The three friends watch sorrowfully as Janal struggles with breathing, struggles to stay alive. The three friends grieve, as their blood rush through their vein, expeditiously turning their hearts to stones.

"D'La, Shi Li, she's so little. She's to young to die," cries Elayne.

"Don't worry Elayne whoever did this will pay," declares D'La.

Shi Li calmly proclaims: "The night of the Black Moon has come! Revenge will be my pleasure!"

"Lord, please help my baby, please," begs Elayne as she gets down on her knees beside Janal's bed, praying for the first time in years.

Paris, France, Candice boards the plane, taking her seat as she thinks back to their beginning, the day the four friends met and there promise. 'No matter what, friends forever.' And that crazy saying D'La would always add, 'Even In Death.' Candice realizes the nature of this situation, and she can only imagine the consequences.

Yes, Janal's incident hits home with Candice as she recalls that tragic night of her rape. The flight is long as she constantly worries about her goddaughter, her only daughter. Candice wonders what Janal had to endure in order to save her own life, as she once did.

The next evening, Candice arrives at the hospital. She stops at the information desk. Then she immediately takes the elevator to her desire floor and walks into Janal's room. Candice spontaneously greets her friends with hugs and kisses upon entering. Their swollen, tearful eyes reveal the fire of hell burning in their souls as Candice walks to Janal's bedside. She is even more shocked and angered as she examines Janal unconscious and battered body. Uncontrollably Candice breaks down as she takes Janal by the hand; the sight of Janal is too devastating.

Hours later and still there are no change in Janal's condition. Candice returns to Janal's room with two cups of coffee.

"Elayne, I have some coffee, I brought you a cup...Elayne, Janal's going to need you when she wakes up. I know she will wake up soon."

Elayne is daunted and she only hears a fraction of what Candice has said.

"Yeah, she will...soon, when she wakes up," she looks at the cup Candice is handing her, "Thank you, Candice."

Candice questions her friends for more information, "Who could do something so terrible to a child?" but they had no answers.

The four friends' cry nonstop, clinging tightly to each other, completely frightened and stressed out of their minds with worry.

"I don't know...but I'm gonna to find out...GOT DAM... IT!" D'La utters loudly and hastily walks out of Janal's room.

Candice abruptly follows her, calling to her, "D'La...D'La, where are you going?"

"I'll be in touch. I got business to take care of."

D'La can only holds what little emotion of her tough image inside as she runs out of the hospital.

Searches for answers, asking questions of anybody in the hood, and paying for any information she can get; but nobody knows anything. Everywhere she goes she comes up empty handed. D'La eventually returns to Elayne's house, in Janal's bedroom and searches through her personal belongings. She picks up a jewelry box that she had given Janal on her tenth birthday, reminiscing as she holds it in her hands. Then suddenly, she notices a piece of paper under it with a name and phone number. She reads it. The number is not familiar but the name sure rings a bell.

"What is this? I know this nasty mother f... How? He'd better not have anythang to do with Janal be'n in the hospital. Uh...I know exactly where to find his rotten as..."

D'La grabs her jacket, exits the house, and drives to the pool hall.

The same place that used to be called Dexx's Place. A few months after Dexx's death, the place was renamed, "The Brotherhood Social Club." A few new faces, but it is the same, same old business, except Dexx Barone isn't there.

D'La hangs around nearly all night waiting for Beauden to come, but so far he is a 'no show'. At that time she decides to shoot a little pool to help pass some time, or waste time, while she wait. Usually the guys will start talking once they become comfortable with you. D'La is out to play the game, obtaining any information is good information.

A few hours later, Leroy comes into the club and sits next to D'La at the bar. D'La knows that Leroy and Beauden are good friends and Beauden will probably walk through the door real soon.

He offers her a drink, she accepts. They shot the breeze, talking jive, drinking and even joking with each other.

What ever it takes, D'La is willing to do to, if it gets the information she needs. Once D'La get p...ssed no mission is impossible.

Finally Leroy is drunk and he starts to talk. He could never hold his liquor, his tongue, or control his brain when it comes to a beautiful woman. He just got to show off his manhood one way or another, ego tripping, boasting as he beats his chest for D'La's approval.

A lot of times that is what got him into trouble with the organization, is his big mouth. Leroy tells D'La all she needs to know about Beauden's thirst for young girls and many of his whores were runaways, between the ages of twelve and sixteen.

Be it as it may, Leroy tries to be discreet, yet is proud of Beauden's style when it comes to controlling his stable; when telling of a certain and most recent night. The night a young girl (Janal) was shot and raped, and about being at Beauden's house, how he thought she was one of his new whores that he was breaking in. He also boast about the news report on the radio, saying, 'that they will never take the shooter down.' He tells her about the missing young girls, the ones that refuse to do business for the organization. That Beauden has raped, killed, and some he even mutilated, and most of those poor souls are buried all over the city, or surrounding suburbs. He even tells her about Beauden affiliation with the Black Connection, that he is crude, crazed and dangerous and warns her not to get involved with him. That life and death were the same to him, and he would stop at nothing to get what he wants. He informs D'La that Beauden never comes to the club on Saturday nights. Friday's and Saturday's are his money making nights, those are the nights that he mainly keeps check of his whores, and he does most of his number collection on those days as well.

Out of jealousy Leroy mimics him, saying: "Beauden favorite words are, 'money, money, and money', everybody got paid tonight and everybody got some money to spend," he continues, "Whether it's the number game or the tricks looking to be satisfied, I gots-ta be out there on Friday and Saturday nights." He also calls them his, 'Big Money' Nights."

He soon gives D'La a seductive smile, touching and rubbing her thigh and poking his lips out hoping she would give him a little kiss. He sticks his tongue out, wiggles it, and begs her as he leans onto the bar with his fist supporting his head. Thinking that maybe, she would break him off a piece for old times. Especially, after giving her all and any information she asked about his friend, Beauden, and everybody that comes into The Brotherhood Social Club.

With a wink of his eye he ask, "How 'bout me and you get'n a room for a little while? You know, you're single and I'm single," glancing down at the crotch, "it still works the same...like it used too. It can make you feel real good, D'La. How 'bout it?"

Before he can close his mouth, Leroy belches a couple of times, looking like a nasty old man that he is.

Not surprised with his proposition, D'La did expect that he would say something stupid, she stares at him as she gets off of her stool, "Drop dead."

MAKING WRONGS RIGHT

CHAPTER 17

After leaving the Brotherhood Social Club, D'La calls the hospital to check on Janal's condition. She impatiently waits as the operator pages Shi Li.

"Shi Li, its D'La! How's Janal?"

"About the same, but I think she will be all right. Still it is hard to say for sure. It is going to take some time, but she is strong."

"Shi Li, I have some news...I found out who did this to Janal."

"What? ...Are you sure, D'La!"

"I'll tell you all about it when I get there. I'm on my way, talk to you later."

Shi Li is intensely excited, and she can not wait to tell Candice and Elayne the good news that she hurries into Janal's room tossing her chart onto the chair.

When D'La arrives at the hospital, the girls look for a secure place in the corridor to discuss and evaluate the entire situation. Afterward, D'La and Shi Li continue to walk the corridor as Elayne and Candice decide to go back to Janal's room. Suddenly, the machine beeper goes off, Janal has stopped breathing and Elayne and Candice hurries into her room.

Brokenheartedly, Elayne starts to yell, "JANAL. JANAL! OH MY LORD...NO NOT MY BABY! NO...O...o...o."

Candice quickly runs into the hallway screaming for Shi Li, D'La, anybody that can help. Shi Li, Candice and D'La rush back into the room along with other members of the emergency staff. Elayne is rapidly pushed from Janal's bedside and escorted into the corridor, shaking horridly. Within seconds, Candice grabs hold of Elayne and D'La as they fearfully watch outside of Janal's room.

"THE LORD IS PUNISHING ME. I KNOW HE IS...PLEASE LORD, PLEASE DON'T TAKE MY BABY FROM ME," cries Elayne as her knees weaken, almost dropping to the floor.

Several long minutes later Janal's stable again and everyone is at peace once more. Elayne leans over her daughter, whispering into her ear.

"Come on baby, you can do it. Please, Janal, honey...Please, open your eyes. Mommy loves you so much. Auntie Candice, Auntie Shi Li and Auntie D'La are her waiting for you to get up, baby."

Shi Li approaches Elayne, caressing her around the shoulders, reassuring her. "She is a strong girl and she is going to make it, Elayne."

But Elayne insists, murmuring again, "The Lord is punishing me for being a bad mother, Shi Li."

"No, he is not. Do not say that. You know it is not true. You did the best you could."

Elayne squeezes Shi Li hands as D'La and Candice embraces each other.

"Did I? ...I don't thinks so," weeps Elayne.

"Yes! Now, do not talk like that. Janal needs you."

"Do she? I wasn't there for my little girl when she needed me most. I'm a drunken slut and The Lord has turned his back to me. I can feel it," Elayne continues to cries.

"Elayne stop it. Janal needs you to be intact, not falling apart like this. You have to be strong for her," states Candice.

D'La quickly adds, "No Elayne. No he didn't Elayne. The Lord didn't turn his back to you. Think about it! The Lord loves you and Janal. The Lord has only love to give and if anybody has turned their back, it was you Elayne who turned your back to The Lord."

"Elayne your Lord is giving you a second chance to be there for Janal. And most of all, he needs you to believe," says Shi Li.

Elayne hesitates before speaking in a soft tone, " I'm so sorry. You're right. I know you're right. I've been so ungrateful to you all. Never saying 'thank you' when I needed too. I was consumed with bad thinking. I'm sorry for all those times, and I do thank you, all of you for being here with me today, and being here for Janal. Thank you. Thank you Shi Li for saving my baby...D'La, Candice, thank you too for being who you are to me and for me...And for being those very special people in my life...I do love all of you. I really do!"

Shi Li is the sensible one, the mother hen and the peacemaker between them whose love has grown overly protective of their relationship. Always reminding them of the importance of being loved and not being afraid to show love among them. Always standing strong which helps them to realize that they are sisters, the four of them, walking together as if they are one.

About thirty minutes later, Dr. Tsetung silently enters and asks, "Dr. Kyi, how is our patient progressing?"

Startled by the sound of his voice, Shi Li swiftly looks back, directly into his face.

"Oh, I am sorry, I did not know you were standing behind me doctor."

"May I see her chart Dr. Kyi? ...I thought...I'd come and check to see how our little trooper is doing, also to see how you were holding up. If you, any of you, need anything don't hesitate to ask...please."

Shi Li hands Dr. Tsetung Janal's chart.

"Come on Elayne let's get something to eat," states D'La.

"Elayne you need food to keep you strong and alert when Janal wakes," agrees Shi Li.

"No, I don't want to leave her." weeps Elayne.

"Elayne, don't worry. Janal is doing fine now. If it makes you feel any better, Shi Li will stay here until we get back," says Candice.

"Yes. Elayne I will not let anything happen to her. I will be right here. Yes, go and get something to eat."

Grief helps Elayne to camouflage her reasons for living. Wishing it was her fighting for her life instead of her daughter as she exits her room, heading for the cafeteria. Constantly looking back, with each and every step, releasing all confidence in the hands of The Lord, her friends, and to Shi Li who is tending Janal's every necessity.

Eventually, Shi Li steps out of Janal's room, down the hallway to the nurse's station. Dr. Tsetung returns and proceeds with his evaluation. Granting himself a personal observation of his young patient. Taking her chart off the door before entering he stands alongside her bed, gently touching her hand. Sympathetically he speaks, "You just hold on my little princess...I'm going to do everything possible to get you back out there running around, enjoying life as you have." He closes his eyes, "Oh my God..."

Shi Li returns as Dr. Tsetung prays. She listens and she is deeply touched.

He continues, "...look at her, she's so helpless. Please God, I'm doing everything I can to save her. Now, her life is in your hands. I pray to you..."

Dr. Tsetung is unaware of Shi Li's presence. She stands there in the doorway, and she is absolutely serene. Resting his head into his hands, his eyes shut, his prayer continues. Her heart goes out to him; she is highly impressed, listening to his every word. Shi Li says not a word as she gradually moves toward him. Yearning to touch him yet waiting for him to finish. Gently she places her hand on his shoulder.

"Dr. Tsetung, thank you. You do not know what it means to me to hear you say the things you said. For you to come here, to care so much."

He immediately turns, "Dr. Kyi, I...I...I didn't know you were standing there. I thought you were with your friends in the cafeteria...I wanted to check on her progress for you, to keep an eye on her. ...She is so young. Sorrow grasps my heart."

"I understand," Shi Li says in a sad tone and with a slight smile. Still and all, her heart is overwhelmed with gratitude, but the pain is too strong and before she could say another word she impetuously burst into tears.

"I love her so much...She is a part of me. I can not stand to see her suffer like this. So innocent, so helpless...it is killing me. I try to be strong for my friends, all the time knowing, deep inside me, that I am just as frightened as they are. I would honorably change places with her, to save her life...to see her happy again."

Dr. Tsetung respectfully takes Shi Li into his arms. "I promise you and your friends that I will do everything I can to help her. Whatever it takes I will not leave her side. And when that day comes, we all will see her laugh and play again."

Meanwhile in the cafeteria the girls are discussing their plans. Elayne refuses to stay at the hospital, she wants to face the man who could do something so horrible to a child. Elayne's heart is pumping iced cold blood and it is starting to freeze with each passing second that her daughter fights for life.

Raymond has been homeless for quite some time, years. Walking the streets, sleeping on park benches and sometimes on the grass, he has no money, nothing. Yet everyday, Raymond faithfully holds a sign that reads: 'HUNGRY- I'LL WORK FOR FOOD'; begging is his only means of survival. Yes, Raymond has hit 'rock bottom' and everything that he touches, ever since the day when he beat his wife and left her lying on the floor, has fallen apart.

However during those incredible and unbearable times, one Sunday morning: What could have posses Raymond to walk into Reverend Jerome Thomas's church? Any church, after so many years is beyond him. Standing near the front doors, the Reverend continues to give his sermon, Raymond Smith speechlessly observes his congregation. Raymond stands in the doorway for several minutes listening to Reverend Thomas preach as the church doors slowly closes behind him. He shouts: "The Lord says. 'Do unto others, as you would have them do onto you.' He didn't say go out here and commit adultery, having no respect for yourself or your mate. Nor did he say anythang to ya'll single peoples 'bout run'n from one lover to another...I said...I SAID. I say to you...if you start hear'n...Yes Lord, I say if you start hear'n some'n talk'n to you, say'n 'Hey, it's ok. She won't know, or he won't know what you're do'n out here. Try it...you gonna like it.' If you hear ANYTHANG like that...you know it ain't The LORD talk'n to you. It's the demon himself, SATAN, The Master of Destruction, do'n all the talk'n. He roars like a lion. And his roar of destruction is loud like thunder. Cause...cause...he's on a mission. And we know what that mission is. He wants to KILL YOU. He wants you DEAD. So repent you sinners, REPENT NOW...Can I get a Amen, I say, can I get AMEN?"

The Reverend Thomas is also preaching about adultery, respect, and sexual disease that is traveling fast through the black community, the white community, all communities, and also informing his congregation on: 'What you do to somebody, somebody will come back and do to you.'

The gospel hits home with Raymond, makes him think even more about the wrong he has done to his family. Raymond sits in the back row, the last row, and makes not a sound as he thinks and waits for the sermon to end.

After church and after most of the members have left, he walks up to the Reverend Thomas, with his head hanging low, embarrassed, and shamefully ask for food.

Raymond's clothes are soiled, tattered, and torn.

"Excuse me, Reverend Sir, but I was wondering if you could spare some change, so I can buy me something to eat?"

His stench is so bad Reverend Thomas has to turn his head when speaking to him.

Although, Rev. Thomas, being a charitable Christian man and after talking with Raymond for a while, he begins to feels the good in him. And gives him not only the food he asked for, but also permission to work the church's ground, cutting grass, mopping floors, washing windows, cleaning anything that needs to be cleaned, and a place to sleep - living in the church's basement. Raymond is also paid a few dollars a week to buy personal things. Raymond soon joins the church and he has yet to miss a Sunday service, any service. Raymond completely turns his life around.

Raymond lived in the church's basement for over five years, almost six. Raymond and Reverend Thomas do realize the day will come for Raymond to leave and that day is today. Raymond is in his basement apartment packing his belongings when Reverend Thomas walks in.

"I see, you've got everythang all packed up son."

"Yes Sir, Reverend Thomas. I guess I'll be heading on out of here soon...Six years! It's been a gratifying six God fearing years...But the time has come, Rev...I got to make my wrongs, right."

"That's right son. I know you're do'n the right thang and I'm gonna pray for you and your family."

Raymond is scared out of his mind about going back to his family, and he is worried about how they will accept him after so many years.

"Thank you Reverend, I got a feeling I'm going to need all the prayers I can get."

Nervously, Raymond goes to the window and looks up at the sky.

"You'll be fine, son. When you get weary from walk'n, The Lord will carry you the rest of the way...All you got to do is ask and you will receive," says the Reverend Thomas, standing next to Raymond's bunk.

Raymond closes his suitcase, shakes the Reverend's hand and that handshake turns into an inspirational hug of gratitude."

"If...it wasn't for you, I would probably be dead today...If I could only find a way to thank you, Reverend."

Reverend Thomas interrupts, holding his cross around his neck, "My boy, The Lord works in mysterious ways."

"Hallelujah! You can say that again, Reverend."

Raymond takes his suitcase off the bed and goes to a car in the parking lot.

"Son, that old car shouldn't give you too much trouble."

Jokingly Raymond replies, "Nah...I doubt it. Ole Bessie and me have become good friends. I know what she likes and what she don't like. And I know she don't like it when I press my big foot too heavy on her accelerator. I got to press real gently, don't choke her...just give her a little gas at a time. Yep, all I got to do is remember that and I'm pretty sure Ole Bessie will take me on home..." Raymond pauses, "...to my family."

Reverend Thomas starts to grin as Raymond face lights up when he talks about his family.

He grins, "Family...I like the sound of that...my family."

Raymond jumps up and down, yelling as loud as he can.

"OH...OH...Ooo...I'M GOING HOME...HOME REVEREND ...THANK YOU JESUS. THANK YOU JESUS. YES LORD."

Raymond excitedly gets into the car, starts the engine and happily drives out of the parking lot.

DO WHAT YOU GOTTA DO

CHAPTER 18

One by one they arrive at Elayne's house. D'La walks up on the porch drinking a soda. A couple of minutes later, Candice pulls around the corner in a Jaguar and parks it in front of the house as Shi Li makes her entrance approximately three minutes later. Never realizing this day would come, as they plan and prepare, bringing all their techniques that was taught to them by life itself.

That night, D'La informs her friends of her findings and the taste of revenge is as sweet as mom's sweet potato pie.

Candice will be the perfect bait, because she knows exactly how to work it. Besides, D'La knows first hand about Beauden's thirst for beautiful women. The plan has been in full operation for the past two nights, and everything is going absolutely excellently.

But on the night of, what a coincidence, instead of meeting Beauden inside the Brotherhood Social Club, Candice meets him as she is getting out of a stolen car. He pulls up behind her and he is alone. Auspiciously, nobody is outside the club or anywhere in sight.

"Perfect timing," says D'La as they watch and wait in another stolen car parked not far away, cars she heist about twenty minutes earlier.

D'La gives Candice the signal, letting her know that he is the man. Beauden's canine characteristics quickly peak reaching an all time high when he sees Candice. With his head hanging out of his car, he tries his best to attract her attention, to make his acquaintances, by yelling at her. Yelling like a hound dog.

"HEY EXCUSE ME...EXCUSE ME, YOUNG LADY. MAY I HAVE A WORD WITH YOU...o...o!"

"With me...what kind of word do you want, Monsieur?" replies Candice.

"Well, hello...could be the first."

"Bonjour monsieur," Candice closes her car door and pretends to be going into the club.

"Are you go'n to The Brotherhood Club, Miss Lady?" Beauden grins, licking his lips as usual, trying to ease the sudden dryness around his mouth.

"No not really...I'm lost and I need some information. I thought, maybe someone inside could help me, Monsieur."

"Maybe, I can help...Why don't you tell me what you need."

Before Candice can respond, he forcefully pushes the door open and practically throws himself out of his own car.

"Umm, do you live around here?"

To be certain of his identity, Candice sways her hips with every step, her seductive and rhythmic motion, and that attractive French accent seem to allure him even more.

"Sorry, but I don't know your name, Monsieur, yet, you say many things and you ask many questions."

"Ex...cuse...me, Miss Lady, I don't mean to be rude or anythang like that. My friends call me Beauden...but you can call me what ever you want...Eee.e..e..u."

"Pleased to meet you, Monsieur Beauden, and my friends call me...Kandy."

Candice realizes that he has bitten the bait. Beauden's uncontrollable nature has struck him hard this time. His eyes begin to roam Candice's contour body from top to bottom.

"A sweet name...for a sweet lady, I'm sure," he adds.

Beauden is motionless, he can barely move his legs as he tries to control his instant erection. Candice's beauty has frozen the so-called Black Stallion and captivated his sexual drive, but not his mouth.

"Since you're lost, maybe, I can show you the way. I know my way around this city pretty good. Where are you go'n again...Kandy?"

He reaches out, opening the door to her vehicle.

"My family owns property and I want to take a look at it. I've been driving for some time now and I'm pretty sure it shouldn't be that far from here. Monsieur, I have directions written on this piece of paper."

Candice hands Beauden the paper for him to read.

"Do you know where it is...I would be so happy if you could show me the way, Monsieur?"

After some pushing and twisting, Beauden finally regaining some normal bodily functions, enabling him to move around again.

Within a blink of his eye his erection returns while watching Candice seductively leans against her car before getting in.

Focusing steadily on her breast and he is not listening to a word she is saying.

"Baby, all you gotta do is follow me."

"Thank you very much, Monsieur, you are so kind."

"Yeah...yeah, what ever you want, cause my time is your time, and you can have all the time you want."

Beauden closes Candice's door, promptly gets into his car. She persuasive him to follow her and they drive about ten minutes before stopping at a traffic light near a 'dead in' street. Earlier the four of them had decided that this will be a perfect intersection.

Loosening the top two buttons on her blouse, looking even more seductive, Candice blows her horn, stops, then pulls her car alongside of Beauden's. And that sensual way of using that French accent, which takes control of him every time, especially when she calls his name: "Monsieur Beauden if you don't mind, I'd appreciated it very much if you would let me ride with you. I don't want to get lost Monsieur...and since we're going to the same place. Maybe, if it's okay, we ride together, Oui!"

Beauden is pleased to hear Candice's suggestion. His smile has increased tremendously. All it takes is a quick glance into his mouth and you can see all his back teeth.

"What ever you want, Miss Kandy."

Candice parks her car on a side street near lots of brushes. Beauden reaches over the passenger seat, pushing open the door of his car. Beauden's nose is blown wide open as he drives away looking for an old vacant farmhouse. D'La, Shi Li and Elayne follow at a safe inconspicuous distance.

Raymond is almost home, a place he left behind so long ago. A place that he was too ashamed to return before. He is apprehensive as his heart beats faster and as each mile brings him closer. Raymond can not wait to see his kid. He unaware of its gender; not knowing if it was a boy or girl, what is his or her favored toy, the kid's name, or anything about his kid. As he drives along the highway he thinks of many ways to approach the family he lost. Every time he would come up with one way of greeting them, a better one would pop in his head. Raymond becomes seriously tense as the distance shortens. Only a few more miles to go before the dream that has been haunting him become a reality. The radio plays as Raymond practice on what to say and how to say it. "Um...Hi. Hello, I'm Raymond. Nah...Elayne knows who I am. Wow...here I am working on my greeting abilities...What, if she has another man in her life. If she does...I know she don't want to talk to me, or hear anything I have to say...Lord, she might not want to talk to me anyway...I don't know why I'm even thinking about coming back after all this time."

As the radio plays it reports on a young girl found shot and nude in a field and warning the public that her attacker is still at large. But Raymond is not paying any attention to the news report; he turns it down, because he is too busy practicing. While driving along the highway he notices a lady in the car that is driving right next to his. He also notices that she looks exactly like his wife, Elayne.

"Hey is that...I think...She's a little older, but still that woman looks so much like her."

He soon questions his sanity, believing that his eyes are playing tricks on him.

"I wonder...is that her?" He speeds up and looks again and even though it is dark he recognizes her, "I'm not crazy. It's Elayne!"

He decides to follow, keeping at a reliable distance, of course. He doesn't want to scare anybody, nor have the people in the car believing he is some kind of a pervert out looking for some action.

Raymond follows the car for miles and eventually arrives at an old abandoned farmhouse.

The first car stops, then the second car stops a short distance. The second car prematurely turns off its headlights before parking. Raymond decides to do the same, he turns his vehicle's light off and drives a little closer, angling in the opposite direction, just far enough to keep his eyes on the two cars; he parks, waits, and diligently watches them.

It is very dark, but thanks to the light from the moon and stars, Raymond can see some movement, and judging by their behavior it is woman and man. He can not identify the two lovebirds as they get out of the car, walking hand in hand to the front door. But in the second car he thinks he knows exactly who they are.

Due to the darkness, Raymond is confidence that they do not see him sitting there. True enough, the girls are too busy concentrating on Beauden than an old beat-up car parked on the other side of the field.

"Why are they going to that raggedy old abandoned house at this time of night? What could Elayne be doing...?"

Raymond has many questions that need answers, but still he decides to wait. As the couple walks toward the house he notices they are still holding hands, hugging, and playing with each other. The woman is leading him toward the house, almost pulling him, making him walk faster.

"Honey...this place is so old, you're gonna need help fix'n it up. And if you do decides to fix it, Darlin, I'm your man."

"You're so sweet Monsieur Beauden, the perfect gentleman...The men in this country are such nice people, Oui!"

"Oui...I won't lie to ya...I think I'm the last of the perfect gentlemen, Kandy."

"Non, that can't be so. But if true, I'm very lucky."

"It's true, Kandy, and you're the lucky one," Beauden grins.

Candice stops and looks at the house, "Really, Monsieur Beauden...I think this place is just magnificent. All it needs is a little paint. Oui, don't you think so?"

Candice appears to be overly zealous about the house.

"Magnificent? ...Honey, you're go'n to need more than a little paint for this old place."

"I want to go inside, just for a second or maybe two, Monsieur Beauden."

Candice takes Beauden's hand again pulling him into the house. Walking that cool pimp daddy stride, he trips over an old broken dusty chair. "Oowl, this place is dangerous in the dark. Kandy, I don't want you fall'n down hurt'n your pretty little self. I think we better get the hell out of here."

"Wait, I want to look at the other rooms, please Monsieur Beauden? It won't take long. And since we are here, Oui!"

"Okay but stay close to me Kandy, my Darlin."

Beauden reaches into this pocket and takes out a book of matches, striking several as they journey through the dark house.

"I think we betta be get'n on back Kandy, you can hardly see anythang, anyway. Plus I'm just about out of matches."

Candice is very persuasive as the two continue to inspect the place before she notices a small piece of a candle; Beauden lights it.

After examining several rooms, Candice makes an alluring request that Beauden finds ever so difficult to decline.

Singing his name," Monsieur Beauden... Monsieur Beauden, would you think wrong of me if I ask you to make love to me?" Candice impetuously places her body in front of him, seductively kissing him, "Ummm...Monsieur Beauden, Oui!"

She begins to kiss his entire face, starting with his forehead, then his eyes, next his cheeks, and finally licking his lips.

"I want to go inside of that room, the one we just come out of...only for a second or so, or however long you may take with me."

Accompanying her alluring smile, Candice winks as she whispers softly into his ear, "Oui, Monsieur Beauden, will you come with me?"

Candice knows her game well, and she is, in fact, disgusted with this man. Every time she kisses him she want to kill him, but she knows she has to wait for the others. She concentrates on her mission, and that is to keep him calm, diverting any suspicion. Despite everything, it is difficult. Though she tries not to think of the man that is standing in front of her as the man that almost killed Janal.

Beauden's aroused, he never has a second thought that a woman of Candice's status would ever give him the time of day, or find him attractive, living the life of a street hustler. He realizes that the whores in his stable can not, and do not, measure up to Candice, nor has he met any woman like her. Yes, Beauden has found a jewel.

Once inside the room, Candice lures Beauden to an old mattress lying on the floor that her and her three friends placed earlier. She stands on top of it. She calls him very sweetly and softly, singing his name again, "Monsieur Beauden."

Beauden's thoughts are pleasing and he is very impressed by the way she calls to him: "Yeah, this got to be heaven cause sh... don't happen like this on earth."

With his head cocked to the side and still walking that old, cool, pimp daddy stride, he approaches Candice, "Umm...Baby."

She rubs her nose against his, kissing him many times while unzipping his pants. She places her hand inside, gently massaging his penis. Quickly kicking off her shoes before slowly unfastening the buttons on her blouse, one button at a time. Without haste, Beauden loosen his belt, swiftly pulls it out of his pant and from around his waist.

"Monsieur Beauden, would you think wrong of me if I ask you to make love to me...right now? It's such a beautiful night. We have a beautiful full moon and the stars shine brightly for us. I believe the sky knew we were coming here tonight...Ummm

Monsieur, everything about this place...umm, how you say. It's turning me on, Oui!"

"Oui, Oui, baby! I can't say I don't like your style, cause I do...Ee.e.e.e.e."

Outside, D'La is keeping track of time, impatiently waiting and counting every minute and every second. She gives the signal. Soundlessly, they enter the old house. Shi Li and Elayne proceed through the back door while D'La goes through the main entrance. Beauden's too occupied to notice the three women watching him with their friend, but Candice does. Shi Li is standing in a corner signaling Candice to move away. Slowly and sexy she moves, playing her part to the end, with that sassy sway Candice gradually moves away from Beauden.

"Where you go'n, baby? You don't have to move that far away. It's big and long sho'nuff...E..e.e...but I don't think my chocolate bar's gonna stretch all the way over there....E.e.e...Come on back over here to your daddy."

"I'm going nowhere, Monsieur Beauden. I'm just putting my blouse, may we say 'out of the way', Oui!"

She hangs her blouse on a stick leaning against the wall.

"Now, that's what I like...a neat woman. Yeah, this is gonna be all right...me and you, Kandy...Oui...Oui...Oui!"

Beauden takes his pants off, folding them neatly, imitating Candice as he lays them on the floor next to the old mattress.

Suddenly, he hears a noise and a voice and it is speaking very vulgarly.

"AYE...Remember me you mother f...," shout D'La.

Beauden jumps off the mattress, shouting, "HEY...WHAT THE F... IS THIS!"

Shi Li steps out of the corner, standing directly behind him.

"You piece of dirt you are about to find out."

Beauden is upset and his temper expeditiously levitates, "What, two more whores? What the f... are you bit... plan'n on do'n anyway? You got me here, now, WHAT'S UP!"

Candice replies, "We're going to f... you, but not the way you thought you were going to f... me, Monsieur Beauden."

Another voice comes out of the dark, F... you up...just like you F... up my daughter, " states Elayne.

"Your daughter. WHO IN THE HELL IS YOUR DAUGHTER, YOU NASTY SLUT?"

"The one you beat, raped, and shot Friday morning you dumb as... Now it's your turn. Payback's a mother f...," declares

D'La as she rubs her knife against her pant leg preparing for the kill.

But Beauden is as cool as a cucumber; he knows he has nothing to worry about, because he has been in many fights in his lifetime and with shadier, tougher, eviler characters than these four little women standing in front of him.

"Ah...that little bit... I should've shot her in the head. Beside, she got what she was look'n for. She wanted some good lovin so I gave her some real good lovin...Hey ladies, don't be jealous, there's more where that come from. I got that big, fat and long chocolate bar right here."

Beauden grabs his crotch, tilting backward and projects it at the four friends and starts to laugh, "Eee..u..u...e..e. So, come and get it you BIT... And when I'm finish woop'n your as..., I'm go'n to f... all ya'll before throw'n you out on the streets where you nasty bit... belong."

Shi Li pulls her nun-chucks from the side of her waist, "Do not worry...we are coming and we are going to give you the same thing you gave, Janal."

"First thing we gonna give you is good as... kick'n" states D'La.

Beauden eases his hand into his jacket pocket reaching for his gun. D'La is not stupid and she is not taking any chances. She keeps watch of his every move. Suddenly she throws her knife stabbing him in the shoulder. Beauden hollers as he drops the gun to the floor. "GOT DAM... IT...YOU CRAZY BIT... YOU."

"Nope...you ain't seen a crazy bit... yet, but that's your problem...Anyway, we're just get'n started so you got lots of time."

Feeling betrayed Beauden dashes for Candice, grabbing her around the neck, choking her, "You funky French speaking whore, I'll kill you."

Elayne jumps on his back, "Get your hands off of her."

Shi Li cracks Beauden over his head with her nun-chucks knocking him back on the mattress as he releases Candice's throat and throwing Elayne on the floor. Wildly, he tumbles off the mattress and to the floor.

D'La immediately picks her knife off the floor, aggressively paces toward him: "Move everybody it's my turn...his black as... is all mines."

"Just save some for me, I am not finished," says Shi Li.

"Com'on you goofy lookin bit... cause this fight has just begun, Ee.e...e. Yeah I rememba you, you knotty, nappy headed bit... Yeah, bring your black, wild, crazy as... to me." Beauden is mad as hell, shouting every obscene word he can think of.

Beauden stands ready, positioning himself, but D'La isn't backing down. She moves closer, staring him in the face, watching, reading his body language. She swings her knife just barely missing him. Beauden is quick, moving from side to side just scarcely escaping her sharp and long shiny blade.

He laughs, teasing her, "Is that all you got, sweetie."

She swings again, he accidentally grabs the blade while trying to grab hold of her wrist. His thumb is sliced off. While gazing at the blood on his hand D'La quickly slides the knife across Beauden's face cutting his cheek. Abruptly he grabs his face, touching it, and feels the blood as it runs down his neck. Insanely, he looks down at his hand and the blood that is squirting from it. D'La has cut his pretty face and he is becoming crazier with each blood drop. His eyes start to protrude almost popping out of his head, he affirms: "You're dead!"

Beauden rushes at D'La, she swings again and misses as he grabs her around the waist, knocking her to the floor. He droops over her, swing with all his might, hitting her with his fist. But the sight of her goddaughter still fresh in her mind enables her to block out all blows. She feels nothing. Shi Li reacts quickly, swinging her non-chucks. Constant blows batter every part of his body. Beauden gets up, he stumbles over his own feet as Elayne runs at him with a wooden, two-by-four plank, barbarously hitting him and screaming: "DIE YOU DEMON, DIE."

Demented Candice grabs a steel pole beating Beauden in the head while screaming, "YOU CRAZY DOG. DON'T YOU EVER TOUCH HER AGAIN...DON'T EVEN LOOK AT HER..."

Remembering their promise, as they caress the bond between them. Embracing their pact with the Devil, igniting the fire of hell that burns in their souls.

Again D'La ferociously attacks him, stabbing him multiple times. Revenge is sweet as his blood drenched their faces and clothing. Nothing can stop them now as Beauden continues to fights for his life. Yet, his injuries are so severe causing him to weaken. Losing control of his defense, he falls and rolls over in his own blood. He tries to protect himself from their blows but it is impossible. Insanity has overpowered the four friends: striking, kicking, cutting and stabbing his entire body with every second. The entire fight goes on for at least thirty minutes or more until there was no fight left in him. Even though, the fight, and the fire was still burning in them.

He lies helplessly, dying as his blood pours from his battered body. As his blood dries on their hands, the four friends watch and wait for his last breath on the night of death, the night they call the 'Black Moon'.

"He'll never have to worry about using this again," says one of the girls as she whacks off his penis.

Another voice says, "Put it in that baggie, we'll throw it in the river...Yeah, feed it to the fish."

The third voice replies, "Leave him here to die like the animal he is. It won't be long now."

A fourth voice adds, "Yes...It'll be our secret, forever."

Elayne opens two garbage bags that were placed in a closet earlier. Inside is a change of clothing, some wet towels, bleach and other bacteria killing cleansers. And before leaving they cleared all possible signs of evidence that can connect them to Beauden and the old farmhouse. Just as they were about to walk out of the door Beauden takes his last breath and dies.

Outside, still sitting in his car for approximately two hour Raymond is becoming suspicious: "What could be taking them so long? ...What are they doing in there?"

Though, after taking a few short naps Raymond still sits patiently in his car. Rubbing his tire eyes he unexpectedly notices Shi Li, then Elayne, and a third woman who he now believes is Candice coming out of the old farmhouse. Obviously, D'La is the last one to leave, and falls behind, closing the door. The four girls take latex gloves, wet rags, some bleach and ammonia, and they cleaned the entire area where Candice sat in Beauden's car as well.

D'La gets into the driver seat, Elayne is the front passenger, Shi Li and Candice gets into the rear doors of their stolen car. There is one person Raymond doesn't see and that is the man that went into the old farmhouse with them.

"Okay, where's he. Where is the other person...?"

D'La drives moderately with her lights off, taking the back roads away from the abandoned house until she reach a main road. Curiously, Raymond drives closer to the old farmhouse. Then he goes into the dark moon lit house; he trips and falls. He feels around the wet floor, wondering where is all the water coming from and accidentally finds the man's body. Raymond tries to wake him but he doesn't respond. Raymond checks for a pulse but there is not one. That is when he realizes the water on the floor is not water at all, but blood. The man is dead. In disbelief, Raymond hysterically runs out of the farmhouse, falling and stumbling over branches, small rocks and his own feet as he quickly charges back to his car.

Not realizing the dead man's blood is on his hand, his clothes and now in his car as he speeds away. After driving for hours, he finally calms down and stops at a gas station to wash and change clothes. He takes the bloody clothing and put them into a large plastic bag that was on the back seat. Consumed with much confusion Raymond is not thinking straight, he tosses the bag into the trunk of his car.

That night, feeling lost, completely mixed up, he ponders the whole night. 'Maybe he should just turn around and go back to where he came from'. Raymond starts to pray, lying his head on the steering wheel: "Dear Lord, help me please, I don't know...What have you put in front of me! ...Why?"

Instead of going to Elayne's house, he needs lots of time to think, and while waiting for answers to his questions, Raymond decides to sleep in his car that night.

The night goes on, D'La drives the stolen car to a dead end street, in another part of the city where mostly old abandoned factory buildings and vacant parking lots are located. Again they wipe, clearing and cleaning the stolen car of all evidence.

Dressed to blend in with the residents in the neighborhood, a rough area of the city, they decided to catch separate buses back to Candice's car. Shi Li and Elayne caught the first bus while Candice and D'La waited on another bus going the opposite direction. Most of all, making certain the tire tracks from the stolen car and Candice's car don't come in contact, keeping both automobiles separated. The last part of the plan: D'La and Candice will double back on a third bus and meet up with Elayne and Shi Li.

DADDY'S BABY

CHAPTER 19

Early that next morning, Shi Li has already left for the hospital when Raymond arrives at Elayne's house. First he knocks lightly on the door, but nobody answered. Then he knocks again, at least three rapid taps, and this time they are a little harder. Candice saunter to the door and she is stunned to see him after so many years.

"Raymond! ...What are you? ...Wait here!"

Before giving him a chance to say anything, she immediately calls Elayne to the door. He waits nervously, standing on the porch and looking about the surrounding area. Placing his hands into his jacket pocket he begins to twiddle with the lint entangled within the lining, while noticing that the neighborhood have not really changed that much.

Elayne is emotionally drained as she drags herself to the door. Raymond is instantly lost for words. She still looks the same, sweet and lovely as he remembers.

"Hey...Hi...I."

Though surprised, Elayne is not happy to see him standing there, not one bit.

He is extremely nervous, blinking uncontrollably. "I want to...What I'm...I know it's been a long time, but I come back to...to a apologize."

P...ssed off, nauseated from his presence, as well as shocked, Elayne seems to be lost for words; she stands there staring at him.

However, he continues, "Is there somewhere we can talk, Elayne?"

Elayne does a complete about-face, swiftly walking away from the door, never saying a word. Instantaneously he follows her into the living room, still with his hands buried deep in his lint filled pockets. Due to intense stress and without warning Elayne's knees begin to weaken. She practically faints because of severe emotional drama that has unfolded within the last week. Raymond quickly grabs her and gently lays her on the couch. Candice observes everything to its entirety and quickly goes to inform D'La of Raymond's unexpected visit.

Candice and D'La hastily walk into the room. Aggressively D'La marches at him. Approaching, as an African queen, a warrior ready to battle: out to protect her people, the ones she loves. Her words burst out of her mouth in full combat. Ready for the kill, ready as the knife she carries: "WHERE IN THE HELL DID YOU COME FROM?"

But Raymond understands that he is on forbidden ground and he deserves every bit of her attack. Despite D'La's courageous aggression Raymond knows to keep his cool. He is not here to cause any problems; he only wants to make a change in the problems he has created.

"D'La...it's nice to see you. How have you been?"

D'La is not interested in small talk or his nice guy routine. Belligerently she yells, "CUT THE BULL AND GET TO THE POINT...WHAT IN THE HELL DO YOU WANT? AND YOU DON'T GOT THAT MUCH TIME...SO YOU BET-TA TALK FAST!"

Raymond can not get a word in as D'La continues to yell.

"YOU GOT YOUR NERVES COMIN HERE AFTER ALL THIS DAM... TIME."

Candice stands along side of D'La, her abusive questioning may seem a bit harsh, but Raymond was expecting it.

"I come back to apologize to Elayne..."

"And WHAT!" she rudely interrupts."

"... and...and to..." he hesitates, "...I want to see my child if I can, please?"

"After all these years you want to see your child. YOUR CHILD! WHERE IN THE HELL WERE YOU WHEN THEY NEEDED YOUR WILD STUPID AS...?" screams D'La, "WHERE?"

Raymond is too ashamed and too embarrassed to answer. He quickly looks down at the floor, then glances at Elayne who sits quietly, waiting for D'La to finish her inquisition.

"D'La...calm down! Let's hear what he has to say," says Candice.

D'La's reply is extremely harsh, "As far as I'm concerned, he's thirteen years too late when it comes to say'n anythang. That's what the f... wrong with these men now days. They think they can come and go anytime they feel like it...and when they come dragging their sorry dumb as... back, we suppose to be calm, sweet, understanding and sit quietly and listen to their S... I don't think so, and I don't care WHAT he has to say. HELL NAH, NOT THIS TIME!"

D'La slowly places her hand on her knife as Candice grasp her elbow.

Elayne is getting a headache from all the excitement and places one hand upon her forehead. Worried about her sluggish demeanor Raymond moderately moves closer and gets down on one knee.

"Elayne...are you all right? I've come back to tell you...that I'm sorry. I'm sorry for all the terrible things I did and the nasty things I said to you and..." Raymond continues to kneel as he moves directly in front of her: "Uh...If it's all right with you, today is the day I start making my wrongs, right."

Bringing her hand down just a bit, Elayne tries to hide her watery eyes. It is very difficult. Psychotic, she loses control and burst into tears. Despite his plea, it is impossible to endure the pain devouring her heart. Raymond reaches out trying to comfort her.

"Please forgive me, Elayne? If you can find it in your heart, I promise I'll do my best to make things right. I'll prove it to you. Give me a chance...Elayne, please!"

Everything is happening so fast and without warning a compelling force seizes her. Elayne unexpectedly slaps Raymond across his face, hitting him several times, all the while screaming at the top of her lungs, "SHE'S DYING! ...SHE'S DYING! ...YOU CRAZY FOOL, JANAL IS DYING!"

Raymond is horrified. But, nevertheless he listens. He needs to understand: why, how could something like this happen?

"She dying? Janal...her name is Janal? ...SHE'S DYING!

Candice hurries to Elayne quickly embracing her. Raymond's heart unexpected skips a beat as the ailing news of his only child trigger sharp pains through his body. Almost destroying any and all hopes and dreams he have. A child he has longed for so many years, just to see her, to touch her and caress her in his arms now rests with fate.

"HOW?" he shouts, "What happened, Elayne? WHAT? ...WHERE IS SHE? I GOTTA SEE HER. Please, please!" he begs as his face reveals his anxiety.

Raymond soon glances up at D'La and she is totally surprised by his emotion. Reason is, she has never known Raymond to be so caring or show concern about anyone except himself. Candice and D'La are touched by his sudden display of sympathy as D'La slowly approaches him.

She explains: "She was raped and shot late Thursday night or Friday morning, nobody knows for sure. A little boy on his way to school found her lying in a field, half-dead and naked."

Caught up, broke down, Raymond can hardly deal with the pain as he imagines the horrible scene. Even blocking out the dreadful description of that night is impossible. Thinking that something so terrible could happen to his daughter, his own flesh and blood is inconceivable.

Helplessly he ask, "D'La, where is she? ...I gotta see her. Please D'La...Tell me where she is? Elayne, take me to her! D'La, Candice, please."

Raymond's ashamed of himself for not being man enough to stand up and protect his family from the evils of this world. His heart is devastated; his tears quickly pour down his face. He brings his fist to his face, slowly opening his hands before covering his face to hide his guilt and his grief.

The Hospital

Standing at the entrance of Janal's hospital room Raymond finds it difficult to control his emotion. Exploding with even more sorrow, weeping from the shock of her appearance.

Impulsively he enters her room and rushes to her side; his needs to take her into his arms, and yet he can not. In all the years when he wanted to see his daughter he never dreamt the first time would be like this. A compelling force to touch her overwhelms him as he gently strokes her face. Touching her for the first time, furthermore, realizing how much of a fool he really was.

Shi Li quietly walks into the room, yet surprised, she stands next to her three friends. With deep regret, she watches Raymond cry. The four friends absolutely are amazed to see a gentle side of him. He is not his usual, egotistical, self-centered person they once knew. An immense change, a change they never thought possible until now.

Raymond is now a caring and a loving individual; and this is the first time they ever seen him display such emotions of love as he acknowledges his daughter for the first time.

He whispers, "Janal...Janal baby, it's Daddy," Raymond bends down and kisses her cheek, "Janal...it's Daddy, baby."

Janal did not respond to the sound of his voice, a voice she waited all her life to hear and always dreamt of, and now she can't.

Raymond's heart is severely broken even more. You can see the tense trauma increasing in his face as he looks back at Elayne and her friends. Hopelessly, realizing that there is nothing even he can do.

For three days, Raymond sits beside Janal's hospital bed, praying and waiting for her to regain consciousness. Moreover, just to be close to her. Everyday, just being in her presence is a wish come true as he lays his head on her bedside. Dreaming of times that could have been, and the things that they could have shared together, if he had not walked out.

On the fourth day, after so many prayers, Janal wakes up and the first thing she sees is the top of the stranger's head. She reaches out to touch him. Spiritually, she already knows who he is and calls to him: "Daddy...Daddy!"

Waking to a tiny, sweet, and lovely sound, Raymond immediately lifts his head. Her face and body are bruised, battered with numerous lacerations, but she is still the most beautiful little girl he has ever seen. Sitting in a chair next to Janal's bed, Elayne is awakened by the sound of her daughter's voice. Seeing Janal and her father together for the first time is more than she can ask for, and most definitely, long overdue. Elayne is overjoyed as she prays for the second time in years.

"Thank you Lord. I just want to say, thank you so much and...I'm so sorry, so very sorry for not trusting in you. I promise from this day on...I'll never turn my back to you again. Thank you Lord for show'n me just how precious life is."

Despite her condition Janal needs answers to many questions. However, today her questions are few, but direct.

"Daddy...Daddy why? Why did you leave me? You didn't like me. Do you hate me? What did I do Daddy for you to leave me? Daddy...you never called."

Raymond takes her hand, looks into her face, her eyes: "Baby, I love you with all my heart. And I miss you so much, Janal, if only words can say how much. But honestly, I was a fool, baby girl. Your daddy was a fool and in some ways, I'm still is. But the truth is, I've never stopped thinking about you or your momma. That day when I walked out that door I knew I was making a grave mistake...but I was afraid to come back. And no, I don't hate you, I never have. Janal you never did one thing for me to hate you or leave you. I was a selfish, egotistical dumb fool."

Joyous tears drips from Raymond's face. His prayers have been answered. "Janal, I promise, I'll never leave you again. You're my angel that came down from the heavens above and always will be."

Raymond clutches Janal's hands: "As long as The Lord allows me, I'm going to be by your side always. I'll never leave you again. Your daddy's home now, Janal. I ain't going to let nothing happen to you or your momma ever again."

Raymond kisses Janal's entire face as he caresses both of her hands tighter.

Elayne, Shi Li, D'La and Candice sobs elatedly, watching Janal smile once more.

"I love you so much Janal. You are the angel in my life!"

On the tenth day of Janal's traumatic incident, about 6:45 PM, the police arrives at the hospital, impetuously flashing their badges as they approach Elayne to question her concerning Beauden's murder.

"Mrs. Smith, I'm Detective Webb and I would like to ask you a few questions about your daughter's attacker. Would you mind coming to the station with me?"

Elayne is astonished, but she agrees by shaking her head before saying a word: "Um...sure. But...but what does that man's murder have to do with me detective?"

Disturbed by the detective and the police's presence, Raymond steps out of Janal's room. Taking an incontestable and convincing position next to his wife, listening to the detective's interrogation of the murdered man. He immediately interrupts, "Umm, excuse me."

Elayne quickly glances into Raymond's inquiring face.

"Excuse me detective, I'm Mr. Smith, Elayne's husband. Can I be of some service?"

"We are trying to put some pieces together on the murder of a man who was found dead in old deserted farmhouse by the owner of the property yesterday afternoon. This murdered man, for some strange coincidence, turns out to be your daughter's attacker. Now your daughter was assaulted and shot and that same DNA that was found on your daughter when was admitted to this hospital just happens to be Mr. Beauden Hamilson's DNA...and after running several tests, I would say the DNA is identical. And that relation between her and the man that was found dead leaves room for questioning."

"There has got to be some mistake detective. My wife couldn't know anything about anything like that," defensively declares Raymond.

"We won't know until she comes down to the station for questioning."

"Excuse me detective, but our daughter is lying in that hospital bed clinging to life because of that man, and you want to take her mother, my wife, at a time like this down for questioning?"

"I'm deeply sorry about your daughter, Mr. and Mrs. Smith and you have my sincere regrets, but this is a matter that needs to be address immediately. It shouldn't take long. If everything checks out Mrs. Smith will be able to return to the hospital as soon as possible. I'll personally drive her back myself."

Raymond reassuring disposition relaxes Elayne only a small fragment. He moves closer, putting one hand about her waist, he whispers: "Elayne, don't worry about a thing, cause you haven't done anything, anyway! And you don't have to say anything without an attorney presence. Do you understand? Don't say nothing until I bring an attorney to the station."

Elayne lies to Raymond. Plus believing her friends are the only people she can truly trust, as well as believing her actions were truly justified.

"Raymond, I have nothin to hide. I didn't do anythang wrong."

Raymond follows the detective and the police as they escort Elayne through the corridors passing Shi Li at the nurse's station. Walking along side of Elayne, Raymond stops at the elevator, they enter and the door closes in front of him.

Shi Li usual demeanor captures Raymond's attention. He goes to the nurse's station, to Shi Li for answers. But Shi Li is quick to make inquiry.

"Where are they taking her?"

"To the station, to ask her some questions about the man who attacked Janal. He was found dead in an old deserted farmhouse yesterday."

Shi Li's face stiffens as she watches each elevator floor number light up as the elevator descends.

"What! ...I got to go."

Before she can leave, Raymond grabs Shi Li by the arm and pulls her to his side, not knowing that Dr. Tsetung is watching from a short distant.

"Shi Li wait. I want to know what's going on?"

Raymond is angry and very worried, and of course, he is extremely serious as he reveals their secret and demands answers.

"That night, when that man was murdered, I saw you there, all four of you...Now tell me what's going on!"

Shi Li is overcome by Raymond's remarks.

"Quit, I can not talk here. Now, let go of me before someone sees you and call security."

Immediately he releases her and yet his demands are persuasive.

"I NEED TO KNOW WHAT'S HAPPENING...and WHY... That's my baby's momma who just walked out of here with the police."

"And my best friend...Now, compose yourself for a moment, I will be right back, " says Shi Li as she quickly goes to a public phone.

"D'La, it is Shi Li. We have an emergency. We need to talk. Elayne was taken to the police station for questioning."

"What! Why?"

Shi Li continues, "Call Candice and meet me at Elayne's house in thirty minutes."

Raymond is eminently focused on Shi Li the entire time. After her telephone call, Shi Li asks Raymond to promptly meet her and the others at Elayne's house.

Not long after their arrival the phone rings, Raymond answers it. The conversation is brief, and after hanging up Raymond is seriously puzzled. He pulls a chair out from the table, scratches his head, sits in a dazed while the three friends wonders who was that on the phone.

Ultimately, Raymond sadly informs the girls of the circumstances.

"That was the police. Elayne is being charged with Beauden Hamilson's murder. The man who tried to kill Janal."

On account of the news, Raymond becomes extremely upset, almost crazed. He gets up, makes a fist and socks the wall as hard as he can, punching a hole straight through it.

"No, she can not be", surprisingly says Shi Li.

"They have no proof", affirms D'La.

"Evidently, they got something", replies Raymond.

"No way, it's impossible", states Candice.

"NOW WHO WAS HE? WHY DID HE TRY TO KILL JANAL...AND WHAT IN THE HELL HAPPENED THAT NIGHT?"

The girls are disturbed about Elayne's arrest and Raymond's assertive demeanor, yet they are composed as they meditate on what to do next. Nevertheless, Raymond is not accepting their reposed dispositions.

"HOLD UP. JUST HOLD UP. I SAW ALL OF YOU THERE THAT NIGHT...AND I KNOW WHY YOU WERE THERE. I AIN'T THAT STUPID...YOU WENT THERE TO KILL THAT MAN FOR WHAT HE DID TO JANAL...I KNOW YOU DID. YOU DON'T HAVE TO BE A ROCKET SCIENCETIST TO FIGURE THIS OUT!"

Candice confronts Raymond: "Yes, we were there that night and we'll gladly go back again if we have too. He had no right doing what he did to Janal or anyone else. He deserved to die."

Shi Li gradually steps to Raymond and proclaims, "Death was too good for him. Raymond, listen to us. Janal is as much your daughter as she is ours. We had to do what we had to do."

D'La's tone even nastier as she defends her actions and her friends, throwing a chair to the table, holding on to her knife that is concealed in a back pouch that is connected to her waist.

"YOU DAM... RIGHT...I JUST WISH THERE WAS A WAY TO BRING HIS BLACK AS... BACK...SO HE COULD DIE ALL OVER AGAIN...AND AGAIN!" Her eyes are iced-cold as she stares into his face. Quickly she releases her knife from the pouch, hastily stabbing it into the table then adds, "THIS TIME A LITTLE SLOWER."

Outraged with the girl's actions and especially D'La's, Raymond continues, "D'La you're going to wind up in HELL."

Very sassy she responds, "If Hell is where I'm suppose to be, then Hell is where I'll finish him."

Raymond is deeply distressed about what he hears and he is even more neurotic when it comes to their relaxed and defensive attitudes.

He stands motionless. "This is hard to believe." Then suddenly he begins to yell, "THIS IS NOT SOME HOLLYWOOD MOVIE...WE 'RE TALKING ABOUT MURDER! MURDER! ...THIS IS REAL. HAVE YOU LOST YOUR MINDS?"

"NO. We have NOT. As long as we are under the sky together, we will always stand strong together...Whatever the cost," confirms Shi Li.

"No, Raymond our minds are intact. Janal is special to us...I love her with my life and I will kill any man who touches her like that ever again. I PROMISE!" replies Candice.

"RAY, we had to avenge Janal. We couldn't LET THAT DOG walk the STREETS ANOTHER DAY, offensively says D'La.

"Who knows how many other girls he has hurt. Can you tell me that, Raymond! Do you know?" states Candice.

Raymond can not answer their questions, though he does understand their reasons as they continue to make known to Raymond Beauden's criminal lifestyle.

However, all he can do is worry and ask, "What if Janal finds out about her momma...WHAT...WHAT ARE WE GOING TO TELL HER AND HOW?" Raymond is saddened by all that he has heard. "We got to do something to get my baby's momma out of this mess. If Janal finds out...I can't let that happen."

Disheartened and baffled, Raymond excuses himself from the table.

Early the next morning, while everyone was asleep Raymond sneaks out of the house and appears at the police station carrying his bag of bloody clothes.

"I want to see Detective Webb. I want to confess to Beauden Hamilson's murder."

Detective Webb overhears Raymond's statement and asks him to have a seat at his desk. Along with a fellow officer who takes the report of his confession.

"So you want to confess to the murder of Beauden Hamilson?"

"Yes. I did it. It all happen so fast."

"Why don't you start from the top, Mr. Smith."

"The top...Oh, oh okay...Well, I've only been in town a short time. I come back to see my little girl. I've never seen her before, and looking at her for the first time, seeing her like that. I had to do something. I had to find the man responsible. So after that...I mean... leaving the hospital...I started asking questions, any information I can get on his whereabouts. Even if that cost me every dime, I had too. I wanted to meet him. Not knowing if he was the man or not I had to know. I had to find out...Who? Why?

So later that day...when I arrived at the pool hall over on Dexter Street. He was about to leave, and he did, alone. I followed him in my car to that old farmhouse. I didn't know why he was going way out there and I didn't care. I just kept following him. I needed information. I still wasn't sure if he was the man or not, but I had to know, I had to be sure. You understand, don't you? ...Well, anyway, when I got there, at the old farmhouse, he got out of his car. There was another car parked there too, I waited for...I think it was about an hour or two. I'm not really sure on the time. All I know that it was getting dark. I was mad and the longer I waited and thought about Janal, the crazier I got. But, whatever they were doing inside it took a long time, cause I fell asleep. It was...just a short nap, and by the time I woke up I saw the other car drive away. I couldn't see who was driving or anybody, by then it was even darker. But his car, Beauden's car was still there. I got out and walked in. There was a candle bit burning in the window...That made it visible. Yet barely, but enough for me to see him.

At first I couldn't say anything, I just looked at him. I remember he was walking kind of funny as he was coming toward me, but I didn't care or even think about that. I was mad. Second, I asked him, is his name Beauden and he said 'yeah mother f..., who wants to know?' He started cussing at me, and he continued cussing through our entire conversation. Then I asked him about Janal. He started to smile. I kept asking him questions. I remember asking him, how can he do something so terrible to a young girl, a child. He started laughing, more and more he laughed, and each time he laughed he got louder. I remember he was holding his crotch and laughing. Saying, pus... is pus..., but you know what, I love it. Especially if it's young and tight.' Then he laughed some more and more as he came closer to me, dragging his foot. That laughing irritated me, 'Ee.e.e..e'. At that point, I knew he had to be the man. I must-ta picked up a stick and hit him.

The raged I felt consumed me. I didn't mean to kill him. I just wanted to hurt him like he hurt my little girl; that's all. By the time I had stopped hitting him, I realized he was lying on the floor. I called to him but he didn't get up. I touched him, shaking him, trying to get him to wake up. He didn't move or say anything...I got scared. So I thought about dragging his body out of the house to hide him under some brushes and sticks, to bury him. Then I stopped, and I started running back to my car, falling over my own feet a few times. I got in my car, I drove around for a while, maybe hours, I don't remember exactly how long for sure. It was too much happening. A lot of things was jamming my brain.

Later that night, I went to a gas station to change my clothes. I had a...pair old jeans, a pullover shirt and tee-shirt on the back seat. I didn't have to ask the attendant for the restroom key, I noticed the door was already open. The lock must have been broken or something, I didn't look to see. I just wanted to get cleaned up, to wash that man filthy blood off of me.

Detective Webb, this man had a bad reputation of recruiting young girls into prostitution and everybody in the hood knows that.

I didn't mean no harm...not at first. I only needed to know the truth, his reasons, why? But his laugh that 'Ee...e...e...e...' I couldn't take it...and I blacked out and he was dead.

"What about the stab wounds to his body and his penis is missing, Mr. Smith?

"I don't know...that must have been the reason he was dragging his foot and holding himself," adds Raymond.

After hours of repeated questioning, Raymond is inevitably charged with Beauden Hamilson's murder. Handcuffed, hopeless and unhappy as he passes Elayne on his way to a jail cell.

She yells to him, "RAYMOND."

He takes a quick look before yelling back to her, "GO ON HOME ELAYNE. GO HOME AND TAKE CARE OF MY BABY...YOU HEAR ME! GO HOME AND TELL JANAL I'M SORRY I COULDN'T KEEP MY PROMISE...DON'T FORGET TO TELL HER, THAT I...THAT DADDY LOVES HER."

Elayne yells again, "RAYMOND!"

"GO HOME ELAYNE...I'LL BE JUST FINE!"

Elayne approaches one of the police officers and inquisitively asks, "What's this? Why is he being arrested?"

Detective Webb walks over to answer her questions, "He has confess to Beauden Hamilson's murder."

"What!" surprisingly she asks.

Shocked and concerned for Raymond's safety and knowing that he has confessed to a murder he didn't know anything about and a murder he had no part of naturally sends chills down her spine.

Elayne hurries to the hospital to inform her friends of Raymond's arrest.

"I...I don't know what to do. He's innocent and we have to do somethang."

"We'll find a way to get him out of there, Elayne," assures Candice.

Elayne begins to cry and plea for her daughter's happiness: "Janal just got her daddy back...I don't want her little heart to hurt anymore. Not ever again...Not for somethang like this; somethang we did."

"Neither do we. She's been through enough," states Candice. "Elayne, don't worry. We'll think of somethang. We all will", affirms D'La.

"Wait! I got it. If anybody can get Raymond out of jail, Jacque can. How about it, should I make the call?" asks Candice.

Shi Li interrupts, "Before we do anything, we are going to have to tell Janal the truth. That is the only way to save her innocent heart from breaking anymore. We can not let her think her father left again, or have her hear about something so terrible like this from the media. She will need to know, what and why. And it is up to us...We will tell her together."

SHADOW

CHAPTER 20

Instead of calling, Candice flies back to Paris to meet with Jacques Crozier. She has to tell him about the murder and their involvement, person to person, and the reason Raymond confessed to a murder he did not commit. Upon arriving, Candice immediately informs him of their dilemma. Jacques is very impressed with Raymond's valorous decision to confess to such a dreadful crime. Sacrificing his life to protect his family, giving up his freedom to ensure his daughter's happiness, something that is very rare, especially in this day and time.

Jacques agrees to give Candice and her friends a hundred percent of his support, by assisting Raymond Smith with his legal defense. Jacques retains the best attorney money can buy.

Why? For many reasons, but one particular reason stands out. That is, Jacques loves Candice so much that he would do anything for her including helping her friends. Another reason is, protecting her goddaughter's happiness and securing that relationship between father and daughter.

With little evident presented the case still goes to trial. Somebody has to pay for a life lost, and after Raymond's testimony the prosecutor wants him real bad. By the way, the prosecutor for the case also has associations with the Black Connection Inc. Mafia.

Raymond sits in jail about a year before his case comes to court. Elayne, Shi Li, Candice and D'La sits in court every day offering moral support. Although, on days when Janal is unable to attend she would send her love from school by writing letters that Elayne hands to Raymond's attorney before the trail.

However, the trial continues for over two years: lots of bad vibes and threatening rumors circulated the courtroom, which led to the rescheduling of court dates, besides missing witnesses and false testimonies.

True enough it was a difficult case due to Raymond's confession. Though many of the testimonies did have his best interest, still things did not look good. Until his attorney did some dirty digging, by hiring private investigators, going undercover, blending into the neighborhood and blending in with the people that lived there. There mission: to bring back any information they can find and they did. They brought excellent witnesses who were not afraid to testify on Raymond behalf, witnesses that were ready to speak out against Beauden and his lifestyle. People in the neighborhoods that were not afraid of retaliation. These people were ready to fight back, people wanting revenge for whatever reason or reasons and at whatever the cost. People that actually had some personal, yet negative involvement with Beauden and his thugs.

Beauden was a man with many enemies and Janal wasn't his first raped victim, of course. And it appears that the Smith's aren't the only parents that wanted Beauden dead.

The courtroom is filled with many undertones as the first witness an elderly woman dressed completely in black takes the stand.

The Old Woman

"My daughter, she's dead now. She was seventeen...He, that Beauden got her hooked on drugs. Then he threw her out on the streets to prostitute so he can wear those fine suits. I ain't stupid 'bout thangs like that. I sees many thangs go'n on around there. And my eyes tells me the truth every time...and my mind's still sharp as a tack. I don't forget nuthin...I was comin home from work one day. I just got off the bus when I saw her and she saw me. She acted like she ain't know me no mo. That day your honor my heart just broke in tiny pieces. She was my baby, my only baby...she was my little girl. Now she is dead. But I promised her that day at her grave, the day she was buried, that he, that murdering fool Beauden would pay somehow, someway...So now since he's dead and I told you the truth. I kept my promise your honor...And I've been wearin black every day to remind me," she then looks out into the courtroom and at the people sitting in the jury, "...Now I can take my black dress off."

The Young Man

Another creditable witness is called to the stand and he testifies on how he seen Beauden beat and kill his brother right in front of his eyes, when he was a young boy about the age of eight.

He soon starts to cry as he relates back to that day, a day that continues to haunt him. He tells how his brother's case was mishandled, and after many appeals the case was eventually lost in the system.

Unknown at that time, the defending attorney had relations with the Black Connection as well. And he accused the young boy of being psychosis and too young to testify in his brother's defense; because, quote: 'kids do lie.'

The courtroom becomes heated. The young man stands and shouts as he continues his disturbing and highly emotional testimony.

"NOW I'M A GROWN MAN," he yells from the witness stand, "I'M NOT A LITTLE KID ANYMORE!" He then sits as he continues to blurt out: "...AND I'M STILL SAYING," he starts to cry, "I saw that man, Beauden, shoot by brother in his head and back five times...in cold blood." He tries to compose himself, but his crying is uncontrollable as he continues, "After he shot him he kicked him. He was trying to get to me. I don't know why he was trying to kill me...We were walking out of the party store that night. My mother sent us to get a loft of bread and a pack of cigarettes. We were minding our own business, wasn't doing anything to anybody...We saw Beauden shoot a man who was standing near the entrance of the store. Charlie was his name. Everybody called him Charlie Brown. Charlie was always doing something to somebody...but we wasn't hanging with Charlie. Charlie was bad news. It was just me and my big brother buying some things for momma...I remember Beauden looking at me and then at my brother. I remember his words, his laugh...he said, 'E...e...e...e...Business is business.' He hit him, my brother, in the head with his gun. Then kicked and stomped him in the leg before he shot my brother dead. Yeah, right in front of me. If it wasn't for my brother's body shielding me. Blocking his bullets when he fell on top of me, I would be dead today...It was horrible. My brother's blood dripped all over me. It kept running down on me, down on my face. It dripped and dripped...Even now I still can't sleep at night. And momma, she still cries, and she keeps on crying for my brother. Wanting him to come home, to come back. Everyday she blames herself for his death. My brother was innocent, Judge. He never hurt anybody...Beauden needed to die" he abruptly stands up and shouts"...AND I'M GLAD HE'S DEAD!"

Similar testimonies came from various witnesses from all walks of life. Beauden was a man with many threats against him. If it weren't for his association with the Black Connection Inc., he would have been dead long before now.

Beauden has a long history of illegal activities and his police record was as long as an average person's legs. Nearly all of the witnesses that testified wanted Beauden dead, as they sat in court cursing his name under their breath each time it is mentioned. There was all kinds of assaults, murders and attempted murder cases pending against him that were brought out during the trial. Beauden is branded a gangster and that information along with his dealing with the Black Connection, Mafia, are most definitely admissible in court, this time.

Meanwhile, the case is getting more publicity than the organization wants, and the night of Dexx's murder, the address books were never found. Ultimately, The Black Connection wash their hands of Beauden Hamilson, scratching his name from recent books, letting dead men lie; also fearing that those missing books might possibly surface during the trial.

At the beginning of the third the year the trail has come to an end. Especially with The Lord's help, Raymond Smith is a free man and is soon released from jail. The newspaper read: "NOT QUILTY" Due To Lack of Evidence. Beauden Hamilson's case is marked unsolved, 'What goes around, comes around.'

Elayne's prayers are finally answered also. The family she always dreamed of has finally come true. On the day of Raymond's release Janal and her mother goes to the jail to bring him home to his family where he belongs. Raymond never forgot his constant prayers, the special ones he prayed everyday when he was locked up. Prayer for his family, for his life, and the Reverend Thomas who taught him about The Lord and being thankful.

Whereas Dexx's love is sealed deep in D'La's heart, she is at last letting go of the past. Reaching on the top closet shelf, she is packing some of Dexx's belongings that are still hanging around her little apartment. Li'l Dexx is getting bigger and she has to make space available for his things.

She notices a large boot box: "I thought Dexx threw this box away a long time ago...What's it still do'n here?" She pulls at it. It falls, slightly striking her on the head.

"OOW! ...What the hell!"

Looking down at it as it lays right side up on the floor, her name is hand written on the top of it. Bewildered, she sits on the floor next to it, lifting the box, putting it on her lap. She has never notices this box before or gave any attention to the top shelf. She stares at the box for several minutes, reading the writing over and over again, stroking her fingers across his name.

It reads: 'To D'La...From Dexx.'

She pulls at the knotted string, opening it. Inside is a letter from Dexx and $750,000 in cash. Ignoring the money, yet desperate, she delicately opens the envelope, the letter reads:

D'La,

I wanted to give you this in person just in case something was to happen to me. The kind of business or should I say, the lifestyle I'm living...Well, what I'm trying to say, tomorrow is not promised...to me, or to us.

Honey, I want you to be happy. I know how much you hate working at the post office, and I know this money can help pay for school or maybe you can start your own business; who knows! But there is one thing I do know whatever you decide I know you'll make the right decision.

D'La Baby, I never met a woman like you before. You're beautiful, smart, strong-minded...oh yeah, I can't forget high-spirited and feisty. Sometimes, maybe a little crazy. (smile) But you're everything I've ever needed and everything I ever wanted in a woman. Every time I looked at you girl, umm...I just wanted to take you in my arms and hold you forever; make love to you till the stars fall from the sky.

De, I'm with you always, til the end of time and then some. You'll always be the only woman for me.

Keep safe.
Loving you always...Even In Death.

Dexx Barone

D'La kisses the letter many times, walking around her apartment reminiscing and crying for hours, caressing his photo, holding it close to her heart. Calling his name repeatedly, "Dexx...Dexx. I love you too, always. Even in DEATH!"

The day has come for Li'l Dexx to meet a very special family member. D'La gets out of her car, and opens the rear door.
"Okay Li'l Dexx we're here."
"Momma is this grandma's house?"
He has never seen her before and he is extremely excited.
"Yep, this is it."
Li'l Dexx runs up on the porch shouting, "Come on Momma before grandma leaves."
D'La is happy and also very nervous. She has only met Dexx's mother once and that was at his funeral. Even though she did speak to her last week before arriving today. However her mind is traveling ever so fast as thousand of questions pops in and out her head that his mother can and will possibly ask.
D'La knocks on the door and within seconds it opens. The woman in the doorway does not say one word she just stands there staring.
D'La greets her with a smile, "Hi, Ms. Barone. I'm D'La, rememba we spoke on the phone last week."
Still the woman says nothing. She keeps looking down at a child whose the spitting image of her son, Dexx, who she severely misses so much.
Rubbing the top of his head D'La continues, "This is Li'l Dexx."
Still Ms. Barone says nothing. She squats in front of the boy and takes him by the hands.
"Hi, Grandma."
Li'l Dexx immediately wraps his arms around her neck, hugging and kissing her face.

She is overcome with strong emotions. Tears quickly fill her eyes. A compelling force controls her every emotion. Instantly she embraces him. She tries to compose herself, but it is impossible. The empty space in her heart where love once lived immediately fills with love again.

"Hi Baby, ah aha...how you doing?"

D'La watches realizing Dexx's mother is very pleased to see them. Showing an enormous amount of affection to Li'l Dexx, welcoming him into her family, into her life, which absolutely settles D'La's nervousness.

Ms. Barone picks Li'l Dexx up, squeezing him in her arms.

"I'm sorry D'La, I don't think you realize the extent of joy you brought into my life today. Thank you thank you, this means so much to me."

D'La is overwhelmed with intense emotions. "I understand. ...This is somethang I needed to do for Li'l Dexx. Ms. Barone, we love you and miss you a lot. We really need you in our lives."

"Thank you D'La.

Stunned and very appreciative, standing on the porch Ms. Barone impulsively opens the door. "Oh, I'm sorry D'La, forgive me. Please come in the house?"

"Grandma, is this your house!"

"Yes it is baby."

"Grandma, you got a pretty house...Pretty like you!" excitedly smiles Li'l Dexx, quickly embracing her around the neck once more.

Time moves on and many things have changed from bad to better since Vanessa Morris ran away from home. Living on the city streets for almost two years did not make things any easier. Vanessa shoplifted area stores for most of her clothing; she panhandled to buy food, beside the many times she had to Dumpster dive for food in rat infective allies. In addition to, fighting to stay alive amongst the many weird strangers she met roaming the city streets in the eerie hours of the night. Findings secured safe haven in abandon houses and sometimes she even had to sleep in nasty public restrooms. She ultimately moves into a shelter for abused and battered women and run-away girls.

Finally one day, she is able to moves out and she gets her own apartment. Social workers at the shelter played an important part in Vanessa's life; she eventually starts receiving government assistance that pays for her housing and other personal needs. She also went back to school, getting her GED, her high school equivalent certificate, which she is very proud of.

One day while shopping at the neighborhood grocery store Vanessa overspends. After all her items are totaled the cashier asks for the amount owed: "That'll be eighty-two dollar and twenty-three cents, please."

Holding her food stamps tight in her hand Vanessa begins counting. She only has sixty dollars in her booklet. Believing she has miscounted she immediately counts them again, but no matter how many times she counts them she doesn't have enough.

'Maybe a few of them are stuck together, but they're not."

She is embarrassed and looks around to see if anyone is watching, all the while, hoping nobody is paying her any attention. But somebody is watching, the next customer in line, Brent Lausen. She quickly hands the food stamp booklet to the cashier, trusting that the cashier total sum will be much higher, but it is not.

Brent Lausen, a military man has only been home from the service for a couple of months. Though he is discreet, he quickly turns his head away from Vanessa, staring in the opposite direction. Trying not to be too obvious about Vanessa's dilemma.

"I think I'm going to have to put some things back. I don't have enough money," says Vanessa, picking through the items. Finding it difficult to choose the ones she can do without, she picks through many of her items, "Let's see, well, I guess...you can take this back."

Before the cashier subtracts any items, Brent kindly interrupts, "Excuse me my Nubian Queen. I don't want to seem too personal but it would be my pleasure if I could offer my assistance."

Brent considers Vanessa's situation and he feels terrible. He remembers the 'hard times', as a child, his family endured. Vanessa wonders,' it's not every day that she'll meets a generous and caring person. She recalls the times when she fought to survive on the streets and asks, "What kind of assistance!"

Without saying another word Brent hands the cashier twenty-five dollars more to pay the balance of Vanessa's groceries.

"Assisting my Nubian Queen in her time of distress. Nothing else."

She is very grateful, eminently impressed with him and his generosity.

"Thank you. I appreciate this very much," she grins as he helps with the packing of the items, and placing her bags into the cart.

"Thanks again."

"No problem at all. I'm just happy I could be of some help to my African sister."

The last conflict, as you know, Lewis and Clarise has been arguing for many years. It seems it has been going on almost every day of their marriage. The Devil's advocate resides in their home, and Lewis has made up his mind that he was not taking Clarise abuse another day, another minute.

He modestly walks of their bedroom, down the stairs carrying suitcases. Places his suitcases on the floor next to the staircase, takes his jacket out of the closet and throws it over them.

Clarise stomps toward him, "Lewis where in the HELL do you think you're GO'N?"

As usual Lewis ignores her, but Clarise is gravely persistent.

"Lewis, are you CRAZY OR SOMETHANG. Hell yeah, you gotta be crazy if you're THINK'N about LEAVE'N ME...If that's what you're THINK'N!"

Lewis continues to ignore Clarise's idiotic behavior as well as her big mouth.

"I said, if you think you're go'n somewhere, you needs to know...YOU AIN'T GO'N NOWHERE! So you need to UNPACK those SUITCASES."

He is very repose, declaring his independence. "Clarise, I'm gone woman!"

"Lewis you gone. YEAH, OKAY, MISTER MAN. I hope you know, ain't no good WOMAN gonna want YOU, if THAT'S what you're THINK'N...Not even the young and DUMB ONES...Cause you know why! Lewis, you're too OLD and you can't WORK IT like YOU USE TO!"

Lewis says nothing, he doesn't want to argue and his reserved disposition is upsetting Clarise even more, insulting her authority. Quietly he walks straight for the door.

"LEWIS YOU BET-TA NOT GO OUT THAT DAM... DOOR...YOU HEAR ME, MISTER. Heed these words, DON'T TOUCH THAT KNOB!"

Lewis opens the door. Clarise runs up to him, raises her hand, like many times before and swings at him. Lewis blocks it, by grabbing her wrist, holding it tight and looking straight into her eyes for the first time in years. Clarise is startled. Lewis has never grabbed her or hit her in his life, yet she believes that day has come. Lewis escorts Clarise, holding on to her arm, to his favorite chair and gently puts her down in it. Still his words are few and soft.

"Clarise, I'm gone."

He walks toward the front door one last time, opening it. Clarise's tone changes, she screams fearfully. Afraid that he is finally leaving her. She quickly thinks about the disgrace to her and her family, once word gets out. 'What will people think about her femininity after being married for so long?'

She proudly shouts, "YOU'LL BE BACK...UH, I KNOW YOU WILL. CAUSE I'M A GOOD WIFE, ONE OF THE BEST."

Lewis never looks back and closes the door behind him. Clarise dashes out of Lewis' chair, runs after him, throwing open the door, yelling like a crazed fool, "LEWIS, LEWIS...COME BACK! LEWIS!"

Lewis goes to his old raggedly jalopy, puts his suitcase in the back seats, gets in and starts the engine.

Disgruntled, Clarise slams the door shut. Abruptly throws her body on the couch, grabs and hastily push back the curtains. Glaring out the window watching Lewis as he drives off.

"He'll be back. We've been together too long for him to be walk'n out like that on me. He ain't gonna find no good woman like me anywhere...Somebody who is gonna do everythang for him like I used to do. Yeah, I know he loves me. He just needs a little time. That's right...Yeah, he'll be back."

Clarise sits day in and day out. Weeks past, and, no Lewis, not one phone call. Inevitably, the weeks turn into months and still Clarise sits by the window looking out and waiting. Everyday Clarise waits and everyday the house become more soundless. Clarise is beginning to feel the pain that Lewis lived with for so long and her heart is gradually ripping to shreds.

Still, every day she sits, hoping, wishing and looking out that same window. Pushing those same curtains apart to get a better view of the front walk just in case Lewis decides to come marching up those steps again.

One day while sitting at the window, and after all those months of waiting, finally admitting.

She whispers, "My husband is gone. He's really gone."

Her tears are immense as they roll onto the sofa pillow. Clinching it ever so tight. Finally speaking the words that Lewis has longed to hear her say, "Lewis Lausen, I love you. I really do love you."

Still, to this day he has never heard them and he never will.

UNDER THE SKY

CHAPTER 21

It is a big picnic at Belle Isle Park and everybody is having a fantastic time on such a beautiful summer day, the year is 1985.

Candice and Jacques were married two months ago, and are expecting their first baby. Shi Li and Dr. Chou Tsetung are engaged and a spring wedding is set for next year.

Things are looking serious between Brent and Vanessa; he absolutely cherishes the ground she walks on. Anton is not sure which girl he likes most. For the moment, he wraps his arm around the one he is with, while strolling through the park; he is definitely sowing his wild oaths as young boys his age do.

Dexx's mother, Ms. Barone, is cleaning another picnic table; it seems as though, more people turned out than expected.

Michael and his two daughters, Tina and Pamela, along with his wife Sophie are playing baseball with Janal and her daddy, Raymond.
Uncle Chung and Aunt Miuki are jumping up and down, cheering for the winning team on the ball field.

Elayne is opening another large box of ribs to barbecue, as the sweet smokes from the grills fill the air.

D'La has graciously accepted motherhood and Li'l Dexx who is about four and a half years old, well he is playing in mud.
"LI'L DEXX...LI'L DEXX...GET OUT THAT MUD AND GET OVER HERE BOY," yells D'La.
Elayne, Shi Li, and Candice pleasantly approach D'La, clutching hands.

"D'La, he's the spitting image of his father. I'm tell'n you girl, goodness gracious. Everyday he looks more and more like Dexx Barone," joyfully expresses Elayne.

Proudly D'La answers, "Yes he is."

Li'l Dexx runs to his mother and he is all covered in mud: his hands, shoes, and his face. As little boys do, he wipes his muddy toy car across his chest, cleaning it with his shirt. From the looks of things, Li'l Dexx must have falling in.

"Mommy, Mommy!"

D'La stoops down as Li'l Dexx puts his arms around her neck.

"I love you Mommy." He stretches out his little arms as wide as he can, "...This much!"

"I love you too, baby."

D'La picks Li'l Dexx off the ground, holds him tight while placing gentle, loving kisses on his muddy cheeks.

" TACT "

' Do What You Gotta Do - When You Gotta Do It '